NO BUGLES, NO DRUMS

No Bugles,
No Drums

CHARLES DURDEN

The Viking Press   New York

First published in 1976 by The Viking Press, Inc.
625 Madison Avenue, New York, N.Y. 10022
Published simultaneously in Canada by
The Macmillan Company of Canada Limited

LIBRARY OF CONGRESS CATALOGING IN
PUBLICATION DATA
Durden, Charles.
  No bugles, no drums.
  I. Title.
PZ4.D955No [PS3554.U67] 813'.5'4 76-91
ISBN 0-670-51419-5

Printed in U.S.A.

For my mother, who got me started
For my friends, who kept me going
And for Tom Guinzburg, who saved
my ass at the eleventh hour
                          but most
especially for the grunts—on
both sides—who did what they
had to do.

NO BUGLES, NO DRUMS

Right off I knew things were gonna be fucked up as a picnic in a free-fire zone. Had to be. Number one in the Jamie Hawkins Index of Worthless Activities is: everything that starts before noon. And here those silly sonsofbitches came at four fuckin' a.m. Two sergeants and the short fat lieutenant, Whipple. Turned on every light in the barracks, like we were still in basic. Yellin' 'n' bangin' on the bedframes. One of the NCOs, an Irish lifer with a whisky-whipped face 'n' bloodshot nose shaped like a cucumber, put a nightstick inside one of our Army standard-issue galvanized garbage cans. Round 'n' round, rappity-rappity-rappity. "Let's go, Kilo. Off ya asses and on ya feet. Shake it up." We got up. Some to conform, some to commit aggravated assault—but it couldn't have mattered less to those Machiavellian motherfuckers. We were outa bed.

"Awright, Kilo, listen up," the lifer yelled and coughed up a mouthful of whisky-flavored cigarette phlegm. He sprayed it into a garbage can. Hundred-proof bile. "You mens quiet it down 'n' listen up."

First Lieutenant Whipple, the Boston bookkeeper, stepped forward a coupla feet. The pissin' 'n' moanin' eased off some. Whipple pushed his glasses up on his nose and flipped open a notebook, one o' those pocket-sized leatherbound looseleaf kind. He dragged a pudgy finger down the page, his eyes in tow, then snapped the notebook shut with a little *pop!* "Right!" he said. Right's ass, I thought. It's all wrong. I know it. I feel it.

2

"It's oh four hundred hours," Whipple announced about five minutes after the fact. "In exactly one hour, at oh five hundred hours, you will be bused to the mess hall for your morning meal. At oh six fifteen . . ." I stopped listenin'. I couldn't get my head into the Army's timetable. Not this mornin'. There couldn't be but one reason for this, one single, solitary, senseless reason. Nam. Today. Now. At four fuckin' a.m. Sweet mother of Mary's mule. I sat down and looked at the rest of us standin' round in Army-issue drawers, cotton, white.

"At oh seven hundred. hours, Kilo Company, officers and men, will depart for Danang, Republic of South Vietnam, for further assignment . . ." The accused, havin' been duly adjudged guilty, will be executed . . . I wondered who was readin' the orders of execution to the rest of us, upstairs. The other eighty combat riflemen of Kilo Company, United States Army. I also wondered, just for a moment, what would happen if we all went back to bed. No way. We'd all seen too many John Wayne movies. Jesus, what he coulda done for the anti-war movement if he'd spent only half his time hockin' up that drawl to say fine things like "Fuck you, Cap'n. If these little Jap bastards want this island so bad, they can have it. I'm hitchin' me a ride back to the fleet." With that he throws down his flame-thrower 'n' wades into the surf. Fat chance.

We got our shit together, purely in the physical sense, and went to chow like men eatin' their last meal. Everything tasted like lumps of cotton to me. I didn't see anybody goin' back for seconds, not even our human garbage disposal, Luke Davis, who normally ate two of everything that didn't wear stripes. I guess we all felt pretty much the same. Even the idiot children among us. Volunteers for Nam, I mean.

The buses didn't show up on time. Two hours late to the airfield, then we had to wait another hour in the rain. Three days to Thanksgivin', and there we stood, life-sized GI Joe dolls, toys taken to the ultimate—real rifles, packs, duffel bags, steel helmets, 'n' weak stomachs. The last word in disposable goods. Soldiers, I mean. Throwaway people. At ten hundred hours, Pacific Coast Time, we got on the planes 'n' flew away. And if we weren't quite like Washington crossin' the Delaware—well, hell, things change.

The plane ride was long 'n' borin'. It's about thirteen thousand miles to No Man's Nam, give or take a few hundred. It woulda been a lot worse, but we stayed stoned. Some of the lifers prob'ly didn't do any dope, and there's always a few of the goody-two-shoes kind, little Peter Purehearts. But in Kilo, a hundred 'n' sixty enlisted men and six officers, the Purehearts were the most minor of the minorities.

Thirty-four freaked-out hours later we dropped outa the upper reaches where the sun was shinin', through a few thousand feet of monsoon clouds, into the puddled rainwater of Danang. Thanksgivin' Eve. It was hard to find anything to be thankful for. Bad enough that none of us looked like John Wayne, or even Steve McQueen. But to get off a plane in a place that looked so much like the one we'd left a day and a half ago was weird. Like it 'r not, we'd all been raised on late-night TV movies that glamourized Americans wadin' ashore under an umbrella of palm fronds 'n' 40mm cannon fire from the fleet. And the only guys who got killed were extras. It was dangerous and exotic. But Danang was only dirty 'n' overcast. It was rainin'. All we could see were rows 'n' rows of American planes. And rows 'n' rows of American hangars. Behind me, someone tuned his Panasonic portable to Armed Forces Radio. The first three songs I heard were "California Dreaming," "These Boots Were Made for Walking," and "I'll Get By with a Little Help from My Friends." Apropos, as the fuckin' French would say. I kept lookin' for some silly-assed dude in black pajamas, with slant eyes 'n' conical straw hat. Anything that didn't say MADE IN AMERICA. I started to flash on our two months of AIT— advanced infantry trainin'. Finishin' school for cannon fodder. We used to attack little hamlets of bamboo huts 'n' straw shacks. And crawl through tunnels lookin' for VC hideouts. What a lotta bullshit that was. Right up to and includin' the last assault we made, at night. Our glorious leader said somethin' idiotic, like "Men, this is it. As close as you'll come to the real thing. Act like it." Then he blew his freakin' whistle. We went rippin' into the hamlet, screamin', "Yi, yi," or some such. Jinx 'n' Poe promptly burned the whole goddamn place to the ground. Zippoed the motherfucker right into oblivion. I think the Army woulda shot Jinx, bein' a spade 'n' all, and put Poe in Leavenworth for a long twenty, but there was a problem. Jinx was one of God's Chosen, a member of the McNamara 100,000. Can't go round shootin' up the retards. And Poe's old man was a US-by-God-senator, a superhawk at that. You don't want to diddle with the senators' sons. What they did was take a stripe away from our glorious leader and fine him two hundred dollars. Dereliction of duty or some such crap. Pity.

Anyway, we were standin' there in Danang maybe ten minutes, lookin' more stoned than stalwart, rubber-neckin' to see what we could, when a jeep roars ass up through the water. A bird colonel jumped out 'n' laid

a big Rotarian handshake-backslap on Captain Jefferson, Kilo's company commander. Then pulled him off
to one side, so we couldn't hear word one. Don't want
the goddamn grunts to know anything. But I was
starin' at 'em. Jefferson's face got longer 'n' longer. All
our asses were draggin', but his was down to his knees
by the time the colonel gave him another big slap on
the back 'n' jumped into his jeep. He roared off, leavin'
everybody standin' round like second-unit extras.

"Yo, mon Capeetan," Jinx yelled. "Where the fuck's
the war? This place looks like McGuire Air Force Base.
We back in Jersey?"

Jefferson gave him a sad little smile, one of those
man-to-man, spade-to-spade specials. "Rest easy,
Troop. I think I just got the inside track on how to find
it."

Everybody started talkin' at once, yellin' questions,
bitchin' 'bout bein' hungry, bitchin' 'bout bein' wet,
pissin' 'n' moanin' in general. Jefferson stood with his
head tilted to one side, waitin'. He's a sharp-lookin'
dude, about five-ten, good build, sorta cocoa-colored.
I call him the Chocolate Soldier. More'n any of us, 'cept
Ubanski, he looks like a soldier should look. His
clothes fit and he carries his gear like a man instead of
a goddamn pack mule. Maybe it's somethin' you learn
after five or ten years. I don't know, 'n' I sure's hell
don't intend to stay in long enough to find out. Anyway, the BS stopped after a while.

"What's the story, Cap'n?" Davis yelled in his thick
hillbilly drawl. "We goan home?"

"Some of you might think it's home. Our assignment is to take up positions around the Song My Swine
Project."

"The *what*?" half a dozen people yelled.

"The Song My Swine Project. We're to be the guardians of a goddamn pig farm."

Bein' it was Thanksgivin', the powers that be let us alone till almost eight the next mornin'. About the time I normally woulda turned over for another two hours of sleep, we were led to the mess hall for breakfast. It was still drizzlin'. We slopped through the mud 'n' water, lookin' more like convicts than coldhearted, steely-eyed warriors. I kept searchin' for some clue to where I was, somethin' that didn't say America. The Vietnamese mess hall KPs wore kitchen whites, and they coulda been Chinese cooks in Cuba for all I could tell. The food sucked. Any army that'd serve powdered eggs on Thanksgivin' can't care much about you. The bacon was half fat and not even half cooked. Tasted like somethin' you'd get in a goddamn Yankee truck stop. A big sign hung over the steam tables: TAKE ALL YOU WANT—BUT EAT ALL YOU TAKE.

"Cute," Poe said. "Fucking cute. I'd like to have two blondes, sunny side up. I could eat all of those they've got."

"I'd settle for real eggs, grits, ham 'n' red-eye gravy."

"All you ever think about is food."

"All you ever talk about is fuckin'," I said. "Maybe that's because I've managed to get laid a lot but can't find much I like to eat. Whereas you eat a lot 'n' can't get laid."

"Funny," he said, 'n' I started laughin'.

"It really is, 'cause your tray's empty 'n' I got a hard-on."

He sneered. "Stick it in your fucking fist, Hawkins, because that's about all there is around here."

"Man, can you imagine gettin' your hand shot off?"

"Better your goddamn hand than your head. Or your prick."

That kinda stopped us both. I was sorry I'd even mentioned the idea. Cheerful fucker, I am. The place was freakin' me. Everything was exactly Army. Long wooden tables. Metal trays. Benches. Soldiers. Signs. Cooks. KPs. Everything. The conversation hummed. Forks scraped against trays. Boots scraped against the floor. Ripples of laughter, waves of conversation. A hundred and however many of us sittin' there like sane men dressed in idiot costumes, thirteen thousand miles from home on Turkey Day, waitin' patiently to be fucked over . . . and you know what they're talkin' about, laughin' at? Blow jobs, real and imagined. Baseball. Football. A book somebody read. Cars, girls, graduation. Grits 'n' fuckin' red-eye gravy. Swear t' Christ. I wanted to throw my goddamn helmet through the window, smash glass, make a noise that'd wake 'em up. Somebody farted, one o' those quick, blatt-soundin' kind like you're shufflin' a new deck of cards. 'Bout fifty people started laughin'.

I got up'n' walked out without a word. Into the rain. Christ! Dumb bastards. Fuck 'em all but eight. Leave six for pallbearers and two to beat the drums.

Goin' back to the barracks I felt like cryin'. But it had been a long time since I'd cried and I wasn't about to start now. Maybe I didn't even know how. Or maybe I was too fucked up. I wasn't even sure what there was to cry about. Nothin' was any more wrong than it had been the day before. Or the week before, for that matter. I guess the way I felt was the way women feel when they go out 'n' buy clothes they don't need. Or the way my mother feels when she starts waxin' floors. I'm here to tell you, when she's got the blues you can end up in a cast quicker than a cat can cover shit. Steppin' on her floors is like tryin' to grab a greased pig. Unfortunately buyin' clothes, cryin' 'r waxin' floors seemed out. So I stole a tape recorder. One o' those Japanese battery-powered things with sixty-minute cassettes. I don't know exactly what possessed me to pick it up. But everybody else seemed to have a camera and there's times when I'll do damn near anything to be different.

The trucks were waitin' by the time we all got back from chow. Fifteen trucks 'n' two jeeps. We got on pretty much by squads, eleven 'r twelve of us to a truck. At least we weren't gonna be too crowded. And the first thing most of us did was start rollin' down the canvas side-curtains. It was still rainin' and the wind was blowin' maybe ten 'r twelve miles an hour. Seemed stupid to get wet. I should say it seemed stupid to everybody but Ubanski, our warm, wonderful platoon leader. A lifer with eighteen years, two Silver Stars, three Purple Hearts and a hard-on for anyone who wasn't wed to the Army. We had him, and we shoulda had the best platoon in Kilo. Prob'ly the whole battalion. Except we were mostly fuckoffs.

"Roll 'em up, First Platoon," he hollered, pacin' up 'n' back. "Let's go, roll 'em up."

"Aw, Sarge, cut us a break," a few yelled, but the goddamn curtains went up. I watched him stomp up 'n' down the line of trucks. A tree stump with movable parts and a whisky-burned voice.

Poe, Jinx 'n' I were all in the same truck. Jinx was rollin' joints. Poe had one o' his supercynical looks on his face. "I wonder if Ubanski's mother had any children that lived?"

"I'm sorry," I said, "but I didn't get all that . . . here, speak for prosperity." I punched the record button on the tape recorder.

"Up yours. Where'd you get that?"

"Stole it. Copped it right off a window sill."

"Here?"

"Over there, somewhere." I waved my arm toward the front of the truck.

"You *stole* it? Ripped off some grunt's tape recorder?"

"Yep."

He didn't say anything for maybe a minute, just stared at me like I'd pissed in his vest pocket. "Whata you care?" I finally asked.

"Man," Jinx snorted, "you don't rip off that kinda shit. If you gonna do in a dude, do somethin' we can be proud of. You dig?"

The trucks started and lurched off toward God only knew where, bouncin' 'n' swayin'. Jinx 'n' Poe were still starin' at me. I'd take it back, I thought, but it's too freakin' late now. "Wha'th'fuck you want from me? I'm sorry. You're right. Except you all piss me off. You sat there this mornin', Thanksgivin' fuckin' Day, in the middle of this misbegotten crotch of creation, eatin' 'n' laughin' like we were spread out round my mother's table. We're about to go off 'n' kill people ain't done a goddamn thing to us and nobody gives two fucks."

"Man, we here," Jinx said. "We here an' they ain't a goddamn thing we can do. What we gonna do? Cry?"

"Maybe it'd help."

"If crying would help," Poe said, "my mother's tears would've stopped this war six months ago."

"She cryin' 'cause her little boy got drafted?" Jinx sneered.

"No. She was crying because I wouldn't take a commission. Her family's direct descendants of the Lees. We're all supposed to be officers and gentlemen. Me being a grunt's about like you marrying Miss Mississippi."

Danang bounced past the open sides of our truck. The wind was still blowin' rain in on us, but it was mostly drizzle. Goddamn near everything was gray. When the French had been here they'd put up some little colonial kinda buildin's. They prob'ly were sorta colorful at one time. But the pastels had faded. The colors were streaked with rust from the tin gutters. Most of what we saw was wood 'n' bamboo. One-story stuff that looked like it'd fall over in the first good wind. The streets were mostly dirt, filled with army trucks, jeeps, Japanese motorscooters, Renaults older'n we were, bicycles and cycle-os—a three-wheeled bicycle with a passenger seat in front of the handlebars. Half the people we saw were wearin' pointy straw hats and shiny pajama-lookin' outfits. Most of 'em looked ancient. But they didn't look like they were made in America.

Jinx lit two joints 'n' sucked a lungful from each one. He started 'em in opposite directions. A minute later he did it again. The grass went round 'n' round, but it wasn't half gone when I realized I couldna grabbed my ass with both hands. I suddenly found myself fascinated with the Indian's bagpipes. I wondered if he could actually play 'em, and why in God's name anybody would drag bagpipes to Vietnam. Then with the insight of a man who's just discovered evil I announced, "Longfeather, either you're stone fuckin' weird or you've got the strangest hash pipe in existence." All twelve of us went off the edge laughin'.

We'd left Danang without my noticin'. One minute it was there, the next it wasn't. When I stopped gigglin' the first thing I noticed was the cold. The next was the gray, wet desolation pocked with green here 'n' there. We were doin' maybe twenty, twenty-five miles an hour, fartin' along the windin' road. The surface was mostly holes. Now 'n' again we passed a cluster of huts, hooches as we came to call 'em. In Nam, we learned, damn near everything was a hooch unless we managed to knock it down. Then it became an enemy structure. Anything from grass huts to teak houses were enemy structures if we knocked 'em over 'r burned 'em down. When the Army's information officers dealt in such things eight grass huts became an enemy base camp. Two fallen logs across a stream was an enemy bridge, a big pig an enemy pack animal.

The screamin' hungries hit us about an hour after we'd smoked. If you've ever been torn out on grass you know what it means. If you haven't it prob'ly can't be explained. It's as different from bein' hungry for lack of food as fuckin' your wife is from ballin' a ballerina in a fantasy. I remember once, visitin' some friends, we got stoned and I ate a ham and cheese sandwich, an inch-thick slab of roast beef, a bowl of cereal, about a dozen pieces of pepperoni, half a bag of Oreos, a pint of ice cream and a can of cold soup. All in less than an hour. Then I drove to a diner and had two chocolate milkshakes. Then ten minutes home, watchin' a movie on TV, I ate a bag of potato chips, half a pound cake, a cold chicken sandwich and drank about a quart of iced tea. I thought I'd die. But that's the screamin' hungries as best as I can describe 'em. Unfortunately, we were in the middle of No Man's Nam and nobody'd seen a Gino's or McDonald's since we left West Coast civilization. The only alternative was meals combat, individual. Better known as C-rations. Now, C-rations are kinda like Philadelphia—they've gotten a bad rap from a lotta people lookin' for a laugh. They aren't all that bad. Take beans, lima, with water. Not very good. But you take three cans of those, two 'r three cans of ham, maybe one of beef, add some pepper, a little hot sauce, some celery salt 'n' let it simmer for fifteen, twenty minutes. Not bad. And if you've got the screamin' hungries C-rations aren't half bad right outa the can. Especially the pound cake 'n' peaches. That was the first thing we went rootin' for. Opened every goddamn carton of meals combat, individual—twelve cartons—and dumped cans all over the truck floor till we all had pound cake 'n' peaches. There musta been a hundred and twenty 'r thirty cans scattered on the floor by the time we had emptied all the cartons. I had my can of cake open and was workin' on the peaches when I saw a truck tire sail into the sky. But before I could mention it the sound of an explosion came rippin' past us. Then another and another. And a lotta little riffs that had to come from automatics. Light machine guns. *Boom!* Rifffff Rifffff . . . *Boom! Boom!* Rifffff. Like a timpani and a snare. With shatterin' glass for cymbals, shearin' metal for strings and my heartbeat for bass. That all took maybe three seconds. In the next I was over the tailgate, on my knees in the mud, between the trucks, squat-crawlin' like a fuckin' crab, lookin' for cover. I thought I was first, but Davis 'n' Jinx were already out, on their bellies. Poe screamed, "Move it," and jumped, almost on top of me. In midair a slug hit the side of his helmet and spun it off. He went face first into the mud, slidin', and came up spittin' 'n' cussin', then started to laugh. Jinx 'n' Davis were lookin' round, then they started to laugh. It took two 'r three seconds before I realized they were laughin' at me. I was still squattin' on my haunches, movin' like a crab, holdin' my M-16 in one hand, the tape recorder under my arm—and that goddamn half-open can of peaches in my other hand. How? You tell me. To this day I don't know how, or why. People were dyin', bleedin' and cryin' all around us. Blake, a kid I hardly knew, never got off the truck. He was dead before he made the tailgate. The truck third 'r fourth behind us had swerved to miss the one in front, turned over and was on fire.

I remember Ubanski runnin' like a striped-ass ape, all hunched over, yellin', "Stay outa the fuckin' ditch. Get back! Get back!" He was firin' into the ditch. Twice somethin' exploded. The concussion from the second one blew him off his feet. He rolled up a few meters from us, kinda dazed, fumblin' to get a new clip in his rifle. I remember thinkin', so that's what they meant— we'd been told about two hundred times not to jump into ditches if we ever got ambushed 'cause the VC'd boobytrap the obvious safe spots and watch you get your ass blown from there to West Texas. Still crab-walkin', I made my way to Ubanski and handed him the can of peaches. His eyes were out of focus. Finally he reached out, took the can, drank some juice 'n' handed it back. I drank what was left. It was all very formal, like a little ceremony. Impossible, right? Shit. I saw a guy from Third Platoon stand straight-the-fuck-up, take a piss and sit down as calmly as though we were campin' out in the California Redwoods. He was cryin' the whole time. I saw another kid, one of those blond beachboy dudes, no rifle, no helmet, runnin' along the side of the road with his goddamn surfboard under his arm. Swear t' Christ. Somebody tripped him and rolled his ass into the ditch before he could get killed. Now, you tell me why'n hell he had a goddamn surfboard in Nam? Later I heard he had a brother at Chulai, right on the ocean, and somebody'd told him we'd be close to his brother. We were close. Thirty miles, maybe. Three to five hours on a truck, if you made it at all.

What happens in an ambush depends mostly on whether you're the ambusher or the ambushee. And how green you are. God knows we were green. There prob'ly wasn't more'n twenty-five or thirty VC across the road, back in the hedgerows. They'd blown the first 'n' last truck so the convoy couldn't go anywhere, then started shootin' the shit outa everything in-between. Six of the trucks were burnin'. Most of the glass 'n' tires were gone. There were maybe ten dead, another dozen wounded. People were screamin', cryin', prayin', crawlin', walkin', yellin', givin' orders, refusin' orders and just plain out of it. Comatose. And it happened so fast there wasn't time to think. All that I've described took, at the most, three minutes. A long traffic light. A wait for an elevator. Less time than it takes to jerk off. And if you're stoned you get straight right quick.

In the middle of all the chaos, Lieutenant Whipple crawled up. Literally, I mean. In one of those textbook styles where you put your rifle in the crooks of your elbows and drag yourself along—right knee, right elbow forward, push; left knee, left elbow forward, push. Over 'n' over. It works okay but it looks dumb as hell and only makes sense when there's no cover. A line of trucks or a ditch bank is about as much as you can expect in the way of shelter, both of which were available. Jinx, Davis, Poe 'n' I were hunkered down in the ditch. We watched him make the last fifteen 'r twenty yards. He was covered in mud. His thick, round lenses were so mud-spattered you couldn't imagine how'n hell he could see. It was sorta funny, but nobody was laughin'. Ubanski was squattin' behind the left rear tire of our truck. Whipple stopped at the front tire of the truck behind ours and eyed the open space. The whole time, mind you, the goddamn VC are layin' down a

lotta lead. It's still rainin'. Trucks in flames. People yellin'
like the last days of Armageddon are on us.
"Sergeant Ubanski," Lieutenant Whipple called.
His voice was naturally soft and the sound of it was
muted by the noise. "Sergeant Ubanski!" Whipple
yelled again, louder this time. Ubanski was squattin'
with his back to the deflated tire, lookin' over our
heads, at nothin' as far as I could see. He turned his
head slowly, like he was in a train station where you
don't pay much attention to people callin' names like
your own. Whipple didn't know what to say, or so it
seemed. He obviously didn't want to yell. I think it
made him uncomfortable. His voice wasn't exactly
Army-issue. He didn't want to leave whatever security
he felt where he was, and if he did, he either had to get
in the ditch with us or squat in front of Ubanski like
two Indians discussin' the price of beaver skins. Ubanski stared. Didn't say a word, just stared. Finally,
with what looked to me like desperation, Whipple
lunged up, jumped toward the ditch 'n' slid in ass first.
Ubanski came in to meet him halfway. "Sir."
     "Sergeant Ubanski, First Sergeant Johnson is dead,
and you're now the ranking noncommissioned officer." He tried to wipe some of the mud from his face
with his muddy hand. It didn't work too well. He
pulled off his glasses and squinted at Ubanski. "Sergeant, I want you to prepare the men for a counterat-
tack, on my command."
     "Where's Captain Jefferson?" Ubanski asked. He
took a little thin cigar outa his pocket and lit it.
     Whipple hesitated for maybe ten seconds, then
said, "I think the Captain is hurt."
     "Where'd he get hit?"
     "I'm not sure he was wounded," Whipple said,

obviously embarrassed. He hesitated again, then said, "He's momentarily immobile."

"Scared shitless?"

Whipple blanched. Swear t' Christ, you could see it right through the mud. "Sergeant Ubanski," he snapped, "US Army officers are *never* . . ." He couldn't bring himself to say it.

"Scared shitless?" Ubanski said for him. "An' the Pope don't pee?" Ubanski laughed, more a snort than anything. "Y' ain't scared, Lieutenant? If y' ain't scared, you lead the fuckin' charge."

"Sergeant, I gave an order!"

"No shit!"

Whipple stared in total disbelief. He'd come on active duty from the National Guard and you could tell nothing like this had ever happened while he was playin' weekend warrior. If you ever saw a mind race you can see exactly what we were lookin' at. It was a weird scene, a noncom fuckin' over an officer in front of grunts. Bad news. Whipple gripped his M-16 till his knuckles turned white. His eyes flashed from Ubanski to us 'n' back. He brought the rifle 'round till it was pointed at Ubanski's chest. I thought I'd shit. "Sergeant, I gave an order. Now get to it." He raised the tip of the barrel maybe an inch, for emphasis I guess.

"Jesus fucking Christ, Lieutenant," Poe started, but Whipple snapped, "Shut up, soldier. Sergeant, get to it."

Not a crease changed in Ubanski's heavy-fleshed face. In a serious, level voice he said, "Lieutenant, t' shoot anybody—me or them gooks or anybody else— you gotta snap off the goddamn safety." Whipple's face crumbled around the edges. *"Baaahhh!!!"* Ubanski screamed, grabbed Whipple's M-16 right outa the lieutenant's hands and slammed it butt down into the ditch bottom. His fingers wrapped around the barrel. His mouth twisted a little. His head shook from side to side, the discouraged parent tryin' to cope with a not-too-bright child. "The fuckin' barrel's cold. Safety's on. Y' ain't fired a fuckin' round at nobody. Y' livin' in a dream world, lieutenant? Y' think this is the goddamn Boston National Guard? A fuckin' war movie? Look at 'em, Lieutenant. None of 'em firin'. They're holdin' their heads. Pissin' their pants. Just like you 'n' Jefferson. Scared shitless. Y' wanna do somethin'? Get on that goddamn radio. Call Battalion . . . tell 'em we're pinned down . . . get some gunships in here. Get these men firin'. The gooks ain't gonna come any closer, they ain't got enough men. Wait 'em out, put some fire in there 'n' let the fly boys take care of 'em." He threw the M-16 back to Whipple. "Move ya fuckin' fat ass like I tell ya an' maybe you'll live long enough t' learn somethin'."

Whipple scurried away on his hands 'n' knees. If he'd had a tail it woulda been stuck between his legs. I fell in love with my first lifer. Like my momma used to say, "Son, if you don't understand somethin', ask somebody who does." I never figured there was many in the Army who knew their ass from the back side of a checkerboard. But this fucker sure's hell seemed to. I musta had a smile on my face, feelin' relieved as I did, because Ubanski turned his anger on me. "Hawkins, wha'th'fuck's so funny? Y' think this is a goddamn circus. Y' think he's a clown?" He pulled the dead cigar from his mouth and spit. "All you peckerheads point your rifles into th' air. Now!" We did, automatically. "Now fire!" Nothin'. Just like Whipple. Poe, Jinx 'n' me. Davis had his shotgun in his lap and looked bored.

"Candy-ass lit'le cocksuckers. You'll all be dead in a day." He spit again. "Awright, First Platoon, open up. Use them fuckin' toy rifles like they was real. Fire, motherfuckers! Fire, goddamn it!" He rammed the cigar back in his mouth and sprayed half a clip through the clearance under the truck.

We all started firin', yellin', scramblin' for a better position. The sound picked up, the other platoons came to life. I started laughin'. Pure fuckin' nervous hysteria. I couldn't see what the hell I was shootin' at and couldna cared less. Jinx's rifle jammed and he banged it butt down in the mud, cussin'. Davis unloaded both barrels of his 10-gauge shotgun. Sounded like a cannon. The shot musta been the size of peanuts. *Boom!* What a fuckin' racket that made. All that lasted maybe thirty, forty seconds, then Henry Longfeather reared up in the ditch 'n' started pumpin' his bagpipes. *Whhheeennnnn . . . whhhheeeennnnnn.* Shit! Blew my mind. Blew all our minds. Freaked the fuckin' gooks, too. The Indian bounced up outa that ditch and started marchin'—marchin' mind you—right straight toward the VC, wailin' on those pipes like the pride of the Queen's Own. He was playin' somethin', but only him 'n' them hotshots in Valhalla knew what in hell it was. He was prob'ly ten meters into our little no-man's-land when Davis jumped up 'n' let out a fuckin' Rebel yell the likes of which ain't been heard since the days of Stonewall Jackson. Curdled my sperm. My balls climbed up inside me like they were retractable. Maybe a hundred of us jumped up then, runnin' 'n' screamin' like banshees, the pipes wailin', and ol' Davis's Rebel yell risin' 'n' fallin', his shotgun boomin'. If I live to be nine thousand and ninety-two, I'll never be that weirded out again. But for all that I don't think we killed a single VC. They split and didn't leave bodies or blood. Nothing but empty shells. And we'd lost another ten or so crossin' the open ground.

We stood there, tangled up like a bunch a little mechanical men bumpin' against an obstacle, turnin' 'n' twistin' into each other. Fucked up like a gaggle of village idiots. What stopped us was the hedgerows, which surprised the shit outa me. I never thought I'd see a hedgerow this far from home. But there they were. Makes a helluva ambush hideout. They were all over the place. Hedgerows, rice paddies, scrub pines 'n' jungle. And when I say jungle I don't mean no Disneyland stuff like Tarzan-baby used to swing through. I felt like I was trippin' out. This can't be real, I thought. But I knew goddamn good 'n' well it was, a lot more real than runnin' through basic trainin' exercises. Now and then, things may seem so real the rest a your life is distant and indistinct. But this shit was like a badly made movie. The focus was all fucked up. I couldn't hear right 'cause my ears were ringin'. It was still rainin', not drops but heavy drizzle. I looked around for somethin' familiar. Anything. Poe 'n' Jinx were standin' a few feet away, smokin' cigarettes. I couldn't remember ever seein' Jinx smoke anything but grass. Davis was squattin' two 'r three feet beyond them, openin' 'n' closin' the breach of his shotgun— click . . . click . . . click . . . over 'n' over, the whole time starin' into space. Maybe a dozen dead 'n' wounded were sprawled in the road, around the trucks. Nobody seemed to care. There ain't much you can do for the dead, but at least somebody coulda covered 'em. It seemed like we'd been there forever. But it couldn't be. Two of the trucks were still burnin'.

"Hit it! Air! Tac Air!"

Wha'th'fuck . . .? was as far as my thoughts got before I went on my ass. Two big fuckin' F-4s screamed in over us doin' about five hundred miles an hour. And maybe thirty feet off the goddamn deck. *Maybe* thirty. The heat from their exhausts was like a blast furnace. The sound you wouldn't believe. Shock waves knocked me ass over elbows. My helmet went flyin'. My flak jacket was damned near ripped off, up over my head. Before I stopped plowin' through the mud they'd dropped four canisters of napalm and were turnin' for another pass. Round they came, unloaded some high-explosive shit 'n' climbed up outa sight. My ears were bangin' like kettledrums. My mouth tasted of mud. It was hard as hell to breathe. The fire from that fuckin' napalm was suckin' all the oxygen right outa the air. The canisters had gone off no more 'n fifty meters from us. I don't know nothin' about brimstone, but if the fires of hell are any hotter than that stuff, we'd all better change our ways.

We got up wobblin' like weak-kneed old ladies. I dug my M-16 outa the mud, then found my helmet. The rifle had about two pounds of shit jammed in the barrel. I sat down, took out the cleanin' rod, stripped the rifle 'n' started cleanin' it like we were gonna have inspection. Two choppers came in over the tree line behind us. They were medical evacuation choppers, mostly called dustoffs. They put fourteen wounded on 'n' tore ass off toward Danang. I watched it, sittin' in the mud with my field-stripped M-16 in my lap. The Army musta told us fifty times, "You're never more than ten minutes from the nearest medical facility." Then they'd say, "If you get hit your chances of surviving are ninety-eight percent." Terrific. But bein' in that two percent that gets hit 'n' dies two hours later sure as hell don't make you any less dead. I never met anyone who said they took any comfort from the Army's numbers. Maybe I don't talk to the right people. Sometimes I think all the right people must live in little rooms, thinkin' up slogans and workin' on new numbers games so the grunts'll keep humpin' for the generals. Course more'n one person has accused me of havin' a bad attitude.

The med evacs were barely outa sight when a loach landed in the middle of us 'n' out jumped a major. A loach, by the way, is a light observation helicopter, LOH, pronounced *loach*. I guess it makes about as much sense as anything else in the Army. Anyway, the major jumped out 'n' took a quick look around. It had to look sad. We'd had our ass kicked right proper. For maybe a minute the major just stood there. Maybe he was makin' mental notes. Or just couldn't believe it. Captain Jefferson walked by. He was as tight as the buttons on a fat man's vest. Strained to the poppin' point. His eyes were sunk an inch deep. His mouth looked like a slashed wrist. His helmet was gone. His flak vest hung open. His clothes were soaked, covered in mud. He'd left his rifle somewhere, prob'ly in the jeep. Both hands were tremblin' so he could barely light the cigarette he took out as he walked. I figured I'd just seen my first zombie.

Ubanski idled over 'n' squatted down next to me, tryin' to eavesdrop, I think. But we couldn't hear a whole lotta what was bein' said. Ubanski took my M-16, one piece at a time, and put it together. Never looked at it. His fingers were as blunt 'n' stumpy as his body, but they suited him as well as the hands of any doctor or card dealer I ever saw. He put my '16 together like some dude whittlin' a stick 'n' starin' at some strumpet struttin' by. My ears were still ringin' so maybe he heard a lot more than I did. The talk didn't last long, three or four minutes. Then the major walked up 'n' down awhile, kinda pissed. He came our way, and stopped when Ubanski got up. The major was a little over six feet, Ubanski barely five-eight.

" 'Lo, Ski."

"Major."

They stared at each other for a few seconds, like two old con men meetin' in a jail cell after a long separation. The major's mouth, as mean and relentless lookin' as the rest of his face, bent at the corners. I think that mighta been his smile. He took a cigar outa Ubanski's pocket without askin', lit it, and spit into the mud. "Wha'th'fuck happened, Ski?"

"We got our ass whipped."

"How many hit you?"

"Two or three dozen, tops."

"You had a hundred and sixty men! You let thirty dinks do this?"

"You, hell . . . I ain't in charge."

"You orta be. What kinda fuckin' flyin' circus is this, anyway? That goddamn nigger musta had his head up his ass to let this happen. Fourteen wounded. Seventeen dead. Fifteen trucks destroyed, or so fucked up they ain't gonna be driven away from here. An' not one goddamn dead gook to show for it? Not even one?" Ubanski shrugged. "Ski, these gold leaves make me a major, but they don't make us any different'n we were last time I saw you. I wore stripes, too. What, by Christ, happened?" Ubanski sighed, then started to tell the story. When he got to the part about Longfeather the major practically screamed, "BAGPIPES? What motherless fuckin' child would bring bagpipes to a goddamn war?"

"Goddamn if I know. But that dumb sonofabitch

damn sure saved some asses. An' that crazy goddamn exec, Whipple, was gonna shoot me for refusin' his orders."

"What?"

"He wanted to charge that hedgerow an' ninety percent of these limp dicks still had the safety on."

The major grimaced. "So you told 'im to go fuck 'imself?"

"I think I probably hurt his feelin's a little."

"You got a way of doin' things like that." He spit between his feet again. "Y'all gonna hafta walk in. Another three miles. Orta make it in an hour or so."

"Bobby, we may not make it at all."

Now it's a fact that sergeants don't ordinarily go round callin' majors by their first name. I figured these two must be pretty tight 'n' that led me to figure maybe we wouldn't get diddled with quite so much as we might've elsewhere. But, truth to tell, I'm sometimes inclined to wishful thinkin'. Anyway, it beat thinkin' about Ubanski sayin' we might not make it at all. I left them and walked over to look at the ones who didn't. Make it, I mean. Seventeen dead, just like that. Welcome to Vietnam. Sure's hell somebody's said somethin' noble about those that die in defense of their country. I'd even bet Bartlett's got it written down somewhere. I couldn't think of anything. Not a fuckin' thing. The first verse of "Flanders Field" came to mind. And that Pepsi ad . . . *You've got a lot to live, and Pepsi's got a lot to give.* Maybe that's the thing, the epitaph, I guess it's called, for this war. Shit, it's all wrong anyway. They didn't die in defense of their country. Any way you want to cut it, we're less threatened by North Vietnam than the Vatican since nobody ever gave a fuck what Ho Chi Minh thought about birth control.

You've got a lot to live. Over 'n' over it went through my mind. Try to remember your mother's birthday. Or your social security number. No way. But a fuckin' commercial you can't get rid of. You've got a lot to live. Horseshit. Their days were done. And I had a feelin' ours were numbered.

"Lookit that," I said to Poe as he walked up.

He jumped into the ditch.

Two bodies were flung back against the reverse side, arms thrown up. Both of 'em had a chestful of holes. And both of 'em looked surprised as hell. You'd think a dead man wouldn't have any expression. At least nothin' the undertaker hadn't fashioned. Swear t' Christ, they both looked like they couldn't believe it had really happened. Both of 'em wore silver peace symbols on long leather thongs. Poe lifted one between his thumb and index finger, then let it fall back. "They don't stop bullets any better than bibles, do they?" he asked.

He tried to close their eyes, like you see guys do in the movies. It didn't work. He shuddered. His face, which normally looks like it was glued on, fell apart. "Jesus fucking Christ." He was shakin', and his butter-soft Virginia voice cracked. "Their goddamn eyes won't even close. Come on, let's get the hell away from here." He pulled his poncho tight 'n' stomped off. I let him go 'n' squatted on the ditch bank, starin' at the eyes that wouldn't close. Well, fuckers, at least you ain't gonna have to hump it over to the pig farm. No more wet socks. No more steel helmet. No more crap from some dumb sonofabitch tryin' to make another stripe. You 'n' your fuckin' peace medals. You shoulda stayed in the bottom of that goddamn ditch like the rest of us chickens. I went into the ditch without even gettin' up, just slid in. There were two bullet holes through the name tag of the guy on my left. Hutton. Never heard of him. Hutton, let's see if you're as dumb as we were. I pulled the M-16 from under his leg. The safety was on. He hadn't fired the first shot. Stupid motherfucker. No flak jacket, either.

I threw the rifle aside 'n' walked up the ditch to where we'd been when Whipple tried to shoot Ubanski. Jinx was standin' there with the tape recorder playin' back the sounds of the ambush. Most of it was static. I'd pushed the record button without knowin' it. Mixed in with the scratchy-soundin' gunfire and explosions were voices. "Oh my God, oh God . . . Christ we're gonna die . . . motherfucker's got us trapped . . . Sergeant Ubanski! I got to pee . . . I got to pee . . . Jesus, don't let me die here . . . my God . . . where are we where are we we're hit they got us I can't see 'em we'rehitohgodchristnothere *UBANSKI!!!*"

Jinx pushed the stop button. "Man, you know who they was?" he asked. I nodded. "Them dudes you heard was us," he said, like he wanted to make sure I knew. I nodded again. "Tha's us on there." He handed me the tape recorder 'n' said it again. "Tha's us. Cryin' like women. You believe that shit?" I nodded for the third time. I couldn't think of anything to say. What would John Wayne say?

A coupla choppers settled into the clearin', kickin' up mud 'n' water. They'd come for the bodies. It didn't take long. The graves registration people zipped 'em right into green body bags 'n' tossed 'em on the slicks. Slicks are what the Army uses to move people, live, dead 'n' dyin'. Just plain choppers with a pilot, co-pilot and a door gunner. If you're lucky you get two gunners. Slow, awkward-lookin' animals. The slicks, I mean.

And they have a tendency to make nonscheduled landings with the least provocation. Cobras, on the other hand, are somethin' else again. Fast 'n' armed to the fuckin' teeth. They go down too, but not nearly so often. When they move people it's usually colonels 'n' generals. Rank really does have privilege, not the least of which is a fair to middlin' chance of stayin' alive a little longer than the goddamn grunts.

We left right after the choppers. Walkin', naturally. Actually, walkin' isn't the right word. Neither is marchin'. When you're dead fuckin' tired, hungry, hung over from dope and half-dazed, carryin' a hundred pounds of gear, you can't rightly call what you're doin' walkin'. Humpin' is more like it, but strictly in a nonsexual sense. Humpin' 'n' gruntin'. We veered off the road about an hour later, though we were still s'posed to be followin' a road of some sort. I never saw any evidence it existed. I can't say I saw much of anything but the backs of heads and the tops of my boots. Lookin' down seemed to help. One foot in front of the other. Think about ballin', body surfin', beer, anything but distance or the pain. And the desire to say fuck it, to lie down by the side of the road. Fantasize. Course, you can get killed like that, daydreamin'. And there's another alternative. It comes wrapped in Alpha cherry papers. Makes some of the horseshit hilarious. When we took a break, about an hour after we left the main road, we got right properly stoned. It's not the only way to fly, but it's cheaper than choppers. And much easier to come by.

We got fifteen minutes to rest. Fifteen minutes to lie in water 'n' mud, shiverin', hungry. It was s'posed to be another half-hour's march to our base camp. The way we were stumblin' I figured it'd take another half-day. Eight of us smoked three joints. Two woulda had us stoned beyond sensibility.

While we humped 'n' grunted between breaks I spaced out and might've stayed that way except some of Kilo suddenly got freaky. You could feel it. Like knowin' you're about to get hit. Guys stopped dead in their tracks, turnin' their heads this way 'n' that. It took five, maybe ten seconds to put it together, for the weirdness to wake us all. Then it hit you: *pig shit.* The fuckin' odor was incredible. Song My was just around the corner. We were home.

Home, some smartass said, is where you dig it. I don't think he was related to the dude who said home is where the heart is. And I don't think the dude who said that was ever in No Man's Nam. The smartass was closer to the truth. He was the only one to hang him up a little sign to that effect, but God knows we all dug holes to call home. Two-man bunkers, four-man bunkers, shithouse bunkers, headquarters bunkers, slit trenches, foxholes, drainage ditches and maybe some I've forgotten. Day after day we dug, then we took all the dirt and filled sandbags to pile on the timbers that covered the holes. The Army doesn't waste much of anything but lives. There we were, the best equipped, best fed, best paid, supposedly best led army in the world, guardin' a goddamn pig farm and doin' convict labor in the rain.

For a week or ten days we dug trenches and stretched wire in the general shape of a clover leaf. A three-leaf clover. Lima Company on one side of us, Mike Company on the other. And us, stuck in the middle—sort of. Except we were *all* in the middle surrounded by rice paddies, hamlets, hooches, trenches and tired people. Us and the Vietnamese. The hard thing to understand was that none of it, the trenches, the wire or the people, were anything like what I, at least, had expected. The Vietnamese, Indians 'n' otherwise, were all around us. Everywhere. And the goddamn pigs. Need I say we didn't immediately overwhelm anybody? We didn't even get right into any heavy stuff. What we controlled was what we sat on. Two hundred meters in any direction you could find Vietnamese wanderin' round, choppin', diggin', buyin', sellin'—goin' on with life and lookin' for all the world like so many Epic extras. In retrospect I think *we* were the extras, but at the time it was hard to tell.

Inside our lines was the village of Song My. It wasn't much, even by their standards. Maybe a hundred people, mostly women, kids 'n' old men. No more'n thirty hooches, close up on each other. All but one of 'em were made out of split bamboo. The one, which supposedly belonged to the hamlet chief 'n' principal pig owner, was teak. That dude knew how to live. He had a refrigerator, lights, a radio and a Honda. He smiled a lot when we wandered by. He should have. With three companies of American tax-paid grunts protectin' his property he had what's known in poker-playin' circles as a fuckin' lock on the board. He couldn't lose.

The rest of the hamlets in the area, outside our protective embrace—or death grip, dependin' on how the whole thing hit you—were growin' rice. Right there, maybe a hundred meters outside the ring of spiraled razor wire we put up to keep out the Indians, little green plants were growin' in dung-flavored water. Every mornin' at first light the fuckers would come out 'n' start diggin' 'n' choppin' in the paddies. Chop chop chop. Dig dig dig. Day after day, like there wasn't a goddamn war bein' fought in their front yard. That's what I call single-fuckin'-mindedness.

It was while we were doin' our diggin' that things began to come together. We tied up with our so-called sisters, Lima and Mike Companies. A bunch of dumb fuckin' grunts, just like us. They had been in the country for less than a month when we got there. But long enough to psych out some of the brass-hats 'n' pick up on what was happenin'. The major who'd come roarin' out of the skies when we got hit turned out to be Major Robert Early. Mighty Major. He was Battalion Operations Officer. That means his job was figurin' ways to do in all the Indians, or takin' some dumbass scheme passed down from God only knows what lofty pinnacle of privy planning and make it work. Course, where I come from a privy is a shithouse, plain and simple, but I wouldn't want to imply that the plans weren't worth a roll of two-ply toilet paper. As plans they may well have been little gems. But the whole time I spent in No Man's Nam I never saw, or heard of, a plan that didn't remind me of our feelin's about an Army career—it sounds good, and it looks good on paper, but you couldn't get ten cents for a tubful of 'em on the open market.

Mighty Major's boss, and ours, was Colonel Levine, Battalion Commander. He came one day, durin' a lull in the rain, and walked round our perimeter with Captain Jefferson. Levine's a runty little dude, maybe five-seven, with a bristly mustache as gray as his hair. Kinda sallow-lookin' skin. I never saw him when his goddamn fatigues weren't starched 'n' creased as stiff as the crack in some tin-god's ass. He always stood tall, as they say. Prob'ly got an A+ in military bearing at the Point. I got the feelin' he liked to walk a wicked pace, quick-steppin' like those crazy Limey bastards in the movies, but the freakin' mud woulda mucked up his boots too much. So he picked his way through the area like some candy-ass little wench cuttin' across a pig sty in patent leather shoes. Three or four times I saw him point to one thing and another, BS'in' with the Chocolate Soldier. Jefferson would write some shit down in his little book. Swear t' Christ, everybody in the country had a little book or an Instamatic. Even me. I got a little book so I could make notes about things. Like Levine, Jefferson and Early.

After Levine left Jefferson disappeared into his hooch. He woulda been happy to spend the whole war in that fuckin' hole in the ground, I guess. Then, maybe an hour later, bunch of us get the word we got to move our mine field twenty meters further out. Mind you, we've already mined everything in sight, from the wire straight out for fifty meters. Now Colonel Levine wants another twenty. Poe 'n' I got a section together, and maybe thirty mines to put down. I, personally, don't trust the fuckers no further than I can piss in a straight line. And that ain't very goddamn far. But who's gonna tell a colonel to go fuck himself? So we put 'em down. Carefully. Very carefully. Maybe halfway through we took a break, starin' into the distance. An old man was off a hundred meters or so, diggin' in a rice patch. Chop chop chop. Dig dig dig. "The Enigma of the East," Poe said.

"Sounds like one of those rum-punch drinks you get in that plastic Polynesian restaurant you took us to."

"Funny."

"You're fuckin' funny. What you really are is goddamn flaky. That old sonofabitch ain't got a lot of choice. But you, you're fucked up like a Filipino fire drill." He didn't say anything, just went on starin' at the Enigma of the East. "You want to know why?" I asked.

"Probably not as much as you want to tell me, but go ahead."

"Because you don't have to be here."

"Nobody *has* to be here, except for papa-san, maybe."

"Yeah, but the alternatives you had seem a lot better'n the ones we had."

"Better for whom?"

"For whom's ass. For you*m* if you weren't so goddamn simple-minded." He laughed. "Listen," I said like he had a choice, "do you think for a skinny minute I'd be sittin' here in the rain with you if *my* old man was a US-by-God-senator? No way."

"But you *are* here, so that's irrelevant. Anyway, what the hell do you think my wonderful alternatives were?"

"At the least, at the very fuckin' least, you could be an officer, right? Be nice to get paid more."

"I've got all the money I'll ever need. And what happened to our platoon leader? Did his gold bars stay the hand of death?"

What had happened to the glorious gold-bar lieutenant was he got blown away. Or so we heard. Durin' the ambush. I didn't see him, but a coupla guys in Third Platoon said he was in the lead truck. Apparently the VC'd rigged a fifty-five-gallon steel drum full of gas with a 105mm Howitzer shell, then wired it for a remote detonation. Tore the whole fuckin' front end right off 'n' Gung-ho took his gold bars to hell in a little yellow basket. "Anyway, I said that was the *least*, right? The most is what counts. You could be in some high-priced school, couldn't you? Spendin' your time chasin' cunt. Ballin' your old man's secretary or somethin'."

"I could," he admitted. "I could be in Harvard Law School. Or Yale. Or Princeton. I could be studying wills and torts while my country makes a mockery of jurisprudence, national and international. I could be waving protest posters and balling the Brandeis girls or the Radcliffe girls. But I'm here, Hawk baby, with you. Two Southern gentlemen in search of chivalrous deeds to do."

"You can shiversly bite my ass. I'm not a Virginia gentleman." Wiseass.

"Ah, but you are a Romantic—even Georgia has a few. Largely illiterate, it's true, and what you do to the language is not unlike what Sherman did to your fair city of Atlanta."

"Not all of us were raised round *proper*-speakin' spinsters and oily-tongued politicians."

"This is a work detail, not a goddamn debatin' school." The voice cut across our heads from the back, but we both knew it was Ubanski. "You two fuckoffs jaw on ya own time. That starts the day you rotate back."

"The Yankee massa is heah," I said. Ubanski, followed by Major Early, walked around so they faced us. Ubanski looked right into my eyes, then hit me in the stomach with the butt of his M-16. Not hard, mind you. Prob'ly didn't even leave a mark. I think it surprised me more'n it hurt. "Wise off with ya wiseass buddies, Hawkins. But when I speak I want y' to pay attention. Got it?" I nodded. He 'n' the major walked off together, prob'ly inspectin' everything from postholes to the captain's piles. "Fuckin' Polack," I muttered.

"Hawk, that man just may save our asses. I heard he and the major are tight as Masters and Johnson."

"Yeah, I heard the fuckin' tooth fairy comes on Thursday." I still couldn't figure what a major was doin' fartin' round with a sergeant. And I don't know Masters but Lyndon Baines Johnson is why I'm here.

At least partly. "I'll tell you one thing . . . two nights ago I had first guard, six to eight. The two of 'em came past me un-fuckin'-armed. Ubanski had a trench knife. The major had a chain. They went off the other side of that buncha hedgerows, walkin'. They didn't come back while I was on, so next mornin' I asked Jinx if he'd seen 'em. He had last guard. He said they came in about five-thirty. Sneaked right up on him. Scared 'em shitless. Said they had two automatics and a rifle. Whata you make of that?"

"AKs?"

"Automatics, man. Whata I know about AKs from BMs?"

"A BM is a bowel movement. An AK is a Chinese sub-machine gun. Supposedly only the NVAs have them."

"So maybe they dinged a coupla Charlie's big brothers. Wha'th'fuck they doin' runnin' round in the bush without rifles? Killin' gooks with knives 'n' chains, for Christ's sake? Show-boatin'?"

"A little recon maybe. You're sure?"

"I saw 'em go out, Jinx saw 'em come back."

"Jinx is always stoned . . ." He seemed skeptical.

"Jinx swears he straightened out like a weddin' night prick. He said the major got behind him. First thing he knew there was a knife blade across his throat. Dull side, fortunately. And Ubanski whispered, 'Jinx, I ever catch y' stoned on guard I'll kill y' myself.' But real calm like. Then they walked back into camp."

"Hunter-killer," Poe said, after a long pause. "Sonsofbitches . . ."

"What's 'hunter-killer'?"

"Two-man teams, usually. Go out with only a knife, or a chain. They go sit where they figure to get a little

VC traffic, out in Indian country. Kill singles, or doubles at the most. No sound. No rifle fire. No explosions. Supposed to spook Charlie the way it would us."

"That's crazy. Jesus jumpin' Christ! Crawlin' round
out there in the goddamn dark tryin' to catch a freakin'
VC by himself. You can get killed doin' that kinda
weird shit." Gave me the creeps. I mean shootin' a
motherfucker at thirty meters is one thing, but that
Lone Ranger stuff's for madmen. "Can you see yourself
doin' that?" He laughed, but I knew damn good 'n' well
he was laughin' at me. "Ain't no fuckin' way they'd get
me out there in the dark to cut people's throats," I said.
"No way."

"We'll see."

"We'll shit if we eat regular." Our relief came and
we went to chow. I fully intended to eat as regular as
possible.

Now, it might seem I don't care much for Bobby Lee
Poe. But that isn't entirely true. A little envious, I'd
guess. He's slick, like the guy wearin' a turtleneck in
a Jaguar ad. Sure's hell he's had a lotta opportunities I'll
never get. And there ain't much I envy people for, but
opportunity is one. I figure I'm as quick as most, but
when you're born suckin' hind tit you spend mosta
your time runnin' to catch up. It's not somethin' I like,
the runnin' or the envy, but I'm fairly much up front
about it. Take his education. It started when he was
born. With the kinda livin' he's done you get educated
to a life style that assures you of your own worth. It
isn't somethin' you question, and it damn sure isn't
somethin' anyone else would question. Which I figure
is a big help. Maybe I'm wrong. Maybe he's gotta prove
himself too, and that's why he's here. But there's times
when I get the feelin' he's slummin', when the soft gray

eyes, sandy brown hair and even his big ears really do look glued on. We get along because I can match wits with him. But he's had an education I could never afford. I've always been so poor I couldn't hardly pay attention, let alone tuition. Not dirt-farmer poor. Lower-middle-class poor, with just enough light to let you know there's a tunnel—but never enough to let you see the end. Anyway, out here it doesn't matter much. We all grunt together. Us 'n' the Song My pigs.

I can't believe it. Guardin' a pig farm. Swear t' Christ, every time I think about it I laugh. It's a long way to come at a lotta expense to baby-sit a buncha pigs. Seems to me it woulda been cheaper to raise the fuckers at home 'n' ship 'em here. Course, that wouldn't win any hearts 'n' minds. I mean, what good are we if we can't guarantee Third World people the right to raise pigs under a democratic system?

I noticed the first time we went through the hamlet that we'd already won a lot of somethin' for our efforts. I think animosity's the word I'm lookin' for. What we were doin' here supposedly had been explained. We came only to guard their pigs. To win their hearts 'n' minds. Apparently what wasn't explained was why their pigs needed to be guarded. Seems that when this area was the responsibility of the Regional Forces—better known as Rough-Puffs, or RFs—the VC used to come in once a month and take two 'r three pigs, grown hogs actually. Like a tax. The Rough-Puffs sure's hell weren't lookin' for a fight over a few pounds of pork, so they stayed the hell outa the way. Then the area's civilian advisor, a WHAMer, started talkin' to a lieutenant colonel in charge of American military advisors around here. Brass-hat didn't think much of the civilian WHAMer, or any of that civilian bullshit about winnin' hearts 'n' minds. He took the opportunity to recommend military intervention. Ship in a boatload of grunts 'n' get Charlie at the meat market. That all sounds reasonable enough, if you go for that kinda crap. But as soon's the area was secure—which meant as soon as it was safe for Saigon tax collectors to show up—tax on pig farmin' went up. Five or six to the tax man for the government, a couple more to the same tax man as a bribe to stay in his good graces . . . and the same two 'r three to the VC. They didn't stop comin', just changed their hours of collection or had the hogs brought to 'em. So much for winnin' hearts 'n' minds.

There's still more to it, though. Like there always is. You think you've got the handle on somethin', then you find out there's another handle, and another. First Lieutenant Winston W. Whipple, Kilo's executive officer, put it in focus the day we made our first long patrol. He was tryin' to impress us with the importance of our mission. "These people," he said, "are depending on us." He meant it.

"How come," Davis asked, "this ol' pig farm is so impor'ant?" He was scrapin' the bottom of a C-ration can, stuffin' the last of his pork 'n' beans into his hillbilly face. "Looks t' me like hit's been heah lots longer'n we 'ave. Who was nursin' 'em afore?"

"Private Davis, we are not here to 'nurse' anyone. The United States has invested a great deal of time and money in this project. It happens to be somewhat more extensive than first meets the eye." He did one of those wide sweep-of-an-arm things. We looked at what we'd been lookin' at for the past two weeks. Pig pens, rice paddies, rainwater, farmers 'n' water buffalo. "This rice crop is invaluable. It's a miracle rice . . ."

"Ah heard gooks don' like hit," Davis cut in.

"The VIETNAMESE haven't as yet acquired a taste for it but it makes excellent food for the . . . the swine."

"They growin' all that for them ol' hogs?" He stood up, all six skinny feet of him, and wiped his thin lips with the back of his raw-boned hand.

Whipple looked like he wasn't sure if he'd revealed a military secret or had just realized no matter what he said he'd appear stupid. He nodded his head, yes.

"Well, shee-it, why'nt they jus' give 'em slops?"

"What?" Whipple asked.

"Slops." He tossed the empty can aside, then absent-mindedly adjusted his helmet. Every time I looked at him I thought of old Ichabod what's his name—the Washington Irving character. Gaunt.

"I don't believe I'm familiar with the term."

"Slops, fer Chrissake. Sir. What this heah battalion don' eat in a day'd keep them ol' hogs happy's a pig in shit. If y'all 'scuse the expression."

"You mean garbage?" Whipple asked. I don't think he'd ever heard of feedin' hogs anything but corn. But how in hell's a Boston boy executive s'posed to know what people feed hogs?

"Looten't, where Ah come from they call hit slops. Call hit any fuckin' thing y'all like. But if'n they don' eat that there rice they grow, where they gittin' the rice they eat?"

"They buy it," Whipple said with some authority, prob'ly 'cause buyin' was somethin' he understood better'n hog farmin'.

"They raise this heah rice," Davis said, imitatin' the lieutenant's arm sweep, "they raise the rice to feed the hogs 'n' sell the hogs to buy rice . . .? Is that hit?"

"Yes."

"*Shee-it!* That don' make no sense at all. Least not t' me."

"Davis, yours is not to reason why."

"Ah s'pose not, Looten't." He shoved his bony hands in his pockets, then locked his black eyes on Whipple. "But Ah b'lieve if Ah'd reasoned hit out ah'da come up with a better idea."

That little five-minute song 'n' dance shook me up. It wouldna taken five minutes if Davis didn't talk so slow. Ubanski was standin' off to one side, watchin'. He said somethin' to Whipple as the lieutenant walked away, then came over 'n' squatted by me. "Y' learnin' anything, Big-ears?"

"I s'pose so."

"Y' sure's hell always hangin' around . . . eh? Big ears, big mouth." We stared at each other for a coupla seconds. I figured fuck him, I ain't backin' up, but I also got ready to roll with whatever he threw. He laughed. "Y' tensin' up, Hawkins." His laugh struck me strange. It wasn't much but I'd never heard him laugh before. "Y' always there. Listenin' an' lookin'. I see the wheels, Hawkins. I hear the gears, click, click. Snap." He snapped his fingers half a dozen times, slowly. "Click-click. Click-click. Other day I saw y' standin' outside the Captain's hooch while Major Early was inside. Hangin' round listenin'. You Poe's bird-dog? You an' him figurin' t' make trouble for us?"

I laughed. "C'mon, Sarge. Two fuckin' grunts? Against all you supersoldiers?"

"All the pros amount t' maybe two percent. Maybe. An' I can't say much for them either. This company's made up of losers an' candy-ass college boys who couldn't cut it with the books. Grocery store bag boys. Bank clerks. Dope smokers. They couldn't find their way out an open door. I been in th' Army twenty-one years. It's been a long time since I saw a more fucked-up company."

"But you *have* seen 'em?"

"Two I can remember."

"Where?"

"Korea. When it was really bad, when we were gettin' our asses kicked all over the last fifty square miles we owned. Y' never saw such a mess . . ." He was flashin' on whatever he could remember. Or stand to remember. The lines in his face looked like they got deeper, for just a second or two. Mosta us were just learnin' to talk when that was happenin'. I wondered how things could still be the same. Actually, I knew exactly how they could be the same, but that's a luxury, a little game I like to play with myself. Truth to tell, it's been the same since man started makin' spears outa pointy rocks 'n' long sticks. "Somebody's always fuckin' up." Ubanski's voice took the thought right outa my mind.

"What happened to the companies in Korea?"

"Dead."

"Just like that?"

"Nothin's ever 'just like that.' What's ya story, Hawkins? Whata y' after, eavesdroppin' all the time?" I shrugged. He hit me, lightly.

"Listen!" I started yellin'.

"No, you listen, punk. This ain't a goddamn sightseein' tour ya on. Take care of ya gear. Keep ya weapon clean, ya ammo clean an' ya goddamn nose clean. Stay outa other people's business. Ya wanna know somethin', ask. Straight out." He stood up and both knees popped.

"I ain't sneakin' round no fuckin' corners." He pissed me off. "You got so many goddamn answers, tell me this: what the fuck we doin' guardin' a pig farm? What was the big hurry to get us here? How come we got shipped out so fast? How come we didn't go to Hawaii or Guam for more trainin'?" He didn't open his mouth, so I went on: "How come they grabbed us from nowhere, guys who'd never even seen each other before—lots of 'em—just threw us altogether, bang-bang, here we are? Why?"

"'Y' got a lotta questions, boy."

"But no answers."

"'Y' know what Tet is?"

"A holiday, right? Chinese . . .?"

"Asian. Get ya gear ready. We're gonna take a little walk in about ten minutes."

"That's it?" I yelled. "Tet? Wha'th'fuck's Tet got to do with it?"

"Ask around."

Jerkoffs. I always gotta end up with the world's jerkoffs. I lit a joint squattin' right where I was. Fuck 'em. I may have to be here, but I sure's hell don't have to suffer all this shit. It started to rain. I skipped into the eaves of the mess tent roof as Davis came by. He took a coupla hits 'n' I finished the joint. It mellowed me out so by the time I finished tellin' the hillbilly about my conversation with Ubanski I didn't feel quite so hostile. Grass can do some wonderful things for a psyche temporarily bent outa shape.

"Thing is," Davis said, "he's right."

"Thanks, futhermucker."

"What y'all want? You 'n' Poe. Y'all wanta make sense from some'in 'at don'? Or y'all want ever'body to ah'gree with y'all? Ah ah'gree. Don' make no more sense'n whistlin' up a pig's ass. But we heah. So we might's well fo'git the philla . . . ah . . ."

"Philosophical."

"Yeah. An' deal with the real shit."

"It still don't make no goddamn sense."

"If you dead, you think hit'll make any mo' sense?"

"Fuck you," I said 'n' laughed. Ol' Davis is okay. He prob'ly seems dumb's hell to a whole lotta people 'cause he's slow-walkin' 'n' slow-talkin'. But he's the kind that can concentrate everything on anything. Diggin' a posthole or partyin', didn't matter. And he's right. Bein' dead sure's hell ain't gonna answer nobody's questions. I think I was gettin' scared. All through basic and AIT they kept tellin' us about bein' the best trained, best led, et cetera. But I lived long enough to watch us get our asses kicked in that ambush. Sittin' there with our heads up our behinds, hopin' to God somebody'd save us. Whipple runnin' up 'n' down like a lost child. God knows where Jefferson was. Coupla guys from Fourth Platoon said he was flat on his ass in the ditch the whole time, clutchin' the radio in one hand and his rifle in the other. They said he didn't open his mouth once. Just sat there, starin' at the other side of the ditch. And Whipple'd said he thought the captain was hurt. But the captain didn't have any wounds. The first sergeant had been killed. Our platoon leader, Lieutenant Peterson, had got himself lit up in the truck that triggered the ambush. Seemed to me our leaders were losers and a lotta this shit was fallin' on us, ready or not. I definitely didn't feel ready.

Most of our platoon left on patrol about half an hour after my talk with Ubanski. Davis, Jinx, Poe, a Mexican named Garcia, Black 'n' Decker—swear t' Christ that was their names, both spades from Newark—me, Ubanski and Whipple were bunched up together. Whata collection. Garcia is an imp-sized Mexican who wants to fight bulls. He's from San Diego 'n' swears he's had about two hundred hours of practice with his cape. If you believe that you prob'ly also believe in the Easter Rabbit. But he's got a scarlet and gold cape about as big as he is. He's funny as hell when he gets stoned, gets out his cape 'n' calls the bulls. Black 'n' Decker are big city spades, hostile as hell. They stay pretty much to themselves. We call 'em the Drill Team. Well, wha'th-'fuck, with names like that there ain't no way to avoid it.

Garcia 'n' the Drill Team, like Jinx, were dubious benefactors of McNamara's brainchild. McNamara's 100,000. It has a ring, like Fortune 500, or 10 Downing Street (which, when I saw it on TV, really wasn't very impressive from the outside). McNamara's 100,000—pulled from the compost heap of America's hopeless. That sounds bitter, but I don't know if I really care much, one way or the other. Maybe I blame McNamara for what happened. I might as well blame God. I don't expect to ever get a chance to talk to either one of 'em. But it was McNamara, not God, who put his name to the program—retrainin' the retards. Takin' people who couldn't read or write well enough to pass the Army's basic entrance exam (geared to a sixth-grade level) and puttin' 'em through a cram course. Teachin' 'em to read 'n' write just enough to pass the test for cannon fodder. Teachin' 'em to write their name so they could sign their own death warrant.

Altogether there were thirty-one or -two of us on the patrol. Most of us knew each other by name but that was about it. We'd been split off in squads, and because of how quick we'd been thrown together 'n' shipped out, we still didn't really function together, or know much about each other.

The first ten minutes or so of the patrol went well

enough. We made it through the circles of razor wire and mine field, into the nearest hamlet. We musta looked like a Pan Am walkin' tour. Half of First Platoon had Instamatic cameras, clickin' 'n' snappin' like the place was a human zoo. The villagers stared back, kinda sullen. Even the kids didn't come round askin' for handouts. They hung to their mothers' hands, starin'. Their mothers didn't seem to like us any better. The old men were mostly off in the paddies with the boys too young to be drafted. Whipple had a Nikon with a big telephoto, musta been 200mm. He kept stoppin' to shoot pictures of little kids. Ubanski gritted his teeth 'n' kept his mouth shut, more or less. He was eatin' Life Savers like a fat lady on diet pills. Butterscotch Life Savers. Yech.

Anyway, Ubanski's love of Lifesavers is the least of his problems. But us and Whipple, we'd have given the Pope an Ulcer Extremus. When he finally couldn't take it anymore Ubanski bellowed, "Lieutenant, can we get this circus on the road, sir?"

"Certainly," Whipple said. "Anytime you're ready."

We moved out. It started to rain again. Off 'n' on, off 'n' on. Sometimes it seemed like it'd be better if it just rained steady till it was finished. Not that it mattered. If it wasn't rainin' our clothes would be sweat-soaked after ten minutes of work or walkin' round in these jungles. Our boots were always wet from wadin' through one goddamn paddy or puddle after another. Ubanski wouldn't let us walk the fuckin' dikes. "That's where they lay mines." Period. This was s'posed to be a friendly area. Tough luck. Wade. We waded. He was up 'n' down the line, findin' fault with everything and everybody. We were too close together. Too far apart.

Too slow. Too fast. We weren't payin' attention. We were too interested in a hut, a jungle flower, another human bein'. Hump it, hump it, keep movin'. Some kid from First Squad was still takin' pictures. Ubanski told him twice to put the camera in his pocket 'n' leave it there. The third time he just ripped it right outa the kid's hand 'n' threw it about fifty fuckin' yards into the middle of nowhere. The kid started to yell, got it about halfway out, saw the look on Ubanski's face 'n' let it die. That ended the happy snaps for the day.

Tryin' to describe the country we moved through is like what old what's his name musta felt tryin' to describe the circles of Hell. Foliage thick as hair on a sow's ass. Lots of times you couldn't see ten feet to either side of the track, or twenty feet straight up. Two 'n' three layers of green growth, vines the size of soda bottles, some the size of whisky jars, sixty to seventy feet long runnin' down trees 'n' across the ground. You'd bust your ass at least once or twice a day. Thorns like twenty-penny nails. Rip you to shreds, rake your glasses off, hang you up 'r tear your weapon right outa your hand. Everything's wet. The ground's muddy. If you don't fall over a fuckin' vine, you slip, twist a knee, pull your back, or just end up on your ass with Ubanski standin' over you glarin'. Then, to make it really interestin', there's mines 'n' booby traps. Some people say seventy to eighty percent of all wounds Americans suffered in Vietnam came from such surprises—bouncin' bettys, deadfalls, pungi sticks, claymores, an assortment of homemade goodies as gruesome as anything De Sade ever dreamed of. Thinkin' about that tends to keep you on edge.

Somehow we managed not to trip anything, or step into any traps ploughin' through the crap. An hour or two after we left Song My we stumbled into a clearin' maybe a hundred meters from a small hamlet. Half a dozen hooches, stone silent, sittin' on the edge of a few acres of rice paddies. The rain had stopped. We collapsed into the mud, gaspin', sweat-soaked 'n' disgusted. Ubanski was up 'n' down the line. "Sit up. C'mon, sit up. Off ya backs. Lay down when ya dead." "That muthafuckah don't never lighten up," Jinx bitched. "He always on somebody's ass." When Ubanski passed us 'n' stopped next to Whipple, Jinx pulled out a joint, lit it 'n' we started suckin' dope. Jinx, Poe 'n' me. I didn't take but a coupla hits. Enough to ease the strain. I watched Ubanski 'n' Whipple. Ski was as wet as we were, and as muddy. But he didn't look too frazzled. Whipple looked like shit. He was sweatin', his glasses mud-spattered. His clothes were twisted round his fat body. The five-seven frame was close to bein' overwhelmed by his hundred 'n' seventy 'r eighty pounds. His '16 was covered in mud, like he'd fallen on it. So was his Nikon. He was heavin' to get enough wind and his eyes were wide 'n' kinda bugged out. He didn't have any color to speak of, sorta pale gray. I could only see Ubanski's profile but you could tell by his hands he was givin' Whipple hell. He prob'ly wanted to go another two hours before we turned back. I didn't think Whipple'd make it. For that matter, I wasn't too certain any of us would last. This was a far fuckin' cry from AIT. This was more like I woulda expected from Special Forces, the green beanie boys. God A'mighty, I wondered, how in hell do they make it out here. I think I'd have given ten dollars for a can of cold beer.

"Shit!" Ubanski said suddenly 'n' stood up. He looked really disgusted. Whipple climbed up, prob'ly to protest. We never found out because just as he stood up a burst of automatic fire cut through the trees over his head 'n' he hit the dirt again. Thump. Ubanski walked maybe ten more feet 'n' squatted down. The rest of us rolled over and stared toward the hamlet. Another short burst came, still too high.

"Carbine," Ubanski muttered.

"How the hell you know that?" I asked. He wasn't more'n ten feet away, squattin' as easily as if this was a firin' range and the crap flyin' through the air was goin' the other way.

"Take my word for it." Whipple crawled up, still hung up on that military textbook style.

"It's comin' from that first hooch," Ubanski said.

Whipple nodded. It got quiet, really quiet. "Well, Sergeant?" Whipple said.

"Well what, Lieutenant?"

Whipple pawed at the sweat on his face. "Think we should rush it?"

Ubanski grimaced. "It's a hundred meters across open ground, sir. Let's wait an' see."

Whipple stared at the hooch. Another burst came 'n' you could see the flash off the end of the barrel. The idiot was still tryin' to shoot out treetops.

"Why don't we just wait till he's tired himself out?" I asked. "Don't look like he could hit a water-boo in the ass with a boat paddle."

"Water buffalo ain't what he's aimin' at, Hawkins. Maybe I'll send you after 'im. Wanna try it?"

I was about to decline when Whipple yelled, "Cover me," and took off like Moody's goose, Nikon bangin', poncho flappin' in the wind. Nobody could believe it. John Wayne, maybe. But Winston W. Whipple the Fourth, fat 'n' outa shape? A retard with a BB-gun coulda peppered him to death before he covered fifty meters. Twice he stumbled and fell. Twice he climbed to his feet. Nobody fired a shot. Not us or the near-sighted sniper. Whipple lumbered 'n' lurched, weaved in and out. The sniper's weapon had to have jammed.

"Crazy muthafuckah," Black 'n' Decker whispered together.

"Stone fuckin' crazy," Jinx agreed.

"I'm a sonofabitch," Ubanski said 'n' lined his rifle on the open window.

There wasn't anything to shoot at. About ten meters from the hooch Whipple fumbled out a grenade. As he passed the open doorway he tossed it inside 'n' flattened himself against the wall. Not more'n two seconds later the hooch disintegrated. The concussion blew out the matted straw walls, includin' the one against which Whipple was pressed. Picked him up and dropped him on his belly in a yard full of muck two inches deep. Stone silence, then Davis's lazy drawl: "Attaboy, Looten't. Y'all jus' killed ah enemy house." We came un-glued. I couldn't say how many of us were stoned 'n' that sure's hell affects what you think is funny. Maybe we shouldna laughed but if you'd seen ol' lard-ass lumberin' across there, then bein' stupid enough to throw a grenade in a straw hooch 'n' back up to the wall for protection . . . I don't know. Maybe when the Good Lord came in to hand out brains Whipple thought He said "trains" and decided he'd rather fly. Fan-fuckin'-tastic. Exactly like the movies, up till the last few frames.

"First 'n' Second Squads, start searchin' the hooches. Dig up the floorboards. Check the wells if they got any. Look for tunnels. That fucker went some-where. See if y' can find 'im."

"Hawkins 'n' Davis, come with me. Where's my RTO?"

Good ol' Ubanski. Work work work. He found his radioman and called for a med-evac chopper. The four of us trotted over to Whipple. I expected to find a bloody mess but he wasn't hurt bad. His pack 'n' flak jacket had taken most all the shrapnel. Far as we could tell he had a few slivers in his ass. He was bleedin', but not bad. Ubanski put his poncho under Whipple's face. "It's okay, Lieutenant. We got a chopper comin'. Have you outa here in a few minutes." Whipple was cryin'. Swear t' God. Ubanski picked up Whipple's glasses and slipped 'em in the Lieutenant's jacket pocket. Then he took a canteen, wet a handkerchief 'n' wiped the mud from Whipple's face. The whole time he was almost whisperin' to Whipple, "It's okay, Lieutenant. Everything'll be okay." I guess maybe Whipple was cryin' more about makin' an ass outa himself than bein' hit in the hindquarters. The dustoff dropped into the center of the hamlet. In less than two minutes they were gone. Very efficient. Ubanski got on the horn with Jefferson for a coupla minutes. Lookin' at the RTO, with his thirty 'r forty pound radio, I made plans to quickly develop a bad back if I ever got picked for that fuckin' job. That antenna wavin' round in the bush must make you a damn invitin' target. Supposedly the three most likely to get lit up are the RTO— the radio-telephone operator—the corpsman, and the point—the first man in a patrol.

When Ubanski got off the radio we wandered through the hamlet. Couldna been more 'n' twenty-five or thirty people there outside of us. All women 'n' kids. Nobody'd seen the sniper. Sure's hell he went down a hole, into a tunnel that led to another tunnel that led to God knows what.

Ubanski walked off to gather up the rest of the

platoon. Davis 'n' I squatted, facin' each other. It started rainin', light but steady. We both tried smokin' —regular cigarettes—but neither one of us could keep one dry long enough to get more'n three or four drags. We musta both been thinkin' about the same thing 'cause both of us started at the same time to say somethin' about Whipple. I nodded at him to go ahead.

"Think he'll be back?"

I shrugged. "Prob'ly."

"Ah reckon maybe he mighta larned some'in today."

"The School of Hard Knocks is one thing, but that kinda course in demolition must lose a lot to attrition."

He shrugged, but I knew from the look on his face he wasn't sure what the hell I meant by attrition. "I mean gettin' a lot of hot shrapnel in the ass is an awful way to learn a lesson."

"Yeah, reckon so. But you sure's hell ain't apt t' fo'git hit. 'Cause anytime you 'bout to put yo' head up yo' ass you goan see wha' 'appened the last time you did."

"Awright, First Platoon, off ya asses 'n' on ya feet. Move. We got a long walk." Long walk's ass. A long walk was an understatement matched only by Custer on the Little Big Horn sayin', "All right, men, don't take any prisoners." What we'd done comin' out was like a warmup exercise. Somehow Ubanski managed to double the distance goin' back, and not once did we use a track—a ready-made trail. We cut 'n' clawed, cussed, bled, badgered 'n' finally begged the sonofabitch for mercy. "Candy-asses," he'd sneer. "Candyass crybabies. Keep movin'." All the kind thoughts I'd had watchin' him bein' so gentle with Whipple went to hell in a handbasket. I thought about killin' him right there. I could stumble 'n' fill him full of holes as I fell. An accident. Sorry, Sarge, I sure's hell didn't mean to do that. But as long as you're all fucked up, how about just dyin'. I fantasized about that for a full ten minutes. But I couldn't do it. I kept on humpin' with the rest of 'em. Prayin' for a break. He'd give us one every hour or so. Let us sit down for maybe ten minutes. And every time he'd wander off, makin' no more noise than an ant pissin' on a ball o' cotton. When he came back we'd know it was time to go. What I finally decided was that the motherfucker had to be as tired as we were. And if he could keep goin', so could I.

Two 'r three hours after we started back—seemed like two days—we stopped for our third break. As usual Ubanski disappeared, but he was back in about two minutes. Finger to his lips. He came down the line 'n' tapped Jinx, Davis, me, Garcia, Black 'n' Decker, got us together and whispered, "The first sonofabitch makes a noise, snaps a twig even, does six months on KP. I found fish in a barrel." He led us into the goddamnedest tangle of vines, thorns 'n' trees I'd ever seen. Black 'n' Decker were carryin' an M-60. Garcia had an M-79 grenade launcher. Looks like an elephant gun and shoots grenades. Davis had his shotgun. I was on the verge of havin' the shits. My heart was bangin' inside my belly like a blown truck piston. We walked so quietly I could hear us breathin'. All of a sudden we could hear voices, laughin' like the war was bein' fought in San Francisco. Then we heard water splashin'. We crawled right to the river edge, still hidden by undergrowth. There, in the middle of fuckin' No Man's Nam, lookin' like they didn't have a care in the world, were nine of Uncle Ho's finest—playin' frisby. You think I'm kiddin'? I couldn't believe my eyes. They gotta be South Vietnamese, I figured. They can't be North Vietnamese 'cause nobody that stupid could be winnin' a war.

"Hit 'em!" Ubanski screamed, emptyin' his M-16 into the thicket of bodies. The chatterin', poppin' 'n' boomin' that followed was fierce 'n' fuckin' frightenin'. My rifle was pointed at 'em but I couldn't squeeze the trigger. I watched the river turn bloody, bodies sink 'n' rise, bone chips flyin', smelled that peculiar odor that gunpowder has, and threw up. It wasn't much, green bile 'n' hot water. I was covered in sweat. My stomach turned 'n' twisted like a snake in a trap. Ubanski tossed two grenades into the river when the firin' stopped. The concussion woulda killed anything that wasn't dead. Like dynamitin' for fish. The poor bastards never knew what hit 'em.

The silence was incredible. My ears were ringin' but I coulda heard any real noise. Nothin'. Everybody just stood 'n' watched the bodies bobbin' in the water, the blood dilute till it mostly disappeared. They looked at each other, then at me. I was on my knees. I musta looked sick 'cause I sure's hell felt it. Ubanski walked over 'n' emptied half a canteen of water on my face, told me to put my head between my knees, then went to collect the slopes' weapons. They'd had a small arsenal, half a dozen AKs, a machine gun called an RPD, I think, Chinese-made like the AKs, and a coupla Eastern European automatic rifles. Some Claymore mines made by us, coupla days' food, mostly rice balls, pretty good pile of ammo. We took everything, includin' their clothes. Walkin' back to Kilo everybody had a souvenir. Mine was nausea 'n' bile puddled in the back of my throat.

It wasn't quite dark when we reached home. I died

in less than five minutes. Just dropped my gear on the floor and my ass on my air mattress. I was s'posed to have guard at two a.m. If anybody tried to wake me they gave up. I woke about three-thirty 'n' drank enough warm water for a hermit's bath. My mouth tasted like a lint factory. Somehow I managed to find my toothbrush without wakin' the dead. That helped some. A cigarette did a little more. Now some coffee, I figured, and I'll be able to face the world. I staggered to the mess hall. There's s'posed to be coffee 'n' sandwiches all night, for the guards. I stumbled in about ten after four. I had a cup in my hand when the cook called, "Yo, y' got guard?" I shook my head no. "Then get ya ass outa here. We ain't open 'cept to guards 'n' KPs till oh five thirty." He glared.

"All I want's a fuckin' cupa coffee and a sandwich. I missed chow last night."

"Tough shit." He crossed his arms over his chest like a goddamn cop. I was tryin' to decide between just takin' the coffee or throwin' the fuckin' cup at Cookie when Captain Jefferson walked in. "Mornin', Sergeant. Coffee fresh?"

"Yes sir."

Jefferson looked at me, at the name tag stitched over the pocket of my fatigue jacket. "Hawkins, bring us both a cup." I grinned. The cook glared. I took two cups of steamin' black coffee to the far corner where Jefferson was sittin'. "Guard?"

"No sir. Either they missed me or couldn't get me awake." He snorted, lit a cigarette, then pushed the pack toward me.

"Hear you had a rough time yesterday."

"Yes sir. How's Lieutenant Whipple?"

"Supposedly they got the lead out of his ass." He

chuckled. "Should be back in a week, maybe less." We nursed our coffee in silence. He lit another cigarette from the butt of the first. He always had filter cigarettes and he always tore off the filter. "What happened at the river yesterday?"

"We got nine of 'em."

"We?" He took a swallow of coffee. "Sergeant Ubanski said you got sick. Threw up . . .?"

"Yes sir." I started sweatin'. The bile oozed outa its hidin' place 'n' made the coffee bitter. Fuckin' Polack bastard.

"You get in close like that . . ." He shrugged. "Gets messy." He drained what was left of his coffee. "Want to get us another cup?"

I took my time, tryin' to think of somethin' to say if he asked me why I hadn't fired any rounds yesterday. Seemed like he might not know. Maybe Ubanski didn't even know, but that was hard to believe. That motherfucker knew everything. When I got back Jefferson smiled 'n' said, "Hawkins, the sergeant's report of your illness was entirely straightforward. He didn't belittle you and I know he doesn't think less of you for it. Just hang loose and you'll be okay." He drank some of the coffee. "You probably had the most honest reaction anyway."

"How's that? Sir."

"Not many of us want to kill people who've done little or nothing to provoke us. What the hell do we care about this fucking place? A pig farm, for Christ's sake." He drained his cup again. "The Army moves in mysterious ways, its miracles to perform."

"I thought that was God doin' that."

"God and the Army, Hawkins, have always been in cahoots." He musta thought that was funny 'cause he chuckled again. "Hang loose, Troop."

Hang it in your ass, you silly sonofabitch. I watched him walk out 'n' wondered what he'd think if he knew I'd overheard him 'n' Major Early goin' at each other. Mighty Major asked him straight out, "You chicken-shit, Captain? You gonna spend yo' whole goddamn tour hidin' in this bunker?" I couldn't hear what Jefferson said at first—if he said anything—then he yells, "Goddamn you, Major! I did my duty here. I got scars on my legs and about a pound of plastic in my hip. I can't walk without limping. I live in pain, Major. This goddamn weather makes it ache day and night. What the fuck would you like from me?" I couldn't hear anything for a few minutes, then Jefferson's voice bellowed "Shit!" A roar of laughter came after it but it didn't sound like he really thought anything was funny. Maybe that was just me, but it seemed a reasonable reaction.

I felt like *I* was unravelin' at the seams. Somethin' was wrong as hell. I'd seen seventeen dead where we'd been ambushed and it hadn't seemed to make much difference. Then I saw nine dinks get blown away 'n' couldn't keep from pukin'. That's pretty fucked up. I don't know. Maybe seein' it done was worse'n seein' the results. But somehow that doesn't make any goddamn sense, either. And wha'th'fuck am I gonna do if I can't start shootin' these cocksuckers, I wondered. Sure's shit stinks there ain't a one of 'em that wouldn't blow me away given half a chance. Here I'd spent a fair amount of time tryin' to live down Life's clichés, or at least those that I thought were a lotta shit. So Life says okay, wiseass, here's your first fuckin' meaningful choice: kill or be killed. I felt pretty much under-whelmed by both of 'em. As choices, I mean. And beyond the point of academic choosin' I couldn't say I was ready for either one.

Crazy Dago and the colonel's son came outa the rain squalls that same mornin'. Separately, of course. When you're a colonel's son assumin' your first command you fly in on a helicopter, have a leisurely chat with your old man, then ride over from battalion headquarters in a cold, wet jeep. Some things even a colonel can't fix. Second Lieutenant Stephen Eric Levine, son of none other than our battalion commander, came to take charge of First Platoon. It wasn't much but you gotta start somewhere. He looked like the All-American Boy gettin' out of his father's jeep. Six-one or six-two, lean, hard, a little Florida tan left, along with a little sunstreaked hair—he had one of those regular Army officer burr cuts. His boots were shined and his clothes fit. That alone was more'n enough to set him off. He was wearin' a Ranger patch on his shoulder. Hot shit, those Rangers are s'posed to be. And he was a Point man. Prob'ly be okay as point man on a patrol, too. What he was—or looked like— was gung-fuckin'-ho.

Poe 'n' I watched his arrival from the eaves of the company headquarters tent. The jeep splashed up. Lieutenant Levine 'n' Major Early got out. Early spotted Ubanski walkin' across the road toward the crapper. "Ho, Ski!" Ubanski came over 'n' got introduced, *before* golden boy even met Captain Jefferson. I took a hit off a joint we were doin', held my breath for about twenty seconds, then exhaled a question: "You gettin' a message?" I asked Poe.

"I'm getting hungry." He put on his clever look.
"Not to mention horny."
"Pay attention, smartass. Look at that." He took
another hit 'n' looked hard. "See what I mean?"
"Nooooo," he sighed 'n' the smoke trailed the
sound outa his mouth.
"You ain't tryin', boy. Note one, that's a new lieutenant, right? A *second* lieutenant?" He nodded 'n' hit
the joint again. "Bein' a *second* lieutenant, he can't be
a replacement for Whipple, right? The Army don't
make executive officers outa second lieutenants. Note,
two, the Ranger patch. Note, three, that he was
ushered over by Major Early, who you'll admit
wouldn't normally piss in a lieutenant's ass if the poor
bastard's guts were on fire, right?"
"Yeah, all you've said probably is true, more or less.
So what? What message?"
"Well," I said with a rush of smoke, "the lef-tenant
must be our new platoon leader. Either that or he's lost.
And Rangers ain't s'posed to get lost. Now, if he's our
new PL and the good major thinks enough of him to
introduce him to Ubanski before—mind you, *before*—
he goes in to see the Black Messiah . . . whata you
think?"
"I think you'd better lay off the dope."
"Maybe. But I got a feelin'. That dude looks like
trouble." I was about to go into a serious discussion of
why I felt like I did when I realized I couldn't remember. The thing about grass and clarity of thought is that
the fuckin' clarity usually lasts about ten seconds.
The arrival of Crazy Dago, on the other hand, was
less thought-provokin' but a damn sight more spectac-
ular. Jinx, Davis, Poe 'n' me were sittin' down to noon
chow. We were first in line when the mess hall opened

at eleven-thirty. All of us were stoned, Davis a little less than us. He always wanted some sense of control. Jinx was half outa his mind, which was normal. Poe 'n' I were floatin' somewhere in between. Jinx was laughin' his ass off at somethin' Black or Decker had said right before they sat down. What we'd been served was s'posed to be chili 'n' rice. I think the cook musta once run a kitchen in a county jail. Only a captive audience would eat that stuff. I had a forkful halfway to my mouth when the shit hit the fan. We all heard two or three guys scream "Incomin'!" About two seconds later two shells exploded on one side. *Boom! Boom!* Then another one—*Boom!*—on the other side. Brackets. Fuckin' food went in the air, trays 'n' benches went on the floor and guys went flyin' out the door. Maybe another five seconds, then the back of the mess hall collapsed. Jinx got up like he was a doctor on call, bitchin', "I'm still hungry." Then he wandered out, holdin' his tray, scoopin' food into his mouth. Davis had taken off like a big bird. Poe 'n' I followed Jinx, both of us carryin' our trays. We're walkin', for Christ's sake. *Boom!* Another fuckin' shell goes off behind us. There ain't another human bein' in sight. Everybody's down in the goddamn trenches, hidin' under a stack of sandbags, rolled into bunkers. And the three of us stroll across the area like the Three Blind Mice. Bad enough. But then, up the road 'n' right into the company area comes a Honda, hell for leather. First I thought maybe it was VC cavalry. One lone madman makin' a bonzai guts 'n' glory run at us. *Boom!* Another round fell about twenty-five meters in front of the Honda. It and the hapless horseman went ass over elbows. Buuurrrpppp, burrrpppp, brup! The Honda died. The rider rolled up on his feet, runnin' toward us.

Jinx was still eatin'. Poe 'n' I were kinda transfixed. *Boom!* Another round took the Honda to hell in bits and pieces. *Boom! Boom!* The shit was gettin' thick and I was comin' down enough to question the wisdom of standin' round in a rainstorm of mortars. The Honda kid kept runnin' toward us, not in the panic you might expect, but definitely hustlin'. When he was about five feet away Jinx says, "Hey . . . man . . . that's some kinda dynamite openin' you got."

Private Angelo Bruno Cocuzza, forever after known, and sometimes loved, as Crazy Dago, stopped dead in his tracks and looked at us like we were talent scouts. Or potential suckers. You couldn't ever be too sure with him. "Yeah, man, but wait till I get my whole act together."

Boom! Boom! Sonsofbitches were gettin' closer. "I think I'll go find myself a hole to hide in," I mentioned casually. And took off lopin', followed by the rest of 'em. We jumped into an empty bunker 'n' watched the mess hall burn. No big loss that I could see. Jinx finished everything on his tray. Poe squinted at Cocuzza's name tag. "Cock'a'zoo . . .?"

"Cah-*coo*-za."

"What nationality is that?"

"Sicilian."

"Hey, hey, a fuckin' Siggie," Jinx said. He acted like he was really happy. "Where you from, man?"

"Jersey. You?"

"Philly, man. Where in Jersey?"

"Plainfield. 'Lantic City. You guys just gettin' settled in, I hear. Where's the action?"

"Shit, man, if this ain't enough for you, you come to the wrong fuckin' place." Crazy bastard. Fuckin' mortars fallin' all over the place 'n' he wants to know where the goddamn action is. Anyway, what the hell can you say about a goddamn grunt that fucks up enough to get himself transferred from a nice safe head-quarters job to a line company—then shows up ridin' a Honda? There prob'ly isn't any rule that says you can't own your own Honda in Nam, but damn sure not many do. For that matter, there weren't many with Dago's flair or flat-out insanity runnin' loose any-where. Crazy people, yes. Crooks, yes. By the thou-sands. But not many Honda-ridin' crazy crooks.

"No, man, I didn't mean this crap. You been here long enough to get it together? There's lots happenin' in Nam. Big money's bein' made."

"My man," Jinx said. "Comes right into a pig farm 'n' wants to set up some action. How 'bout ribs 'n' pizza? Get us a franchise goin'."

"Fuck, man, I'm talkin' about money. Big money. Who's got the numbers here? The lottery?"

Mind you, the whole time, the goddamn war's still goin' on. Mortars were fallin'. The mess hall was burnin'. At least some of Kilo musta been scared. And those two are havin' an investment meetin'. J. P. Morgan . . . meet John Jacob Astor.

The shellin' stopped after twenty 'r twenty-five rounds. Two KPs and the cook had gotten hit. The KPs were okay, small stuff that got 'em out of the kitchen. The cook got some iron in his big fuckin' belly. He got evaced out 'n' we never saw him again. I was ready to invite some VC to lunch for what may be the only humanitarian mortar attack I'll ever see. We went to fightin' fires once the mortars stopped. There wasn't much to burn and most of the rounds had fallen be-tween bunkers. Everything was back to normal in less than an hour. Everything but the mess hall. That was goin' to need a little reconstruction. Crazy Dago went

to check in with the company clerk and get his assignment. He was back in ten minutes, shakin' his head.
"Who the fuck ever heard of an Apache 'at plays bagpipes? That guy trippin' or what?"

"Henry Wadsworth Longfeather *is* a trip. We just
don't know which one," I said.

"Yeah, well I been in this fuckin' country over five
months but I never saw nobody with bagpipes. He
really a goddamn Indian?"

"Who knows?" Poe asked. "Am I really a senator's
son? Are you really a bookie? Is any of this for real?"
He flopped down on his air mattress. "I wouldn't take
bets on anything I've seen in the last month."

"Drop your gear if you wanta sleep in here." All he
had left was a pack, which he put down in a corner of
the bunker. Everything else he'd had went up with the
Honda. I led him outside.

"Who the fuck's he?" Dago asked.

"A senator's son. Name's Poe." We sat down.

As soon as Crazy Dago 'n' I were alone he started
talkin', callin' me Hawk. Right off. That's a thing with
a lotta Yankees. Take a guy with a name like Yaroskovitch. God knows he's got enough problems like it is. All
his life the poor bastard's correctin' other people's pronunciation, forever spellin' his name. Then he meets a
buncha friendly Yankees. First thing, Yaroskovitch is
'Roskovitch, then Rosko, then Ros, then Ya. *Bam bam
bam.* His name is obliterated. And what's worse,
there's a lotta guys from Philadelphia, Newark, Brook-
lyn, Boston who yell "Yo" instead of "Hey" or "Pardon
me." So they take Yaroskovitch, reduce it to Ya 'n' then
run around yellin' "Yo, Ya." I mean how the fuck
would you like to be called Yo Ya? Yankees are strange
people. Friendly enough, but strange.

Anyway, Crazy Dago gets to talkin' as soon as we're

outa the bunker. "Hawk, y' look like a sharp dude so I'll lay it on the line. I wasn't BS'in' when I said there's money to be made. I can't do it all, y' know? I can use help. How'd y' like a piece of the action? We get things organized, with you as my main man, y' could prob'ly make ten 'r twelve in a year." He dug out a thin gold— gold, mind you—cigarette case, opened it and took out a joint. There musta been another dozen in there. "How long you guys been here?"

"Who the fuck knows? Seems like forever." I took a drag off the joint, the most perfectly rolled one I'd ever seen. When Jinx rolls one it looks like something a straight artist would do to illustrate copy on *The Evils of Marijuana*. Three hits later I was on my ass. "We got here Thanksgivin' Day. How long is that?"

He looked at his watch, which had a calendar. "Three weeks, give or take a day."

Three weeks coulda been three months. I felt like somebody'd strapped my brain to a boomerang 'n' sent it whirlin'. Maybe that was the dope. "Whata . . . wha'd you say 'bout me bein' your main man?"

"Sure. Easy, y'orta pick up ten, twelve a year."

"Ten or twelve what?"

"Ten grand, minimum."

"You gonna pay me ten thousand dollars for bein' your lieu-ten-ant?" It was gettin' damn near impossible to get the words out.

"Yeah. Y' interested?"

"For ten thousand dollars I'd volunteer for Lucifer's Royal Dragoons." Visions of great wealth went past me in a stream of images: sports cars, airplanes, beautiful girls, grand houses. I must admit that right at that moment it didn't occur to me that ten thousand wouldn't buy all that. Fact is, it wouldn't buy very much at all. But fantasy's no fun if you fuck it over with facts. I don't know how long we sat like that, me in a stupor. I remember at one point Crazy Dago pulled three throwin' knives from a little case he had hitched to his waist. He threw the first one at a corner post of a bunker. It was on the mark. Then a second one, which stuck in maybe two inches from the first. "That's some trick," I mumbled. He threw the third 'n' split the distance between the first two. "That's the fuckin' trick," he said. He did it three 'r four more times. Didn't miss once. Ubanski, Lieutenant Levine, Davis 'n' Garcia walked up and watched him do it the last time. The lieutenant was introduced 'n' said something stupid like "I'm sure we'll work well together." I could see him checkin' us out while we each shook hands. Fuck you and your Ranger patch, I thought when our eyes met. The corners of his mouth turned down in a mockin' smile, like he knew where my head was. A minute or two later he and Ubanski strolled away. Davis and the wetback sat down with us. Crazy Dago said, "That's a cheerful twosome. A cherry Ranger lieutenant and a bad-ass lifer. All they need is Mighty Major, y' know, and they'd prob'ly win the war by themselves." He smiled with that soft, spaced-out kinda smile people get when they're stoned. "Man, the stories I could tell you about Mighty Major'd make ya fuckin' hair stand up. Y' think Ubanski's a bad-ass, this fuckin' guy—Early's his name—he makes the Sarge . . ."

"What's his name?"

"Early, Major Early. He . . ."

"He's here," I said. "He's OPs officer for the Battalion."

"Jesus, Joseph an' Mary. Ya shittin' me? He's here?

He was gonna be sent the hell home. Oh, goddamn. Listen, I'm gonna, y' know, tell ya a coupla stories. No bullshit, man. This shit really happened. I seen it with my own baby blue eyes . . ." For some fuckin' reason he aimed 'em at me . . . "Hawk, man, you know I wouldn't BS, right? This is straight, man. That mother-fucker's crazy. Stone fuckin' crazy. First thing, he ain't afraid of nothin'. Nothin'! He'd sooner hunt dinks than take a sure bet on the Jets. God's my witness, last August him 'n' me was out together with a buncha ARVNs. I was with a battalion HQ group in Chulai, right? Mighty Major is American advisor to an ARVN battalion. For six months he's been doin' that. Bad job. Really bad. Fuckers won't fight, won't patrol, sleep on guard, start late, quit early, throw away their equip-ment and they're stupid. Y' know? There's like a few good ARVN outfits, but ninety percent of 'em are chick-enshit. I mean they recruit most of 'em at gunpoint, right? So wha'the'fuck?

"Anyway, I been in HQ for maybe two weeks when in comes Mighty Major, lookin' for another RTO. He don't go no-fuckin'-where without a round-eyed radio-man. That's my job, right? Last one he had, and the one before that, got greased. One dead, one fucked up. So some idiot lieutenant I had some words with picks me, right? An' I, y' know, man, I don't know from nothin'. I'm in-country like maybe two fuckin' weeks. He wants an RTO, I figure it beats hangin' around that place arguin' with lieutenants.

"First day he goes, 'Cocuzza, you stick with me. When I say do somethin', do it. When I say move, move. Yo' don't question what I say, not for a second, 'cause if yo' do y'all prob'ly end up dead.' All in this weird fuckin' Reb talk, right? No offense, but it's hard to understand Rebs when they slur words the way he does. He hardly ever raised his voice. Take 'im ten minutes to say 'good mornin''—not that I, y' know, ever heard 'im say it. I heard 'im tell a general to go fuck 'imself—no shit—but never a nice word. Almost never . . ." He got quiet. His eyes looked far away, but not like he was stoned. Garcia lit a cigarette. Dago ran his hands through his hair. It was longer'n any army hair I'd ever seen. It musta been three months or longer since he had a haircut. He didn't wear a helmet, unless it had gone with the Honda. He was a nice-lookin' guy, with a lotta laugh lines. But he didn't look so happy now. Finally, maybe five minutes after he got quiet, Davis said, "Ah'm waitin' fer yo' story 'bout the Major."

"Well, I'm with him 'n' the slopes for two, three weeks. Every day, man. Every day, it's a fuckin' fight, y' know, between him an' the gook captain. Mighty Major wants to patrol, like push out, keep movin'. The dinks wanna lay on their asses. They go out an hour, rest two, come back. No contact, right? They tell their bosses everything's, y' know, secure. Mighty Major's tellin' *his* bosses these bastards won't do their job. There's bad trouble comin'. I know it, man. An' one day Mighty Major, he goes to the dink captain, he goes, 'These men are worthless as soldiers. An' soldiers always reflect the worth of their leaders.' *Bam!* The shit hits the fan. That fuckin' dink captain gets 'is bowels all in an uproar. Calls out the whole fuckin' company, right? Has their ass. Tells 'em what the major said. He's gotta save face, so he tells 'em to draw a week's rations and ammo, to get their ass in gear 'cause they're gonna show the fuckin' round-eye who's worthless and who ain't.

"So us an' the gooks take off. Mighty Major's happy as I'd be if I was Joe Namath. Three days we humped it. He still couldn't get 'em started before nine, ten o'clock. But they kept movin' away from the base, into Indian country. By the end of the third day everybody but Mighty Major's draggin' their asses. He's not even tired at night, y' know? He goes out at night by 'imself —or with me once—and looks for the bastards. Stone fuckin' crazy.

"On the fourth day, like about eleven in the mornin', we're walkin' through these rice paddies. The dinks're strollin', draggin' their ass an' their weapons. The point man's fuckin' whistlin', *whistlin'* f' Chrissake. All at once Charlie opens up with machine guns, automatics, everything but rocket-powered punji sticks. Fuckin' ARVNs start fallin' like bowlin' pins. What doesn't fall starts to run, y' know, but they're runnin' AWAY. Throwin' down their rifles, screamin' some shit in Vietnamese. 'Get air in here,' Mighty Major goes to me. I was already on the phone. Next thing he trips a dink runnin' by, grabs the fucker's M-60 an' starts bellowin' *'Dung lai, dung lai,* cocksuckers!' But they don't even slow down. I mean, man, them dudes was cuttin' it for high country. Before he'd even stopped yellin' he opened up. *On the fuckin' ARVN!* He ran through a whole fuckin' belt. Then he grabs another belt from the guy he'd tripped—he'd kept a foot on the little fucker the whole time, right?—and he takes off for the ambush. Dead at 'em. Firin' the whole time.

"I'd got the fuckin' Air Force on the horn right away. They had a coupla F-100s in the air goin' somewhere. They were there in like two minutes. I told 'em we had an NVA company pinned down. They love to get those bastards from the North. I popped some

smoke, sent 'em over the tree line where Charlie was
dug in. That was a show to see. Man, I'd come here a
cherry. I never seen nothin' like that. Napalm, rockets,
machine guns. Those flyboys did a number on the
gooks you wouldn't believe. Mighty Major had got
knocked on 'is ass a coupla times. First time around
took his boot heel off. I mean, can you believe it? He
damn near drowned in that slimy paddy water. But he
came up roarin' an' firin' an' got another round through
the leg. *Bam!* Down on 'is ass again. I don't think he
got to kill a fuckin' one of the VC. What the 100s hadn't
done in musta been long gone before he got there,
limpin' like he was."

Dago stopped, outa breath. We were all hangin'
there, disbelievin' on one hand, but somehow knowin'
on the other hand it prob'ly was true. We knew Early
'n' Ubanski had gone out at night—a hunter-killer team
Poe had called 'em—and you could just see Early doin'
exactly what Crazy Dago said. He was that kind. Stone
crazy.

"Ah ain't nevah heerd of nobody shootin' down 'is
own men," Davis said.

"He didn't, y' know, shoot his *own* men. They were
dinks, y' know? I mean a goddamn gook's a gook. If the
fuckers in Washington had any sense we'd be fightin'
with Charlie. Sure's hell we'd win the war a lot faster."

I started chucklin', seein' Early screamin' 'n' yellin',
runnin' across the paddies, shootin' the shit outa everybody. It isn't funny, but it is. South Vietnamese may
be the most useless soldiers since Mussolini made privates outa all those grape pickers.

"Y' think that's funny, y' shoulda been there when
the honchos came in. First thing when Mighty Major
comes limpin' back, y' know, the dink captain goes

crackers. He's yellin' an' screamin' insults, doin' a number on the major. Mighty Major, he doesn't say a word. He raises the barrel of that M-60 till the gook's lookin' right into it. Mighty Major's got his finger on the fuckin' trigger. The gook gets stone quiet. Then the major says to me, 'Get Battalion on the horn. Explain our situation to 'em.' Maybe ten minutes later half the choppers in Nam came in. Two generals, more colonels than I got cousins, great fuckin' gobs of majors an' captains. Corpsmen, doctors. I say to myself, Major, ol' buddy, you been had. Ya ass is grass an' these dudes gonna mow y' down.

"First thing, this one general, he's been in-country about three weeks, he starts givin' the major hell. He rants for five minutes, threatenin' court-martial, firing squad, Leavenworth for life—an' Mighty Major listens the whole time, till the general's outa breath, then says, 'General, you can go fuck yo'self.' I mean this guy's got brass balls like the size of cantaloupes. The general, a brigadier, goes white. He's prob'ly gonna explode, but the other general, a two-star dude, calms 'im down, says they can't solve anything there an' they get in the major general's chopper with some colonel. Me an' the Vietnamese captain get in another, an' off we go.

"F' like maybe two weeks, y' know, y' couldn't tell what was happenin'. I musta told ten different people the story. They kept layin' down this rap about how I wasn't gonna be charged with anything. But they had my ass under wraps. House arrest. I couldn't go ten feet to take a crap without my guard. Then, *bam!* it was over. Like nothin' had happened. I go back to HQ. An' it's like nobody knows from nada. They give me my old job and I figure wha'th'fuck. I mean, what am I gonna do, right?"

"Ah cain't b'lieve hit," Davis says after we had digested it for a minute or so. "Ain't no way Ah can b'lieve an American Army major would do hit, an' Ah cain't b'lieve hit could be kept a secret if'n he did."

"Reb, maybe where *you* come from it couldn't happen. But where I come from it happens all the time. It's called payin' off."

Welcome to the real world, sports fans. How the fuck do you like them apples? I believe it. Crazy Dago might be a hood but I sure's hell don't think he could, or would, make up a story like that. Fuck me. It's funny, like low comedy, 'cept the dudes didn't get up after the scene was shot. But there's somethin' else, too. I mean, wha'th'fuck's the forces of freedom comin' to? If we're gonna go round doin' in our Partners in Peace, dingin' our slope-headed Allies . . . I don't know. Maybe that's the way real wars are fought. And what I found out later helped explain it a little better. The whole thing. Early's adventure, fuckin' up the Friendlies—as they're sometimes called—comes under the TOG Rule. The TOG Rule covers a lot of things, accidental and elsewise. You fire off a salvo of 155s and they fall short, right into an ARVN infantry company; you drop your bombs in the wrong place 'n' wipe out a platoon of ARVN grunts; you ambush some slopes and they turn out to be on Saigon's payroll—right away, first thing, you scream TOG Rule, TOG RULE!! It's a little like King's X in a game of tag. The TOG Rule— They're Only Gooks—has kept a helluva lot of round-eyes outa trouble. And it applies to civilians, too. Prob'ly even more than the military, but I can't swear to that.

That night Davis 'n' me were sittin' guard in a hole

on the perimeter, starin' over the barrel of our big-ass M-60 when he says, "You think ol' Cockatoo knows 'is ass from a jug of apple cider?"

"Dago? 'Bout some things I guess he does. Why?"

"Well, Ah was thinkin' on what he was sayin', 'bout Major Early. Don' seem right, somehow."

"What Dago said? Or what Early did?"

"They both wrong."

"Luke, you stare at them fuckin' water-boo and I'll take a nap. Wake me if the Polack shows up, okay?"

"Hawk, you b'lieve 'im?"

"Luke, I believe the worst of everybody."

"You mus' be a right unhappy feller."

"It's old age. Makes me tired 'n' unhappy."

"How old are you?"

"Twenty, goin' on ninety-six."

"Ah'm goan be twenty-two in three months. Helluva place to spend mah birthday, ain't it?"

"I figure any birthday I live through can't be all bad, so I ain't gonna bitch about where I am."

"You better hurry to the next one. 'Banski says you won't live long." He said it in the same flat fuckin' drawl. It's rainin' out. Your pants're on fire. You're about to get lit up.

"Did that Yankee sonofabitch say how long I've got?"

"He says a month, at the most. You, Jinx 'n' Poe, them niggers Black 'n' Decker. Says y'all goan git hit right quick 'cause you fuck off all ah time." He spat a wad of phlegm into the darkness. "Hard to say, 'bout you . . . I 'spect Sarge jus' don' cotton to you 'n' that sometimes blinds a man. He might be right about them niggers, but you 'n' Jinx, way I figure it, y'all goan git by. Poe, he ain't goan be here long 'nough to git in any trouble."

"Luke, how come you call Black 'n' Decker niggers, but Jinx has a name?"

"He's yo' buddy, ain't 'e? I wouldn't no-ways call yo' buddy a nigger." He spat into the darkness again. "Anyways, he ain't like them sorry bastards." He stood up 'n' pissed over the edge of the hole. "They's always fuckin' off, stayin' stoned, cain't find 'em when there's work 'ats gotta git done. Don' do their share. They fuck up with me 'n' I jus' might light 'em up myself."

"Like Early?"

He studied the question for a good two or three minutes. Looked at it from about nine different angles. "Ah guess you right, Hawk. But how you goan feel if'n they git us lit up 'cause they fuckin' off?"

" 'Bout the same's I would if it was you, Poe, Ubanski . . . don't matter much who it is."

"Ah reckon. Anyways, Ah wanta ask a question . . . how'd you git to be a peacenik?"

"A *what?*"

"Ain't that what they calls somebody who don' shoot people in a war?"

"They're called conscientious objectors."

"You one, ain't you?"

"I don't know."

"You ain't fired a round yet, is you?"

"I shot at the bushes when we got hit comin' out."

"But the other day, at the river . . . ?"

"No."

"How come?"

"I couldn't."

"How'd you git like that? It ain't natural."

"It's a defect, like bein' black, or ugly, or growin' old."

"Cain't the doctors do nothin' fer you?"

"I don't think so."

"Well, what you goan do? If we git lit up 'n' we need you, you goan be there?"

"I'll be there, Luke."

"Good. Makes me feel a mite bit better."

I said it with a lot more conviction than I felt, but I sure's hell didn't think I could say no, forget it, I'm goin' home 'n' go to sleep.

I leaned back against the sandbags 'n' closed my eyes. But I was as far from sleepin' as I was from San Francisco. And that was a long fuckin' way in more ways'n one. Ubanski thinkin' I was gonna get greased didn't bother me much. I didn't like his goddamn attitude any better'n he liked mine. What bothered me was feelin' we were all gonna get the shit kicked outa us. We weren't more'n half-ass ready, the way I saw it. Sure's God we didn't have our heads together. Seemed to me there wasn't one in fifty that took this seriously. I couldn't make up my mind whether it all was a farce or some fuckin' far-out reality I just couldn't cope with. This whole thing of killin' people might be okay for movies. And seein' some other dudes dingin' people on Huntley-Brinkley is fine 'cause I can change channels. But the bare-ass brutal truth of it all is it ain't just dinks that die. Up to the point where we came on stage there'd been several thousand round-eyes who'd gone home wearin' those funny-lookin' squared-off tin containers with handles on the sides. Must mean the Indians were doin' somethin' right. And besides that there's the whole business of all this bein' for nothin', or next to nothin'. You didn't have to be two days in Army basic before you heard the first, or the fifth, or the fiftieth story about how completely fucked up Nam is. The cadre, as they're called, our drill sergeants 'n' platoon leaders, all had been here, killin', burnin', blowin' away everything in their path. Damn near everyone of 'em, even the ones that think we should light up Hanoi with A-bombs, say Uncle Ho's children will sit down to dinner in Saigon six months after we finally get out. So why'n hell should I go around shootin' up the dinner guests?

"You 'sleep?"

"No," I grunted.

"What time is hit?"

"Ten till two."

"Who's our relief?"

"Dago 'n' Garcia. That's a great combination. Garcia'll go cape a water-boo and Dago'll give eight to five on the buffalo."

"Man's gotta be crazy's hell to let a bad-ass bull try 'n' run 'im down whilst he jus' waves a tablecloth inna air."

"Luke, sittin' out here in the mud like we are, babysittin' a bunch of goddamn hogs, it makes it a little hard to judge another dude's sanity. If we ever . . ." We both sat bolt upright at the same instant. I felt Luke's fingers tighten round the handles of the M-60. "You want a flare?" I whispered.

"Wait up a minute . . ." He turned his head, one way, then the other. I couldn't see a fuckin' thing. The juice was joltin' my stomach. "Luke . . ."

"Hit's a hog."

"How can you tell?"

"Ah can smell 'er." A flare went up, off to the left. *Pop*. Weird white light 'n' there the fucker was, a big goddamn sow right in the middle of our mine field. The flare died. I heard footsteps comin' up behind us. Lieutenant Levine squatted in front of our bunker. "Davis . . . ?"

"Suh?"

"Who fired the flare?"

"Cain't say, Looten't. Off the other side there. Ain't nothin' but a big ol' sow. But if'n she don' step lightly there's goan be a lotta bacon fer breakfast."

"How in hell did a hog get into those mines . . .?"

"Walked, I reckon."

I giggled. "Want me to waste her?"

"Not with that machine gun. Give me a flare." I fired a round outa the flare gun. Levine sighted 'n' squeezed off three rounds, ding, ding, ding. The sow squealed a coupla times, rolled on her side 'n' died without settin' off anything. The light died almost as fast as the hog. Levine got up 'n' strolled off, back to bed I s'pose. Everything got stone quiet again. I slumped back against the sandbags, sleepy, just startin' to drift when Davis drawled, "You know, Hawk, we sho' got some right funny looten'ts. First 'un kills a house, next 'un kills a hog. Too bad we ain't fightin' hog growers 'n' meat packers. Slaughterhouses 'n' hogs'd be easy."

Ol' Luke-baby knows just where to put the knife when he wants to cut through the crap.

Next day was one of those days that would have driven my English teacher stone crazy. Ol' Witherspoon. I used to blow him out with my stories. He'd get all bent outa shape 'cause I'd make everything happen at once. Or bring in some totally unexpected BS at the last minute, somethin' that would unhinge the hero. No warnin'. Nothin'. Like he'd get hit by a car just about the time he got his head together. Or one time I wrote a story about this dude who dreamed incredibly beautiful, weird far-out paintings. Better'n Pollock, better'n Picasso. And he *knew* they were dynamite. But he couldn't paint a kitchen cabinet and make it come out right. He bought maybe a hundred tubes of paint, brushes, canvases . . . nothin'. He'd dream these paintings, try to put 'em on canvas, fuck 'em up, have a goddamn fit 'n' finally just throw everything against a wall. Couldn't figure it out. So he decided to take art lessons. He spent two or three years studyin', drawin', mixin' paints, readin' about dudes who painted. And all the time he's half crazy with these dreams. But he can't put 'em on canvas. Finally he gets to where he can do a fair job of mixin' to get color, he knows about proportions, relationships of one part to another, all the academic shit. He spends three years doin' that, gets his degree in fine arts or whatever, and *bam!* his dreams change. Now all he dreams about are stick men, like the kind a three-year-old would draw. They're all exactly proportioned, bein' a fine arts man, but the wild, incredible visions that he'd seen in his dreams are gone. Witherspoon tore that story to pieces. Yack yack yack. Finally, in exasperation, he says, "It doesn't make sense. What happens to him now?" I just shook my head. "Oh, man, what else, he becomes a fuckin' art critic." I got suspended three days for sayin' fuck. Witherspoon didn't like it, not because the dreams stopped, but because there wasn't any advance indication *for the reader*. It's unfair, he says. I said who the fuck ever heard of life givin' any warnin'? He says but this is literature. "I ain't writin' about literature, I'm writing about life." Dumb bastard couldn't understand that. But English teachers aren't the most gifted of God's little door prizes.

Anyway, that's all beside the freakin' point. The next day woulda put ol' Witherspoon up a tree, but that sure's hell didn't stop it from happenin'. First thing, I'm makin' coffee, up walks Lieutenant Levine. He's watchin' me screw around with some rocks, tryin' to make a little hearth for my canteen cup. I flunked hearth-makin' during my Boy Scout trainin'. He squats down, not a word, and arranges the rocks so the cup, half full of water, balances perfectly. I put a piece of C-4 about the size of a golf ball under the cup 'n' put a match to it. That shit's somethin' else. You can heat a gallon of water in less than thirty seconds if you use enough C-4. It's plastic explosive, but if you don't put a fuse in it the damn stuff just burns. Hot as the gate posts to hell. I mixed instant coffee, sugar 'n' sat back. Mind you, he hasn't said a word.

"Got a minute . . . ?"

"You askin' for real? Shit, I got most of a year."

"Looks like we're all in the same boat."

"Looks is deceivin', Lieutenant. How's the view from the top?"

"The way the world's standing on its head you may be a lot closer to the top than I am."

"I might also be your fairy godmother, but don't take no freakin' bets on it."

"Hawkins, let me lay it out for you. I like wiseass dudes okay, as long as they're funny. But I don't intend to take a lot of shit from a private. Not in this army, nor the next."

"Private first class, sir."

"You can be a private before you finish that coffee."

"I couldn't freakin' care less. Sir." I took a mouthful of coffee 'n' rolled it round, like I'd seen people in movies do with brandy. "Anyways, ain't it against the law for officers to talk to grunts?"

"Probably. But I don't like tyranny, even for the sake of discipline. I'd rather talk sense to a man."

"I just bet your old man wonders where he went wrong." He laughed. Did you ever know, not just feel but absolutely know, you were gonna like some dude because of the way he laughed, or some screwy thing he did, the way his mouth stretched out when he smiled? I knew right then, when that fucker smiled, I was gonna like him. That blew me out, 'cause you aren't s'posed to like officers. Not for friends. Breaks down morale, disrupts command. Maybe ten, fifteen seconds went by like that 'n' he just looked at me.

"What's it like, bein' a colonel's son?"

"About like being a private."

I laughed. "How come you like wiseasses?"

"Because they usually have a little more smarts. And they're funny. I don't think my father ever told a joke in his life. There wasn't much humor in my home."

That blew me out, too. Some dude sittin' there

sayin' things most people never admit, even to themselves. He wasn't upset or overfriendly. Just straight up, said what he wanted to say. "Why you pitchin' me?"

"I want a tight platoon. I don't want anybody to die because they were off on their own trip. Everybody does his job, works together, keeps his head straight . . . we'll all make it."

"Bullshit!" He got up, smiled that smile of his and walked away. Not a word. Fuck you, Lef'tenant, you 'n' the horse you rode in on. But I liked him anyway. What the hell, we're all full of crap, one way or another. He wants to BS about us all makin' it, can't hurt. Bullshit keeps us goin' at times.

Next thing, a little later, was mail call. Now, let me say first off, there's two kinds of mail call in the Army. One way is you check the mail room, just like some dude walkin' into a post office to check his mailbox. Civilized, more or less. Then there's the other way, usually confined to basic trainin' and transient situations. Kilo's mail clerk, a big, strappin' corn-fed clodbuster, a corporal we'd picked up in California, evidently thought we were transients—which was a fact, looked at in one way—and proceeded to handle the mail in an appropriate manner. It was like the last minutes of a weddin', when the bride throws her flowers to her collection of co-conspirators. Letters come sailin' out over the heads of a hundred guys half starved for something to put them in touch with their idea of the real world—it leaves you scramblin' like a buncha fuckin' refugees for a handful of food. "Brown, Adams, Adams, Smith"—he sniffs the letter—"smells like a French whorehouse . . . Peters, Adams . . . man, that loan company is after yo' ass . . . Tompkins, Baker, Smith—sealed with a kiss—Zimmerman, Smith . . . tell 'er to use cunt juice, man, it smells better . . . Parker, Brown . . ." On 'n' on. The corporal, a lifer with four years, was named Cellars. When he'd finished he yelled, "That's it for you fuckin' grunts. NCOs can pick up their mail inside." He spun around and headed inside.

"Corporal Cellars, you got a minute?"

"No," he bellowed, without even lookin' round. Typical lifer attitude. Lieutenant Levine was up the stairs in two jumps, through the door. Jinx came up 'n' grabbed me by the arm. "Hey, man . . ."

"Ssshhhh. Watch this."

"What . . . ?"

"Quiet, man. Listen."

Levine's voice came out of the mail room, loud but even. "Corporal, when I ask for a minute I want one . . ."

"I'm busy, Lieutenant. I got more goddamn paperwork piled up here than you got days in the Army."

We couldn't hear what was said next, but then Corporal Cellars yells, "What kinda fuckin' . . ." Next thing he comes through the screen door. Backwards. His feet a good ten inches off the ground. Him 'n' the door hit the ground, maybe a yard from Jinx 'n' me. Levine comes through the openin' where the door had been. He jumps down 'n' walks over to Cellers. "Mailboxes for every man in this company, Cellars. By tomorrow." Cellars scrambles up, pissed, big as a goddamn bull. He had to be six-four and Levine is maybe six feet, can't weigh no more'n one-eighty. But the lieutenant was all muscle 'n' meanness. Cellars glared, pawin' the ground. Levine gave him a smile, walked off two or three feet, then turned around. "Cellars, you want me to take off these bars?" Cellars didn't say a word. The lieutenant starts to unbutton his jacket. When it was open—mind you, he didn't even get it off—Cellars did a little dance into the distance. I'm here to tell you, he made a good choice. Levine was one solid slab of muscle. His belly looked like a goddamn washboard. If you hit him you'd prob'ly break your fist. When Cellars walked off the lieutenant started to button up, as calmly as he'd unbuttoned. He smiled at Jinx 'n' me, that little half-ass grin.

"I like a man who reasons with people," I said. "No fuckin' tyranny with the troops." The smile grew about half an inch on each side. He walked off to do whatever he'd been goin' to do before he'd kicked Cellars' ass.

"My man," Jinx said.

"I think he's gonna be all right."

"Them goddamn Ranger dudes mus' spend alla their time liftin' weights. You see the muscles on that cat? 'N' that little Jew star round 'is neck? He don't look like no Jew I ever seen."

"He don't act like no fuckin' Army officer I ever saw. Must be an experimental model."

That's all before eight a.m., right? Helluva way to start your day. About ten-thirty we got some replacements, dudes from other companies scattered here 'n' there. They didn't look no more like us than a motor-scooter looks like a Maserati. Two or three months in No Man's Nam, as a grunt anyway, and you get right lean in the flank, poor's a sharecropper's mule, mostly muscle 'n' bone, with a wary look and a bad-ass view of life. Bein' shipped off to do time with a bunch of virgins like us didn't do much to sweeten their disposition. There were six or eight of 'em. They all went to Second Platoon. We were still light a few men, but so was almost every line company in Nam.

A little later another dude shows up, well fed, his

clothes all neat 'n' starched, his boots shined. Simmons, L.D. Another corporal. He gets us, or we get him, dependin' on how you look at it. He gets the bunker Black 'n' Decker are holed up in. They're out somewhere, screwin' around. He's in there long enough to drop his gear 'n' change. Out he comes, wearin' a goddamn judo-karate-kung-fu getup. And proceeds, just like this was the Eastern Regional Quarter-fuckin'-Finals, to scream *Ha! Haaahhhh! Ah!* And other such insanities. The whole damn time he's choppin' the air, flingin' himself this way 'n' that, kickin' 'n' jumpin' like a barefoot spastic steppin' on hot coals. Maybe a dozen of us form up in a half-circle, starin'. He don't pay us no more mind than a gnat on a gnu's ass. For ten, fifteen minutes he goes on with it, then just as suddenly as he started, he quits. All sweat-covered, blowin' his chest in and out. Ellis, a skinny little punk from some North Jersey slum, pipes up, "All right, folks, now you've seen him in action. Supersoldier—breaks bodies nine ways—now, what we're gonna do, for jus' twenty-five cents, that's right, one quarter, for one quarter we're gonna let you feel this man's muscles. That's right! You can actually touch them. They're all there, folks, right on top of his shoulders. One quarter, two bits for two minutes with Supersoldier inside his bunker."

Simmons doesn't think it's funny. Simmons has a sense of humor that would've made Hitler happy. "You wanta try it, punk?"

About six guys, all at once, go "Ooohhhhh." Simmons glares. Then somebody in back, outa sight, yells, "Does the money go to the society for retarded children . . . ?" Simmons yells, "C'mon up front, wiseass, so we can see you." This time we all go "Oooohhhhhh." He's really gettin' pissed. So I gotta get into it, right? I say, "Hey, Simmons, is that thing you're wearin' a short-sleeve straitjacket? You really a road-show exhibit for the mentally retarded?" Now, I don't know *why* I had to say that. Maybe I really am a wiseass, but everybody laughed 'n' I love to make people laugh. Simmons comes toward me, really pissed. I figure it's an odds-on bet I go home a cripple 'cause I damn sure don't know anything about that choppin' 'n' bone-breakin' shit.

He's maybe three feet from me when I hear this loud clank behind me 'n' Davis says, "Hawk, Levine wants t' see you." Simmons stops dead, starin' over my shoulder at Davis. I give Simmons my best up-yours smile and split, leavin' ol' Davis lookin' at Supersoldier over the barrel of that fuckin' shotgun he carries. The sound of that 10-gauge clackin' shut would put fear into the heart of Quasimodo himself.

Right honorable Lef'tenant Levine I found sittin' outside his bunker, surrounded by Ubanski and half of First Platoon. He had a map on the ground, pointin' to this checkpoint, that river. There were a lot of crayon marks here 'n' there, but one of 'em ran a big rough circle that had to cover twelve or fifteen miles. It didn't look good to me and I didn't even know for sure I was included. I tried to fade into the background when he looked up. "Hawkins, go get a radio."

"Sir . . . ?"

"A radio, Hawkins. An RT with which we communicate over great distances."

"Sir . . . ?"

"Hawkins," Ubanski snarled, "get ya goddamn ass in gear. Move it!"

I got a radio, neatly mounted on a pack frame and weighing no more than eight hundred pounds. I got it on without too much of a problem and immediately sank four inches into the mud. Now, let me tell you a little somethin' about Army radios. They don't really weigh eight hundred pounds. Eighty pounds, maybe, but if you go bare assed, unarmed and without water, you prob'ly aren't carryin' any more'n you'd normally lug around on patrol. But the thing about radios is they gain weight as you go. Seriously. They feed on human sweat 'n' the longer you carry one the heavier it gets. They also tend to attract bullets, which add to the weight. I mean, you go out for two, three days 'n' that bastard will weigh about half a ton by the time you get back. If you get back. I pointed that out to the Lef'tenant while we were standin' round waitin' on everybody to get their gear together. "Listen," I said, offerin' what I thought was a reasonable alternative. "Listen, Lieutenant, sir, how about I leave this motherfucker here 'n' take a drum. A snare drum. Really, listen, man, we don't need this thing unless we get in trouble, right? So if we get in trouble I'll beat hell outa that drum 'n' we'll split. Makes more sense to me."

"I can imagine. Where's your weapon?"

"You mean I gotta *defend* myself, too?"

"No, but you damn sure better defend that radio."

"I can hardly wait." I got my little plastic pop-gun, two hundred rounds of ammo, six goddamn canteens of water and six grenades. In ten minutes I'd gained a hundred pounds. And not from carbohydrates. Right off, first thing, before we took ten fuckin' steps, I knew me' 'n' that radio weren't no-ways gonna get along. I'd sooner carry a big sack of monkeys in heat than that thing. Sonofabitch is dead weight. Just for drill I tried joggin' a few steps. Imagine the hunchback of Notre Dame tryin' out for the Vatican track team. I wasn't laughin'.

"Hawkins . . . ?"

"Sir?"

"What the hell are you doing?"

"I give up, Lieutenant . . . what the hell am I doin'? This is Dago's job."

"You don't look too happy."

"What gave me away, Sherlock? Sir."

"Hawkins, I don't want Dago, and I don't want you runnin' off with my radio. I want you here, at my side, in my pocket."

"Lieutenant, would you consider lettin' me pull this motherfucker along in a little wagon?"

"That would ruin your image. You look good. Like one of those posters they use to recruit Airborne troops." The sonofabitch was smilin', like it was all a big fuckin' joke. "You're going to be a fine-looking soldier, Hawkins. A real poster child."

I was walkin' close, in his goddamn pocket, so to speak. The BS that was goin' back 'n' forth was quiet, between him 'n' me, so I figured to hell with it, let's see where the line is. "Lieutenant, with all due respect to you, your goddamn Ranger patch 'n' them fuckin' gold bars, you can hang it in your ass."

"Don't be bitter, Reb. Ol' Stonewall Jackson would think you a fine speciman of Southern manhood, a soldier if he ever saw one. Think what Lee could have done for you at Gettysburg if he'd had radios."

"With Longstreet sittin' on his ass, radio 'r no radio, we'd still have got our asses kicked."

"Any of your family at Gettysburg?"

"My great-grandfather and his brother on my mother's side."

"They make it okay?"

"My great-grandfather's brother got killed on the second day. He was with those crazy bastards that breached the Union lines. Supposedly there weren't more'n twenty or thirty that made it to the top. Looked round and wasn't another fuckin' gray uniform in sight."

"And your great-grandfather?"

"Third day—he was with Pickett—when Pickett started down the hill my great-grandfather looked at him for a while, sittin' his horse up on the ridge, then said fuck it, they're all crazy. He packed it in. Went home."

"Just like that?"

"Yeah. When he made up his mind to do somethin', that was it. Kept tellin' people the war was over. They kept sayin', 'We ain't heard no news about it.' And he'd say, 'That's 'cause the dumb bastards runnin' the war don't know it yet. But she's over 'n' done, and I'm agoin' home.' "

"Well, at least you've got a family tradition of reluctant warriors. I was wondering if you were the first."

"Nope. And I ain't likely to be the last, either."

"I hope not."

Well, shit. Wha'th'fuck you gonna do with a dude like that. I had a half-assed feelin' I was bein' suckered. Lef'tenant Levine, whatever he is, is sharp. I kept tellin' myself, don't forget it, stupid. He's sharp. But the thing is, if I really like a dude, I like him. And if I get suckered I don't get pissed, but it hurts. Like fallin' in love with a liar, or findin' out your mother tried to abort you. I'd just as soon not get close with too many people, 'cause they're gonna sell you out if it gets really rough. When it comes to the crunch, as they say, you're gonna be left to pull your own little wagon. And don't think that don't go in war just like it does elsewise. I used to believe all that crap about battle makes buddies outa everybody. The fuckin' movies have done more to make romantic bullshit outa bad business than any single industry ever known. I'll tell you this, if movies had made up as much BS about the glory of missionary work as they have about makin' war, the whole goddamn world would be populated by Jesus freaks. I sure's hell ain't suggestin' we'd be any better off, but a war to repel Christianity makes about as much sense as one to contain communism, or repel nationalism, or expand capitalism, or whatever the fuck we were s'posed to be doin' in No Man's Nam.

Havin' said that I'll say this, too: I'd still rather be with dudes I know than those I don't. And I didn't know two outa ten on this not-so-fine fuckin' rainy-ass day. Names were no problem 'cause the Army, in it's infinite wisdom, has you sew that across your chest on the right side. Ubanski, Davis, Levine, Jinx, Poe and Garcia I could figure to one degree or another. The rest of 'em were little more than strangers. I didn't like that. I like to have some idea of who a dude is 'n' what he's apt to do. I figured to stay close to Davis 'n' Levine. Fuck the other fifteen of 'em.

About an hour out we pulled up alongside a track and dropped our shit for a while. Levine 'n' Ubanski went off on their own. Davis came over 'n' took a hit off the joint I'd lit. "What you make of the Looten't?"

"Beats me. But I can tell you one thing, me 'n' this goddamn talkin' box ain't gonna be the best of friends no matter how long I lug it around." I kicked at it, and missed. "You got the faintest of faint fuckin' ideas what we doin' out here? Or how long we're gonna stay?"

"Did you sleep all through basic? We *patrollin'*." He said it like I'd forgotten my part of the responsive reading in church. "We goan back tomorrow."

"TOMORROW!!? You mean we're gonna be out here all night?"

"Damn, you dumb sometimes. How else we goan

go back tomorrow if'n we don' stay heah all night?"

"Are we lookin' for trouble, Luke? I mean, ain't it enough that trouble's gonna find us?"

"Hawk . . . Ah don' know, man. What you think we doin' heah? We come a long ways jus' t' sit on ou' asses 'n' farm pigs. Ah ain't much fer givin' advice. Ain't often Ah feel hit's mah place. But Ah'm goan give you a lit'le. Git yo' shit together, man. This heah's the real thing. We heah t' kill people, t' hunt 'em down 'n' waste 'em. You a soldier—ain't no way to change hit less'en you git lit up. This ain't no sightseein' trip you on."

I think that's about as serious as I ever heard him. He drawled along, huntin' words, tryin' to be helpful, I guess. Looked to me like everybody was pretty much agreed that we were here for something other than an idle life, and that I'd better get it together. Thing is, I knew it. I'd known it from the day they put my name on the list for No Man's Nam. But I sure's hell had a great reluctance to admit it, 'cause then I was goin' to have to deal with it in an altogether different way. In or out, Hawkins. In or out.

Except for the pain in my back I did about as well as I needed to do. Nothin' happened. We didn't see diddily-shit that I could tell. I didn't sleep more'n two or three hours all night. We were wet. Cold. Caught up in playin' at some strange game of hide 'n' seek. I looked at the faces, and what passes for understandin' just wasn't there. Ubanski, I guess, knew what was happenin'. Levine was puttin' all that Ranger stuff to some practical use. But the rest of us could as well have been back in camp, or out to lunch. We musta covered fifteen miles and I didn't see a fuckin' thing worth walkin' across the street for. Shit, it all looked the same to me, then and forever after. I never did learn to tell one freakin' hamlet from another. Like walkin' through swamp country. Who the hell can tell one cluster of shacks from another? But that didn't bother me as much as my fantasies. I've always had fantasies, seein' myself the hero of this or that, or seein' myself dead 'n' all my friends 'n' family sorry they'd treated me like they did. I've solved crimes, defended criminals, won games, broke the bank at a hundred casinos, caught huge fish, fucked the most beautiful women in the world, fought duels 'n' done ten thousand sorts of things I doubt I'll ever get to do in *real* life, as they say. But I'd never fantasized killin' people. Even the duels were relatively bloodless. I'd just wound the dude. But while we were sittin' there in the dark, wet, shiverin' 'n' shakin' like a dog tryin' to shit a peach pit, I musta killed two hundred slopes. I saved Levine's life, and Davis's life. Ubanski got greased, but you can't win 'em all. I lit up the equivalent of two companies of Ho Chi's finest. All by my fuckin' self, which is even more unlikely than me doin' in a bunch of dudes in some heroic fashion. The thing that bothered me, though, was feelin' that if I was to the point of fantasizin' about doin' in Indians, I was bound to hell in a handbasket. I don't mean in any religious sense. I don't pay no more attention to God than he does to me. I mean the only reason I could see for that kinda fantasy would be acceptance. If I kill, I'm one of the boys. There was too much I didn't know for me to come to any real . . . wha'cha call it, the French thing that means an absolute. And sure's hell there wasn't nobody to talk to about it. Maybe Levine or Poe. Maybe. But that was it, and I wasn't too sure I wanted to talk to them. The chaplain would give me some shit about God 'n' man, and how their laws sometimes seemed to be at odds, but they only *seemed* that way. I heard that bullshit in

Basic. I just got up 'n' took a walk. Nobody said a word. The fuckin' headshrinkers'd say I was havin' an anxiety attack, give me a pat on the back, make a note in my record. Fuck that. How in hell was any of us not s'posed to have anxiety? Goddamn people out there tryin' to blow you away 'n' some asshole says I'm anxious.

We got back about eleven in the mornin'. And I'm here to tell you, the boys had been busy. Now I know how hard it's gonna be for you to believe this, but you 'n' ol' Witherspoon can get fucked. While we were out chasin' Charlie the rest of Kilo had built us a new mess hall. It looked exactly like a Howard Johnson restaurant.

"Good God," the Lef'tenant sighed.

"Remember," I said, "you coulda been a Green Beanie. Bet there ain't no HJs in Laos."

"Hawkins . . . ?"

"Sir?"

"Fuck off, and take that radio with you."

I went to find my bunk, but where I'd left it there was a solid wall of telephones, radios, files, reams of paper, a sort of tote board 'n' two or three clerks.

"Hey, Hawk baby, how's it goin' buddy? Wha'cha think of our HQ?"

"Our what?"

"Nerve center, man. This is where it happens."

"What happens? And where's my goddamn bunk? Wha'th'fuck's goin' on, Dago?"

"We're in business, man."

"Which fuckin' one?"

"Lottery. Numbers. Money changin'. Smugglin'. Don't matter. Anything 'n' everything that'll make us a buck. Beats gettin' ya ass shot off, don't it?"

"Dago, I'm just a poor-ass ol' country boy. And I ain't rightly got no idea of wha'th'fuck's goin' on. My ol' mammy done warned me 'gainst big city women and big city ways. But she ain't said a goddamn thing about no big city dudes like you. And just as soon's I wake up I'd sure be mighty pleased to have you explain all this. *Now where's my goddamn bunk?*"

"Cmon, man, it's all set up."

It was, and that's a fact. He'd moved us into a hole big enough for six people, prob'ly the best sand-bagged goddamn hole in the compound. The two-by-fours were fuckin' paneled. It was raw lumber, but damn sure it looked better'n anything else in the area. The walls were covered in pinups, bright cloth, peace signs, posters of Ho, Mao, LBJ, Nixon and some dude I'd never seen before. Turned out he was a forcibly retired Sicilian gentleman named Lucky somethin' or other. "I clipped that picture from a newspaper 'n' sent it to a place that blows 'em up. Prob'ly the only one in Vietnam."

"I sure's hell hope so. How'd you do all this?"

"Friends, man. I got a lotta friends." He gave me a big smile and it hit me again how good-lookin' he was. "My friends 'n' me, we look out f' each other, y' know? You 'n' me, Hawk, we friends, y' know?"

"Dago, you're stone fuckin' crazy. Wha'th'fuck are you doin'? Explain it to me, and remember, I'm a country boy."

"Okay. First, the numbers. Simple. Guys bet a number, any number over fifty. Maybe they dream somethin', y' know? In the dream there's the number seventy-seven. So they bet seventy-seven. If it hits, they collect four hundred to one. Easy enough, right?"

"Who decides which number wins? How do you get to that?"

"ARVN body count."

"*What??!!*"

"Dead ARVNs. Can't use VC dead. People fuck with them, y' know? Even more than the ARVN dead."

"You got GIs bettin' on how many South Vietnamese get wasted in a day?"

"Sure. Wha'th'fuck, they're only gooks."

TOG Rule. "What happens if maybe twenty guys bet a number 'n' it turns up? You gonna pay out a lotta money at four hundred to one."

"No way, man. I got hit men in a dozen different places. I got a line right into ARVN HQ in Saigon. Shit, I can have half a company lit up in less'n an hour."

"You'd blow away our sorry-ass allies in this piss-poor war to keep from payin' off?"

"Is the Pope Catholic?"

"You really are stone crazy. Man, you can't go round greasin' those dudes like that."

"Y' kiddin' me? Christ, Hawk, I pay out good money every day of the week, y' know, to keep those dudes ready to move. Shit, they're ARVNs too. If they don't care, why'n the fuck should I?" He opened a little electric refrigerator 'n' pulled out two cans of beer. *Pop . . . pop . . .* Ah, America, we see your face in every snap-tab can of Schlitz. "Hawk, listen, man. They got dudes in Saigon, Nha Trang, Danang, Can Tho, Pleiku, Cam Rahn Bay . . . they make me look like a canoe laid up next to an aircraft carrier. Americans, Koreans, Indians, every kinda goddamn gook known to man. This ain't a war, this is high finance. There's more payoffs, kickbacks, black market deals, money swaps, an' shit stolen than you can imagine. Man, half the Koreans in this country —we're payin' 'em somethin' like fifty dollars a day to fight over here, apiece, I mean—half of 'em are moonlightin' as guards for every double-dealer between the

DMZ and the U-Minh Forest. And that's as fuckin' far as you can go in this country. Whole shiploads of shit, just, y' know, disappear. Turns up on the streets, for sale. Stereos, radios, cigarettes, clothes, guns, medicine. Don't matter. Y' know there's dudes that specialize in stealin' penicillin an' plasma to sell Charlie? They—"

"You gotta be lyin', Dago—"

"Wise up, man. Walk down a street in Saigon, one block, you'll see if I'm lying." He drank off half the can, then smiled again. "Hawk, I might shaft you for a whole helluva lot of money. Or kill you if you shafted me really bad. But I wouldn't lie to you, y' know? No profit in that."

"Who's doin' all this?"

"G-fuckin'-Is, man. Civilians. Officers. NCOs. Everybody that can get a piece of the action is grabbin' with both goddamn hands. Y' wanna little truth laid on you? At least half—half, man—half the goddamn film cans that the network boys send back is packed tight with dope. I heard of this one dude in Saigon, a bureau chief, he made a stone fuckin' fortune sendin' back dope he had flown to Saigon from Laos. If he's doin' it, man, bet ya ass they're all doin' it. Who the hell looks in a film can? Customs? With that big fuckin' network tag on it? No way. A kilo a day. Easy. No risk. More if he's greedy. He's workin' with a dude in New York. The dude mails 'im back the money, Saigon guy puts it through the money changers, fifteen hundred for a thousand . . . round and round, Hawk. And that's small shit. Believe it or not, I heard the fuckin' CIA was flying opium from Burma to Hong Kong to be processed, an' doin' it for the fuckin' Chinese Army we pay up there."

"Hey, Dago, wait! Wait, man, I'm willin' to believe anything almost, but the fuckin' CIA and the Chinese Army? C'mon, man."

"Y' ever heard of Air America?"

"No. Wha'th'fuck's Air America?"

"Buncha airplanes flown by people paid by the CIA." He shook his head, side to side, like he was as disbelievin' of my ignorance as I was of his information. "I don't know how y' got along without me." He finished the beer. "How long did you say y' been in-country?"

"I don't know. We got here Thanksgivin' Day."

"That's not even a month. Even so, haven't y' learned *any*thing?"

"Man, we been diggin' holes 'n' walkin' round in the goddamn bush huntin' Indians."

"There ain't no profit diggin' holes. An' y' can get killed out there . . ." He waved at everything beyond where we were.

"Dago . . . ? Can I sleep now?"

"Sure, man. I'll wake y' f' chow."

Well, as the good ol' boys down home say, I ain't never. Exactly what they ain't never depends. In this case I'd say it was a safe bet the good ol' boys would say I ain't never heard the likes of no such carryin's on in all my born days. Me neither. But what freaked me out even more'n Dago's descriptions of money-grabbin' and double-crossin' was his sayin' "That's not even a month." How in hell, I wondered, am I gonna survive another fifty fuckin' weeks of this shit?

Dago had said he'd wake me, but it was Davis, or the rain. I woke with a start, out of a dream, some weird shit that didn't make no sense. Everybody was laughin' at me 'cause I was runnin' round in a big cage, like you see at a zoo, grabbin' fifty-dollar bills people were throwin' to me like peanuts to a monkey. All the fifties had Dago's smilin' picture where ol' Ulysses Grant's shoulda been. "You 'n' me got guard at six. Wanta eat first?"

"I s'pose so. Who turned on the shower?"

"Gooks. Sarge says we can look t' git hit tonight if this don' let up."

"I can hardly wait." I sat up 'n' lit a cigarette. "This freakin' war's bein' fought by absolute madmen. Ain't no man in his right mind that would go out on a night like this. Looks to me like it could be postponed, at least. Hell, they been fightin' for forty fuckin' years anyway. What's another two or three months? Luke . . . ?" He looked up from the pieces of my rifle. "Why're you cleanin' my pop-gun?"

"Hit needs cleanin'. Looks like you spent the night stabbin' worms with the barrel. If'n we git lit up tonight Ah don' want yo' rifle t' jam up."

"Why's everybody bein' so good to me? You cleanin' my weapon so I can blow away people. Dago tryin' to educate me to the ways of the world so's I can make a bundle of money. Lef'tenant Levine tryin' to make me a soldier so I can redeem the honor of my ancestors. Y'all just too good to this ol' boy."

"We love you, Hawk. You what we all wish we was."

"What's that?"

"A nine-year-ol' kid who still thinks there orta be some sense t' things."

"Go fuck yourself."

"Hain't ameanin' it badly. Don' take no offense."

We stared into each other for a moment, past all the shit we all wear on the surface to keep people from seein' inside. "I don't." And I didn't, truth to tell. I still can't see no virtue in bein' all man 'n' no boy. 'Specially when bein' all man means killin' or never questionin', just sorta lyin' down so's you don't get in the way of those that think they know how everything should be. I heard a lot of people sayin' a man's gotta do this, do that. A man's life is this way or that way. Those that said it to me, I most often told to stuff it. But a lotta us dumb fuckin' Southerners believe we got a responsi-bility to our country. And we don't look no further. So I go off to answer my country's call, to defend it against aggression, to help maintain peace in the world, and next thing I know I'm in this silly-ass place to shoot people who ain't no more a threat to my country than the Beatles are to Beethoven. Any country that's been around long as this one and still uses two sticks to pick up one grain of rice and one stick to pick up two buckets of shit ain't likely to keep me awake nights wonderin' when they're gonna invade California.

Davis 'n' I came into chow behind the biggest human bein' I've ever seen. Absolutely. I ain't but five-nine, so a lotta people look large. But this motherhumper had *feet* long as my legs. His boots had to be special made. He was at least six-eight, straight up, and damn near that goin' round. His fuckin' field jacket looked like a two-man pup tent. "Who the fuck's that?" I asked Davis.

"New first sarge. Minnow's 'is name."

"*Minnow!* Minnow?? My God, he'd scare Moby Dick and his name's Minnow?"

"Who's Moby Dick?"

"Forget it. When did *he* get here?"

"Yesterday, while we was out."

"No shit. He got his own truck?"

" 'Is own truck?"

"To carry his shit around. Man, he couldn't get a change of underwear in one of our duffel bags." Man Mountain Minnow went through the chow line with two trays and the freakin' KPs didn't open their mouths. They just shoveled the shit on 'em and tried to keep their eyes from poppin' open too far. The sarge nodded his bald head 'n' smiled. He had the most goddamn cheerful face I think I ever saw. Not handsome or strong, particularly. Cheerful. He looked like he was stoned on himself. When he sat down at a table he took most of the bench on one side. I pushed Davis ahead of me 'n' we sat down opposite him. But not before I asked if it was okay. No way. We BS'ed a little. Then I said, "First Sergeant, I know there's prob'ly been ten thousand guys . . ."

"Six-nine, three-hundred and twenty pounds. Give or take a few. Everything I'm wearin' is special made. And every time I re-up it takes a special act of Congress, or something close to it. Anything else?"

"Yeah . . . anybody ever say no to you?"

"Not since I was fourteen or fifteen . . . I forget which." He was chucklin', not bothered a bit by bein' a curiosity. When he finished eatin' he sat back, lit a big cigar, and belched. Almost blew Davis's hat right off

the table. It thundered through the room—the belch—
and twenty people cracked up. He couldna cared less.
He looked at the name tag on my chest. "Hawkins
. . . where you from?"

"Georgia."

"There was a family of Hawkins up where I'm from,
but I think they were from Virginia originally."

"Where y'all from?" Davis asked.

"Iowa. Hogs 'n' corn. Looks like I come to the right
place. But in my thirty years in this man's army I think
this is the first time I ever saw a US Army Infantry
com'ny raisin' hogs. My brothers should be here. They
own a hog farm in Iowa. They'd laugh like hell at this,
though."

"How come?" I asked.

"The fuckin' porkers looks like war orphans. Feedin' 'em *rice.*" He said "rice" about the way I'd expect
the Pope to say "birth control." "But I 'magine I can
take care of all that. Week or two.

"Shee-it," Davis put it. "Ah told that fat fuckah,
Looten't Whipple, we orta jus' slop 'em with these heah
lef'ovahs."

"Damn right. Whole battalion here. Plenty good
stuff to feed 'em."

It had to happen. Had to. Americans are all alike in
some ways. Can't leave well enough alone. They got to
do it better. And it ain't no accident that it's called
Yankee ingenuity. If there'd been one of us with Moses
while he was tryin' to get the Jews to the Promised
Land you can bet your ass there'd be oil in Israel. For
$4.98 you coulda had a copy of the Ten Command-
ments, suitable for framin'. And the Red Sea woulda
had a toll bridge when the Egyptians came thunderin'
up. Bet on it.

The two of 'em sat there, talkin' hogs, grain, prices

on the hoof, like a coupla farmers in a Sioux City bar. I left, smoked a joint with Jinx 'n' went to the hole. Davis wasn't there so I relieved the dudes from Second Platoon by myself. It was rainin' like the first days of the Great Flood. Had to be four inches of water in the bunker. Not that it mattered. Everything 'n' everybody was wet, soaked. I sat in the water 'n' stared at nothin'. It was stone black. Couldn't have been more'n ten feet of visibility. The elements, as they say, sucked. I tried to keep my mind on what I was s'posed to be doin'. The more I stared into blackass nothin'ness, the less I could see. I tried closin' my eyes, lookin' away, constantly shiftin' focus. I could just as well been jerkin' off. A fuckin' company of VC coulda crawled up to the wire 'n' I would never have seen 'em. Mind you, it wasn't but a quarter after eight. If it got any darker before this dawn I didn't want to know nothin' about it. I kept tellin' myself no reasonable human bein' was comin' out in this shit no matter how much they wanted to win a war. You already got it won, you stupid bastards. Stay home tonight. Cut us a break. Somethin' moved, maybe ten feet off to the left. I heard it but I couldn't see a thing. My ears strained to the poppin' point. I heard it again. "Hold it right there, motherfuckers!"

"That's not quite the proper phraseology, Hawkins."

"I ain't one to stand on no ceremony, Lef'tenant. You could die out there like that."

He slid into the hold. "I didn't think you were into shooting people."

"I was thinkin' more of you drownin'."

"Where's Davis?"

"I left him with the first sergeant."

"You making out okay?"

"You kiddin' me? This is like shittin' in high cotton. When I was a kid I always wanted to get in a tub, a pool, anything like that, with my clothes on. I thought it'd be fun to go swimmin' like that. The US fuckin' Army has made another wish come true. Christ, what a sorry-ass goddamn existence this is."

"Hawkins, you got it made."

"C'mon, Lef'tenant. Don't jerk me off."

"You're eating, every day. You sleep damn near every night. You got clothes to change, music, good boots, more ammo than you can shoot up in a month. And you're sitting in the middle of a fucking fortress. How'd you like to be out there with Charlie?"

"I cried 'cause I had no shoes, till I saw a man with no feet . . . ?"

"Something like that."

"You ever hear the end of that idiotic song 'n' dance? The dude with no shoes kept on humpin' it. Barefoot, naturally. His feet got infected, and he died of blood poisoning. But the dude with no feet got evaced home, bought two Nubian slaves to haul him around in a wagon, and died a rich old man." He was chucklin' by the time I finished. I was half-laughin', half-pissed. All my life I heard that shit about how it can always be worse. It's true. And just as goddamn true it can be a helluva lot better.

"Hawkins, you know the story about the child psychologists who wanted to study attitudes of optimism and pessimism?"

"Nope."

"Well, listen up, as the sergeants say. The psychologists took two kids. About five years old, one a born pessimist, the other a natural optimist. They put the pessimistic kid in a room filled with everything a child could want, every toy, sweet food, every imaginable form of entertainment. Then they put the optimist in a room full of horse shit and gave him nothing but a shovel. The day passes, and they went back to the pessimistic kid. He's sitting in the middle of the room, disgusted, grumbling, 'That one broke, this one's stupid, this stuff's going to spoil before I can eat it all . . . and, anyway, somebody's going to take all this away from me.'

"The psychologists shook their heads and went away to see what sorry state the other kid would be in. They walked into the room and the kid's there, a big smile on his face, laughing and throwing shit every way imaginable. They couldn't believe it. 'How come you're so cheerful?' they asked. 'Because, man, with all this shit there's got to be a pony here somewhere.' "

I thought I'd bust a fuckin' gut to keep from laughin' out loud. There we were, sittin' in four inches of cold water, in a clammy mud hole, God only knows for how long, waitin' for a bunch of banzai bastards to come rippin' through the dark 'n' waste us—whisperin' like two school kids after lights out. There's gotta be a pony somewhere. Fuck me.

"It's going to get worse, Hawkins."

"No way! How? How in hell is it gonna get any worse'n this? I thought you was the kid with the shovel."

"I stopped being a kid when I was six."

"How old're you?"

"Twenty-three."

My God, we're all children. "I got a cousin same age as you. He's still tryin' to pick up girls at the Dairy Queen."

"You laid any of the girls in Xap Dong?"

"Shit. Who's had time? Between diggin' 'n' hump-

in' that freakin' radio round for you . . . listen, Dago's
an RTO. How come he ain't doin' it?"

"Because I want you, but I'll see if I can give you an
afternoon off." He crawled out in the rain, and stopped
on the edge. "You fired any rounds, to see if that
thing's dry enough to work?"

"No."

"Checked the ammo, to see if it's dry?"

"No."

"Checked the flares?"

I sighed. "No."

"You got any grenades?"

"No."

"How much ammo you got?"

"Twenty rounds, in the '16."

"Hawkins . . . ?"

"Sir?"

"My patience is not without end. If they come
through you without even having to slow down, they
might get me. I don't want some fucking gook to get
me, Hawk. Okay?"

I didn't answer. I couldn't see his face, and only
heard him sloppin' away through the mud. For the first
time since I'd said "I do" to the major givin' the oath
I wished I wasn't such a fuckup. Davis crawled into the
hole before I could get very deep into the idea of re-
form.

"Sorry, Hawk. "Me 'n' the first sergeant was jawin'
'n' Ah clean fo'got."

"No sweat. Levine was out here holdin' my hand."

"You think maybe he's queer 'r some'in?"

"Do I think *what*?"

"He's nice 'nough, but he's funny-actin'? You
know?"

"Luke, for Christ's sake."

"Ah s'pose so. You check this piece o' shit?" He thumped the handles of the M-60.

"Go fuck yourself. I'm gonna take a nap." I leaned back, stretched out my legs, and closed my eyes. I was stoned enough so that four or five inches of water didn't seem too bad. I think I might even have gone to sleep but Davis got up to check the flares, moved some boxes of ammo around. "Shit!! Luke? How am I s'posed to sleep if you're gonna make all that noise?"

"Hawk . . . ?" He sat down 'n' I grunted. "Ah sho's hell wish you wouldn't sleep tonight. Them fuckahs is out there."

"You spooked, man?"

"Ah feel 'em."

"You think we're gonna get hit?"

"Yeah. Maybe not tonight, maybe not tomorrow. But we goan git hit." He spit into the water between his feet, like the leader of a lynch mob that ain't quite been got together. "Less'en we git 'em first."

"I can hardly wait."

The night, as they used to say, passed without incident. Well, almost. Comin' off guard, Davis 'n' me split up. He went off his way 'n' I headed toward the chow hall, to see if the new cook was any more generous than that last SOB. Just as I cut past the corner of a bunker a big fuckin' arm goes round my throat, tightens down 'n' somebody starts to say somethin'. At the same moment, without thinkin', I slammed him in the balls with the **butt** of my rifle. Turned out it was Simmons, the hotshot karate freak. Whatever he'd started to say came out in a gaggin' scream. Before he hit the dirt I'd spun around, jacked a shell into the chamber, clicked off the safety and was half a hair's breath from blowin' the dumb bastard away. About a dozen guys were there in less than ten seconds. Somebody threw a light on us.

"Wha'th'fuck's goin' on?" I heard somebody ask. "Hawkins . . . that you?" The light came up to my face, then switched to Simmons. He was gaggin' good. I musta waffled the shit outa him. "Who's that on the ground . . . ?"

"Simmons."

"What's goin' on?"

I walked away. My hands were tremblin' and I almost fired off a round tryin' to get the safety on. Then I heard big heavy footsteps runnin' up behind me. I spun around 'n' snapped up the barrel of the M-16. Simmons stopped about four inches from the end.

"I'm . . ."

"You're gonna shut your motherfuckin' mouth, you stupid sonofabitch, 'n' if you ever come anywhere near me I'm gonna blow you away like a big wind." His mouth was open, but whether in fear or to give one of them dumb-ass chop-chop yells I didn't know, and couldna cared less. I flipped the fire control selector to automatic. "Twenty rounds, motherfucker. Either shit 'r get off the pot." I coulda jabbed him in the eye. We were that close. And I knew I'd kill him. He was stone fuckin' crazy. Had to be, to grab somebody like that. He took a half-step toward me, more like a rockin' motion, then back. I clicked off the safety. It doesn't make much noise, but we both heard it. "Get—the fuck —away." My finger tightened on the trigger. He backed up, slow 'n' careful, maybe two feet.

"Simmons! Get the hell back to your bunker." Levine's voice was like a fuckin' rifle shot. I almost lit up Simmons accidentally, I jerked so hard. "Move your goddamn ass, Troop."

"Lieutenant, I want to bring charges against this man for assaultin' a non-commissioned officer, assault with a deadly weapon, disrespect to—"

"Simmons, you've got five seconds to disappear. One . . . two . . ." Simmons turned away 'n' walked into the darkness. "You okay?" I was so scared I couldn't say anything, and started cryin'. We stood there, him waitin', me cryin'. The rain was still comin' down. I was shakin' with cold 'n' fear. And prob'ly shame. I felt so weird I couldn't stand. I went down on my knees, leanin' on the rifle, and stayed there for a coupla minutes. He gave me a lit cigarette. I took a coupla drags, then got to my feet. "You ain't got a joint, have you?" He chuckled. "Officers aren't supposed to smoke dope. You okay?"

"Fuck no, I ain't okay. I almost killed that stupid sonofabitch, and it wouldn't be no loss to the world if I did."

"What's his problem?"

"Beats the shit outa me. 'Less he's still pissed 'cause I wised off at him. He grabbed me comin' off guard. Jesus Christ, Lieutenant."

"Lef'tenant."

"Will you tell that motherfucker to stay away from me? So I don't have to kill him?"

"I think he believes you."

"Good night, sir."

" 'Night, Hawkins."

Night it was. But not much good. I didn't sleep worth a damn. I kept havin' dreams about killin' Simmons. I wanted to. I wanted to light his ass up 'n' put him outa my mind.

Dago came wanderin' in, about eleven o'clock, and we smoked another joint.

"How's business?"

"Not bad, except f' my lottery. I can't understand it. Numbers, craps, poker, football pools, don't matter— fuckin' grunts'll bet on anything. But I can't do no good with the lottery. Can't figure it." He got us a beer each. "Heard you an' Simmons had at it tonight."

"Fucker scared me half to death."

"I heard it the other way around. Coupla guys said if he'd sneezed you'd have wasted 'im."

"I guess." I could feel something in the back of my mind, some sorta idea, one of those bright-light kind that usually pops out like a spring-loaded fun-house clown. "You know, Dago, I'm gonna lose the war."

"By y'self?"

"Not this shittin'-ass mess with whoever we're fightin'. The one with the Army."

"Y' fightin' the Army? Hawk, why don't y' take on somethin' more your own size?"

"Who the fuck ever gets to choose? Did I pick the fuckin' VC? Or Simmons? The goddamn Army picked me. They're winnin'. They put us here like this, all bunched up, nothin' to do but wait to get killed. They give us guns, cannons, airplanes, bombs, every fuckin' kinda shit they can ship in here. Then they wait. Sooner or later, man, you're gonna kill *somebody*. I might kill Simmons. Ubanski. Maybe some dude I don't even know, just somebody who fucked me over at the wrong moment. But sure's shit stinks, man, I'm gonna end up killin' somebody."

"Listen, y' want me t' get rid of Simmons? I can have him, y' know, scratched off by tomorrow night. Say the word."

I thought about it for a few minutes. But it seemed about the same. "Naw, fuck it. If it has to be done I'll do it."

"Okay. But don't get ya ass busted if it isn't necessary. I can have it done while ya off in the boonies. No way they could get you for that."

"I ain't sure it matters, Dago. I mean, if I grease the sonofabitch I gotta expect somebody's gonna be interested to see that I pay up, so to speak. And anyway, it ain't gonna be tonight 'cause I'm sackin' out if you'll so kindly shut the fuck up for five minutes."

"Say good night, Hawk."

"Good night Hawk."

Next day turned out to be Sunday. Could just as easily have been the third Thursday in the first week of Never. I'd never have known, 'cept Dago woke me fuckin' round gettin' ready for Mass. Some stray Catholic chaplain was in camp to sing that "Body of Christ, Body of Christ" bullshit and stick them silly-ass wafers in people's mouths. Bunch of guys went, not more than a third of 'em fish eaters. Not me. My attitude toward the Church ain't no better'n my attitude toward the rest of the world's power-grabbin' futhermuckers. Anyway, I figured goin' to church is a lot like hangin' round company HQ. Somebody's gonna take notice of you. I didn't want God lookin' down and seein' me hangin' round. Outa sight, outa mind.

But it bein' Sunday didn't help Garcia. He got caught jerkin' off. Whipple. Figured. The fat fucker'd come back like a straight dude, quiet and mindin' his own goddamn business. But when he walked in on the Mex makin' love with his fist the shit hit the fan. Took about six hours to clean it up.

"Man, what I know? I think ever'body's at Mass," Garcia told us that night. "It's Sunday, right? What's officer doin' in enlisted men's shithouse on Sunday? Prob'ly he comes to sniff seats, no? Dumb fuck. He take me to first sergeant an' he tell first sergeant, 'I want to write up thees man.' First Sergeant, he say, 'Why?' 'He commit indecent unnatural act,' fat fucker say. 'What's that, Lieutenant?' Fat fucker, he no want to say, so I say, 'I flog my dong, First Sergeant. Nobody ever say me it unnatural. I do all time. Is natural to me, no?' First Sergeant say, 'Lieutenant, you gotta be kiddin'.' Fat fucker say, 'Sergeant, I want you write thees man up. And send to see battalion psy'atrist . . .' Head doctor. I no can say. First Sergeant shrug. He make report. I get ride to head doctor. He work Sunday like ever' day. Head doctor, he say 'Mmmmmmm, yes, I see, mmmmmmm.' I say, 'That it, Señor Head Doctor, sir?' He say, 'No, no, sit down.' He ask me if I like girl. I say sure I like girl. 'You got girl here?' He say, 'No, yes, but no. They nurse.' I say, 'I no mind. I like nursie.' He say, 'You like father?' 'Sure,' I say. 'He good man. He fishman, have big boat.' He say, 'Mmmmmmm, yes, I see, mmmmmm.' I say, 'That it, Señor Sir Head Doctor?' 'No, no,' he say. 'Sit down. You like mother?' I say, 'Sure. Good woman. Make best tortilla in San Diego.' He mmmmm ag'in. I say, 'Señor Major Head Doctor Sir, Private Garcia can please go now?' 'No, no,' he say. 'Now, when did you first start . . .'' he say word for floggin' dong. 'I no remember for sure,' I say. 'But I think I am six.' 'Six?' 'Si, six, or maybe before but I no remember.' 'How often you do it?' he say. 'Two, three times.' 'A week?' 'A day.' 'A day!?' 'Si, unless we on patrol. Then maybe only once. Very tired on patrol.' He say, 'Mmmmmmm.' I wait. He say, 'You no do it with girls? You not proud of penis?' I say, 'Not proud? I got biggest cock in ghetto.' An' I jump up, unbutton pants, I show him. 'No, no, Private,' he say. 'Not necessary. How come you no do it with girls?' he say. 'What girls?' I say. 'Vietnamese girls.' 'Ho, no see. An' they got mucho VD, no?' 'Yes,' he say. 'But it's natural with girls. Floggin' dong no good.' 'Better I get VD than flog dong?' He say, 'Mmmmmmmmm.' I say, 'Señor Sir Major Head Doctor, Garcia can go now?' 'Yes,' he say. I go."

Now, as ol' Witherspoon would say, let's put it in perspective. As far as the Army's concerned, jerkin' off is still the cause of mental disorders, disrespect to officers, acne, cavities 'n' bad breath. There are maybe ninety-two kinds of VD in No Man's Nam, and about ninety-two percent of 'em are incurable. Fuckin' grunts tell stories of dudes whose brains rotted, whose eyes fell out, whose nervous systems came completely unglued, who were shipped off to some secret hospital to die and were reported KIA. But the Army asks only that a grunt with VD report to the medics before his cock falls off 'r his intestines become a massive pus pocket. Just please tell good ol' doc so we can shoot your ass full of drugs 'n' try to stave off permanent damage. But let a dude jerk off, 'cause he knows if he gets fucked up with VD he'll wake up one mornin' to find his cock crawled off to die, and the Army wants to lock him up on a funny farm. Somebody told me it was written down in Army Regulations that enlisted men were forbidden to shake their dong more 'n' twice when they finish takin' a leak. I don't know if it's true, but damn sure the AR's full of strange tribal laws.

I been sittin' a while, readin' back, thinkin' of Witherspoon pissin' 'n' moanin' about the way I write. I know what he'd say. Too ambiguous. We need to know more about the first sergeant's reactions, and Whipple's. Well, I can tell you this: The first sergeant didn't give two shits about Garcia, a fuckin' Chicano ghetto kid with some crazy idea about bein' a bullfighter. And Whipple was a Boston closet queen who prob'ly pulled his pud every night of the week, under the covers. Who cares what he thought about it. Garcia didn't. Anyway, life's ambiguous. All Whipple wanted was to make trouble. And all the first sergeant wanted, so Dago says, was a piece of the action. Damn sure he got that, but I doubt it was what he had in mind.

We went walkin' the next day, and the next, and about half of the day after. Lookin' for Indians, Lef'tenant Levine said. We'd walk an hour or so, watch a track for two, walk another hour. I don't think I've ever been so tired 'n' so bored in my life. We didn't see a single goddamn slope the whole time. "They're here, Hawk," the Boy Ranger says to me. "Bet your ass they're here."

"How the hell can you tell? We haven't seen a goddamn thing but thorns, vines 'n' Ubanski's varicose veins when he took a crap yesterday. No wonder he's always in such a shit mood."

"You haven't seen anything because you're walking around with your head up your ass."

"Oohh! That ain't nice. Here I carried this fuckin' radio round without bitchin' 'n' you say somethin' like that." He smirked. "What the hell am I s'posed to be lookin' for, anyway?"

"Litter. Footprints. Broken twigs. Food. Butts— roaches you call 'em. Cloth snagged on a vine. All the crap we'd leave behind if Ski wasn't back there sweeping the track."

No shit. I wondered why Ubanski was followin' us like a retard, drag-assin' along. And sure's hell I hadn't seen any of the stuff the Lef'tenant was talkin' about. "You see any of that stuff?"

"Enough."

"Well? I mean, what happens now?"

"We'll get back to Kilo in another two hours. I'll put what we found with what everybody else found. Like a Mulligan stew. That's what intelligence is most of the time. Put all the pieces in a pot, stir like hell, and see how it smells."

"Who cooks?"

"Lots of people."

"My old lady used to say too many cooks spoil the broth. 'Course, she liked clichés."

"So do a lot of the people who work in intelligence."

"We really gonna get back in two hours?"

"If we don't get lit up first."

"You think there's slopes layin' up out here waitin' to do us dirty?"

"Hawk, I'd bet we walked through at least five hundred of 'em in the last two days."

"Man, you jerkin' me off? Sir?"

"I haven't got time to jerk myself off. Damn sure I haven't got time to waste on you. Private."

"Private fuckin' First Class. Jesus, cut me a break, sir."

"Hang it in your ass."

"Another month, you'll sound just like us. The great unwashed."

"I'm not all that sure we'll be around."

"Jesus fuckin' Christ! You 'n' Ubanski. Give me the goddamn creeps."

"Good. Maybe you'll get your head together. Might keep you alive."

"You really give a shit, one way or the other?"

He twisted his mouth around in that goofy smile he had.

"Why do you think I keep trying to teach you the

difference between your bowels and your goddamn brains?"

" 'Cause you always wanted to be a brain surgeon?" He got really thoughtful for a coupla minutes. I figured either I'd pissed him off or he was bored with the bullshit. Then he says, "I always wanted to be a tugboat captain."

"A what?" I wasn't sure I'd heard what he said.

"A tugboat captain. My father was stationed around New York a lot, when he was home at all. I used to go to the East River and hang around. The guys got to know me, and let me ride around on the tugs. It's a beautiful life, hard at times. But beautiful."

"You serious?"

"Sure. You ever been on a tug, pushing a big barge, or a ship along a river? You can smell the ocean, feel the engines through the soles of your feet, watch something being done and know you did it well. It's a good feeling." He gave another smile. "What are you going to do if you ever grow up?"

"Be smart enough not to figure it out." He laughed.

We made it back without gettin' lit up 'n' I still didn't see sign one of evil lurkin'. I even looked. Mud 'n' misery. *That* I could see. But no Indians, or arrowheads. I headed for my bunk, figurin' to be asleep in five minutes. It took ten to get my boots off. They'd been wet for three days, or the most part of three days. Another day and I'd have had to snip tendrils. They smelled like last week's fish left out to cure. I cut off the fatigues, what was left of 'em. And I didn't look any worse'n anybody else. For about five seconds I debated on a bath, said fuck it, wrapped up in my blanket and went to sleep.

"Lef'tenant Levine woke me three hours later. "Get

up, Hawk. We got school." He thumped me in the back. "You awake?"

"No, but keep tryin'."

"Come on."

"It's okay. I got an excuse note. Tell the teacher I'm sick."

"Off your ass, Troop."

"Aw shit, Lef'tenant. Wha'th'fuck?"

"Come on, wiseass. You're driving."

"Drivin' *what*?"

"A jeep. We're going to your bar mitzvah."

"I don't drink. Bad for your liver."

"Up!"

I got up, into a half-comatose sittin' position.

"What's a bar wha'ch'ma'callit?"

"It's a Jewish ritual where the community acknowledges the boys as men, and the boys acknowledge their responsibility to the community. More or less."

"Maybe I'm not old enough."

"Thirteen, Hawkins. Thirteen. Even you have to be that old."

"But I'm not Jewish."

"Oh hell, yes you are. You may not know it, but you are definitely a Jew."

"Then how come my mother never told me?"

"She probably assumed you had enough problems. Come on. Move your ass. Take a bath, for God's sake. You smell like a grunt, and the colonel doesn't like grunts. I'm going to try to pass you off as the court jester."

"Which colonel?"

"The one who runs this battalion. He's also my father."

"I can hardly wait."

I took a bar of soap 'n' walked into the storm. No shower I've ever seen could put out that much volume. Course, your feet tend to be a bit muddy when you're finished, but my feet had been muddy since we got to this goddamn misbegotten armpit of the world. At least I smelled better. I put on the last of my dry clothes, wrapped up in a poncho 'n' went to the chow hall to meet Levine. I wasn't happy. We ate 'n' he talked.

"What you're going to hear will probably be classified top secret. What you're going to see will be considered sacred. Keep your mouth shut, and watch. Listen. You want some answers, and you might get a few. But don't ask questions, not even of me. You're my driver. Keep it at that. Okay?"

I nodded, swallowed a mouthful of chili 'n' beans, and asked, "Why you doin' this? Why me?"

"Why not?"

I shrugged. Why not. Beats the shit outa me. We picked up Captain Jefferson. I drove. Well, I pointed the jeep's nose in the general direction suggested, and let her fly. We got there. Jefferson was on the floor in the back. I couldn't tell if he was scared or slid off the seat. Prob'ly both. The Boy Ranger grinned. "Come on, Hawk." We wandered around the battalion HQ compound, found the right bunker 'n' slipped in. It was full. Captains, majors, lef'tenant colonels, colonels, charts, maps, graphs 'n' God only knows what else. There were two other grunts in the bunker, both of 'em there to fetch 'n' carry. They were starched 'n' pressed stiff as two book ends. One black, one white. When it comes to menial shit the Army doesn't discriminate nearly as much as people might imagine. They fuck over everybody. The lot of 'em were standin' round like they were waitin' to view the last remains. Whisperin', noddin' yes to this, shakin' nay to that, everything in hushed tones. I found a dark corner. Levine came over. "Remember, keep your mouth shut. And no dope smoking," he said, as he walked off.

All of a sudden, just when I thought I might go to sleep on my feet, the fuckin' flaps over the bunker door fly open. In come three chicken colonels. Somebody bawls " 'Ten-hut!" Ol' Pavlov's dogs couldn't have done better. The colonels stomped through the metamorphic mop handles and took their seats at the front. Everybody but the book ends, a major and me took a seat. The book ends served the chicken colonels some coffee. The major whipped out a telescopic pointer, the kind that comes out like a radio antenna. With that in his left hand, he pulled down a multicolored map. It unrolled like a window shade, over some others that evidently did the same thing. When it was down he snapped the pointer round, *pop!* right on the battalion's position. The map rolled up like a window shade. Thuuuuuppppop. The major pulled it down and hooked a small eyelet over a conveniently placed tack. The major, evidently, had had problems before. What followed may well have been a classic briefin'. I don't know, because it was my first 'n' last. Three battalions placed here, here 'n' here. Artillery here 'n' here. Tanks. The Air Force at Danang. The Navy in the South China Sea. And God in heaven. How could we lose.

Five gold-leafed majors, two silver-leafed colonels and one chicken colonel spoke. The war should have ended the next day. The guts of it was that intelligence reports, patrol reports, agent reports, reports by deserters, spy satellite, U-2 overflights, and two itinerant salesmen for Coca-Cola on the CIA payroll all confirmed the absence of any large bodies of NVA troops.

It took forty-five minutes and eight brass-hats to say that. Maps 'n' charts were rolled up 'n' down like a J. Walter Thompson client conference. When it was done, or I thought it was done, and wondered why in hell Levine had dragged me to this shit, the other Levine got up. He was a picture of military propriety, but nowhere near the All-American his son was. The colonel would never have given anyone a goofy smile. "Gentlemen . . ." I assumed that excluded us grunts but I listened anyway. It was, in a way, I guess, like wantin' to know somethin' about your girl friend's father, without havin' him know you were gettin' together a picture.

"Gentlemen," he says, "we've heard from the best intelligence analysts available that the NVA's Three-Eighty-Second is nowhere around. They've gone up in smoke, whether ours or something more ethereal we don't know. But, say the experts, they are not here, at hand. Agent reports, air reconnaissance, patrols, all the instruments upon which we normally rely for advance information, all of these, gentlemen, say it's no go. The Three-Eighty-Second has quit the field.

"Gentlemen, I submit that this is nonsense. It is my contention that their very absence proves—*proves*—that they are here." He snapped off a knuckle-thump against the map, then another 'n' another. All of 'em landed goddamn close to where we went walkin'. "The lack of evidence proves their existence." That, as they say, is some heavy shit. I mean, can you imagine havin' that sonofabitch on a jury? Reasonable doubt would disappear at the mere mention of your name and the fact some crime had been committed.

"They are out there, and I propose to find them."

No shit? By yourself, birdman? Or you plan to send

us fuckin' throwaway grunts out to root 'em up? I suddenly got a slightly sick feelin' in the pit of my stomach. I flashed on why the Boy Ranger had brought me along. He wanted me to be the first in my neighborhood to know the good news. For some weird reason he wanted me to know *why*. I mean, I wanted to know, but why did he want me to know why? Shit. You get an answer to one stupid question 'n' there's two more.

There was a lotta whoopin' 'n' shoutin' when Colonel Levine sat down. Majors arguin' with light colonels, captains with chicken colonels (but not too loudly), back 'n' forth. I slipped out 'n' lit a joint. No dope-smokin's ass. I did half a joint, snubbed out the fire 'n' climbed in the jeep. Few minutes later out they came, still yackity yackity yackity. Jefferson and the Levines came over to the jeep. Standin' no more'n five fuckin' feet from me they laid it out. The colonel laid it out. The colonel's son and the captain went yes sir, no sir, yes sir. I kept quiet. What he said was: Find 'em.

Then he said, "I've got an idea. Competition." He got one of those tight-ass corporate executive stretched-lip looks on his face. I can't call it a smile. No way. I've seen more humor in a dead man's face. "Competition. A silver loving cup for the company that kills the most gooks in any given month. And any company that wins three of them gets an all-expense-paid R and R." Whoop-de-fuckin'-do. Prob'ly send the survivors to Saigon for a Saturday afternoon picnic at the race track. A fuckin' lovin' cup for killin' gooks. Good God. The sonofabitch was as fuckin' crazy as Dago. *Had to be.* "Americans love good competitive situations. The troops'll eat this up. Gentlemen, I think we'll see some body counts that will surprise a lot of people when the word gets around. I'll put it out tomorrow." He patted the Boy Ranger on the shoulder. "Naturally, I expect Kilo Company to take the first award." Naturally. The Chocolate Soldier and the Boy Ranger got in. Everybody said good night. The colonel walked off into the darkness. Whistlin'. The Lef'tenant said, "Let's go." I lit the roach, cranked the jeep 'n' tore ass off into the rain. "I told you no dope smoking, didn't I?" "This ain't dope, dummy. It's Laotian licorice." I shoved it into his hand. "And you'd better get your shit together, learn what this stuff's all about. 'Cause we're gonna need somethin' more than them fuckin' C-rations if we're gonna win the lovin' cup and make Daddy happy."

"Hawk . . ."

"Sorry." Jefferson didn't say shit. The fuckin' wind was roarin' round in the jeep so maybe he didn't hear. Who cared? Jail looked good compared to what I knew we were about to get into. Breakin' rocks didn't seem no worse'n breakin' my back humpin' through God knows what lookin' to get killed, blown away by a bunch of fuckers that weren't there. Or who were there 'cause they weren't there. One more fuckin' joint and I could prob'ly say the alphabet backwards. When we got back 'n' just the two of us were standin' in the dark drizzle, I asked him straight out, "Your old man crazy?"

"No, he's a colonel. And he wants to be a general."

"You think he's right?"

"Morally or tactically?"

"Yeah."

"Morally, no. Tactically . . . he might be. You get a sense of things, Hawk. A feeling. I had it out there, more than once. He might be right."

"I might be the fuckin' tooth fairy too, but I ain't

gonna go round peekin' under pillows to prove it."

"Yeah, but you don't want to be a general."

"What's your name? Your first name?"

"Stephen. Stephen Eric. My friends, the two or three I've got, call me Eric. But they aren't privates."

"Private fuckin' first class, Eric." We grinned at each other, like two shit-head kids doin' somethin' we weren't s'posed to be doin'. Which wasn't far from the truth. Then I said—without intendin' to say anything— "We on the way to gettin' our asses kicked."

"I know." His goofy grin came and went, real quick. "Good night, Hawk."

There's times when you can look back 'n' see a point at which you changed. Some single simpleminded shit made a difference and forever after you weren't no way the same. Other times, rare I think, you know *right* then, at exactly the moment mayhem strikes. Course, most often I don't think you know diddly-dork. You just change and if you're lucky maybe somebody'll tell you a month or a year after. I changed 'n' I knew it that instant. I still didn't know if the Army'd won. I did know I had to get *my* shit together.

Next mornin' about eleven, Jinx wrote him 'n' me a pass to Xap Dong. "Fuck R 'n' R, man. This is I 'n' I"

"I 'n' I?"

"Intoxi-ca-tion and in'er-co'rse. Booze 'n' broads."

Xap Dong was the place for it. I 'n' I, VD, soft dope, hard shit, black market money changin', booze, broads, or about anything else the League of Mothers would look down on. Xap Dong was a hell-raisin' slum of maybe five hundred people supported by sex-starved, dope-hungry, greedy grunts. There were maybe fifty or sixty shacks strung out along four or five streets, mostly bars, whorehouses, Coke stands, opium dens and three clothin' stores owned by Indians. Bombay Indians. They traded money on the black market, made tailored fatigues, sold the whores their mini-skirts, and sold information to the other Indians. VC 'n' NVA. The Chinese owned opium smokin' houses, sold hash, grass 'n' information to both sides. The hookers sold a fast fuck for ten bucks, all night for twenty, twenty-five. Two or three old crones did laundry 'n' if you were really hard up would give you a blow job for five bucks. If you could get by the black teeth—or no teeth—but not me. I never in my life been that freakin' horny. God alone knows what Xap Dong was before the American Army came. It was in the middle of nowhere, far as I could see. Didn't seem to me that it coulda been a market town. In fact, the only purpose I could imagine for a town there would be whorin' 'n' hell-raisin'. But considerin' that the war'd been goin' on for over thirty years if you go back to the Japs, it didn't need any other reason for existence. Where there's an army there'll be booze, broads 'n' dope. Don't matter whose army it is.

Jinx 'n' I went to The Ace of Spades, a quiet little bistro made outa rustin' corrugated tin, bamboo 'n' thatched somethin' or other. Palm fronds maybe. There wasn't much to choose between Ace of Spades, Queen of Hearts, Jack of Diamonds, Latin Quarter, Flamingo, Mom's and maybe twenty other gin joints. When we finally get the good sense to get the fuck outa here the owners will just change names, cut prices and go on doin' business with the NVA. Hell, they already were doin' business with 'em. After curfew.

An old Momma-san, about fifty, gave us a gold-tooth grin. "Hello, GI. You like drink?"

"Ho, Momma-san. Two *ba-me-bah.*"

"*Ba* who? Where the fuck did you learn that jazz?"

"That's about it. Means beer, like Schlitz."

"*Ba-me-bah?*"

"Yeah. Thirty-three."

The old broad brought us two beers, ice cold. The label said "33," and some other stuff I couldn't read. "What if we want a '21'?"

"We in deep trouble, man. *Ba-me-bah* is it. And I'm not entirely sure tha's the way to say it."

"You must be doin' somethin' right." The inside of the place was as dog-eared as the outside. A long, dark wooden bar, stools with red plastic seats, ratty wicker tables. Maybe ten seconds after the bottles hit the bar top two miniskirted girl-sans sat down, one on either side of us. "GI Number One. You buy drink?"

"*Khong.* Di-di."

"Tai sao?"

"Di the fuck di."

"Cheap Charlie, Number Ten."

They flounced to the end of the bar 'n' started jab-berin' with the old lady. She shrugged. "I got the drift of that, but what did you say to piss 'em off."

"Nothin', man. I tol' 'em to fuck off. Cunts."

"That one with the long hair's not bad."

"Man, they take you for twenty bucks 'fore you can get it up. You know what you get for 'twenty bucks? Giggles, man. Giggles. They might ball but you'd pay the price of gold to get it. You want to get laid, we'll go to Madam Ming's."

"Madam Ming's?"

"She's about a thousand years old. Half-slope, half-French, half-Chinese. Funny ol' broad. Got the cleanest broads around. Couple with big tits. These goddamn dinks ain't got shit for tits."

We drank the beer, ordered two more 'n' stared into circles of water that pooled under the bottles. The inside of the bar was as dismal as the freakin' rain outside. I wished he hadn't sent the girls off. For a real giggle twenty bucks didn't seem like much to pay. I sure's hell didn't have anything else to spend it on. I looked at the long-haired one. She prob'ly wasn't more'n seventeen, eighteen. Good legs. Big eyes. Too much eye shadow. Her hands were beautiful. Long pale pink nails filed to a near-point, elegant fingers. I finished the beer 'n' ordered us two more. *Ba-me-bah*, as badly fucked over as the pronunciation mighta been, always worked.

"Ho, momma-san. How 'bout layin' a little Stones on us."

Momma-san went behind the bar to a tape deck,

diddled with it for a few minutes, and Christ is my witness, out came Mick Jagger. "I Can't Get No Satisfaction." No shit. The tweeter in one speaker had seen better days but, considerin' we were a long-ass way from Panasonic's prime sales region, it wasn't bad. Armed Forces Radio, which we could get most of the time, was okay. But they didn't play much Stones, or Grateful Dead, or Who. The chickenshits that diddled with their programmin' either didn't know or, more likely, much like hard rock. We downed the last of the third bottles 'n' ordered another. The bar was beginnin' to look more homey. It was nice to have it all to ourselves. I smiled at the long-haired girl. She was lookin' good. "Coupla more of these ol' *ba-me-bahs* 'n' I just might marry that long-haired girl-san."

"Wouldn't be the first grunt that let 'is prick fuck 'is mind around."

"Wouldn't be bad for a week 'r so."

"Cool it. We gonna do Madam Ming's."

"How you so hip to what's happenin' in this place?"

"Black 'n' Decker."

"They been doin' recon round here?"

"Damn, man, where you been. They livin' here. At Madam Ming's. They split a week ago."

"AWOL?"

" 'Less Jefferson gave 'em a pass, they AWOL."

"Ain't nobody missed 'em?"

"Who knows where anybody is? You could take a walk and it'd be a stone fuckin' month before you was missed. Everybody'd think you was off doin' somethin' f' somebody else. You dig it, man? We don't mean nothin' individually. I might miss 'em, or you. But I wouldn't go runnin' to the first sergeant sayin', 'Hey, my buddy Hawk is missin'.' You know? Sooner or later somebody'll start askin', but they figure to be into Cambodia by then."

"They figure to be in *Cambodia*? Are they stone fuckin' nuts, man? Why'd anybody in their right minds wanta go to Cambodia? There's more fuckin' Indians there than there is here."

"They goin' to Sweden. They tryin' to negotiate with the VC political dudes for political asylum an' a ticket to Sweden."

"C'mon Jinx, don't shit yo' ol' redneck buddy."

"You seen 'em in the last week?"

I hadn't. I didn't even have to think about it. You don't think about somethin' like that, but when it's brought to your attention—*bam!* You know. "Sweden?"

"Sweden."

"So much for McNamara's Hundred Thousand, huh?"

"Get a nigger behind the trigger . . . then give 'im a ticket to Nam. Dig it? But some of us gonna survive. Sooner or later some of us niggers goin' home."

"They got some poor-ass white people with that program, too."

"Yeah, but it was us they wanted. Get the young blacks off America's city streets and into Nam's backwoods. They finally figured a way to kill spades 'n' slopes at the same time." He emptied the last of his beer down his throat. "If we was smart we'd get together. Niggers of the world, unite!" He banged the bottle down on the bar top. And laughed.

A rabbit hopped over my grave. Do you know that expression? That's what my granddaddy used to say when he'd shiver for no reason. I imagine everybody has had that feelin', but they may have another name for it. Maybe it comes from knowin', without knowin' what you know—if you know what I mean. I didn't dwell on it. "Who else is hip to this Sweden trip?"

"Nobody. Few guys might've noticed they ain't been around, but nobody's hip to what's happenin'." He dug out a wrinkled joint 'n' we lit up. After a coupla hits I knew I was in love with my first bar girl. Well, hell, after three or four weeks in No Man's Nam some guys fall in love with water-boo, goats, grass, opium, bunker buddies, first sergeants, the mail clerk . . . the list is endless. "Listen," I said, "if I insist on marryin' her and you can't talk me out of it, how about bein' my best man?"

"C'mon, man, it's time to see Madam Ming. She'll fix you up with Mary Ann. She digs it, man. She'll come twice before you realize she's fuckin' *your* brains out."

"Jinx . . . ?"

"Yeah, man?"

"I can't move." I couldn't. The beer, which musta been about fifty-proof, and that half-joint, had locked my ass to the bar stool.

"C'mon, you fuckin' candy-ass honkie." He picked me up like a sack of meal 'n' carried me off on his shoulder.

"We didn't pay—"

"It's cool, man, I got credit."

"How you in so tight . . . how you in . . . oh, fuck it! Just don't drop me." He carried me through the streets, two or three blocks, into another ratty-ass place 'n' dropped me on a bed. I went to sleep before he got straightened up. Passed out prob'ly is a better word. And passed in maybe an hour later. Still half stoned.

I heard music before I came awake, way off in the distance. Stones. Beatles. B. B. King. Crosby Stills Nash 'n' Young, doin' "Wooden Ships." One of 'em, Stills or maybe Neil Young, was doin' some wicked shit with a guitar. I can never keep musicians straight. I opened my eyes. Madam Ming's looked like a fuckin' convention for a Vietnam Chapter of Black Panthers. Black 'n' Decker, Jinx, half a dozen other black dudes, lot of 'em with wildass Afros 'n' everyone with a mustache. They were passin' a pipe. Jinx looked over after I'd been awake a coupla minutes. "Hey, man, you livin' or dead?"

"Yeah."

"Shit, give that fuckin' honkie a hit off the pipe 'n' bring his ass back to life."

One of the girls, out of about a dozen hangin' round, brought the pipe to me. I hit it twice 'n' she went back to the circle. "Beer. Cold beer, amigo." The same girl brought a beer from a cooler in another room, poured it in a glass, then sat down on the side of the bed 'n' smiled. I downed about half of it, chugalug. My blood started to move a little. I smiled at her. She chattered somethin' in Vietnamese to the other girls. They all laughed. One of 'em said somethin'. They all laughed again. Back 'n' forth, back 'n' forth. "Wha'th' fuck am I, some sorta curiosity piece?"

"She wants to ball you, man," Jinx said.

"What the hell, tell her I'm cheap. She can have me for two hundred piasters." Madam Ming said somethin' to Jinx 'n' he repeated what I'd said. She spoke to the girl, and they all giggled. Then the girl moved to the foot of the bed 'n' opened her blouse. She wasn't wearin' a bra and had about a thirty-five-inch set of chalubbies. I'm here to tell you, they were bigger than anything I'd seen in No Man's Nam. Nice round little devils. I almost creamed my pants. "A hundred, Jinx. Tell her a hundred." The old broad says something else. They giggle. The girl opens the blouse wider, so they ain't just peakin' out, but standin' there for God and all the world to see. "Fifty, man, tell her fifty." They went through the translation—or the put-on—and off comes the blouse. Creamy white. She musta had some French blood. She stood up, unzipped her skirt, let it drop. She had on bikini pants, yellow ones with Tuesday written on the cheek of her ass.

"Well," Jinx said.

"How much?"

He said something to the madam. The old lady translated 'n' all the broads went into a gigglin' fit. The girl said somethin' which Madam Ming translated to me as "For love." Black 'n' Decker howled. Coupla the other spades yelled, "Shit, fuckin' Whitey's gonna make out like a champ. Ain't none of these cunts ever give us shit for love."

The girl pulled a white cotton netting down. That was privacy. She got on the bed with me, took off my clothes 'n' we fucked, bang-bang the first time, then long 'n' slow. Long 'n' slow for me. Would you believe five minutes? The second time she got off, or gave a fuckin' good imitation. Everybody cheered, applauded, turned up the music and went back to the hash pipe. We lay in bed for another fifteen 'r twenty minutes. I was stoned, half-drunk 'n' fresh fucked. The world could have ended at that moment and I don't think I'd have even walked outside to watch. Finally the girl said somethin' to the others. One of 'em brought the pipe. She held it for me to hit, but wouldn't take any herself. I did it twice again. It was potent shit. I got up to take a piss 'n' almost fell on my ass. I came back and sat down in the circle with the spades. Round 'n' round the pipe went, and I got more 'n' more stoned, but it wasn't the paralyzin' stuff we'd done in the bar. This just blew your head out. Madam Ming told one of the girls to change the tape. First cut up was the Doors doin' "Light My Fire." Musta been, real time, a seven 'r eight minute cut. That mother-fucker went on forever. I took chopsticks off a table 'n' started drummin' on an empty beer bottle, then two, then half a dozen arranged round me like a set of drums. I got into the drummin' 'n' music like never before. I lost any sense of where the hell I was, who I was, why I was, or why I had ever cared. Wasn't noth-in' but me, music 'n' the sticks. One cut after an-other, probably thirty minutes. Jinx 'n' Madam Ming were doin' the boogaloo, or the water-boo stomp. Every-body was dancin', singin', stompin, their feet, and grabbin' ass. We were all dancin' around our open graves, laughin'. The fuckin' war was over 'n' we knew it, knew it absolutely, knew it the way you know you've done somethin' good or made somebody happy even before they can say it. We knew it, and if nobody else did, that was their problem. The war was over 'n' we were celebratin'. One beautiful moment, snatched outa the clenched fist of reality. Who says you can't make a silk purse from a sow's ass?

'Course, reality has a way of snatchin' right back. You don't fuck reality around too much. About four o'clock I bid a fond farewell to the girl with the big bazongas. Jinx 'n' me went back to the bunkers 'n' bullshit. Sure enough, nobody knew the war was over. Lef'tenant Levine even insisted that it was at that moment goin' on, and we were goin' to look for it that very same fuckin' night. "Why? Why don't we just sit here a spell, see if it'll go away?"

"My old man expects us to win the Loving Cup. Remember?"

"We can frag him. Him 'n' all the other field grade officers . . . man, s'posin' the grunts blew away all the officers. They couldn't try us all, couldn't do nothin' but let us go home. Everybody just quit."

"Hawk . . ."

"I know."

"Anyway, I'm an officer, even if I do let you get away with that kind of crap."

"Yeah, but you're a grunt first. I wouldn't let 'em frag you."

"Spoken like a true Olympian."

"Up yours, I don't know what that is 'n' I could care less, Sir."

"Private Hawkins, get your gear in order by eighteen hundred hours this evening. We are going on a night patrol. You, private, will carry the radio in your usual conscientious manner."

"Why me?"

" 'Cause you my main man."

"You sound like a nigger."

"I am, man, I am. We're all niggers, regardless of race, creed or color. Try not to forget it."

Now, I'll tell you a little somethin'. I've never been big on walkin' round in No Man's Nam, and most especially at night. There's too freakin' many ways to muck up. It's a fact we'd been lucky as hell, not fallin' over any booby-traps or steppin' in shit, so to speak. Ubanski 'n' Levine had prob'ly helped, but we'd been lucky. Three guys from Fourth Platoon had gotten

fucked up less'n two hundred meters past the pig village limits. Three others, from the Second Platoon, got
zapped on patrol the first week, two KIA, the other
dinged right through his legs with an AK-round. Altogether, we'd lost prob'ly twelve, fifteen guys since we
got dug in, four of 'em, to what's known as a short
round. That's when your own artillery—or mortar crew
—fires at a target and the round falls short. On you.
Makes you wonder about the marvels of modern firepower.

The whole world was the color of a crow's ass when
we left. No rain, but it was there, ready, waitin' for
whatever the fuck called it forth. I never have understood why it rains, stops, rains, stops, and all in the
same hour. We went out steppin' light, the Lef'tenant,
Ubanski, Davis, Jinx, Garcia on the point, Poe 'n' me.
I was surprised to see Poe. He'd been made a corporal
and put in charge of the pigs. The first sergeant had
wanted Davis, but Levine said no. Poe was logical, his
old man bein' a senator. Keep his son from gettin'
blown away. Or lessen the chances.

"How come you leavin' them babies alone? Ain't
you in charge of hand-holdin', sloppin' and general
welfare?"

"I am a man of many talents, Hawk. And like the
true stereotyped American executive, I've delegated the
responsibility for their safekeeping to lesser beings."

"Who?"

"Lieutenant Whipple."

"Good luck." We plodded along in silence. Through
the fuckin' paddy water, round the shacks, away from
anything that was alive. It was so freakin' dark I
couldn't see Garcia on the point. We were walkin' slow,
stoppin' every few minutes to listen. Nobody was talk-

in'. My man knew his shit. When we were maybe two hundred meters past a small hamlet, halfway up a ridge on a slope, he stopped us 'n' we set up for ambush. Davis 'n' Ubanski put out some claymores, wicked fuckers that throw out little ball bearings, prob'ly a thousand of 'em at a time, with a mean blast. You could fuck up a bunch of people with one of those. We were prob'ly no more'n a hundred meters off a track leadin' right into the last hamlet we passed. When we were set, Eric called in some coordinates so we could blow the shit outa everything around us. I whispered in his ear, "We waitin' for the Indians to come home to roost, or can I sleep?"

"You go to sleep and I'll kick your goddamn ass."

"How come we're so far back from the track?"

"I got that sonofabitch zeroed in. Stay awake, maybe you'll learn something."

We sat for four fuckin' hours. Nothin'. It rained twice. Four hours. No talk, no cigarettes, no movin' round, no coughin' or throat clearin'. Nothin' but a wet ass 'n' leg cramps. Then we packed it in and started back. Slow. Really slow. A different route. Stoppin' 'n' listenin'. An hour, hour 'n' a half. I didn't have the faintest fuckin' idea of where we were. Then in the middle of a paddy that looked exactly like every other one I'd seen I almost fell over it . . . an arm, a clenched fist stickin' out of the water. I was fourth man back and at first I couldn't believe it. Garcia, Davis, and Eric had walked right by it. It couldn't be what I knew it was, or they'd have seen it. I reached out 'n' grabbed Eric's jacket by the tail. He froze. Everybody froze. Telepathy, maybe. Fear smells, too. Maybe they smelled it. I went right up to his ear 'n' whispered, "Man, some dude's arm is stickin' outa that water back there."

He backed up. I could see his head turn this way 'n'

that, like he was sniffin' the air. "Here," I whispered, and pointed the barrel of the '16 at the arm. He dropped down and pulled on the wrist. The arm was stiff. He stuck his hand into the water, gropin'. He came up with a piece of black cloth. It wasn't one of our grunts. Slowly, without a sound, he pulled his knife free of the scabbard 'n' started probin'. He covered prob'ly thirty feet, in a line. The rest of us had bunched up somewhat. Dumb. We coulda been takin' the bait, maybe ten seconds from gettin' lit up. He spread us out, moved us off on a line, away from whatever the hell I'd found. Hundred, two hundred meters. We crawled into a hedgerow, close up to the Lef'tenant. In a hoarse whisper, he said, "Either it's a mass grave or we're getting sucked in. Let's sit a while." It was close to three a.m. by then. Three, maybe four hours to light. We waited, thirty minutes, an hour. Nothin' moved, not us or them, if they were out there. Eric went under his poncho with a map and a tiny light. When he came out a few minutes later he took the receiver off the hook. "Seven-five, two-one. Fire mission. Over."

"Roger, two-one. This is seven-five."

Levine read some numbers into the phone. The night watchman at the artillery fire base acknowledged 'em. "Give me one round illumination."

If I hadn't been in his pocket I'd never have heard him. "Seven-five, two-one. Fire."

"Roger, two-one." In less than a minute the whole goddamn world lit up. Pop. Like snappin' on a big fuckin' fluorescent light. Weird greenish-white light. We all looked like wax dummies, taut, eyes strainin' to see, hunkered down. Nothin' moved. The hamlet looked like somethin' on an overexposed film, stark, ugly. Eric whispered into the phone again. "Seven-five, two-one. One round H 'n' E."

"Roger, two-one. One round H 'n' E."

"Seven-five, two-one. Fire."

"Roger."

A fast-fuckin' freight roared over our heads and exploded about two hundred meters in front of us, maybe fifty meters off to the left. He corrected, told 'em to fire, and another freight slammed over us, into the paddy. The illumination round died. After the white light we couldn't see a damn thing. The third H 'n' E screamed in. Bright light, earth, fire 'n' water leaped a hundred feet into the air, then it was black. The Boy Ranger talked to the cannon man again. My ears were ringin' and all I caught was "Salvo." Over they came, two sets of four, spaced out on a line. The whole damned world trembled, fire, earth 'n' water. Flames, steam, noise. I closed my eyes. At that moment I was infinitely more thankful for what the dinks didn't have than for all the firepower we did have. The fires fizzled, the light was gone, the thunder stopped ringin' in my ears. The world went back to bein' stone black. We waited, half an hour, an hour. Nada. If there were any people in the hamlet they musta been too fuckin' afraid to come out and see who was blowin' away their rice crop. It began to get light, barely noticeable, straight up more than at eye level. "Let's go," Eric said. We went.

I don't know what had been buried there. Twenty, fifty, a hundred bodies. You couldn't tell. There were pieces everywhere. An arm here, a leg minus a foot there, scraps of clothes, pieces of metal, bone—with 'n' without flesh. The smell was putrid. We were spaced out, pacin' up 'n' down. Poe squatted off to one side and picked up two skulls, pretty much intact. "Alas, poor Yin and Yang. I knew them, but not well."

"Madre, mucho dead VC, no?" Garcia took a skull

from Poe. "Look like Major Head Doctor. Maybe I send heem."

"All or nothin', Wetback. You can't have Yin without Yang."

"Why?"

"It's like having one ball."

"No good." He threw the skull back to Poe. "Fuck Ying Yang." He wandered off, his rifle slung, searchin' the ground for God only knows what. He was close to fifty meters away, near the hamlet, when suddenly he threw down his M-16 'n' ripped off his fatigue jacket. We heard the rifle hit the water, and him yell, "Ho, toro-boo. Haaahhh. Sisssttt. Ho, toro." In the faint light, barely visible, a water buffalo was wanderin' around, maybe curious, more likely fucked up by the concussion of explosions. Garcia was naked to the waist, wavin' his jacket, yellin', "Ho, toro . . . ho ho. Stupid gook cow, you never see matador? Ho!" The water-boo came closer. "Ho toro. Sisssttt." Suddenly the water-boo got the smell of a round-eye, or maybe because he liked the idea of playin' some stupid-ass grunt's silly game, he thundered into movement. A thousand pounds of flesh 'n' muscle roared through the water straight at Garcia. It musta scared the shit outa him. He turned to run or grab his rifle or say his prayers. Who knows? The horn, three feet with a sharp point, speared a hundred-'n'-thirty-pound nineteen-year-old kid, flipped him about ten feet straight up on the run. The buffalo cut a circle 'n' came back, head lowered. Garcia was screamin'. Ubanski turned loose a burst. The buffalo staggered, made a final flick with his horn, and pitched over on his side. We got to Garcia in about ten seconds. Vomit spilled outa his mouth. His crotch 'n' upper thigh were laid open like the belly of a filleted fish. His cock was hangin' by a shred. Everything was bloody. The last thing he did was reach for his balls. They weren't there. Maybe that's what killed him. Or maybe he choked to death on puke. Or bled to death. But he died. In less than two minutes he went from bein' a dumb grunt to a dead man. I couldn't look. The fear, the bile, juices from that place where we never look, boiled up through my stomach into my mouth. I sat down in the water 'n' shook. Eric took the radio off my back 'n' walked away. Fifteen minutes later a med-evac chopper settled close to the ground, throwin' water everywhere. Garcia was tossed in. It never touched the ground. In and out. Speedy Garcia was gone.

I figured that was it. Whatever *it* was. The Lef'tenant was on the phone with his old man. When he finished he got us together. "We're going to check out that hamlet. Carefully. I've got it plotted. If we get hit, *one* fuckin' round, get out and I'll light it up like Times Square. We got maybe an hour before all hell breaks loose."

"What sorta hell?" Davis asked.

"We are about to become the subject of electronic journalistic curiosity. By tomorrow night we may all be famous." He rinsed his mouth with water from a canteen, then squirted it off to the side, disgustedly. Coulda been the taste of the water. "Naturally, if we are, we'll be forgotten two days later. So don't count on a movie contract.

"All right, let's go."

The six of us moved off toward the hamlet. Davis was on point, twenty meters ahead. We were still fifty meters from the hamlet, in the misty half-light of first dawn, when an old broad comes tear-assin' round the corner of a hooch, beatin' a track straight to us. Yellin' 'n' wavin' her arms. Hot to trot. "Watch her," Eric said. Shit, you couldn't help but watch her. She had the whole fuckin' stage. Davis stopped when she was within ten feet. Yackity yackity yackity. He shrugged. She got really pissed. Yap yap yap. The tone went up ten decibels. She pointed toward the dead water-boo. Levine walked over. She was close to hoppin' up 'n' down by then. Jinx stopped to listen. Levine said somethin' to her in English, "I'm sorry," or some such. Jinx asked her somethin' in Vietnamese. She yapped a little slower. "She wants five thousand piasters for the water-boo."

Levine looked at him like wha'th'fuck? "Ask her if it was hers."

"I can't."

"Why not?"

" 'Cause the only things I ever buy is booze 'n' broads. It ain't a relevant question since damn sure cunt 'n' beer belongs to them that's selling it. Right?"

"Right. Fuck her. Let's go." We moved on, her hoppin' along with us for another ten seconds. Then, without even the faintest warnin' the Boy Ranger spun and pointed his M-16 right at her goddamn belly button. "Di di."

Dee-dee hell, I thought. Drag ass old lady or you're gonna be choppin' rice with air whistlin' through your belly. She twisted her mouth round in a half sneer 'n' walked away. Yap yap yap. She wouldn't shut her face. I was afraid the Boy Ranger was goin' to blow her away. I'd never seen him pissed like he looked now. Not even when he was hasselin' with the mail clerk. "Hey, man, cool it," I whispered when I walked by him.

"Hawk, remind me to show you something when we get back."

"You think we will?"

"I may have to part the sea with 155s, but we'll get back."

There wasn't a fuckin' thing in the hamlet. Old men, women, few kids. Some hogs. Ducks 'n' such. Weird. We coulda been walkin' round on top of an NVA hospital for all we knew. Freakin' slopes been diggin' tunnels here since about 1930. End to end they'd prob'ly reach from Hanoi to Sydney, Australia. But we didn't find any. So we stared at the people 'n' they stared at us. Unless one of us wanted to get laid, or buy a beer, Jinx's Vietnamese was worthless. I started laughin'. Not too loud, 'cause it wasn't a belly-laugh kinda thing. But it suddenly struck me funny's hell that we were standin' here, couldn't even tell the old lady why we'd shot her fuckin' water-boo, and that she'd get paid for it. Or was s'posed to. I pulled Jinx off to the side. "You got a joint?"

"Does a cat cover its shit?"

We got stoned.

The brass-hats arrived. Boy Ranger's old man, Early, two dudes from intelligence—one of 'em about as far from it as he could get, to judge by his attitude—a network TV crew, reporters from AP 'n' UPI, coupla freelancers and a specialist fifth-class hotshot from the *Stars 'n' Stripes*. He acted like he thought he was a military writer for *The New York Times*. I was standin' behind him when he asked Lef'tenant Levine if there was any resistance. "One old biddy waving her arms." The jerkoff wrote, "Patrol met lgt resist." I walked off laughin'. Fuck me. Lgt resist's ass. From a distance the whole thing was even funnier. When you couldn't hear, all the gestures, shrugs, shiftin' of bodies, became a weird pantomime. Super-slick dudes with cameras, pencils, paper flutterin', faced off against a bunch of grungy, stinkin' grunts, circled by brass-hats, which were balanced on one side by Huey gunships, on the other by pissed-off gooks.

"And now, through the miracle of modern electronics, we take you to the scene of today's big victory in No Man's Nam. Our man in Nam, Peter Pureheart" (dissolve to Nam stock footage) "has an exclusive interview with an American infantryman forty miles west of Danang. Peter . . . are you there . . .?"

"Yes, Chasper. I'm here, amid the carnage of another great battle, a stunning victory for American forces in the fight to rid South Vietnam of Vietnamese. I have here, at my side, an American infantry private, a grunt as they are affectionately known in the Army. Soldier, what's your name?"

"Hawkins."

"What unit are you with, Private Hawkins?"

"I'm only permitted to give my name, rank and serial number."

"No, Private, it's okay. We're the American Press. The good guys. Ha ha."

"That ain't what I heard. I heard you Eastern effete shitheads were atheistic commie-lovers."

"Ben . . . Ben. Come quick. It's Jamie. He's on the TV."

"No, that's not true. Not at all. Why there've been hundreds of stories unfavorable to the American soldier that we've not shown to the public at home."

"Elsie, that ain't Jamie. You know Jamie's in Veet-nam."

"That's from Veet-nam, Ben. Fix the color. His face is purple."

"He always was a funny-looking kid, Elsie."

"Private Hawkins. That's all I can say."

"Okay, ha ha. Good to see our boys so security conscious. Tell me, Private, how did all this happen?"

"Lit 'em up with H 'n' E. Course, they were already dead, but we dug 'em up right quick with that high-powered shit."

"Private Hawkins, this is *live* television, bein' beamed into the family homes of millions via satellite, right at the moment you speak."

"No shit?"

"*Elsie, ain't that boy ever gonna learn not to cuss in public?*"

"*Ben, his head's too long.*"

"*And he's a right smart too big for his britches, if you ask me.*"

"Private Hawkins, how do you see your personal role in this stunning victory?"

"I was humpin' the radio."

"*Elsie, don't that boy know he's on TV. He ought not to be talkin' about radio.*"

"*He always was fair-minded.*"

"And the radio is a crucial, vital link with support units, correct?"

"It's heavy's hell, and that's all I know."

"We understand you met some light resistance entering the hamlet. Can you tell us about that, and do you think it's indicative of enemy troops hidden in the area?"

"Huh?"

"*Ben, what'd he say?*"

"Huh?"

"The resistance . . . can you tell us about that?"

"Yeah. An old broad came runnin' out wavin' her arms, uptight 'cause we'd greased her water-boo."

"Greased . . . ?"

"Lit him up, man. Blew him away. One apprentice bullfighter and one water-boo, KIA."

"What happened to the—bullfighter?"

"Got gouged in the gonads."

"Ben, his face's purple again."

"It ought to be, talkin' like that on TV."

"Ben, what's it mean, gouged in the Nomads?"

"I ain't sure."

"Private, one last question. How do you look at your role as an American in Vietnam?"

"With a goddamn jaundiced eye."

"Well, Chasper, that's it from here . . ."

"Thanks, Peter. Good news, and good night."

"Good night, Chasper."

"Say good night, Elsie."

"Good night Elsie."

The brass-hats and hotshots all left on the choppers that brought them. They left without us. We walked back. The great unwashed, once they served their purpose, were forgotten. It figures, I guess. I never took a monkey home to dinner when I visited the zoo. We were lucky to get back. Alive, I mean. Maybe Ubanski 'n' the Boy Ranger were into it, but the rest of us might's well been stoned we were so spaced out. Garcia's death was as stupid as anything I'd seen here. We regret to inform you your son was killed in hostile action against a water-boo. It went round 'n' round in my head, like that fuckin' Pepsi commercial. The birdman had told us we'd be officially credited with one hundred and nine enemy KIA. One-oh-nine. Nice number, one-oh-nine. Wha'th'fuck, one-oh-nine or nine-oh-one. Who cares?

Coupla hours after we were back Eric came into my

bunker. Dago was over at the nerve center doin' whatever the hell he did all day to make money. I still hadn't figured out what my job was s'posed to be. I hadn't seen any money, either. Boy Ranger threw a book on my bunk. "Open it at the bookmark and read."

Few had forebodings of their destiny. At the halts they lay in the long wet grass and gossiped, enormously at ease. The whistle blew. They jumped for their equipment. The little gray figure of the colonel far ahead waved its stick. Hump your pack and get a move on. The next hour, man, will bring you three miles closer to your death. Your life and your death are nothing to these fields—nothing, no more than it is to the man planning the next attack at G.H.Q. You are not even a pawn. Your death will not make the world safe for your children. Your death means no more than if you had died in your bed, full of years, and respectability, having begotten a tribe of young. Yet by your courage in tribulation, by your cheerfulness before the dirty devices of this world, you have won the love of those who have watched you. All we remember is your living face, and that we loved you for being of our clay and spirit.

I read it twice. Slowly. "It's beautiful," I said.
"I thought you might like it."
"It's also bullshit."
"I also thought you might feel that way."
"How can anything so beautiful be so much bullshit?"
"Because if it wasn't for the BS we'd all quit. Not only war. We'd quit living."
"That's it?"

"What else is there? Bullshit's all there is. What matters is what you do with it. Like the Army, if you can believe it. I want to be the best fucking platoon leader in the Army. The best. I don't want to lose any men. None. And I'm going to see how many gooks we can kill without losing anyone else."

"Garcia . . . ?"

"Some things are out of my hands."

"Why kill dinks, man? I mean, why don't we go out 'n' sit in some comfortable bar, get half in the bag, then wander back. Who's gonna know where we been or we ain't been?"

"I'll know. Listen, I don't give a damn about the Vietnamese, one way or the other. They could be pop-up targets for all I care."

"They're human, man. They got a right to somethin' besides this shit."

"Sure they do."

"So why kill 'em?"

"Because they're there. If they don't want to fight let 'em go home."

"But this is their country. They *are* home."

"Home, Hawk. Back to the rice paddies and fish boats. Hawk, they're here because they're playing the same game we are. If we leave tomorrow—I'll be happy to leave—but if we do, do you believe they'll be free or happy, or without some other kind of misery. Life is all bullshit. We happen to be the active ingredient at the moment."

"Wha' th' fuck . . ."

"Exactly." He gave me that goofy smile. "Think about it, Hawk. It could keep you alive, if you care."

Too muckin' futch. I mean I've felt that way for a long time. That it's all bullshit. But I got these ambitions. I want to change it. Make somethin' outa life that's worth the goddamn effort I put into it. But I couldn't figure the Boy Ranger. As old Witherspoon would say, it was out of character. He believes every character should have a personality to which he holds, steadfastly, as he'd say. He likes words like that. Steadfastly. Heretofore. Christ, Eric looked like the All-American Boy, like he really believed in what he was doin' on some level other than this. I couldn't get it together. Didn't make any sense. But people usually don't. 'Cept in fuckin' fiction, where everybody is steadfast. Maybe I just never meet the right people. The Army takes anything. And the infantry takes the worst of the lot.

Nobody seemed to notice that Garcia was dead. First coupla days there were some jokes. But nobody gave a fat rat's ass Garcia was dead. Tough shit. Might be me tomorrow. Count your days 'n' keep your ass covered. "Yet by your courage in tribulation, by your cheerfulness before the dirty devices of this world, you have won the love of those who have watched you. All we remember is your living face, and that we loved you for being of our clay and spirit." Chicano slum kids don't come from middle-America's clay, or spirit. I mean, what fuckin' Iowa pig farmer, Mississippi share-cropper, Westchester County Jew, California grape grower, Harlem spade, or Spokane shop owner is gonna admit bein' of the same clay and spirit as some dumb wetback who got his ass ripped in Nam? Those who have watched *us* have done it through the bottom of a beer glass in sleazy bars, or lookin' over a forkful of potatoes. We were lucky to get three minutes between an Anacin commercial and the stock market report. We were a pain in the ass, and just so many numbers on some dude's board in Saigon, the Pentagon, and the international desks of the networks. Once a week the voice, for thirty seconds, became somber and the announcements seeped into the ether: Forty-five Americans were reported killed in Vietnam this week. The Dow Jones Industrial average was off today, down three points to 983. No one loved us for bein' of their clay 'n' spirit. They were grateful to those of us who went away quietly, without makin' too big a fuss 'r screamin' Hell no, we won't go!

Four days after Garcia got it, First Sergeant Minnow called Poe, Dago 'n' me to his office. "Garcia's parents have asked for a body escort, someone from his outfit. You three have been chosen."

"Why me?" Dago asked.

"We ain't got any other Mexicans."

"I'm Italian."

"Same thing. You're leavin' tomorrow mornin' for Danang, where you'll pick up the body for flight to Oakland, then San Diego. You'll be briefed. Get your class-A's ready."

"That's it?" Dago asked. "We don't know shit about escortin' bodies, First Sergeant. What's the scoop?"

"You'll be briefed, Cocuzza."

Dago looked a mite pissed when we left. I was stoned out on the idea of gettin' outa Nam, even if it was only for a few days. Poe was quiet. "Man, how come you're so fuckin' down on it?" I asked Dago.

"It's a setup. I know it."

"How?"

"I don't know, but I feel it. That fucker's settin' me up, y' know?"

I couldn't see how, but I wasn't into Dago's doin's

enough to know anything except he was apparently makin' a shit-load of money. When he'd gone off to make arrangements for his absence, Poe said to me, "I can't go."

"Wha' th' fuck's with you two?"

"I can't go."

"Why?"

"I can't trust Whipple alone for four or five days with my pigs."

"I got your fuckin' pig hangin'." I grabbed my crotch. "Here's your goddamn pig."

"You aren't supposed to talk to the Corporal of the Pigs like that, pfc Hawkins."

"Stuff it. Do you realize we're gonna see the land of the Big PXs? Round-eyed girls. Clothes that ain't olive goddamn green? Food . . . think of it, man. Real food."

"It's supposed to be a funeral, Hawk. For a fallen comrade."

"That can't last more'n half a day, right? We got time."

"I hope you don't seem that delighted that Garcia got it while you're standing by his grave. His parents might not understand."

"You think that's why he tried to tie it on with that water-boo? So we'd get a chance to get outa here?"

"I think you're flaky." He stopped at the openin' to his bunker. "You're changing, Hawk."

"Ain't we all?"

"May be. Just may be."

Next mornin', about an hour before we were s'posed to leave. Dago went out. He wasn't gone more'n fifteen minutes, and I didn't think anything of it till he came back, dropped a duffel bag on the floor 'n' said, "Put your clothes in here." The bag was almost full. I picked it up. I *tried* to pick it up. I made maybe two feet before it thumped back to the floor. "Put my clothes where?"

"In there."

"You shittin' me, man? That fucker weighs about a hundred pounds now, and the room that's left ain't enough to change your mind in."

"It weighs eighty pounds. Y' got room enough for all y' need."

"Wha'th'fuck's in there?"

"Grade-goddamn-A Thai grass. One thousand dollars a pound, wholesale."

My mind went through some rapid-ass tote-boardin'.

"*Eighty thousand dollars!*"

"For that one. There's two more. One f' you, one f' Poe. You both get a cut."

"A quarter of a million dollars?" My voice squeaked. "Two hundred 'n' fifty *thousand* US dollars?"

"I may not get more'n two hundred thou' since I'll hafta dump it quick. But that's minimum."

"Dago . . . we'll be shot. They won't bust us. We'll be shot down on the streets like gooks in a free-fire zone. You're crazy. You know that? *Crazy.* How in God's name do you think you can smuggle—how much is it?—anyway, don't matter. You can't get away with that shit!"

"No sweat." He snapped his fingers like he was in the Top of the Mark and wanted the check.

"'No sweat,' he says. How much is there?"

"A hundred keys."

"Two hundred 'n' twenty pounds?"

"Actually, it's two-forty. But twenty pounds is f' my friends."

"Two hundred 'n' forty fuckin' pounds of grass . . . no sweat? Am I s'posed to believe *that*?"

"Have I steered y' wrong yet?"

"No, man."

"Well?"

"I mean, no! I'm not goin' to do it. You're stone flaky. Cracked at the seams. No way."

"Not even f' twenty-five percent of what ya bag brings?"

"Not even for—twenty-five percent?" Whirrrr . . . "Twenty thousand?"

"Give that man a big cigar! Twenty thousand it is."

"Even if *I* do, Poe'll never go for it."

"He's already agreed."

"He doesn't need twenty thousand any more'n I need another year in Nam."

"He's agreed, Hawk. Would I lie?"

"What's in it for him?"

"Votes."

"Votes? Votes for what?"

"Votes f' the senatorial seat in the next election of a Virginia senator."

"You're from *Jersey*. How you gonna vote in Virginia?"

"Not me, y' dumb fuck. Teamsters. My uncle's a teamster, tied in with their political wing. I tell 'im this dude did me a favor an' he needs votes. All the fuckin' truck drivers in Virginia are gonna line up to vote f' Poe."

"His *old man*'s already senator."

"Poe's gonna run against 'im."

"Fuck me. Anyway, he can't be that old."

"He'll be thirty, two days before the election—three years from now. Anyway, we gonna get us a mess of round-eyes 'n' party till the cows come home . . . ain't that how you fuckin' rednecks say it?"

"What we say is hang it in your ass. I'll do it, but I still don't see how."

"Just do what I tell y' to do, no questions. An' keep ya goddamn mouth shut. Dig?"

"I dig."

"My, my, you aren't as dumb as I thought."

"And you may fuckin' well not be as smart as you think."

"Y' better hope the hell I am."

Longfeather drove us to Danang. There wasn't ten words of conversation. I s'pose everybody was into thinkin' about us carryin' a quarter-million in grass. I couldn't believe no fuckin' grass, I don't care how good, would sell for a thousand dollars a pound, wholesale, retail or at gunpoint. But I did want to see how Dago planned to pull it off. Why else would I be draggin' round eighty pounds of shit on my way to a funeral?

Instead of goin' to the processin' center where we were s'posed to be briefed on procedure, Dago had Longfeather drive us to the body shop. The place where they try to fix up dudes who've been had. They plug up the holes with cotton, I think. That's what somebody told me. And they paint over 'em with makeup. That's the exposed part, face 'n' head. Cover up the body with a new uniform. Don't want him goin' home in rags. Dead's okay. But he's gotta be neatly dressed. That's the rules. Dago went inside, was gone a few minutes, then came out. "Bring 'em in." We took the bags inside. "Put 'em here an' go wait in the jeep." We dropped 'em and left. He was back in another five minutes at the most. We went to be briefed on how to act at the funeral of our fallen comrade. They said act natural. I thought that might not be too cool. If we acted natural, which is crazy, poor old Garcia's parents would fuckin' freak right out. They said where the coffin is marked "non-viewable" the family of the deceased is not to be permitted to view the body under any circumstances. That's because the Army doesn't want our tax-payin' mothers 'n' fathers to see their son's head shredded by shrapnel—or see his body with no head. It happens. Heads get blown away exactly like feet 'n' arms, cocks 'n' balls. It's all the same to a mine, booby-trap, or grenade. What it hits is what it gets.

The whole thing was depressin'. When it was over we went to the grunts' club for a beer. Round noon we got on the plane. There were three dozen caskets. I counted. Morbid. There were another fifteen guys. Some of the caskets wouldn't get an escort until they reached Oakland. All the escorts were grunts, right outa the field. All pfcs 'n' corporals. Dago started rappin', doin' his shit and out came some grass. The plane's crew were all busy flyin' or sacked out. In less'n half an hour everybody but us was asleep. Zonked. Stoned into oblivion. "You drug 'em, man?" Poe asked.

"That's the weed we're carryin'. Give 'em half a joint, they're gone for an hour or two at least."

"Why do that?"

"Hawk, we gotta check the casket. It'd be hell if I tried to sell a hundred keys of that stuff 'n' there wasn't nothing but a body in there."

"In where?"

"In Garcia's casket."

"You put grass in with Garcia? You sonofabitch, you ain't got no goddamn respect for anything."

"Where the hell did y' think I was gonna put a hundred keys of grass? In my goddamn shoes?"

"But in the *casket*, for Christ's sake? With the body?"

"Not with the body."

"*Not* with the body?"

"Hell, no. Even as light as Garcia is, or was, it would weigh so much somebody might get suspicious."

"Well, where the hell is the body?"

"I had it thrown away."

"You threw Garcia away? Dago—"

"Hawk, don't get all excited like that. Ya blood pressure goes up too high. Y' want a heart attack?"

"You threw away Garcia's body? Right?"

"I didn't. The body men did."

"How did you get 'em to do that?"

"Five grand each. Garcia's body don't mean nothin' to nobody. He's fuckin' dead. No body—I can't stop that . . ." He giggled. "No *one* gave a damn about him when he was livin'. So how come it matters now?"

"I don't know . . . I guess I'm just old-fashioned."

"Last month would y' have believed you'd be smugglin' dope? Never mind my ingenious plan. Anyway at all, could y' see y'self smugglin' dope? Yes or no?"

"No!"

"Well, what's the big deal? You've already come a long way, Hawk. Why stop here?"

"Where the fuck *do* we stop?"

"It beats me." His voice was suddenly sad, like an old man who's weary of life with its hassles 'n' bullshit.

"Poe . . . ?"

"Garcia's dead, Hawk. You and I watched him die and we were glad it was him and not us. It's too late for a sermon."

"I'm gonna be sick."

"No ya not," Dago laughed. "Ya gonna learn, baby. Ya gonna be just as goddamn stinkin' fucked up as we are. Kill gooks an' pray y' get a chance to get rich off it just like us. Ya days of bein' a nine-year-old are over."

"He's right," Poe said. "I wish he wasn't but he is."

"Not yet, motherhumpers. Not yet. I'll go with this, and maybe I'll go with some more shit, but you haven't got me yet."

Dago made a quick check of the coffin, opened it, and poked round inside. When he'd locked it tight he came back, a big goddamn grin on his face. "Right on. We're in like a porch climber."

"What happens to Garcia?" I couldn't get it straight in my head. I mean I knew it really didn't make any difference, but I couldn't reconcile the intellect and the emotion. I had the feelin' my difficulty wasn't gonna be more'n a fart in a whirlwind compared to Garcia's parents. "What happens when his parents open that casket and don't see nothin' but dope?"

"First off," Dago, "his parents aren't gonna open that casket. It's tagged 'Remains not f' Viewing.' Second, the Mex went up in smoke about an hour ago. No sweat."

Poe laughed. "Hey, how are you going to get the dope from the casket to your contact?"

"'I haven't figured that yet." He smiled, lit a cigarette, settled back. "But it'll come to me. F' that much money, believe me, it'll come."

We flew to Japan, picked up some more caskets,

then to Oakland, direct. In Oakland we were checked, caskets and escorts matched, unescorted bodies picked up by escorts, and sent on our way. Somebody was with us the whole time. And Dago hadn't come up with an answer, or he was keepin' it a big fuckin' secret. We were put up for the night, restricted to the base. Next mornin' we got on a plane to San Diego. The grass was still in the coffin. The plane landed. Some dip-shit lieutenant met us at the airport, the casket was loaded on a hearse, and off we went. To Garcia's house. I was watchin' Dago. Sonofabitch was cool as a morgue slab. We stopped in front, and three of Garcia's brothers came out. Dago, Poe 'n' I took one side of the casket, the brothers took the other. The lieutenant left with the hearse. We were s'posed to sit with the family for a few hours, then all of us, includin' the casket, would be taken to the church. From there to the graveyard. I saw a quarter of a million dollars in grass goin' down the drain. There wasn't no way that fucker could get it out now.

The house was a four-room shack, filled with gaudy icons, greasy cookin' smells 'n' prob'ly fifteen or twenty mourners. Candles burned in the front room, where we put the casket. The furniture was shabby, the floor bare, the plaster peelin'. Everything was clean, but it looked 'n' smelled of a scrape-by existence. Garcia's mother was prob'ly forty, plump to fat, dependin' on how you see such things. She was puffy-faced from cryin'. His father was short, lean, lotta muscles. His hands were leathery as boot soles, his arms and handshake like iron. Two minutes after we were in the door, before we could even get seated, his mother tried to feed us. We were his good friends, his comrades, spared from the same awful fate. God forbid we should die of hunger. They were bein' so nice to us, so worried about us while we were jerkin' 'em off, I woulda liked to eat my heart. And for nothin'. No way were we gonna get that grass out. Poe 'n' I refused anything to eat. Dago said sure, whatever you've got. He went into the kitchen with the old lady. Poe 'n' I sat on a threadbare couch, starin' at Garcia's brothers, sisters, aunts, uncles, cousins, neighbors, who knew? There was a roomful of people and we were the only white-asses in there. Maybe ten minutes went by, then the old lady yelled for Garcia's father. He excused himself and disappeared into the kitchen. Another ten minutes, then he called in the brothers.

"Wha'th'fuck's Dago doin'?" I asked Poe, like he should know.

"Beats me. But I'll bet you a month's pay he's conning them. Some way or other, he's givin' them a snow job."

We waited. Whatever he was doin' was takin' time. Ten, fifteen minutes. Then all of a sudden the whole goddamn lot of 'em burst into the room, laughin', smilin', cryin' with happiness. They circled the casket. Dago starts to open it. Poe rolls his eyes. I about shit. Up goes the top. Dago brings out the duffel bags, one, two, three. Garcia's mother throws her arms around Dago, laughin' 'n' cryin' at the same time. The other people in the room, me 'n' Poe included, don't know what's goin' on. The old man starts yabberin' in Spanish, machine-gunnin' words around that room like a verbal M-60. Even if I'd known Spanish I'd never have gotten the first word. I got up, grabbed Dago by the arm, dragged him off, outside. Poe came. "Wha'th'fuck did you do, man? Are you totally fuckin' insane?"

"Shit, Hawk. Y' didn't think I'd let them bury that dope, did you?"

"What did you tell 'em?"

"I told 'em Garcia's not really dead. That he, y' know, was sent on a secret mission to Laos. That he couldn't write 'cause they're supposed to believe he's dead. But that he didn't want them to worry, so he picked us—his friends—to come back with the casket, to tell 'em the truth. I also told 'em that twenty grand of that money is theirs, Garcia's share, which he asked me to see that they got. I made him a hero, instead of a dumb-ass that got wasted by a fuckin' water-boo."

Poe cracked up, walked off down the street in hysterics.

"You sorry sonofabitch," I said to Dago. "I ought to kill you right now, right here." He laughed. "I mean it. You motherfucker, how they gonna feel when he don't come back? Or don't you give a shit?"

"They're gonna have a hero for a son. The whole fuckin' parish is gonna remember Garcia 'cause he died on a *secret* mission. The truth is, Hawk, the truth is I gave Garcia another year of life. F' them, he's alive, in Laos. They'll pray for 'im, talk about 'im, live with 'im, just like he's alive, doin' 'is thing. An' when I hafta report 'im killed on his secret mission, they'll believe he died bravely. Don't that beat gettin' done in by a goddamn water-boo?"

I shuddered. There was a certain logic in what he was sayin'. It was against everything we been taught about right 'n' wrong, truth, whatever. But he was right. The sonofabitch was stone fuckin' right. They wanted to believe their son was alive. And he would be, for another year. Dago, for an instant, was God, and a damn sight less arbitrary. Fuck me. I felt like somebody was takin' hold of everything I'd ever thought was right, makin' it wrong, makin' all the wrong right . . . and laughin' 'cause I couldn't keep up.

It needed some more thought. I thought about it right through the Mass, the burial, the ride back to the house. I prob'ly was the only one who looked somber enough to be at a funeral.

We escaped from there about five in the afternoon. Just walked away. We were s'posed to report to someone at the Naval Air Station for a flight back to Oakland. What we did was go AWOL. Dago had laid a big green bundle of money on Garcia's parents, told them they couldn't, under any circumstances, write anyone about Garcia without fuckin' up the secret mission, and we caught a plane to Las Vegas. Rather, Poe 'n' I did. Dago went on to New York. He gave me a five-grand advance. "Go to the Desert Sands, ask for Papa Angelo. Tell 'im ya buddies of mine, an' I'll be there tomorrow night. We gotta be in Oakland in less'n seventy-two hours. Up to three days they don't do anythin'. Report you to ya company, but no hassle, y' know?"

"You figure everything, don't you?"

"I try, Hawk baby. God knows I try."

It wasn't until we were ridin' to the airport that I noticed it was Christmas. Two days after, in fact. Trees, lights, tinsel, all that Noel shit was on the radio. The cab driver had a little plastic Santa Claus hangin' by a string from his rearview mirror, and a plastic nativity scene on the dashboard. It musta been close to sixty degrees. The streets were filled with well-tanned people in shirtsleeves, light jackets. The sun was shinin' but it didn't cheer me the way I had expected. We hadn't seen the sun since we'd been in No Man's Nam. Now, here it was. It seemed as unreal as the Christmas carols. I wished, in some weird way, we were back with Kilo. The flight hadn't been long enough to even get drunk.

Poe 'n' I went to the Desert Sands and asked for Papa Angelo. Poe explained that we were friends of Dago, etc. The guy said, "Papa's dead. Heart attack."

"This dyin' shit's spreadin' like fertilizer in a high wind," I said. The goon really got his ass up on his shoulders.

"Who else is dead?"

"A friend of ours," Poe said.

I walked off, toward the casino restaurant. The place was crawlin' with short-skirted women. I shoulda been happy as a pig in shit, but nothin' was worth it. Everything was fucked up. We looked like the only two gringos at a Mexican weddin'. Outa place. I passed the restaurant 'n' went into the casino. It was seven-thirty, eight o'clock. The place was fairly crowded. Poe found me and we watched some dudes shootin' craps. I couldn't figure it out. I mean the basics I understand, but all the side bets 'n' shit was so fuckin' fast I couldn't make heads or tails out of it. Everybody talked 'n' pushed chips round like they knew exactly what the hell they were doin'. Craps, blackjack, roulette. We stopped at a roulette table. Maybe five or six people were playin', small stuff. Dimes, quarters, half-dollars. A hunch hit me. "How old was Garcia?"

Poe looked at me with a blank expression, then grinned.

"Twenty, I think. Nineteen or twenty."

"Okay, count nineteen turns of the wheel, then I'll bet nineteen. If that doesn't pay, I'll play twenty. I feel it." We counted. After the eighteenth spin I asked the broad runnin' the wheel, "What's the limit?"

"Two hundred, sport. Can you afford it?"

"Two hundred on each number, or total?" I pulled out the fifty hundred-dollar bills Dago'd given me. Her fuckin' eyes popped. She mighta seen more, but not in the hand of a fuckin' grunt.

"Two hundred, total. But you can probably get it raised, honey."

"Honey's ass, spin the motherfucker." I put a hundred on 19, fifty on 1 and fifty on 9. Twelve came up. She looked right pleased. The wheel went round again. I put a hundred on 2, another on 20. Zero came up.

"So much for hunches," Poe laughed.

"Close. We're close. What's today's date?"

"Twenty-second."

"Nineteen, twenty, twenty-one . . . next time." The wheel spun, the twenty-first time. I laid off. On the next one I put a hundred on 2, another on 22. "Two, black," the crier cried.

"I'm a sonofabitch," Poe said.

"I'm rich!" I yelled. Everybody started yackin', yap yap yap yap yap yap. About nine casino goons popped outa the woodwork. The broad counted out thirty-five hundred-dollar chips. I threw one at her. "There you go, *sport*." Poe grabbed me by the arm. "Let's go," I said. "I don't like this goddamn place."

I cashed the chips. Thirty-four hundred dollars. Jesus. I never even saw that much money before today, let alone had it in my sweaty fist. My hands were shakin'. I had to piss, but I was afraid to go to the bathroom. Altogether, I had a little over eight thousand dollars in my pockets. "Let's get a cup of coffee." I said to Poe.

"Can we afford it?" He laughed all the way to the cafeteria.

We sat in a booth and I kept fingerin' the money, then took it out 'n' counted it again. Eighty crisp, green pictures of Benjamin Franklin starin' off into some vision I couldn't see, plus some twenties. It wasn't real. The money, I mean. Intellectually, I guess I knew I could spend it; buy a car, buy all the steaks in the restaurant, buy the biggest goddamn stereo system in town, buy damn near anything I wanted. But it hadn't settled into my guts yet. One minute I'm playin' with plastic chips, the next I'm foldin' green money in my hands. Monopoly money I could understand, but this was unreal. I owned Boardwalk AND Park Place. Poe finished his coffee, starin' at me. I fucked around with mine. I didn't know what the hell I wanted to do, and finishing the coffee meant I had to decide something. Poe finally asked me, "What's the most money you've ever had at one time? Before tonight?"

"Three hundred and seventy-five dollars." He smiled. "You?"

"My grandmother left me a hundred thousand dollars, in trust, but I get the interest as an allowance. Eight grand a year."

"What the fuck am I gonna do with all this money?"

"Spend it, probably. That's how it usually works out."

"On what? My own M-16 import-export company? Wha'th'fuck do I need money for in Nam?"

"Buy a hog farm, man. Buy a hog farm in Nam, next thing you know you'll have two, three hundred grunts around to keep you company."

"Poe . . . ?"

"Yeah?"

"I already got that."

"Let's go get something to eat. I'm hungry."

"In a minute." I found a bathroom, emptied my bladder 'n' started back to the cafeteria when I saw her. She hadda have forty inches of chalubbies, thirty-eight of which were hangin' out. Super-fine legs, short-ass dress, thick, black hair, big brown eyes, a pink mouth with beautiful teeth, tan and healthy-lookin'. She was tough enough. "Where you going, Blue-eyes . . . ?" I almost wet my pants. Never in my short sweet life had anyone who looked that good even looked at me, let alone spoke. My blue eyes about popped outa their sockets. I mumbled somethin' about the cafeteria. "How about a drink?" Her voice was like warm glue. I hung on every word. "Well . . . ?"

I cleared my throat. Three times. "I'll give you eight thousand dollars to go to bed with me."

She almost fell off her high heels laughin'. Finally she said, "Blue-eyes, you can have me for a lot less than that. Let's talk about it."

"Wait a second," I said in my hardened combat infantryman voice, that squeaked twice tryin' to get those three words out. "I gotta get my buddy."

"I don't ball doubles."

"We ain't goin' bowlin'. We're gonna have a drink 'n' talk." I was at the table, reachin' for Poe's arm when I realized she'd said ball, not bowl. Fuck it. No pun intended. "Poe, c'mon, man, I found us a sex goddess. Maybe she's got a sister."

"Hawk, around here they're called hookers."

"I don't care how you call 'em, man. Her fuckin' bazongas are bigger'n anything I seen in the last three months. Like honeydew melons, and prob'ly as sweet."

"Your eyes are shining, for Christ's sake."

"I'm in love." I dragged him back to the spot where I'd left her. She was there with another girl, a cocoa-colored blonde, flat-chested next to mine. And she had skinny legs. "For God's sake, Susan, they're kids. Probably virgins."

Right away I figured mine was named Susan. She says, "I'd hate to make book on it."

The blonde sighed, but the kinda sigh that goes with bein' or feelin' coerced into somethin'. So I said, "Listen, split-tail, don't put yourself out none for us. Where we just came from mosta the people your age are already dead."

"What are you, a wiseguy or something?"

Susan pulled my arm toward a bar. "Come on, Blue-eyes, let's get drunk and you can tell me war stories." We walked past the reception desk, six doors to the casino, and sat at a big, dark, mahogany bar. The bartender gave me a funny look, like he knew I wasn't old enough to be in there. But I don't think he gave a shit, 'cept he said we should move to a booth. We moved. I kept lookin' round for Poe. About the time we got a drink he came in, alone. "Where's ol' Tweezer-legs?"

"Who?"

"The bowlegged blonde."

"You got any friends?" Susan asked.

"Nope."

"I can believe it. Do you insult everybody?"

"So far. But I haven't met the whole world yet."

She smiled at Poe. "Would you like company? I've got another friend. A sweet girl from Alabama. She talks slow as hell but what she says might make your motor race." Poe shrugged, not really indifferent, but sorta restrained. Susan called a waitress over, BS'ed with her for a minute, then asked her to go find Alice. Let me say this about Alice. She came, right through the lookin' glass. She was some sorta weird chick. That's what Susan said. I said, "Holy shit!" Poe's motor raced 'n' the poor girl hadn't even opened her mouth. She was easy five-eleven. Easy! She was wearin' a jump suit, white, with big goddamn holes cut outa the sides, slit down the front, no back, and the fuckin' straps didn't look none too substantial. She was built like a brick shithouse, with Doric columns. Stone black hair, trailin' down to her ass, earring hoops the size of saucers, almost no makeup. She didn't look like no Southern belle I'd ever seen. Dyna-fuckin'-mite. When she said "Hi" it stretched out across the table like a big velvet rug.

We drank, twice around, BS'in' about where we'd been, Nam, my winnin' three thousand dollars on the roulette table. I was just beginnin' to wonder exactly how to say I'd like to go fuck when their pimp came up, sat down, uninvited, pushed back his hat 'n' said, "Well, boys, how's the Army treatin' you?" He looked like he'd been ridin' range in West Texas for the last month. He didn't smell but his jeans, boots 'n' chambray shirt were perma-wrinkled, stained and prob'ly woulda stood up by themselves. He was wearin' a Stetson-style hat, rolled brim 'n' all. It had been pearl gray once, five or six years ago. It had more sweat stains than I had money. He took it off. You wouldn't believe it. His sideburns were thick, black 'n' two or three inches below the earlobe. With his hat on he looked like he had hair as thick as a horse's mane. When he took it off all you could see was a shiny dome, like a big fuckin' egg layin' in a nest. Across the top of the dome he'd combed all thirty-seven hairs he had left, from front to back. They musta been a good twelve inches long. I stared, tryin' to figure what was wrong. His face had a lotta acne scars, really heavy beard shadow, a weak chin . . . but there was somethin' else. Poe was talkin' to him. Susan 'n' Alice were quiet. I wasn't even listenin', just starin', when it hit me. "You are the first dude I ever saw with acne scars on the *top* of his fuckin' head." Just like that, I butted in. He looked at me like I'd called his mother a cocksucker. "Those are scars from an operation I had." I wanted to say "Lobotomy . . . ?" but I couldn't think of the goddamn word. "A hair transplant," he said when I couldn't get the word out. "These priceless hairs you see cost me thirty-five hundred dollars. What's left of 'em."

After two beers 'n' maybe half an hour that seemed like an hour we paid him seven big bills for the pleasure of the girls' company. *I* paid him seven hundred. It was my treat. Wha'th'fuck, the casino paid, or some dimwit from Des Moines. Who the hell knows where the money came from.

We all went to dinner, spent another two hundred with wine. It wasn't Dago red, but that's about all I know about grape juice. Prob'ly was good stuff 'cause it didn't lay there on your tongue after you'd swallowed. Half a glass of some of the stuff I've had and you can eat garlic without knowin' it. We screwed around in the casino, went to two or three others, blew a fistful at blackjack. I wanted to learn how to shoot craps but Poe said it wasn't the place. Even through the whisky fog it occurred to me he might be right. The whole time, mind you, I'm sniffin' Susan's neck, gettin' ass rubbed all over me, pattin' Alice every chance I get, and generally about to come in my Class-A Army-issue underwear. They both smelled good enough to eat normally. But when you figure we hadn't smelled anything but pig shit 'n' paddy water for over a month you can imagine what waitin' round was doin' to us. Or me. Poe's cool about that kinda shit. Not me. At one point, Susan was sittin' next to me at the blackjack table. She stroked the inside of my leg, absentmindedly, while she was watchin' the game. I took a hit on seventeen. I woulda hit blackjack at that point. Finally I couldn't keep it together any more. I said, "Hey, how'd you like to come up 'n' look at my collection of M-16s?"

It occurred to me that I didn't even have a room. We hadn't bothered to check in. The four of us went back to the Desert Sands, got adjoinin' rooms and went upstairs. We had brought two bottles of cognac—fuckin' Poe's always gotta come up with somethin' I never heard of—got some ice 'n' commenced to get more in the bag. We partied, got stoned off some Nam stuff—I couldn't believe we'd had two hundred 'n' forty *pounds* of Thai shit and didn't even think to take a pinch. I don't know how long that went on but I suddenly had the flash of inspiration. I grabbed Susan 'n' pulled her to the bathroom. "Let's take a shower together." She gave me a big smile 'n' started takin' off her clothes. Wha'th'fuck, I figured, if she takes off hers I guess I gotta take off mine. I felt kinda shy for some weird reason. I mean I sure's hell wasn't a virgin. But I'd never even seen a bare ass that looked like hers, let alone got into a shower with it. We musta been in there two days short of forever.

When we finally got out, Poe 'n' Alice-baby were in the other room, ballin' their brains out. You ever watch anybody fuck? I here there's a whole sorta cult that really gets off on that. I fell on the floor laughin'. Couldn't help myself. Ol' Poe's skinny white ass was doin' some movin' and it was so fuckin' comical I thought I'd bust a goddamn gut. Susan, maybe a little less stoned, drunk 'n' depraved, hauled me away, to the bed. She had a super fuckin' body, rich an' creamy. And tan all over. *All* over. That blew my mind. But not as much as not bein' able to get a hard-on. All evenin'

I'd been thinkin' how I'm gonna fuck her brains out, eat her ass till she comes a quart, a million fantasies. We get in bed and—nada. I wanted her and she was more'n willin'. Hell, she did everything she knew, I guess. And I shouldn't say I couldn't get an erection. I'd get up like a goddamn knight's lance. Coupla times we even started to ball. But sure's a rockin' horse has a wooden wee-wee, I'd flash on Poe's little skinny white ass and I'd see how absolutely ridiculous people look while they're fuckin'. Thuuuppppp. Wet spaghetti. I coulda cried. Could, hell. I had to fight not to cry. The more I tried, the worse it got. I finally rolled over in pain 'n' self-disgust. Susan got up 'n' closed the door between the rooms. She left a bathroom light on, closed that door all but three or four inches, turned out the rest of the lights and got back in bed. She switched on a radio. Somebody was playin' soft stuff: Beatles, Brazil 66, Mamas 'n' Papas, some broad named Nina Simone, who I'd never heard of. Really fine voice. We were laid out, close.

"How long've you got?"

"We're AWOL. Prob'ly go back tomorrow, next day."

"You going to get into trouble?"

"I been in trouble since I got my orders to Nam. Lots of people over there seem to want to kill me. That's about as much fuckin' trouble as I ever want."

"The girls over there pretty?"

"None that I've seen. After a while some of 'em look pretty good, except they got bad teeth or flat noses. I like round-eyes better." I squeezed one o' her bazongas. "And I ain't seen the first fuckin' one with two to equal one o' these."

"They're delicate, aren't they?"

"Yeah, but they're strong. Prob'ly from throwin'

grenades 'n' haulin' ammo for the goddamn VC. Ah, what the hell, it's their country 'n' we're just there to fuck 'em around—and let a few guys get rich." I lit a joint 'n' hit it twice, then gave it to her. "How come you drag-assin' round with that dumb bastard who took the money? What's his name?"

"Myron. He's okay. He doesn't hassle us. Lot of guys fuck girls around really bad, beat 'em, take all the bread. Myron's a faggot, so we don't get too much crap. He keeps us straight with everybody, takes care of any bad-news bastards. It works out okay."

"He's a *faggot*, for Christ's sake?"

"Yeah. Got a girlfriend, guy's maybe six-one, two hundred pounds. Keeps house for Myron; cooks, cleans, goes shopping, nags him. They're cute when they're having an argument."

"*Fuck me.* You serious?"

"Sure. Don't you know any gay people?"

"Hey, I don't even know any *happy* people."

We killed the joint 'n' I was beginnin' to relax. My head wandered away, back to Kilo, the Boy Ranger, Jinx, Ubanski, Davis, the karate champ. I felt guilty. They might all be dead by now. Garcia flashed in my mind, and I couldn't picture him dead. My mind wouldn't let me see him castrated, bloody, cast off, burned 'r thrown in Danang harbor, unwanted right to the fuckin' last. I saw him in a matador's suit, the suit of lights I think he called it, graceful, gliding across the sand on an arena floor, passin' the best bulls in Spain . . . I saw the scarlet cape float past while the Mex spun in a tight circle . . . *Ole! Ole!* Fifty thousand crazy beautiful bullfight freaks screamin' for Garcia, over 'n' over, the goddamn bull big as a Ferrari and damn near as fast, black, all muscle 'n' bone 'n' bare-ass meanness with unbelievable horns. . . . The sound of my voice startled me. I couldn't remember when I'd started talkin'.

Susan's soft voice jarred me out of my fantasy. "You ever had a blow job?" I think my mouth musta fallen open. "I mean a real one . . . I want you to come in my mouth . . . would you like that? Just lay back and get off on my mouth, see yourself unloading all that sweet white cream, wipe it on my tits . . . you want to lick my boobs, Blue-eyes? Suck 'em . . . ? I'm going to suck you, eat your cock, stick my cunt into your mouth, come on you. . . . Will you make me come, Blue-eyes . . . ? Make me come. . . . The whole time she's talkin' to me she's lickin' me, jerkin' me off with her tongue on the head of my cock. My balls got hard 'n' swollen, and when I came I was afraid I'd drown her. The last things I remembered were screamin' and my head comin' unglued. I tripped out. Acid can't be any better. Lasts longer, but can't be no better. I went into an orange sunset that stretched from horizon to horizon. Waist-high grass as green as any oat field I'd ever seen, blowin' in a gentle breeze. Everything was orange 'n' green. Soundless. Totally soundless. Then it exploded, in silence. Huge columns of earth 'n' fire, still orange 'n' green, rising fifty, seventy-five, a hundred feet into the air, twistin' 'n' spinnin', sheets of flame. I musta freaked out altogether. Susan's voice came through, softly. "Hey . . . come on, baby . . . come on . . . it's okay."

"Just like the fuckin' movies, huh?" She had her arms wrapped around me, my head pulled into her breasts like mother 'n' child. Charmin', I thought. Fuckin' charmin'. A three-hundred-dollar whore wet-nursin' one of the Army's "Ultimate Weapons." That's what they call us. It's bullshit. They know it 'n' we know it, but they put up a statue of a chargin' grunt and called it "The Ultimate Weapon." The ultimate in throwaway people. That's what we are. The ultimate luxury of a throwaway society.

"You want to talk?"

"What's to fuckin' say? The whole world's turned to shit and I gotta come back as a roll of two-ply toilet paper. All I want's to be let alone. If nobody'd fuck with me I wouldn't fuck with nobody. Is that unreasonable?" She shook her head no. I took a slug from the cognac bottle. I was beginnin' to like the stuff. "You don't act like a high-priced . . ."

She laughed at my shrug. "Whore," she said. "A gold-hearted whore, just like the movies."

"Nothin's like the movies. Why are you fuckin' round with me?"

She shrugged.

"How old are you?"

"Twenty-two," she said. "You . . .?"

"Twenty, goin' on a hundred. I'm agin' in a hurry."

"Is it that bad?"

"Lotta people dyin'. Which might be okay, but they want me to contribute to the totals. I'm not sure I wanta give 'em that much."

"I had a brother over there. He used to fly guys in and out. Grunts, he called 'em."

"Chopper pilot?"

"Yeah. They shipped him back in pieces. Alive, but in pieces."

"How's he makin' out?"

"He's dead. Killed himself one night. Left a note that said, 'Fuck it.' That's all. 'Fuck it.'"

"I know how he felt."

"You going back?"

"Sure." I said sure, then I thought about the question. "I have to go back."

"Go to Canada."

"I don't think I can."

"It's easy. Hell, I'll drive you if you're afraid to go alone."

"It's not that. I got a friend in Nam. Coupla friends, I guess. I s'pose we're sorta in this together." I hit the bottle again. "I never had a friend before, so I'm not too sure about it, but I think at least one of 'em is."

"Is he a grunt, too?"

"Supergrunt. A Boy Ranger. You'd fall in love with him." She laughed. "No shit, man. He's a really fine dude, even if he is a goddamn Yankee Lef'tenant. He's got his shit together."

"I think you're in love with him, from the way you talk."

"Prob'ly. But that ain't acceptable. Hey! You got a picture of you? Somethin' really sexy . . . maybe with those beautiful chalubbies standin' straight out."

"No, why?"

"I'd like to take him one. Like this was for both of us. If it wasn't for him I wouldn't be here now."

"You like him that much . . . ?"

"More." She looked at me . . . how much more? "I can't leave him over there to lose the war by himself."

"What time is it?"

I looked at my watch. It was three a.m. I couldn't believe it. "I think this thing's broken. Says three a.m."

"That's about right." She picked up the phone, gave a number to the operator, then spoke to someone, conned him into bringin' a camera over. "Polaroid, okay?"

"Sure." I started laughin'. "Goddamn straight it's okay. Dirty pictures. He'll love it. The All-American Boy Ranger. You're beautiful, you know that?"

"I know it, but not many other people do. I'm glad you feel it."

"How'd you ever get to be a prostitute?"

"You ever tried being a secretary? This is less work at ten times the pay."

"You must do okay."

"I do. And I save it. Another year, maybe two, I'll get outa here. I got money in three Mexican banks, paying me nine percent. I'm buying a house in California. I own land in Wyoming, speculative stuff that's being sold by land hustlers."

"Wha'th'fuck you gonna do with all that money when you retire?"

"Blow it on some jerk. I'm stupid about love. I keep falling for gamblers. I could walk into a room with five hundred people and one gambler. We'd find each other in five minutes, or less."

"You wouldn't consider an inexperienced roulette player, would you? I could learn to shoot craps if it'd help."

"You in love with your first hooker?"

"I'm in love with your money."

She hit me, hard, right in the goddamn stomach, and laughed.

"Well, hell, Susie-Q, at least I'm honest. Anyway, I like you."

"I don't even know your name."

"Hawkins."

"That's it?"

"Hawk."

"A Hawk with blue eyes and a bad mouth. Were you always a little boy?"

"Sometimes I feel like I never got a chance to be a kid."

She smiled. One of those if-you-only-knew smiles,

but before I could chase it somebody knocked on the door. It was the camera.

I took maybe a dozen pictures of her, some posed like something out of a porno magazine, some artsy-fartsy stuff, and one just of her face in a slight profile. That one was for me. When we'd finished we went to sleep. It prob'ly was five a.m.

I woke at seven, slept for another hour, then had to get up. It takes more than a coupla days to get human again. At ten Dago came bustin' in. Damn near kicked the door off the hinges. "Hey, y' dumb fucker . . . we're rich." He threw twenty-five thousand dollars into the air, all fifties 'n' hundreds. Just ripped open a big paper bag 'n' threw everything into the air. They went all over the goddamn place. "I got a good price. Ya share's twenty-five Gs. Good enough?" He grabbed me round the neck. "I heard y' hit last night . . . on roulette yet. Y' must be a lucky motherfucker. Nobody beats roulette, man. Y' know?"

"Maybe I should give the goddamn money back." I walked back 'n' forth across the room a coupla times to see what it felt like to wipe my feet on twenty-five thousand dollars. Susan was starin' at us like we were slightly demented. "Susie-Q, this is Crazy Dago."

"Who's fighting the war? Half the goddamn army is in Vegas."

"Who's she?"

"My wife, so watch your mouth."

"Your wife's ass. Where's Poe. If that sonofabitch let you get married to some chislin' allotment-chasin' snatch I'll kill 'im. *Poe! Poe*, goddamn it, where *are* you?"

"Poe's married too. We had a double ceremony."

"Poe's got more smarts than that. You, maybe. But not Poe. *Poe!*" The door between our rooms opened.

Poe 'n' Alice, still dressed in that all-but-not-there jump suit, came in. Dago whistled, low 'n' soft. "Maybe he did . . . it sure's hell would be a temptation." Alice almost fell outa her shoes when she realized she was walkin' round on a rug of money. "Is that stuff real?"

"It's real," Dago said. "An' I got a lot more of it."

"Why is everybody in *my* room, walkin' round on *my* fuckin' money? Wakin' up *my* wife? Why?"

"We're all leavin', Hawk. Poe an' me an' the Suit are goin' downstairs for breakfast. If y' wanna join us, we'll be in the Saddle Room. Let's go." They went. I sat down on the floor 'n' fondled some of the money. It wasn't any more real than the bills in my pocket. Now I had over thirty thousand dollars and it coulda been thirty thousand pig's ears.

"What did you steal?"

"*Smuggle's* the word."

"Dope?"

"Hundred keys of Thai."

"Good Christ! You could turn on a whole fuckin' city."

"I think he's tryin'." I started pickin' up bills, makin' a pile of fifties and a pile of hundreds. "I don't know wha'th'fuck to do with all this. You need any money?"

"No, thanks. Don't you remember? You married me for my money."

"Right. I forgot. Hey, why don't you take this 'n' open an account for me, in one of those wetback banks where you got your money."

"I can't. They won't let somebody open an account in anybody else's name."

"Shit! I can't put this in an American bank. Somebody'd start snoopin' sure's shit stinks. No taxes. I'd get screwed."

I had stopped makin' piles. "Hey, you take the money, put it in your account 'n' when I need bread I'll write. You can pay me six percent. Keep the rest. Whata you say?"

"You're crazy. My God, I thought I was easy with money. If I wanted to split, man you'd never know where I was, and you couldn't prove it was yours, anyway."

"You wouldn't do that."

"Why not? Why the goddamn hell not?"

"Because you're beautiful."

"What if you get killed."

"Keep it."

"What about your family?"

"They'd get ten thousand from the government. That's what they pay for a would-be Hemingway, or Picasso, or Jeb Stuart. Or sharecroppers 'n' slum kids, for that matter. It's all the same. Yes, that's right, madam, we're returning your son, little Goody-Two-Shoes, who we borrowed. He's dead, of course. But here's ten thousand dollars. And if you want to bury him in a military cemetery, it's free. Fuck 'em. The Army, the U.S. government and my futhermucken family."

"Hey, Blue-eyes, easy . . ."

"Aw, shit! You know, I don't even know my father . . . he 'n' my old lady split when I was three or four. He came back *once*, one fuckin' time. And my step-father told him to clear out. Never saw him again. I don't know if I got any brothers or sisters, halfs, as they call 'em. My mother showed me a picture of him once, one she found in a shoebox full of shit. That's what happens to people you throw away. You put the remains in an old shoebox. She actually *sneaked* the picture to me. Can you dig it? A conspiracy between her 'n' me so I could know what *my own father* looked like. Would that chill the ass on a polar bear? You'd think she'd had a goddamn sneaky affair with him."

"Do you like your stepfather?"

"He's okay. But whatever he is, he ain't my father. It wasn't his sperm sprayed in my mother's belly that took root. And whatever I am, I'm my father's son."

"You really want me to take the money?"

"Yes."

"Why?"

"I told you."

"Tell me again."

"Because you're beautiful. Inside. Outside, you're not so bad, either."

She messed around for a minute, lookin' for her pocketbook. It was one of those suitcase-sized sonsofbitches, so it took another five minutes before she found a pen and a business card from some car rental place. On the back she wrote, "Susan Dancer—Oak Lane, San Luis, California."

"I forgot the goddamn zip code, but it'll get there."

I didn't say anything. I picked up the rest of the money 'n' handed it to her. She took it in fistfuls, stuffed the bag.

"I'll always get mail sent to that address. May take a few days more, but I'll get it."

I dressed without sayin' anything else. Wasn't anything to say. We went downstairs for breakfast with Dago, Poe 'n' Alice. I ate without talkin'. Finally Dago snorted, "What's with you?"

"He's ready to go back," Poe said.

"He's nuts. Hawk, y' ready to go back? Really?"

"Prob'ly. I don't know. Seems like we should."

"He is nuts," Dago said. "A flat-out freak. We can easy get away with another day, maybe two. Fuck, man, they ain't gonna do a damn thing to us." I shrugged. "Well, y'know, what can they do? Send us to Nam? Two, three days, they don't give a fuck, man."

"His conscience is bothering him. Doesn't matter what they do . . . it's what he's doing to himself."

Dago grumbled, "A goddamn headshrinker?"

"There're three kinds of people who understand human nature—gamblers, politicians and fishermen. I was raised around politicians."

"He right, Hawk?"

"Prob'ly."

"Okay. Let's take a walk. C'mon. You 'n' me."

"Where?"

"I'm gonna give y' somethin', clean up ya fuckin' conscience."

We walked outa the hotel, down a street. It was sunny, warm, not too many people, and those that were there were smilin', laughin', havin' a good time. It was everything Nam wasn't. He gave me a joint. It looked like a cigarette, rolled in white paper, very exact, tobacco at both ends. Later he told me it had a pinch of Thai stuff in it. I got blown outa my mind in maybe two minutes. He was right, though. I stopped feelin' guilty. I stopped feelin' pain. I stopped feelin' anything that didn't blow me out. I thought he'd soaked it in coke or STP. We stayed two days. I smoked three or four times a day. I don't remember a lot about it, and it doesn't matter anyway. Unless you've been blasted on that shit you wouldn't understand. And if you have, you know. Fuck Witherspoon.

Altogether we were gone a week. One lousy fuckin' week. What can happen in a week? Somethin' happened. I changed . . . Kilo changed . . . the whole goddamn world changed . . . I don't know. Some things were immediately obvious. The Indians had blown away half a dozen bunkers, killed a few guys, includin' Mister Karate, sent three to the hospital, and put the colonel on the warpath. The colonel this, the colonel that . . . for the first few fuckin' hours all I heard was the colonel. The Boy Ranger, Davis, Jinx 'n' Ubanski were out. Jinx was bein' written up for a court-martial. Black 'n' Decker were officially listed as AWOL. But it was more'n that. Somethin' had changed. Jefferson was out, prowlin'. The whole time we'd been in Nam, he'd stayed in his goddamn bunker. I always figured he signed papers and decided whether to send out one patrol or two. He wasn't worth a shit for anything else that I could see. Now he was participatin', playin' the game, givin' orders, checkin' to see if they'd been carried out. Pain in the ass. I heard half the fuckin' battalion was out in the sticks, lookin' for whoever'd wasted Kilo's little fiefdom. Some new guys were wanderin' round the company, replacements. I felt old 'n' worn next to them. Six weeks and already I'm a vet'rin. I still wasn't sure I could find my ass with both hands.

Somethin' was different. Looked the same. Smelled the same. Pig dung 'n' paddy water don't change. I went back to our bunker. It hadn't been touched by the mortars. It was the same. It's me, I thought. I'm fuckin' weird. Dago came in before I could pursue that. He threw his helmet across the bunker. It smacked the picture of the Chairman. Mashed in his nose. "That motherfucker. I knew it. I knew the pig-fuckin' cocksucker was settin' me up the goddamn minute I was picked to go back with Garcia . . . I knew it." He glared at me. I'd never seen him really pissed. He was fit to be tied. "That whore-humpin' motherfucker."

"Who?"

"*Who!?* Who the hell do y' think who?"

"Wait a minute, I'll get my list."

"Fuck you." He stomped up 'n' down for a few minutes. "I knew it, and wasn't a goddamn thing I could do, y' know? Cheap chislin' sonofabitch." I didn't say anything. "Well, I'll fix 'is fuckin' ass. *He'll* never spend it. I hope 'is wife's fuckin' private E-2s."

"Dago . . .?"

"He couldn't be satisfied with a cut. I mean, I gave 'im a fair share, right? Shit, man, I didn't hafta give 'im a fuckin' thing. Then he pulls some shit like this. But he fucked with the wrong dude this time." I figured from that it must be one of his partners in crime. But which one I didn't know. I didn't even know how many he had. "Wha'th'fuck ever happened to honesty, Hawk? How the hell can we do business if some bloodsucker like him is gonna grab grab grab?"

"Beats me."

"And him a fuckin' first sergeant. Well, tough shit. He died and don't even know it."

"Minnow?"

"That's right."

"You gonna light up the first sergeant?"

"I give a fuck what he is! He's had it."

"Dago, you flipped out? You snap a spring some-where? You can't go out 'n' waste a fuckin' first ser-geant."

"Why the fuck not?"

"*Why not?* Man, if I gotta explain it, I might as well hang it up."

"He's a thief, a ripoff artist. He deserves t' die."

"Thief is one thing, man. Murderer is another."

"Murderer? I waste a thief and you call it murder?"

"I sure's hell don't call it a matin' call."

"Hawk, he lit up a whole goddamn ARVN com-pound, blew away forty, fifty guys. He orta be hung."

"He *what?*"

"He got somebody to give 'im the numbers, after somebody else had bet a block. Then he lit up that slope compound about ten miles from here."

"Dago, I know I'm stupid, but I don't understand."

"Four nights ago. About nine o'clock, accordin' to the Indian . . ."

"Longfeather?"

"Yeah. Accordin' t' him, the first sergeant got the number of ARVN dead for the day. Longfeather said he'd taken a block bet—all numbers from fifty to one fifty—a hundred dollars on each number. Guy brought in ten grand cash. From Lima Company, a fuckin' pla-toon sergeant. Figure there ain't no more'n twenty, thirty ARVNs a day get it, at the most. No way they gonna go over that. So then the first sergeant takes a mortar crew out—fuck, might only have been him an' the dude from Lima Company. I don't know. But they hit that ARVN compound, blew away fifty-six slopes. Hundred-dollar bet, paid off forty grand. Four hundred to one. They made thirty grand off me. But they ain't gonna live to spend it."

"You're sure?"

"Hawk, I may misjudge a man's character, but I don't make no mistakes about money. Count on it."

"What kinda goddamn stupid war is this? Holy mother of Mary's mule, nobody, *no-body* would believe it . . ."

"Believe it!"

"And you gonna kill him?"

"Y' crazy? Of course I'm gonna kill 'im. Y' think I want every goddamn cheap chislin' bastard comin' down on me? I got to kill 'im, man. Y' know?"

"How?"

"I don't know yet. But don't hang out with 'im. He may go anytime. If I frag 'im I don't want y' gettin' hit."

"God, Dago. Not a grenade . . ."

"Maybe not. I'll hafta see." He picked up his helmet 'n' started for the door. "When it happens, y' know nothin' from nothin', right?"

"I know nothin' from nothin' right now. That ain't gonna change."

He was gone, a plague swept in and out by the winds of fortune. Or misfortune. Kismet. Kiss my ass. How the fuck we ever gonna explain this to our children . . . if we ever have any. I'm weird, I said to myself. I'm weird, I'm weird, I'm weird, I'm fuckin' weird. It's my perspective that's all fucked up. Mine. The right-thinkin' people—the ones who said North Vietnamese PT boats attacked American destroyers in the Tonkin Gulf, when it later turned out there prob'ly wasn't a fuckin' Indian within twenty miles of an American ship—the silly bastards who keep sayin' we're winnin' when we're gettin' our asses kicked—all this shit of supportin' a military dictator so the people can have a democracy—bombin' hospitals 'n' schools and sayin' ooops! That's the right attitude. It must be. There's gotta be a hundred million Americans who say it's right and a hundred million Americans can't be wrong. Fuck the French, it's Americans who gave us Fords, frozen food 'n' free-fire zones. Mass production, goopy strawberries 'n' legal murder. I'm weird. I like Italian cars, fresh fruit and I'm goddamned if I'm gonna go round lightin' up people without a better reason than I've gotten from anyone yet. Fuck 'em. "Fuck 'em!"

"What the hell are you doing back here?" I almost had a heart attack. The Boy Ranger's voice jumped right into the middle of my fantasies. "You stupid fuckin' retard, I sent you back to the States so you could go AWOL. What are you doing here?"

"Fantasizin'. I was about to tell a general court-martial board how I never intended to do in anybody, not from the beginnin'. And that I didn't give a fat rat's ass what they did to me, in the end it was them who'd lose."

"Were they impressed?"

"I think you came in right before they gave me fifty years at hard labor. They didn't look too impressed."

"Serves you right. What—are—you—doing—here?"

"I don't know . . . what am I doin' here?"

He sat down with a sigh. He looked bad, shabby, dirty, disappointed. Whether with me or the way things were goin', I couldn't tell. He hadn't shaved in three or four days, which wasn't like him. But it was his eyes that got me. Bloodshot, circled with black rings. "Christ, if I'd known you weren't going to split I'd have gone back myself." He looked around the bunker, like he was seein' it for the first time. "Some layout you got here."

"Dago."

"It'll probably be yours soon. The CID was around, asking about him while you were gone. What's he into, anyway?"

"Name it."

"He came back too?"

"Sure. He's gettin' rich."

"He's got his ass in a sling."

"He'll prob'ly buy off the whole fuckin' CID. Or have 'em wasted. He's made a mess of money." I jumped up. "Hey, I brought you a present."

"Officers aren't allowed to accept gifts from enlisted men. Army regulations."

"Well, grunts aren't s'posed to have what I got, so s'posin' I turn myself in and give you the stuff as evidence."

"Let's see it, Troop." I dug out the pictures of Susan. He looked through them carefully, one after the other. "Who's she?"

"She ain't my fuckin' sister."

"The sister part I can believe."

"She's . . . look, I know this sounds stupid 'n' all, but she was for us. I'd never have made it back there if you hadn't done it for me. I told her about you and asked if she'd let me do the pictures. She's some kinda broad."

"Prossy?"

"Who?"

"A prostitute?"

"Does it matter?"

He looked at me for a minute, then gave me that goofy smile. "Fuck no, I was just wondering how you had time to get it on with somebody who wasn't."

"Shit, man, I'm slick as a greased eel when I get started."

"Maybe. But you weren't slick enough to get the hell out when I gave you a chance. What are you doing back here?"

"I don't know. It's got somethin' to do with you."

"Hawk, we're on the way to getting our asses lit up . . . *you* said it. The colonel's getting flack from Saigon, Division, Regiment. He wants Charlie. He wants bodies. He wants that regiment of NVAs, if they exist. We've been going every day."

"See anything?"

"Not much. But I feel them. They're out there. And everybody in this goddamn battalion is tight. You can feel it. Just waiting for something to snap."

"*That's* what it is. I felt it."

"You see Jefferson?"

"The Chocolate Soldier? Yeah, I saw him. Wha'th'- fuck brought him out of hidin'?"

"Tension. Pressure." He laughed. "Pain?"

"Give him a goddamn Anacin, see if he'll go away."

"Wouldn't matter. There'd be another one."

"You've changed. A week and you look like shit."

"I feel like it. We're going to get it, Hawk. If we don't find them first they're going to wipe our ass."

"I can hardly wait."

"I don't think it'll be long. Week, two maybe." He put on his helmet. "We're going out again tomorrow morning. Since you were gallant enough to come back I'll assume you're dumb enough to hump that radio for me."

"Why me?"

"Why not?" He grinned and walked out into the rain. Fuckin' rain. That hadn't changed. Hell, nothin' ever really changes. Appearances may be such that we think it's changed, whatever the hell *it* might be. The appearance, the feelin' of Kilo seemed different. Uptight, strung out. But what the hell had changed? Shit, I thought, I ought to quit fuckin' around lookin' for some kinda truth. Nothin' changes, but everything seems to change. How's that for a truth? I've always had the feelin', since I was a little kid, that I was too goddamn smart to be stupid, and too fuckin' stupid to be smart. Hung up in the middle with you, like— you've got a lot to live, and Pepsi's got a lot to give. It's the real thing. I walked over to the bunker door 'n' pissed into the rain. Piss on the world. I went lookin' for Davis 'n' Jinx. I had a dozen boxes of shotgun shells for the Hillbilly and half a dozen joints of Dago's Thai dope for the spade—stuff Dago gave me in Vegas. I'd kept another dozen or so for myself. If it got bad enough I'd get stoned and stay stoned. Prob'ly could go for days 'n' never give anything more than two seconds of concentrated thought. Too much thinkin' wasn't good for me anyway. I never knew what to do with the mess I made in the process.

Jinx met me on the way to the chow hall. "I heard you was back, man. You fuckin' blew it."

"I got the same feelin'." I handed him the joints. "I know you're gonna think it's like givin' bullshit lessons to Rap Brown but wait till you try it."

"Good?"

"I don't remember. I went into orbit after three hits and didn't come down for days."

"I'll save 'em. Where I'm goin' I don't know what to expect." He smiled at my inquirin' frown. "You didn't hear, man? I'm up on charges for deckin' that dumb-ass you almost killed."

"Supersoldier? I thought he got lit up?"

"He did. Next night we got a loada shit from Charlie. But I did the deed before that."

"Wha'th'fuck, if he's dead he sure's hell ain't gonna tell on you."

"There was 'bout fifty witnesses. In the chow hall. Wasted his ass. Kunged 'is fu with this ol' number ten."

"You musta been pissed."

"The sonofabitch. We were at the same table, him 'n' me, Davis, first sergeant, coupla other dudes. Somehow they got this dumb fuckin' discussion goin', you know? I didn't say much. They talkin' 'bout why we here, how we helpin' to defend democracy . . . stupid bastards. Davis says he ain't so sure anymore. The karate king says to Davis, 'Who you think we fightin' for?' Davis says he don't know. The bullshit's flyin' back 'n' forth. Then the first sarge says, 'Jinx, who you think we fightin' for?' But real sarcastic. I was just gettin' up to leave, so I stood there, you know, real cool like. I put my hands in my pockets and I feel something. A piece of paper. I pull it out. It says 'Inspected by Number Eight.' It was like a goddamn Chinese fortune cookie. I knew, right then, this whole fuckin' war was bein' fought for some silly muthafuckah who puts little pieces of paper in pants pockets. 'Number Eight,' I said. 'This whole goddamn stupid fuckin' war's bein' fought for Number Eight.' I threw the paper on the table top. Mister Karate grabs it. 'Dumb fuckin' nigger'd be the only person who'd think of somethin' like that.' I unloaded. He never even saw it comin', man. When he hit the floor I tried to take 'is goddamn head off. I woulda killed the muthafuckah if that big fuckin' first sarge hadn't pulled me away."

"So who's pushin' a court-martial?"

"Jefferson."

"*Jefferson?!* Shit, man, he's almost black as you."

"That fuckin' dude's an Oreo, man. Don't you know that?"

"Hey, I'm just a poor little country boy who ain't hip to all this spade slang."

"Oreo, man . . . black on the outside 'n' white on the inside."

"So?"

"So he gonna make it bad f' me so he look good to the white dudes that look at HIM."

"Shit!"

"No shit."

"You gettin' a summary or a special court?"

"Special."

"How's it look?"

"Three months in LBJ."

"That's s'posed to be a rough place to do time."

"Tha's where *he* was before he come here. Doin' guard. Can you dig it, man? They gonna send my ass down to Long Binh Jail to do time, guarded by 'is friends, and me a nigger."

"Maybe you won't get time."

"Maybe if a frog had wings he wouldn't bump 'is ass when he jumps. But I wouldn't take no bets on it."

We'd walked to the chow hall while we were talkin', filled our trays 'n' now we were eatin'. I looked around the room. There weren't many grunts in yet. We were more or less alone. I felt a blind rage buildin' up in me. Dago was as big a thief as walked the earth. He had people wasted like a quality control man discardin' faulty parts. The first sergeant had lit up a whole goddamn ARVN compound. We were s'posed to be out here killin' people so what was left could live with . . .

what? Dignity? The right to choose their own government? Shit, if we still go round callin' each other niggers, kikes, wops, spics, frogs, krauts, honkies, wha'th'
fuck's the good of killin' people because they're com-
munists. I call Jinx a spade, but I don't do it with
malice. Jefferson's the Chocolate Soldier, Eric the Boy
Ranger. I'm a fuckin' redneck. But there's a difference.
Besides which, that motherfuckin' karate freak needed
his ass kicked. I shoulda lit him up myself. Or let Dago
take him out. "When's the court?"

"A week, ten days. I won't be here."

"You figure on a vacation?"

"I'm goin' over."

"Over where, for Christ's sake?"

"Over to the other side."

"VC?"

"Shhhsss, be cool, man." He put a forkful of beans
in his mouth.

"Be cool?" I hissed, tryin' to keep my voice down.
"Be cool!? You are freaked out. Black 'n' Decker, okay.
They're dumb as shit anyway. But not you, man. Anyway, wha'th'fuck's the VC Army doin'? Runnin' an
underground railway?"

"Beats LBJ."

"Shit, Jinx, maybe . . ."

"Maybe, maybe, maybe . . . c'mon, Hawk."

"Who's gonna roll my joints?"

"I'll be around, man. You can always come over 'n'
blow a little weed with me."

"You'll be *around*? Around where?"

"Around here. I'm gonna be an advisor to the VC
Army."

"Have—you—fuckin'—flipped—out?"

"Ain't no VC ever called me a nigger."

"You mean to tell me you gonna fight with them? Against us?"

"It's the only game in town."

"Fuck me!" He laughed. "Shit, man. You're puttin' me on, right?"

"Tomorrow night. You 'n' me got midnight guard. I need ten minutes."

"Hey, man, listen. I ain't never said this to a spade before. Never really knew one. We were all separate but equal when I was growin' up . . . okay? I mean, forgive me my fuckin' prejudice 'n' all. Man, I like you. You're a good dude. Don't do it. You gotta get fucked over sooner or later. *Think*, man. How long's it gonna be before everything round here is wasted, and you with it."

"Don't matter. Charlie's gonna waste what the round-eyes don't. It don't matter where I die, if I die. What's the difference if I get lit up by an AK or a '16. A B-12 rocket ain't no better'n a 105."

"Jinx . . ."

"You gonna give me ten minutes?"

"You can't ever come back, man. You know that . . . ?"

"Back to what? To West Philadelphia? To horseshit! Hey, you think if we was back in the Land of the Big PX you'd have time for me? You think this buddy-buddy shit goes on 'n' on? You know what I got to go back to? Smack. Shit jobs. Humpin' for a livin', never gettin' enough to sit back 'n' enjoy it. Cheap booze, second-hand cars, cops hasslin' me, somebody always tryin' to rip me off, black and white. A system that's goddamn well gonna insure we don't ever get more'n a bare-ass minimum existence. That, or I can hope to be a token middle-class Oreo pet for the liberals. I'm tired of havin' people pull my chain, dancin' to their little tunes."

"You think the goddamn slopes ain't gonna do the same thing? See the token American who deserted. Look, runnin' dogs . . . we got one of your boys. You gonna be a prize exhibit in every fuckin' newsreel from now to when we finally get the fuck outa here."

I was sick with desperation. I've never been one to try talkin' nobody outa doin' what he wants to do, but this was all wrong, fucked up.

"Ten minutes, Hawk."

"I gotta think about it. Jesus Christ, Jinx, I gotta think." I left my tray on the table 'n' walked off. Walked off . . . that's a joke. There wasn't anywhere to walk off to. We lived in each other's pockets. There wasn't anywhere to be alone. Always some dude to walk up and say wha'cha doin'? What the fuck am I doin'? I'm playin' with myself, for Christ's sake. I'm fuckin' meditatin'. I walked round in circles for a few minutes, then it hit me. What the hell . . . I went to the Boy Ranger's bunker. "Permission to speak to the Lieutenant, sir."

"Come in, Private."

"Private First-fuckin'-Class, sir. Hawkins."

"What can I do for you, PF-fuckin'-C?"

"Jinx is up for a special court, right?"

"Yeah."

"Can't you talk the captain outa that shit?"

"I tried."

"How about your old man?"

"He says it's good for discipline."

"Nothin' . . . ?"

"When it's over I'll talk to my father. Once there's a conviction I should be able to talk him into reducing any confinement to restriction. May have to give up a couple of month's pay."

"He's gettin' the shaft."

"I know." We stared at each other. "What do you want from me?" I shrugged. We both knew what I wanted. "Hawk, don't make me into something I'm not. Okay? I don't do miracles. Moses I'm not. I don't do magic tricks. I'm not God. I'm a Ranger lieutenant in the US Army Infantry, and that's all." I felt pain like I hadn't known in a long time, not since I quit lettin' people get close to me. He got off his bunk, found a cigarette, threw the pack at me. When he had his lit he walked to the doorway of the bunker 'n' stared into the gloom. His voice came back over his shoulder. "He going AWOL?" My heart had a two-second spastic fit. "Forget it. I don't want to know. I guess I'm just thinking of what I'd do in his place. Black and Decker are gone. Six grunts from Lima Company, two from India. Not AWOL. That's what the Army calls it. Deserted is what it really is." He snorted, a cynical explosion of air 'n' maybe a vision of somethin' I couldn't see. He flipped his half-smoked cigarette into the drizzle. "You got a joint?"

"A *what*?"

"A goddamn joint."

"Yeah," I stammered. "I mean, sure I got one. I got a fuckin' dozen."

"Give me one. Let's get stoned."

"You . . . ?"

"Hawk, for somebody who's so cynical you sure as hell are naive. Light up, Troop." I got out the little plastic case I carried my weed around in, took out a regular, lip up 'n' passed it to him. He took three straight hits, one, two, three, then passed it back. "You ever heard the stories of grunts leading VC platoons, advising companies, and working in their operations units?"

"No."

"It's a fucked-up war."

"It's true? The stories?"

"I haven't met any of them. But I heard from too many people to think it's all bullshit. I also heard there's a bounty on their heads. "He giggled. Swear t' God. A fuckin' Ranger lieutenant. I grinned. "Maybe we should give up this and go look for them. Except I can't even find a goddamn regiment of NVAs, so it isn't likely I'd be able to find half a dozen round-eyes runnin' through the bush, right?"

"Maybe they're all on R 'n' R." We giggled. "Wonder where the fuckin' VC go for R 'n' R?"

"Saigon. Phnom Penh. Dalat."

"Dalat?"

"It's a little resort not too far from Saigon. Pretty."

"Why you lookin' so hard for the Indians?"

"Why'd you come back?"

"It ain't the same."

"How do you know?" He smiled. "You intend to smoke that whole joint by yourself?"

I gave it to him. "I don't know, but . . . I don't know. Maybe it is."

"We find them or they get set up and waste our ass. They may do it anyway, but I'd like to make it a little harder."

"You think they're out there, don't you? No shit, just yes or no."

"Yes. They have as much of a problem with this rain as we do. Thing is, they're methodical as hell. They'll work and wait, dig tunnels, position themselves, and one day, or one night, here they come. Mortars, sappers, the whole show. We might hold them out, if there's enough of us around. But there'll be hell to pay."

"And if we find 'em first?"

"Depends. If we can catch them in the right place we should fuck them over pretty good."

"How come when the philosophical dudes do their number, war's always like chess? All exact 'n' precise. But when we're out here in the fuckin' boonies it's *if* this, *if* that, *if*'s ass."

"I think it's called the breaks of the game."

"No, man. I'm serious."

"So am I." He laughed. "Really." We started gigglin' again. "Really. It's the breaks of the game. Do you think if the velvet-jacket jerks that write strategy had to hump it through this place day after day there'd be any goddamn strategy books? Giap did for a while, I guess. Some English ass, Thompson, I think his name was. Or is. But I'll promise you one fucking thing, and I've told my old man this: If the silly sonsofbitches who vote for war in the Congress and the generals, colonels and munitions makers had to spend just half their time walking point, we'd damn sure have a hell of a lot fewer wars. You know it. I know it. They know it. But here we are. Breaks of the game."

"Maybe I ain't gonna play no more."

"You had your chance. I gave it to you. You fucked it up."

"You think we'll be friends after we're outa here?"

"You think we'll *get* out of here?"

"C'mon, Eric, don't fuck me around."

"Let me tell you something, Hawk . . . straight out. I wouldn't give you ten cents for our chances of getting out alive. If we find them, we're just as apt to get our asses whipped as not. And if we don't they're going to light up this whole fucking pig farm."

"Why you so sure?"

"Because damn near every one of us is counting

days. This fucking war was supposed to be over four years ago. Kennedy, Johnson, McNamara, all of them said we had it won, victory's right around the corner. Bullshit. You know it, don't you?" I shrugged. "Sure you do. And let me ask you something else . . . are you here to win, or to do your time and try to keep from getting blown away?" I shrugged again. "You want to win, yes or no?"

"Win what?" He laughed, and I started gigglin'. "C'mon, Lef'tenant. Win what? I wouldn't give *you* ten cents for ten acres of this fuckin' place. If God had made the world as a man, we'd be sittin' in the last four inches of his intestine. This is the ass-end of creation. Do you know—I looked it up—do you know that aside from gettin' greased, we stand a fair to middlin' chance of catchin' cholera, smallpox, bubonic plague, leprosy, typhoid, malaria, amoebic dysentery, eczema and swamp fever? Just for openers."

"How long did it take you to memorize that list?"

"About ten fuckin' seconds. But when I read the list I was in a state of shock for an hour."

"You left out typhus, hepatitis, spinal meningitis, sunstroke and fourteen kinds of VD."

"I don't wanta know nothin' about that. I got enough worries like it is."

"I'll give you one more."

"No more."

"One."

"What?"

"We're going to get hit tonight."

"C'mon."

"No shit."

"By who?"

"Charlie. Who else?"

"Around here you can't ever tell." I thought about tellin' him about Dago, Minnow and company. We gonna get hit?"

"I feel it. I felt it the other night, while you were gone."

"Mortars?"

"Yeah. You'd better get yourself straight."

"Fuck it." I lit another joint, took two hits 'n' offered it to him. "Wanta sit this one out?"

"Why not?" We smoked it down to the last tiny bit, like I didn't have enough left to turn on the whole goddamn platoon. "When you think it's gonna happen?"

"Soon. They may even come for the wire tonight."

"There's two fuckin' miles of mines out there for 'em to come through."

"You ever see them work bangalors? Bamboo tubes stuffed with plastics? Blow a hole right through those mines. Hell, a good mortar man can blow a path through there with half a dozen rounds. And they got some *good* mortar men."

"You think we ought to find us a place to sit, somewhere high 'n' dry?"

"I'm open to suggestions."

Before I could open my mouth to offer a suggestion three rocket rounds exploded inside the perimeter, one two three. The ground shook 'n' the noise put a cold edge of fear in me. Before the thunder had rolled away the mortars started, walkin' down through the mines, through the wire, through bunkers, back 'n' forth. Off a hundred yards or so to our left somebody'd been playin' his tape deck. Concussion, coincidence . . . who knows? The volume went up. "Light My Fire" screamed out into the flame-swatched darkness, guitars 'n' organ risin' 'n' fallin' over the sound of screams, cries for medics, chatterin' of machine guns, M-16s, M-79 grenade launchers, explodin' fireballs, bellowin' sergeants, bawlin' grunts, squealin' pigs . . . "Come on baby, light my fire." I looked at the Boy Ranger 'n' laughed. "I forgot my pop-gun."

"The rules are very exact, Hawkins. You can't shoot anybody without your rifle. You know that."

"Could you loan me one?"

"That's not permitted. I'm sorry."

"Well, shit, man, s'posin' the dinks don't know I ain't playin' 'cause I forgot my rifle. You think they gonna ask?"

"Not likely. I'd suggest you sit here while I go win the war. And next time bring your goddamn rifle if you want to play."

"You can't go out there, you stupid bastard. You're too fuckin' stoned." We started gigglin' again.

"I got to go. I'm an officer and a gentleman by an act of Congress. It's in the book."

"Well . . . have fun. If you find my rifle give a yell, okay?"

"Right."

And by God, he put on his fuckin' helmet, picked up his M-16 and went out into the end of the world. I laid down on his bunk. Through the open door I could see people runnin', yellin' to each other, flashes of light when the mortar rounds exploded. Maybe five minutes after the Boy Ranger left Whipple crashed into the bunker. It was dark 'n' he couldn't see exactly who was on the bunk. "Eric, you hurt?"

"It ain't Eric. It's Hawkins. Sir."

"You injured, Hawkins?"

"Nope."

"Why aren't you on the line, soldier? Every man's needed."

"I'm not participatin', Lef'tenant. I ain't got my weapon. The Boy Ranger says I can't play 'less I got a rifle."

"Hawkins . . . !"

A mortar round crashed nearby, close enough for the concussion to blow Whipple inside. He hit the floor, groaned once 'n' got quiet. I checked him for a pulse. It fluttered a little, then steadied up. Good enough, I figured. The fucker'll be safer in here than out there, runnin' round givin' orders that nobody's gonna follow anyway.

I started toward the nerve center, as Dago calls it, to get my gear. About halfway there it dawned on me I coulda taken Whipple's. I stopped dead in my tracks. Flashes of fire were rippin' open the darkness, confusin' my pupils enough that my eyes wouldn't focus on anything. I could make out people runnin' here 'n' there, tracers rippin' through the air, fireballs, earth clods the size of fuckin' footlockers. But the sound was what got me. Rockets whinin' 'n' screamin', then an earth-rattlin' boom. Shrapnel whippin' past, buzzin' like a flock of hornets. The machine guns chatterchatter-chatterchatter, two or three different pitches accordin' to what kind they were. The '16s poppin'. The M-79 grenade launchers . . . when they go off it sounds like somebody's pulled the cork on a twenty-gallon wine bottle, sort of a deep *pong!* Grenade explosions, mines blowin', gasoline goin' off, screams from the dyin', screams from the livin', pure fear personified in falsetto vibrations so unreal in other moments that a man would deny he's ever made noises even remotely similar, and prove it by tryin' and failin' to imitate himself.

Kilo was gettin' fucked over. Ubanski took two rounds in the back of his helmet. They traced a circle round his head, barely breakin' the skin but sure's hell scarin' ten years off his life. Poe died. I saw him runnin' across the far side of the quadrangle. I yelled at him, but he ducked into the officers' latrine. God 'n' Poe alone know why. Maybe he had to take a crap. The latrine buildin' went up in a cloud of fire 'n' smoke. It came down in splinters. Everything was covered with earth 'n' shit that had piled up in the bottom of the hole. We never did find much of Poe. If he'd been anybody but a senator's son they'd have said fuck it and covered him up where he lay, in pieces. But bein' he was a senator's son the graves registration people had to get down in the shit 'n' shell fragments to pick out what they could. But that was the next day, and by then Poe was a memory, already growin' faint. Whipple hadn't been hurt. Davis took two small pieces of shrapnel in the arm. He was treated and back in three or four hours. Four guys from First Platoon were KIA, all four in the same hole. A rocket round fell right on top of 'em. As they say in the movies, they prob'ly never knew what hit 'em. I don't know if that's a consolation or not. Altogether we lost seven dead and a dozen wounded seriously enough to be evaced. Plus another handful with give-'em-a-bandage-and-a-pat-on-the-back wounds that don't get you anything but a tin medal. At least a third of the bunkers were wasted, the roofs of three or four were blown away, the company office demolished, the chow hall reduced to rubble, most of the mines . . . and First Sergeant Minnow. I think Dago killed him. There's no way to prove it. Minnow died with a shredded belly, like he'd fallen on a grenade. No ballistics, no witnesses, no more fuckin' with Dago. Maybe it was an accident, but since there weren't any Indians inside the perimeter that's hard to believe. I never asked Dago, straight out. And he never volunteered any information. The first sergeant was dead. Tough shit.

Poe's death freaked me out. It wasn't that I liked him so much. I mean, he was okay, but if we'd crossed paths somewhere else he prob'ly wouldn't have had the time or inclination to ask my name. The thing that blew me out was realizin' I didn't know a fuckin' thing about him. Not really. Ol' Witherspoon would say he was badly developed as a character. And he'd be right. Poe was the senator's son. Cynical, maybe bitter at times, but I don't know why. I'd guess he's like a lot of us, or was. He heard too fuckin' many stupid people talkin' outa both sides of their mouth. But I'm guessin'. Which is what most of it comes down to, in the end. Guesswork.

About Minnow I know even less. A hog farmer, a killer, a crook, a lifer with thirty years, a lousy excuse for a human being . . . but that applies to most of us. Minnow'd been in the Army longer than Poe'd been on earth. So what? Sew buttons on your fuckin' vest. Poe died young. The sorry-ass fact of it is I still think he was slummin', breakin' his old man's balls. Funny . . . three days later a set of orders for him came, along with a direct commission to second lieutenant. Bet your ass they buried him in an officer's casket. Their caskets are different from ours. On an officer's casket the handles stand at attention.

Truth to tell, it also bothered me that he died in the latrine: If you're gonna die it doesn't really matter where . . . I know that, but I know nobody's gonna pick through an acre of shit to find me and I don't want to be left in a Vietnamese shithole. And if Poe got killed in one, so could I. For three days I couldn't take a crap.

Every time my bowels got in an uproar my paranoia acted like paregoric. Lookin' at a latrine was as good as puttin' a big stopper up my behind. It mighta gone on for weeks but my belly swelled up like a balloon. Somethin' had to give. Finally, I took my entrenchin' tool, the army's name for a short-handled shovel, and went lookin' for a place to trench. I walked here 'n' there, but every time I'd stop to dig somebody'd come up and ask me what I was doin'. Mostly they were just curious, I guess. But I never could take a crap with somebody standin' round watchin'. So I'd say I was checkin' the water table for Lef'tenant Whipple. They'd go "Oh . . ." It was exactly the sorta stupid thing he'd have somebody do, and besides, isn't one in fifty that know what the hell a water table is. It worked, but it didn't help me with my problem 'cause the dumb bastard would always stand round and wait for me to do the check. I'd usually dig up a shovelful or two, write some numbers on a piece of paper and wander off in search of more privacy. I spent mosta one day doin' that.

That was the third day, I think. Third or fourth after the attack, which had come on the tail of the New Year's truce. That broke me up. Day before New Year's Lima Company had a patrol out, they got hit and half the fuckin' company went tearin' ass out to kill Indians. But the next day everybody's sittin' round, fuckin' off, and the war's stopped. Like a coffee break. Course, there were always vi-ooohh-*la*-shuns, as the fuckin' news readers call 'em. It's too bad somebody doesn't invent baritone keys for a typewriter . . . that word has to be heard to be appreciated. "The US Military Command in Saigon reports there have been three hundred vi-ooohh-*la*-shuns of the temporary cease-fire agreement during the first fourteen minutes . . . " No shit. The whole goddamn war's a violation of everything this fucked-up country supposedly stands for, and the Army's cryin' foul because the Indians don't have any particular regard for our New Year Celebrations. But I guess the Army figures that if we're willin' to stop fightin' for Buddha's birthday the fuckin' slopes ought to be willin' to stop long enough for Guy Lombago to play "Auld Lang Syne."

Anyway, my diggin' expedition wasn't goin' worth a shit, so to speak, and the gas pains were gettin' worse. I was afraid to fart. Finally, after maybe an hour of that nonsense, I'm alone, back near the goddamn hogs, diggin' like a sonofabitch, when Whipple himself walks up. "What exactly are you doing, Hawkins?"

"Attemptin' to comply with those stupid fuckin' orders we got this mornin'."

"Orders? What orders?"

"The orders regardin' the fertilizer campaign for the benefit of the Vietnamese National Land Restoration Program, sir."

"I don't recall seeing any such information. What was the nature of the orders?"

He's really serious. So I figure I'll play it for what it's worth. "I think the orders were only for enlisted men, sir. Here, read 'em for yourself." I tossed him a folded paper. What was on the paper, near as I can recall, was this:

TO: *American Ground Forces, Vietnam.*
FROM: *Defecation Detachment,*
Military Assistance Command, Vietnam.
SUBJECT: *Vietnamese National Fertilization Program.*
RE: *DD/MACV Ord No. 70–2345/BS*

In our efforts to assist the people of Vietnam in their search for peace, self-determination and fertile lands, a special military group known as the Defecation Detachment has been formed with the goal of restoring Vietnam, or at least that part under friendly control, to prewar conditions. One step in that direction is refertilization. Your name has been selected as an individual particularly suited to our purpose. A profile of your military test scores, aptitudes and general conduct was programmed for our IBM 12–5, fondly known as the Built-In Shit Detector, or BSD. Yours was one of several thousand names fed to the BSD, which determined that you have talents particularly suited to this program.

In accordance therewith, we have placed your name on our list and request that you give your usual half-assed cooperation to this project. It should be ample. This is strictly a volunteer program, but we believe you will see the wisdom of it and wish to participate fully.

What we are asking is that you pick a spot—there are many indicated on the enclosed map—and take a shit, at your earliest convenience. You will note that several of them, such as the Presidential Palace, the Hue Citidel, ARVN General Army HQ, etc., may seem inappropriate, but consider it further and ask yourself, "What greater contribution can I make to the Vietnamese nation than to take a crap in one of these places?" If you feel you know a better location, then by all means go there and do your duty.

If you should encounter any difficulties with Vietnamese Nationals while attempting to enhance this farsighted program, just show the questioner a copy of this directive. It should quickly end any objections.

If by any chance you are constipated, please pass this directive on to a buddy who, while he may not be as full of crap as you, undoubtedly will jump at the chance to show our allies that we've really got our shit together.

(SIGNED) *Harvey Fartz*
Colonel
Defecation Detachment Commander

Pure fuckin' genius. I never did find out who wrote that goddamn thing. It really did come in the mail. Damn near everybody in Kilo got one. I'd like to think damn near everybody in No Man's Nam got one. While Whipple was readin' I finished diggin' and dumped maybe two pounds of unadulterated shit into the hole. We finished about the same time. I felt much better. He was outraged.

"This is outrageous."

"Ingenious."

"Hawkins, you'll be court-martialed."

"Wha'th'fuck for?"

"Possession of obscene material and conspiracy to defame the Vietnamese National—" He couldn't think of a word.

"Not defame, Lef'tenant. Defecate. There's a difference."

"Hawkins!"

I jumped half a foot into the air, stomped my boots into the soggy earth 'n' shouted in my best British military voice, "Sir!"

"Hawkins, you've made a mockery of everything good military discipline and customs stand for."

"Sir! I suggest, sir, that the goddamn military mind is a mockery in itself. And that it is impossible to mock what is a mockery already. The mindless, manic, mediocre military mind can't be mocked any more than a hole can be punched in a hole, you fat fucker." I had blown him out. He didn't even hear "fat fucker." His eyes crossed about midway through the sentence. "Sir!" I did another one of those jumpin' boot-stompin' tricks. "Permission to cover my shit, sir!" He started to cry. Not loudly, or anything. Just big, soft tears, like a girl. His face went to mush, soft putty. It was all too much for him. I threw some dirt into the hole, then walked over 'n' put my arm around his shoulder.

"C'mon, Lieutenant . . . it ain't worth gettin' all upset. Really. I know everybody gives you a hard time, but you gotta learn to ignore it. Hell, don't even talk to grunts. They don't appreciate it, anyway. Stay in your office and sign your name to stuff. Eat with the officers, drink with 'em, and fuckin' ignore us. We ain't worth the effort you put out. If I was you 'n' I saw a grunt even walkin' on the same side of the goddamn street, man, I'd cross over 'n' cut him dead. Fuck the goddamn grunts!" He perked up. The tears stopped. His face went back to borderline firmness, which was all he ever managed, even under the best of circumstances. "C'mon, let's hear it—fuck the grunts."

"Fuck the grunts."

"Too goddamn timid. Put some iron in your voice."

"*Fuck* the grunts!"

"Bravo. Suck it in and let 'er rip. Give me a clenched fist, and a fine steely tone."

"Fuck the grunts!" He did a half-assed black power salute.

"Beautiful. Every time you see one of us, let go with it, just like that."

He stretched his little cupid's-bow lips across the bottom of his face. That was his smile. "Thanks, Hawkins."

"Sir, I'm a grunt, too. There can't be no exceptions."

"You're right. Fuck the grunts!" He stomped off, a

new man. I felt good. Maybe now the dumb sonofabitch would stay outa the way.

Impossible. What kinda weird-ass world is this?
Did you know that Napoleon was late for the Battle of
Waterloo because of his goddamn hemorrhoids. Uh?
You ever see *that* in a goddamn movie? Ol' short-stuff
soakin' his ass, in too muckinfuch pain to sit his horse?
War's s'posed to be all brave men, bad men, heroes,
enemies who die, sacrifice, romance, glamour . . . who
the hell ever heard of John Wayne missin' the invasion
because his goddamn hemorrhoids was givin' him a
royal pain in the ass?

After Whipple left I took a walk, out through the
mine field, which had been replanted, into the hamlet.
I went by myself, lookin' for Jinx. He hadn't waited
until we had guard. I think he split while we were
gettin' lit up. It was possible he'd been blown away.
Completely, I mean. It happens. Some dude gets
dinged with a rocket round, *boom!* Vaporized. What's
left wouldn't make *foie gras* for a cannibal. He'd been
listed as missin' in action. It looks a lot better than
listin' him as a deserter. The Army'd rather have you
dead than deserted. Deserters mean the system's got
flaws.

I went through the first hamlet, past a bunch o' rice
paddies, through another hamlet, some hedgerows,
into the third group of hooches. It was larger, so maybe
it was a village. I never understood the difference, 'less
one had five and another had fifty. Even then I didn't
find him. He found me. I was drinkin' a Pepsi. He
walked up behind me, quiet, put his arms round my
neck. "You come in peace, white man?"

"I'm gonna come unglued if you do that very often."

"What you doin' out here? You alone?"

"Yeah, I'm alone. You think anybody else is dumb enough to come lookin' for you?"

"Wanta beer?"

"*Ba-me-bah?*"

"Schlitz."

"C'mon . . . "

"Cold."

"I'll take it."

We walked to a teak 'n' brick building that looked like a combination house 'n' village headquarters. It was furnished in wicker, but nice stuff like you see in the movies where dudes in white suits sit under ceilin' fans. I flopped down while he got the beer from a GE wha'cha call it. Side by side. Brand new. Copper-colored. The place had two air conditioners in the windows, but they weren't runnin'. Wasn't hot enough, I guess. A Fisher reel-to-reel, amp 'n' pre-amp were sittin' on a table near the door. In the kitchen I could see, on a counter, an eight-speed blender, a pop-up toaster, electric frypan, electric can opener.

"You must be usin' half the fuckin' voltage in the village, man."

"Don't matter. This is the only place wired for electricity."

"Who lives here. Besides you, I mean."

"Village elder and the head of the political cadre in this area."

"You shittin' in high cotton."

"Beats sleepin' in a bunker. Wanta move in?"

"Naw. Dago's got us a nice place. 'Cept we don't have a goddamn electric can opener. Where'd you get this shit?"

"It was here when I moved in. But they bought it."

"The fuckin' VC got PX privileges now?"

"Watch yo' mouth. You never know."

"Where's the Head Nigger, if you'll excuse the expression."

"You tryin' to be funny?"

"C'mon, Jinx. Don't get touchy just 'cause you moved in with high-class slopes."

I watched him wrestle with it for a few seconds, then he snorted. "I bet if you was talkin' to the President you'd be the same."

"Ho Chi or that other jerkoff?"

"Would it matter?"

"Nope. I wouldn't piss in his ass if his guts were on fire, don't matter which one. Anyway, you gonna give me that fuckin' beer or I gotta swear allegiance to the party first?" We drank in silence for a few minutes. "You know, if they'd let us run this goddamn world for a few days, wouldn't be no wars."

"Maybe." He belched. "You really come out here to find me?"

"Yeah."

"What for?"

"Fucked if I know. I guess I wanted to make sure you were alive. They got you listed as missin' in action."

"It's true, in a way."

"You hangin' round or goin' to some other place?"

"I'll be around."

Well, there it was. It'd stopped bein' so much bullshit. He really was gonna take up arms, as they say, against his own country.

"It ain't my country."

I almost shit. "How'd you know what I was thinkin'?"

"It ain't hard, Hawk. I said all the same things to myself before I did it."

I shrugged. "Wha'th'fuck, man, it's your life."

"You really don't understand."

"It's hard."

"Not if you try." He finished his beer 'n' got us a couple more. "You know where all the electric stuff's from?"

"Land of the Big PX, looks like."

"Right. Beer, soda, fifty cases of grenades, ammo dump out back, a hundred cases of '16s, plasma, drugs, bandages, whisky, shavin' cream, toothpaste, you name it . . . we got it. You know why? How? Grunts, man. Cam Rahn Bay Commandos. They steal anything you want, for a price. You want a shipload of stuff, and you got bread, it's yours. You want the whole goddamn ship, you can buy it. And a crew to sail to Hanoi. *Americans*, Hawk. They stealin' 'n' sellin' everything they can get their goddamn greedy hands on. Slopes steal too, but it's nickels 'n' dimes. Half the fuckin' Korean Army is moonlightin' as guards for grunts that're stealin' to sell to us."

"C'mon, man. This kinda crap"——I waved the beer at him, "maybe. But guns, ammo 'n' medical supplies? You expect me to believe that?"

"No. But it's true."

"Ssshhhit," I sighed.

"How else?"

"You say you got it. Maybe so. But I ain't seen it. Have you?"

"I'm a special weapons advisor, Hawk. Everything from .82-millimeter mortars to some ol' BARs that come right outa Army storage in Virginia."

"Is that the shit we got hit with the other night?"

"Partly."

"Poe got lit up."

"Too bad. He paid for his ol' man's sins."

"And me?"

"Keep yo' ass covered, man." He smiled at me. He looked happy enough, like he was sure of what he was doin'. "I'm gonna be gone for a few days. Don't try comin' back in till at least the twelfth. Come alone, if you wanta come out. Sling yo' rifle barrel down, clip out. I can maybe ninety percent guarantee yo' safety."

"That's better'n I get drivin' through Atlanta."

"Do me a favor, okay? Try to fix it so you get my mail, if I get any. And mail this for me." He gave me a letter, sealed, addressed to his mother in Philadelphia. "I don't want 'er to worry."

"Ain't you afraid she'll raise hell? Call the Army—"

"She's got a cool head."

I was about to tell him again that he was crazy when in walked the girl from Madam Ming's, the girl I'd balled. She smiled. I smiled. This might turn out to be a better trip than I'd expected.

"This is Mary Ann . . . you remember her?"

"Do the Indians remember Custer?"

"We're married."

"I'm a motherfucker!"

"Not yet. She's not pregnant."

"Ah . . . I . . . uh, look . . ."

"Cool it, man. It's okay. It's 'er job. Right, Mary Ann?"

"Yes."

"She speaks English?"

"Sure. How else would she get information?"

"She balls grunts to get information?"

"You rather be tortured?"

"Well . . . you got a point. But why pretend she doesn't. In the house, I mean."

"It works better. Or so she says."

I looked at the two of 'em, half-smilin', havin' fun with me, and I knew I could snap out right there. Whipple I could handle. Dago. Shippin' grass back in Garcia's coffin. But this was too much. "I gotta split, man. Before your buddies get back."

"If I don't see you before the twelfth, try to come out in the afternoon. Think you'll make it?"

"Why the twelfth?"

"Why not?"

"I'll make it. I'll just take a walk, and if anybody asks where I'm going, I'll say the theater . . . to watch the biggest fuckin' comedy of errors since the goddamn British were let loose on the world. You're crazy, Jinx. You know that? Stone fuckin' crazy. I don't think you're what McNamara had in mind when he authorized Project 100,000."

"I sure's hell hope not."

Goin' back, not quite out of the village, I passed an Indian patrol. We looked at each other. They all had AKs, plenty of ammo, water, boots. They didn't look ill-fed or poorly equipped to me. In the States all you ever heard was how they were badly equipped, badly fed, demoralized. More BS. I mean, they didn't sing 'n' dance their way past me but they didn't look any more unhappy than I did. And damn sure they were a sight less scared. My spine felt like it was made outa hot cake dough. But nothin' happened. Maybe, I figured, Jinx really could guarantee me ninety percent safety.

Even so, it was weird. I'd accepted the idea of bein' surrounded by people who might or might not be "the enemy" on any given day. I'd accepted the idea that this war, at least, wasn't like the movies had made all other wars seem—we didn't capture towns or take control of anything further than a rifle shot from where we were dug into our holes. But even acceptin' that it was stone fuckin' strange. Seein' an Indian patrol wasn't an everyday event. But they slept in the hamlets at night, with their wives, played with their kids, visited their families—all right under our noses. And nobody could stop that because you never knew, unless one of 'em pointed an AK at you, exactly who was who. Maybe it really didn't matter. But I kept thinkin' it did. Or should.

I came through the wire, past the newly planted mines into camp. Nobody paid any attention. Bein' back didn't help. I'd begun to really feel like I was ODing on absurdity. You can. Things get so outa hand that nothin' makes sense. I was losin' my perspective . . . which was fucked up to begin with. Alice in Wonderland was gettin' to be timid shit next to this. I remember readin' a book called *Catch-22* and I said this dude's gotta be crazy. He was. But he wasn't crazy enough. Or maybe it was the difference in the wars. In the Second World War I think there were people who really believed we were doin' somethin' that had to be done. There musta been fuckups, like the book said. But I can't believe it was as fucked up as No Man's Nam. My mother used to say, "When I was a girl . . ." And the bullshit started. And *her* mother'd start with the same stuff . . . always worse. Maybe it's true with wars, too. Maybe everybody's war is the worst. But I'm here to tell you, sports fans, if the next one is any more fucked up than this one I don't want to know nothin' from nothin'.

I was sittin' over a cup of coffee in the chow hall a few minutes later, wonderin' if I should say anything about Jinx and the arms piled up out there, if they

really existed. Ubanski came in, filled a cup 'n' took a
seat across from me. We hadn't said fifty words to each
other in the last two weeks. I tried to stay outa his way
and he'd quit fuckin' with me since the Boy Ranger
kinda took my side. Not against Ski, but for me. Ubanski stirred some sugar into his coffee, lit a cigarette—
one of the few I'd ever seen him smoke—tasted his
coffee, nodded, and said, "Y' find 'im?"

I almost dropped my fuckin' cup. "Who?" It came
out in the range of a high-C.

"Who, hell."

"Who?" Middle-C.

"Who who who. Y' got feathers on ya feet? Y' sound
like a fuckin' owl." He drank some coffee, watchin' me.
I shrugged. "Jinx, who the hell else?"

"He's missin' in action," I tried to say with a
straight face.

"That's for damn sure. I was curious if y' found the
MIA misfit."

"Why you think I'm lookin'?"

"Hawkins, f' Chrissake, don't you ever give nobody
a goddamn straight answer?"

"On occasion . . . birthdays, anniversaries . . ."

"Y' wasn't out lookin' f' Charlie, the whorehouses
is the other direction and I don't think y' was on no
cultural tour. So what the fuck else was y' doin' in
Indian country? Takin' language lessons?"

"I went for a Pepsi." He put his helmet on the table
'n' rubbed his baldin' head. "Wha'th'fuck, Ski?"

"I'd like t' help 'im, Hawkins. If he comes back now
we might be able to keep 'is ass outa jail. If he waits
too long ain't a goddamn thing to do for 'im. Simple
enough?"

"I ain't his keeper, Sarge."

"You saw 'im?"

"Yeah."

"What else?"

"Gooks with AKs and new boots."

"How many?"

"Nine, ten. I didn't want to seem too interested."

"Nine or ten . . . ? And they let y' pass?"

"I'm here, ain't I?"

"Christ, y' could fall in a barrel of shit 'n' come out wearin' a new suit of clothes." He shrugged. "What's Jinx doin'?"

"How the hell do I know what he's doin'? He's smokin' dope 'n' drinkin' beer."

"You were there . . ."

"I'm here too, but I don't even know what I'm doin'." I stood up, pissed, but even more unsure about what to do. I decided on another cup of coffee. There's always time to stomp out. "You want more coffee?" He pushed his cup toward me.

"Y' want t' help 'im?" he asked. We were stirrin', sippin', lookin' at each other. "He's ya buddy."

"I learned a long time ago not to try helpin' somebody that doesn't want help. They're apt to get a mite pissed."

He thought about it. The cams turned, the wheels spun, click, click, whirrrrr, clickclick. "Y' right. But he could get shot for desertion."

"Ski . . . ?"

"Yeah . . . ?" I started gigglin'. "What . . . ?"

"You got any fuckin' idea how much *better* his chances are of gettin' shot if he *don't* desert?"

Whirrr, click clickclickclick—spuuttt.

"Well, what about 'is honor?"

"Honor? *Honor!!* What'th'fuck's honor got to do

with it? I mean if he's dead, and he died for some stupid fuckin' reason like honor where there ain't none, they ought to mark his stone, 'Here lies Jinx, he was one stupid sonofabitch.' *Honor?* Whose honor, for Christ's sake? The fuckin' thieves, war profiteers, black-market motherfuckers, the ego-centered, bigoted bastards lookin' to get promoted, jerkoffs like the colonel who gives out lovin' cups for the most VC KIA? Or your fuckin' buddy, Early, who shoots down fifty ARVNs for runnin' away? Or the first sergeant, who lit up an ARVN command to hit the numbers? Whose goddamn honor you talkin' about?"

"His own!" He slammed his fist into the table top. "He owes somethin' to himself, his family, his goddamn country."

"What he owes himself is a long life. I don't know about his family. And his country . . . ? His fuckin' country is spendin' twenty-five million dollars a day—a fuckin' day—to keep this war goin'. But you can bet your ass they wouldn't give *him* shit to grow a garden if his fuckin' belly was welded to his backbone. He could starve. Fuck his country, my country, your country. It sucks. Political pigs, corporate dictators . . ." I never saw it comin'. I was on the verge of listin' a dozen more collective groups I don't like—next thing I was on my ass. I hit the floor, rolled over 'n' was on my feet almost before my mind caught up to my movements. There wasn't more'n another ten people in there with us. They were up on their feet. A fight's always more interestin' than the food the Army serves. Ubanski came toward me, prob'ly ready to kill me. Wha'th' fuck, kill me, kill a gook. Musta been the same to him. I grabbed my '16, jacked a shell into the chamber 'n' flipped off the safety. Where I'd felt a cold sense of dread with the Karate King, with Ski I thought I couldna cared less. We looked at each other over the length of the barrel. Everybody else in the place was frozen, like a wax dummy layout. Grunts at war. There's a French name for that kinda shit but I couldn't remember what it was. And I swear t' God I don't know why it even came to mind. I can never seem to keep my head straight when it comes to killin' people. I guess I did care. I put the safety on, dropped the barrel. "I can't kill you, man. If you wanta kick my ass, go ahead." I walked past him, outside, sad, almost cryin'. It seemed so natural, blow him away, blow away the karate freak, blow away anybody that don't agree with you. Four or five rounds in the belly. The ultimate argument.

I walked around in a circle for a while. Mortar holes got in the way. Maybe the engineers were gettin' tired of fillin' in our little garden spot. Or maybe the smell of pig shit didn't appeal to those delicate souls. We were gettin' quite a reputation, anyway. From the duty, I mean. The whole battalion was known as Pig Wardens. Battalion HQ was known as The Pig Palace. I heard there'd been some fights in Xap Dong, between grunts from our battalion and some of the others south of us. That's what I heard. Somethin' about the battalion's honor. I never talked to anyone who said he'd been stupid enough to fight for that kinda shit. Anybody that goddamn dumb I wouldn't walk across the street to tell the motherfucker he was on fire. Anyway, the third time my erratic circle took me past our bunker I looked in to see if Dago was hangin' round. I wanted to get totally fuckin' stoned. He wasn't. I rolled a joint, partly the Thai stuff. What I did was take too fuckin' much. I smoked the whole goddamn thing.

I say I smoked the whole thing, but I'm guessin'. After three hits I couldn't hardly find my mouth. The last thing I remember is tryin' to whistle "Waitin'on the *Robert E. Lee*" while I was changin' clothes. Dago said he found me packin'. I was wearin' my Levis, a sweat-shirt with a picture of W. C. Fields on the chest, jungle boots and a headband I'd gotten from Longfeather. Accordin' to Dago, I said I was goin' home, fuck the war 'n' all the horses the warriors rode on. Seems rea-sonable enough to me. I vaguely remember thinkin' I'd collect a few people worth collectin' and we'd all drive to Danang, steal an airplane 'n' fly somewhere. Any-where. Didn't matter.

"I wonder why I didn't?" I wondered out loud.

"The lieutenant said y' couldn't go 'less y' had a pilot's license."

"Which lieutenant?"

"Whipple."

"*Whipple??* I tried to get Whipple into that."

"I think what y' said, more or less, was 'If I don't save ya fat fuckin' ass, who's gonna?"

"What'd he say?"

"Fuck the grunts. But he didn't write y' up."

"What time is it?"

"Seven, seven-thirty."

"A.m.?"

"Yeah."

"What happened after Whipple?"

"Y' drove somebody's truck into a shell hole."

"How. . . ? I can't drive a truck."

"We noticed."

"You shittin' me?"

"Look over by the officers' latrine."

"Forget it. Was that it for the night?"

"Y' really don't remember?"

"Oh, fuck me . . . what else?"

"Y' made a midnight requisition, y' know? Spray paint."

"Spray paint?"

"Those little cans." He laughed. "Scared the piss outa Sergeant Pyke, wavin' that Thompson around . . ."

"Thompson? As in sub-fuckin'-machine-gun?"

"As in."

"Oh motherless child. Why didn't somebody stop me?"

"I don't know nobody dumb enough to argue with a Thompson at close range."

"Wha'th'fuck did I do with the paint?"

"Painted pigs."

"*All* of 'em?"

"Nope. A couple. Then y' started sprayin' initials, y' know . . . ? On their sides."

"Initials . . . like . . . ?"

"LBJ, RMN, RSMcN. I gotta give y' one thing . . . you may not be worth a shit as an artist but y' sure's hell have got a beautiful eye for findin' pigs that look like the people you named 'em for. That one y' named RMN is the only goddamn hog I ever saw with a nose that turns up on the end."

"I did all that?"

"That's all I remember, but I was laughin' so hard I may've missed somethin'. So was everybody else. Or almost everybody."

"I don't wanta know who *didn't* think it was funny. Let 'em surprise me. Christ on a crutch. Where the hell did I get a Thompson? I never even fired one of 'em."

"Really? Y' did a helluva job last night."

"*Firin'??!!*"

"Y' shot McNamara. Said it was bacon for this mornin's breakfast."

"I think I'm gonna be sick."

"I'd bet more on y', like, bein' in jail." He was smilin'.

"You don't have to look so fuckin' happy about it."

"I'm not smilin' at that. You were funny, man. Y' know?"

"No, I don't know."

"I guess y' hadda be there."

"No shit. Where's the Thompson?"

"Under ya bunk."

I looked under the bunk. There it was. Ugly-lookin' motherfucker. Jesus. I musta been really weirded out. I really never had fired one. I couldn't imagine hittin' a bull in the ass with a bass fiddle, let alone shootin' one of those things at a goddamn hog.

Actually pointin' it at somebody was ridiculous. But not even bein' able to remember it was worst of all. I'd heard drunks talk about that kinda crap, but I always found it hard to believe. Obviously I've never been drunk enough. "I think I'm comin' unglued," I said. Dago nodded like we were discussin' theology and I'd said I think God's out to lunch. "I think maybe I'm in big trouble." Same thing. "Maybe I'll just quit. Go home."

"Good luck."

"I'm hungry. Let's get somethin' to eat." I climbed off the bunk just as Ubanski came through the door. I sat down.

"Levine wants to see y'."

"Which one?"

"The lieutenant." I looked at Dago. He shrugged.
"Let's go, Hawkins." We went. Wha'th'fuck, there
wasn't anything else to do.

Ski left me at the Boy Ranger's bunker with a smile
that woulda frozen Dracula's dork. I went inside like a
finalist in an Aztec Lucky Virgin contest. Wasn't no
way I figured to come outa this with my ass in one
piece. Eric was sittin' on his bunk, feet propped on a
chair. He was bare-chested, and wearin' a bush hat.
One of those with one side of the brim folded up, the
kind heroes wear in jungle movies and documentaries
on big game huntin'. Truth to tell, it is kinda sexy. It
fits the image. I did my best British boot-stompin' drill-
sergeant routine.

"Sir!"

"Ah . . . Private Hawkins, I believe." He didn't
crack a smile.

"Private fuckin' First Class . . . Hawkins. Sir!"

"Wrong again, Hawkins. Private. E-fuckin'-One."

"E-One, huh?"

"E-*fuckin'*-One. You rank right after Arab camel
drivers and nursing school dropouts."

"E-One, huh?"

"Plus thirty days' restriction to the area."

"When did this happen?"

"This morning."

"Sounds like a court-martial. Sorry I missed it."

"You're lucky you didn't get a goddamn court-martial. What the hell ever possessed you to write 'Head
Nigger's Hooch' on Jefferson's bunker?"

"I did that?" He closed his eyes 'n' shook his head.
"You're shakin' your head no but I gotta feelin' you
mean yes . . . yes?"

"Yes." He lit a cigarette 'n' blew the smoke out like

a dude about to get into the heavy shit. "Hawk . . . ?"

"Sir?"

"I'm getting bored with saving your ass. I suppose I could go on indefinitely but it's boring."

"Yes sir." The silence was hangin' in the air like sulphur. "Is that all, sir?"

"No, that's not all, sir! Where's Jinx?"

"Beats the shit outa me."

"Hawk . . ."

"I really don't know. He said he hadda split for a while."

"But you saw him?"

I shrugged. His jaw muscles started jumpin' round. "Wha'th'fuck . . . I saw him. So what?"

"Changing sides is bad form."

I shrugged. He took a big drag off the cigarette. The smoke trailed out his nose. I thought he looked a little bit like a defeated dragon. It was sorta sad. I mean, there we were, sittin' in a hole in No Man's Nam, both of us hatin' it as bad as Jinx, me a total fuckup and him all bent outa shape 'cause he hated it but couldn't stop tryin'. I think somewhere, way back in that part of the mind where you keep old phone numbers 'n' ten-year-old memories, he'd stored the idea that he'd like to win the goddamn war. As long as he was here, I mean. He'd prob'ly have been just as happy to go home, but as long as we were here . . . . If a job's worth doin', it's worth doin' right. But to do the job right we'd *all* have to change sides. Any idiot could see the Indians were the only ones who knew what they were gonna have to do, and were willin' to do it. The silence got heavier. I walked round the bunker, back to the door 'n' stared out. It had started rainin'. Again. Still.

"I heard Jinx had some interesting things to say,"

he finally muttered, to break the silence.

"I heard we were winnin' the war . . . you hear all kinds of shit round here."

"Yes or no?"

"Why ask . . . ?" I shrugged. "Give me a cigarette." He threw a pack across the empty space between us. And it was empty. The space, I mean. I knew what was comin' and I didn't want to have to choose. "Whata you want me to say?"

"Where is he?"

"Out there . . ." I waved at the dark rain-soaked sky. "Out in the shit."

"What's he doing?"

I ignored him, walked over 'n' picked up his helmet, put it on, then looked in a small shavin' mirror hangin' from a beam. I grinned at myself, turned to Eric. "Whata you think?"

"I think you'd better quit fucking around and tell me what Jinx is doing."

"Special weapons advisor, whatever the fuck that is." I said it deliberately. Detached. And the whole time a part of my head's screamin' no, no, goddamn it. But the voice is way off, in the distance, unimportant. I wondered a lotta times if that's how judges sentence people to be executed, how cops shoot people . . . or for that matter, how I'd have to be to shoot a gook.

"Sit down."

"Why?"

"You're shaking. You're pale. And . . ."

"And I just took another giant step to becomin' an asshole like the resta mankind." That came rippin' out like a rifle round. I flopped on the floor. "I'm sorry. You've been a good friend and it's not your fault you're an officer." I fumbled around, lit another cigarette.

"Wha'th'fuck they need with a special weapons advisor? We been over here long enough, they got to know everything we got, how it works. He said they got a hundred cases of '16s . . . a hundred *cases*. Fifty cases of grenades. Ammo. Medical supplies." I laughed. A sideways snort that mostly came out the left nostril. "The fucker's got an electric can opener, for Christ's sake. That's too fuckin' much."

"Cool it, Hawk."

"Goddamn it, I like him. Now what? We goin' out'n kill him? Light him up?"

"You want to wait? Till he comes for you? Throw me the cigarettes. He'll come. You know that, don't you?"

"No."

"Believe it. He'll come for us, him and the rest of them. He's got to."

"To prove himself."

"Got to."

"Maybe not."

"What's that thing you say about the tooth fairy?"

"Jinx is gone. Out somewhere. Said he'd be back the twelfth."

"We should be back by then."

"Where we goin'?"

"Hunting."

"When?"

"Tomorrow."

"I heard they got some great beaches down near Chulai . . ."

"I heard we were winning the war."

"You gettin' to be as big a wiseass as I am. Listen, I got to carry that goddamn radio? I mean, I'm not trained as an RTO."

"You're doing fine."

"How many's goin'?"

He did a quick count. "Five, six . . . six."

"Six?!"

"Six. You, me, Ski, Davis, Dago, and Suchow."

"Who's Suchow?"

"Replacement. This is his second tour."

"Lifer?"

"Yeah. E-5."

"Another fuckin' sergeant. Kinda rank-heavy."

"Since none of you fucking privates want to fight this war we're having to do it with NCOs."

"They ought to do it with field-grade officers and generals. That'd put an end to this shit in a hurry. How far out we goin'?"

"Forty miles."

"Shee-*it!* We'd be in Laos."

"That's right."

"You kiddin' me? We gonna walk to Laos? In a week?"

"First class. Choppers."

"Fuck me, I ain't goin' to *Laos*. I know there's got to be a rule somewhere says American grunts can't go into Laos."

"Well, you get all the books you can . . . for reference. And the radio. You can read while we're on the OP." He laughed. "Anyway, you look like a goddamn civilian."

"I *am* a civilian."

"Then you won't have any problem in Laos. Just tell everybody you work for the CIA. There's a lot of them over there."

"Wha'th'fuck, man, they make a lotta bread, right? Let them go huntin' for us."

"Hawk, get your shit together. This one isn't a

walk-on. The colonel says they're out there, and he says he knows where."

"Then why the fuck doesn't the colonel go find 'em himself?" I ripped the helmet off 'n' threw it across the bunker. "I know . . . that's not what they pay colonels for." I picked up the helmet 'n' hung it on a nail. "Forty miles?"

"Twenty, actually. For openers. We're not going to Laos just yet."

"What'll we use for protection if we run into a bunch of 'em? We ain't got diddly-shit that will reach that far."

"Part of it's covered by some 175s. Anyway, we're supposed to stay out of sight. Like a camera safari."

"What time we leavin'?"

"First light."

"Terrific. T-fuckin'-riffic."

"Hawk . . . ?"

"Yeah?"

"Stay out of Jefferson's path, okay? And Sergeant Pyke?"

Maybe an hour later it hit me. What he was really sayin', I mean. When I told him Jinx wouldn't be back till the twelfth, he said we *should* be back by then. Should, hell. Why wouldn't we be? Wha'th'fuck would we be doin' runnin' round out in Indian country for that long? Overnighters made me nervous. Campin' out for a goddamn week was too fuckin' much like the real thing. Christ, next they'd have me actin' like a real soldier, shootin' people for no better reason than that they happen to cover the sights of my pop-gun. The freakin' fact of it is that the longer you're out there lookin' for trouble the more likely you are to find it. If we were gonna be out there that long, sure's hell

I'd have to take it seriously or run a good chance of gettin' my ass blown away. The whole goddamn prospect was depressin'. Well, I decided, there's always the option of goin' AWOL, shootin' myself in the knee, or declarin' the war won. Fuck 'em. Fuck 'em, we won. Let's go home.

"We fuckin' won, Luke, goddamn it. Don't be so freakin' hardheaded. Fuckin' war's over. It came to me in a vision and you know you ain't s'posed to fuck with the prophet's visions. Remember what happened to that goddamn Egyptian dude when Daniel—was it Daniel? yeah, it was Daniel—when Daniel did his thing?" Davis was cleanin' his shotgun, swabbin' the bores, and I wasn't sure he was even listenin'. "Luke, you listenin'?"

"Ah'd hafta have a peck of pig shit in my ears not to."

"Well?"

"Watah."

"Funny."

"Hawk . . . "

"Well water, well done, well-to-do, why the fuck can't we just say we won and split, man?"

"We ain't won, Hawk." He snapped the breach shut. If I didn't know him better I'd swear he was tryin' to act like a fuckin' movie star. 'Cept he don't fuck around like that. "An' not only ain't we not won, Ah ain't so sure we a-goan to win."

"No shit, Sherlock. What gave you the first clue?"

"Ah ain't sure. Hit may be you did." He put the shotgun across his knees 'n' reached into a canvas bag at his feet. Out came a bottle of lemon oil. Swear t' God. "We ain't won. Ain't goan win," he added.

"Is that a goddamn gun or a piece of furniture?" He ignored me. A little oil on a rag 'n' he started rubbin' the stock, up 'n' back, up 'n' back. "Ski 'n' Suchow was talkin' a while ago. 'Bout how they pullin' out whole battalions, down south, ovah in the highlands. Suchow says grunts is gettin' theyah asses kicked right smart 'cause ever'body's sorta tryin' t' play hit safe." Up 'n' back, up 'n' back. The wood was beautiful. The whole goddamn thing was beautiful till you saw the two orange explosions and knew that somethin' or someone had died. "Suchow's com'ny got did up in a ambush. Whole fuckin' com'ny. They was already down to 'bout a hundred guys. Six got out."

"Six?! Six fuckin' dudes outa all them?"

"Six." Up 'n' back. "Next day a fuckin' regiment went in. Nothin'. Not one fuckin' slant-eyed slope." He turned the shotgun over 'n' started on the other side. "We been lucky, Hawk."

"If we were lucky we wouldn't be here."

"Ah reckon, but bein's we heah, we lucky we ain't got the shit kicked outa us."

"Well, I'd say they ain't done too bad like it is, Luke. Long as they can keep knockin' hell outa us with those fuckin' mortars 'n' rockets they ain't gotta come in too close. How come we didn't read about Suchow's company? How the fuck can a hundred dudes get wasted and we don't even hear?"

"Ah s'pose theyah's ways. He says prob'ly half the KIAs is hid from the newspapers. On account of the protesters."

"Yeah, or maybe 'cause they figure if we knew we might just tell 'em to go get fucked next time they say 'Let's go.' "

"Hit ain't right."

"I don't think that's one of the things they worry about." He'd finished oilin' the stock. I reached over and took the shotgun off his lap. It was heavy but so well balanced you hardly noticed it. I thumbed the breach open and the barrels fell forward a few inches so I could see through the long blue tubes. Clean as a whistle. "Nice piece," I said 'n' tried to snap the breach shut with a wrist motion I'd seen him use six dozen times. Nothin'. I tried again, and again. He was gigglin' by the time I gave up.

"Sweah t' Christ, Hawk, you fuckin' city boys ain't worth the powder it'd take to blow yo' ass outa bed."

"Luke, when you gonna learn to speak English?" I handed him the goddamn gun.

"Ah don't rightly reckon hit matters, Hawk. Ain't nobody payin' no attention to what Ah say anyway." He opened the breach, put two shells in and snapped it shut with the wrist action I'd tried.

"Smartass."

"You et yet?"

"Nope. I'm trying' to stay outa sight."

"Some Cs under my bunk."

"Fuck that. Christ, we gonna have to eat fuckin' C-rations for a goddamn week."

"Naw. Ski says we gonna git some of them pouch foods."

"Some what?"

"Pouch foods. You put water in 'em an' they make food."

"Dehydrated?"

"Yeah, tha's hit."

"Yech. Jesus. I'd as soon eat fuckin' rice balls 'n' monkey meat."

"You ever et any Viet food?"

"Where the fuck am I s'posed to get any of that? McDonald's don't serve fish heads 'n' rice, or twenty-nine flavors of *nuoc mam*."

"Hit ain't bad, once you git hit past yo' nose. Hit's jus' fish gravy."

"Gravy?!! That's shit's rotten, pure 'n' simple. Fish guts."

"Well, hit's fermented."

"You really eat that stuff?"

"Yep. Me 'n' Ski been whamin' them people in Duc My."

"Where?"

" 'Bout half a mile south of here. Duc My Two. There's four or five hamlets."

"Ski?"

"Yep."

"Luke . . . Ski ain't about to try to win nobody's heart or mind."

"He's right friendly with 'em. Brings chocolate 'n' soap, some Cs . . ."

"Fuck me."

"You orta give Ski a chance. He's a good ol' boy."

"Luke, wha'th'fuck's the matter with you? Uban-ski wouldn't wake up from a nap to save the whole goddamn world. Why you think he'd give two shits about them fuckin' slopes you're takin' chocolate to?"

"Ah ain't often been able to unn'erstan' *why* anybody does anythin'. But 'e does it, so tha's all 'at matters, right?"

"Wrong, Luke. Dead fuckin' wrong."

"Maybe. You hungry?"

"Yeah, I'm hungry. You plannin' to take me to lunch at Duc My's Four Forker?"

"Ain't got no forks, you dumb fuck. They eats with chopper sticks."

"One stick to pick up two buckets of shit 'n' two sticks to pick up one grain of rice."

"They ain't eatin' pouch food . . ."

"You're as relentless as the goddamn rain. Let's di-di."

He put a double handful of shells in his pants pockets, snapped on his Reb cap—which he claimed was authentic—and off we went. I was still wearin' my Levis 'n' sweatshirt, which ain't the most inconspicuous outfit to try sneakin' round in, so I dropped a poncho over my head, put on a helmet and tried to look innocent in case I ran into Jefferson or Pyke. Pyke might be ready to forgive me for pointin' a loaded Thompson at him, but it'd be a cold day in hell before the Chocolate Soldier would forget I called him a nigger. People are weird like that. We stopped by Dago's 'n' my bunker so I could collect my '16. He was workin' on his books. He looked up from under his green eyeshade when we came clumpin' in.

"Stockade?"

"Restriction. And I got busted to E-1."

"Ya the luckiest motherfucker I ever saw."

"Jesus loves me."

"He may be a Jew but he ain't Jesus."

"Who?"

"The lieutenant."

"You think he saved me?"

"Does Manischewitz make wine?"

"Who?"

He dropped his voice. "Christ, anybody ever tried to court-martial you, y'd have 'em so fucked up they'd probably apologize. Forget it. Goddamn rain. My books're off seventy-five dollars. I got to go huntin' slopes with you dorks tomorrow. A man can't make a decent livin' anymore."

"Wanta go eat gook food with us?"

"Hell no! Where y' goin'?"

"Wing Fat's Wonder World of Oriental Delicacies."

"Duc My," Davis put in.

"Thank you, Corporal. It's nice to get a straight answer. Ya both nuts. Y' got a better chance of gettin' lead balls than flied lice."

"They right friendly. Ah et with 'em afore."

"Good luck an' get the fuck outa here so I can balance my books."

I picked up my pop-gun and we went. It was drizzlin' and the sky was the color of rifle barrels. Maybe ten minutes of sloshin' 'n' slippin' through the mud got us to Duc My Two, which looked to me exactly like Duc My One to One Hundred, and like goddamn near everything else I'd seen of No Man's Nam. Ugly. A wizened old man stood off to one side as we passed, noddin' a greeting. Davis nodded back. About three steps past him I jerked my head around, half expectin' to see him whip out a long, curved knife. He just stared back, his head still noddin' up 'n' down.

"Luke . . ."

He grunted.

"This place stinks . . ."

"Wind's blowin' from the pigs back yonder."

"It ain't that, Luke . . . it ain't that." He stopped to look at me. "A feelin' . . ." I shrugged. "Man, I'm weirded out . . . I don't know. A feelin' . . . you know?"

Luke turned his head, like an animal before it goes to a water hole, sensin', smellin'. Which mighta eased my mind if I hadn't eaten as much venison and squirrel as I have. "Hit's okay. You jus' spooky."

We were at the edge of the hamlet, or whatever the hell it was. "Come on," he grunted. I let him move ahead of me four or five steps, then followed, but I moved off to the side, goin' downhill from spooky to scared shitless. About fifty yards in front of us there were some people, mostly women 'n' kids, standin' round yackin'. I caught up to Davis just about the time a little girl, maybe three or four years old, busted free of the group, runnin' toward us, yellin' 'n' squealin' like Davis was her daddy. Any tension he mighta felt went the way of the wind. He tossed me the shotgun. "Tha's my lit'le girl . . ." and started to trot toward her.

"*Luke!*" The fear was in my throat. I was shakin'. "Luke . . . !" The girl was maybe ten meters from him when she raised her arms . . . I raised the shotgun . . . she was still squealin', shoutin' somethin' that sounded weirdly like Luke's name. I couldn't see his face but I knew he had a big dumb grin spread all over it. The spoon from the grenade fell out of her dress . . . he stopped dead in his tracks . . . I fired one round . . . the gun boomed and slammed back into my hip . . . her tiny chest turned to bloody jelly, the bone, flesh, 'n' blood flyin' . . . the grenade exploded and she disappeared in a ball of smoke 'n' orange flame, blown to bits. Somethin' moved in a hut to the left . . . I emptied the other barrel. The front of the thatched bamboo shack shattered 'n' someone screamed. I was yellin', "Luke, Luke, Luke . . ." over 'n' over, runnin' toward him. He was on his back, blood seepin' from a dozen wounds in his stomach, chest 'n' legs. I remember he said, "Help me, Hawk," and I started pullin' him backwards through the mud. Somebody opened up on us with an automatic, stitched a line through the mud. I lurched to the right 'n' Luke screamed with pain. I dragged him through a door, into a hooch.

There was an old woman crouched on the floor, her

eyes big as saucers. I tore off the poncho 'n' spun the M-16 round to cover her. She covered her face with her hands. The automatic had shifted positions and a dozen rounds ripped through the wall about waist high. "Luke . . ." He groaned. I popped open the breech on his shotgun, dumped the empties and dug out a handful of shells. They were slick with blood. My stomach turned over 'n' I thought I might puke right there. Fear fought the bile. I gagged but nothin' came up. I pushed two new shells into the breech 'n' snapped it shut. I tried to duckwalk backwards, draggin' Luke toward a stone hearth in the rear of the room. Vertigo hit me and I fell over on my side. Two more long bursts came through the walls, lower. God help us, don't let us die here . . . not like this. I emptied both barrels out the door, at nothin' I could see, re-loaded 'n' pulled Luke further back into the hooch. We were fucked . . . the old woman wailed . . . I pulled Luke behind the hearth, next to a protective wall about two feet high. It was dark and I was shakin' with cold 'n' fear. The old woman wailed again and I screamed *"Shut the fuck up."* One of the automatics emptied half a clip through the wall behind her and I blew her, the wall 'n' the automatic into bone dust 'n' bloody froth. I grabbed my M-16 and went over the hearth, out the door in two bounds, screamin' somethin' I doubt I'd have understood if I'd been listenin'. Goin' through the door I hit the mud, belly first, rolled over two or three times and ended up facin' the door I'd just come through. I had one goddamn clip, twenty rounds . . .

"All right, you chickenshit cocksuckers . . ."

Stone fuckin' quiet. I rolled over 'n' ran with my belly no more'n a foot off the ground, around the end of the shack and grabbed the dead dude's automatic as

I went past. Nothin'. Not a shot, not a soul in sight. There had to be another sonofabitch somewhere. I'd heard two automatics and I couldn't account for more than the one dink bleedin' into the mud where the wall was half-gone and the old woman was twisted into the splinters 'n' fragments of bamboo. Five seconds, six, seven . . . I couldn't sit there and I didn't know where the fuck to go. I ran around the hooch 'n' stopped short of the narrow street. My heart was poundin' so loud I prob'ly couldn't have heard a half-track in the front hall. The M-16 was hangin' from my shoulder by the strap and I pointed the AK at the hooch across the street. I squeezed the trigger and the sonofabitch went off so quick most of the rounds sailed over the roof. I slung it, empty, over my shoulder and started backin' away with the pop-gun pointed at the hooch. Nothin'.

I ran back to the dude who owned the AK, hopin' he'd have some more ammo. He was barely alive, holdin' mosta his guts in with his hands. His eyes were closed. I shot him once through the head. He didn't have any ammo, no grenades, nothin'. I was standin' there tryin' to figure out what to do when I heard the jeep whinin' 'n' grindin' gears, comin' from the direction of Kilo. Ski, Dago 'n' Suchow were bouncin' 'n' slidin' along the track. Suchow standin' up in back, both hands wrapped around the handles of a swivel-mounted .50. He fired off half a belt at nothin', just random bursts down the street. Ski was out, runnin' before the jeep slid to a stop. "Where's Davis?"

"Inside, hurt."

"You hit?"

I opened my mouth to say no 'n' vomited all over my boots. My knees sagged 'n' I went down. Dago ran past us, inside, then popped out. "Call dustoff, Sarge.

Tell 'em to hurry." He shook his head. "And tell 'em to bring a lot of plasma." Suchow was on the radio before Ski could say anything. Ubanski looked down at me, then reached out 'n' wrapped his fingers around the barrel of my '16. It was cold. I hadn't fired but one round with it, to finish off the sonofabitch I'd wasted with the shotgun. He started to say somethin', then sniffed the breech. I got to my feet 'n' started to wobble toward the jeep.

"Hawkins!"

I turned around. "If that kid dies I'm gonna kill you." Way off in the distance of whatever was left of my rational mind a younger, angrier version of me started yellin'. He ripped off his helmet 'n' threw it down between us—a gaunlet, maybe—but it was comical, a stupid, idealistic throwaway kid in Levis, W. C. Fields sweatshirt 'n' headband. I started laughin'. Shakin' 'n' laughin', quietly, then out loud, then hysterically, laughin' 'n' laughin', a crazy puke-smellin' punk with spittle droolin' from his mouth, his clothes crusted in mud, his hands smeared with dried blood cracked 'n' peelin', the right hand wrapped round the rifle grip, finger on the trigger . . . laughin' and laughin' and laughin'.

The first thing my mind processed in the way of information was sounds. Weird. I mean I wasn't aware of my body or where I was. Just sounds. Low voices, sorta hummin', then a chopper. Whack-whackwhackwhackwhack . . . whackwhack . . . whack . . . whack. I opened my eyes, expectin' to see a dustoff comin' for Davis. What I saw was the inside of the battalion hospital, people runnin' round in hospital greens the color of anemic pea soup. I was stretched out on a canvas cot, most of my clothes cut away, hangin' in tatters. And a big goddamn white bandage around my right leg, below the knee. Fuck me. I moved the leg. Seemed to work okay. I started gropin' myself, like some dude absentmindedly lookin' for a match in his pockets. Nothin' else wrong, but for all that I didn't even know what was s'posed to be wrong with my leg. When I sat up 'n' swung my feet to the floor nothin' hurt. From the new angle the bandage didn't look so big. I tried standin', with most of my weight on my left leg. That worked. Wha'th'fuck, I put the weight on the right leg. A little sore, but I figured I could walk. And I was on my way out when Jefferson and the Boy Ranger came into the room. Mind you, this wasn't a hospital room like you'd picture. More like a receivin' room I guess; big, filled with wheeled tables 'n' cots like mine. There were some other dudes stretched out here 'n' there, some out, some awake but out of it, couple like me, prob'ly wonderin' what the hell they were doin' there.

Jefferson saw me first 'n' almost smiled. They came over. He said, "Hawkins . . ." and I said, "Sir . . ." He grimaced. I shrugged. "That's some uniform you've got there." I grimaced. He shrugged. "Good thing we aren't married," I said.

His face went from more or less neutral to first-step firmness, makin' ready to remind me I was talkin' to an officer. "How's that, Private?"

I shrugged. "We'd sure's hell have problems communicatin' with nothin' but shrugs 'n' grimaces."

He grimaced. Swear t' God, he did. "We have that without benefit of matrimony," Jefferson said, and damned if he didn't grin. "Reports from Corporal

Davis are that you're quite a hero. Of course, I haven't spoken to him myself, but Sergeant Ubanski says Davis can't say enough good things about you."

"He goin' to be okay?"

"Doctors say there's nothin' they can't fix. He'll be evaced out tomorrow. Japan. But you apparently saved his life. I'd like the story from you, if you feel up to it."

"I'd like to forget the whole fuckin' thing, if you feel up to that."

"Hawkins!"

"Captain Jefferson . . . I . . . look, I don't mean any disrespect, you know? But today I killed a little girl, maybe three years old. An old broad, prob'ly sixty, and two dudes—or one, I'm not sure about the second—and I would like nothin' better than to forget it. I know that ain't possible, but I don't see no reason why I should break my own balls to satisfy your curiosity." He started to say somethin', but I cut in, "Or anybody else's."

His mouth got tight. I shrugged. Fuck him. He shrugged. "Private Hawkins, on the recommendation of Corporal Davis I intended to recommend you for both the Purple Heart, by virtue of your wound, and the Silver Star, for risking your life to save that of a fellow soldier. I still need a full written after-action report on the events that transpired." He let that hang there for maybe three seconds. "At your earliest convenience." I nodded. He turned to Eric. "Lieutenant, I'm going to see if Corporal Davis can receive visitors." He walked off.

Eric 'n' I stared at each other. "How's the leg?"

"Do *you* understand?"

"Sure."

"My leg's okay. I don't even know what they bandaged."

"Frag wound, we heard."

"I'd like to get the fuck outa here."

"You want to see Davis?"

"I guess. He's gonna OD on visitors." We wandered off in the direction Jefferson had taken.

Jefferson was leavin' the ward as we came in. "Five minutes . . .?

Eric nodded for the both of us. Ubanski was sittin' by the bed. He nodded.

"Hello, Ski . . ."

Luke looked over when he heard my voice. He worked on a half-assed grin that got all fucked up. Tears filled his eyes 'n' he turned his head away. I looked at Ski. He looked away. Lord fuck a duck.

"Luke . . ." He sniffed, and slowly raised his hand to wipe at his eyes. "Luke . . . ?" He turned his head back toward me. "Luke, did you tell those motherfuckers I was a food critic for *Stars 'n' Stripes*?" He shook his head no. Dead serious. "Then next time how about lettin' me pick the place for lunch. Or let's stick to pouch food." He got a grin together and his eyes came to life.

"Man . . ." He shook his head, slowly. "You somethin' else with 'at ol' Greener. Evah'time Ah looked up you'd done blowed away anothah slope." He coughed and the pain went through him like electricity. He musta had two dozen frag wounds; legs, stomach, chest 'n' arms. "Ah'm cold, Hawk." I pulled the sheet up over his chest, leavin' his arms free. He nodded. "Good. Listen, Hawk, Ah ain't much with words, ain't really too good with English, but Ah can say Ah 'preciate what you done."

"Shee-it! I was just tryin' to save my ass."

"You coulda took off." He grinned. "Gone fer help."

"I'd have got lost by myself. Anyways, you kept sayin' you weren't goin' nowhere till you spoke to the manager."

"You done good by me, Hawk."

"I guess . . . listen, we gonna leave so you can rest. Take care. And write, okay?"

"Ah will." We held each other's hand for a minute, and I almost weirded out right there. I started to the door. "Hawk . . .?" I stopped and turned my head more'n my body. "You keep the Greener, okay? That ol' gun was made fer you."

I nodded. My eyes were fillin' with tears. Not from gratitude. From pain. From the realization that, in his eyes, and prob'ly in Ubanski's, Jefferson's, maybe even Eric's, I had grown up. I'd slaughtered people and symbolically earned my manhood. My mind snapped out and I saw myself through a camera lens, a long, slightly out-of-focus shot that slowly zoomed in, sharper 'n' sharper—Hawkins, the hunter with his boots, jungle fatigues, bush hat 'n' .10-gauge shotgun, stalkin' . . . I missed the corridor to my right and stalked into a huge square room lit up like a freeway fillin' station—six tables, twelve 'r fourteen people dressed in blood-spattered pea-greens, doctors, nurses, corpsmen, chatterin' 'n' chatterin', machines beepin', people dyin'—a skinny giant with a mask coverin' mosta his face looked up holdin' a saw in one hand, an arm in the other. The arm was weirdly bent at the elbow. The severed bicep was a bloody smear. "You missed your turn . . ." I felt my knees buckle a little. A flood of perspiration washed over my forehead,

into my eyes, along my cheeks, rivers of sweat . . .
"Back out, Troop, out the door, down the hall . . . move
it!" I backed out the swingin' door. The last thing I saw
was the arm tossed into a plastic trash can liner . . .
thump!

I backed into a wall 'n' slid down, soaked, faint,
freaked out. From about a hundred meters away, a
corpsman peered at me, curious, bird-like, chirpin',
flutterin' a hand on my face, another on my wrist. The
Boy Ranger came up beside him. They chirped together. The corpsman fluttered away for a second, then
came back 'n' broke a glass tube under my nose. Am-
monia. I think I smiled. Another one, practically in the
nostril. Tears mixed with the sweat in my eyes. The
two of 'em came in close, the corpsman pullin' at my
eyelids, still chirpin', passin' the vial back 'n' forth
under my nose.

"Okay, okay, motherfucker, okay." I jerked my head away 'n' tried to get up. Each of 'em grabbed an arm, got me on my feet. Eric passed his hand in front of my face. "Four fingers. Get me outa this goddamn place." We lurched out together, into the rain. It felt good; cold, clean. We stopped by the side of a jeep. Eric got in. I leaned on a fender, my face turned up to the bowel-black sky. Three, four, maybe five minutes. My back started to hurt. I straightened up and found Eric starin' at me. "The war is over."

"That sounds like an audition line for The Famous Actors School. 'Can you convincingly say "The war is over"? If so, you may have hidden talent that will bring you fame and fortune as an actor or actress.' " He looked disgusted. "I didn't even realize you were fighting. Who won?"

"The goddamn fuckin' Army won!"

"No shit. Won what? Your soul? Christ, Hawkins, why don't you get in the goddamn jeep and let's go back to Kilo. I'm hungry."

"Eric . . . ?"

"Don't give me that betrayed-friend look. I've saved your ass more times than you can count." I shrugged. Wha'th'fuck could I say to that? "But the day you start feelin sorry for yourself is the day I start kicking your ass." We stared at each other. It was another one of those little moments in life when my mind separated from my body and I could see us as we were, like lookin' at a freeze-frame on a movie screen. I had to decide if I was goin' to play it out. "I know you don't think much of John Wayne, but is playing James Dean any better?"

"Am I so fuckin' simpleminded . . ."

"Obvious, Hawk. Not simpleminded. Obvious. You're exhausted, dirty, fucked over, feeling unique, and nobody wants to take you seriously when you talk about your soul or your agony. Damn! You haven't got the good sense to get in out of the rain. You want to play the angry young man, go ahead. But it'd better be good or I'm going to let you walk back." He started the jeep's motor. "And that's seven long fucking miles." I sighed 'n' got in on the passenger side. He took out a joint 'n' handed it to me. "Present from Dago."

I got it lit, took a coupla hits 'n' passed it to him. "What kinda sick sonofabitch would wire a kid with a grenade?"

"Same kind that napalms villages."

I started to say there's a helluva difference between the two, but my mind caught up with my mouth. Kill your own kids, or someone else's, what's the fuckin' difference? The pretense is there, but the goddamn reality is we're all kids. Most of us, anyway. Garcia, Poe, Davis. And me. I'm still fuckin' nine years old.

We bounced along, fallin' into 'n' climbin' out of water-filled holes, the jeep lurchin' from side to side, hittin' the joint one for one. It took the better part of an hour to get back. It was dark. "What fuckin' time is it, anyway?"

He glanced at his watch. "Six-forty."

"Jesus H. Christ! Is *that* all? Feels like it should be next week."

"Listen, Hawk, I don't usually lecture people. Or give a lot of advice. But I'm going to say something to you that you can take any way you like . . ."

"I'm too stoned 'n' tired to listen to a long lecture."

"I'll make it short. You made a decision today. You can't go back. Your life is changed, for better or worse. Accept it. And accept yourself, however you see it."

"That's it?"

"That's it."

"Good night, Lef'tenant."

"Good night, my friend."

Dago was out when I got to the bunker. It was dark 'n' cold, everything was wet, and I was completely weirded out. The dope had numbed me, but nothin' was right or funny or even worth an effort. My mind was messin' with about forty thoughts a second, which was the same as not thinkin'. I couldn't think, couldn't focus on a fuckin' thing long enough to even get dry clothes on. I stood there, in the middle of the bunker, starin' at nothin'. I don't know for how long, or how much longer it woulda gone on if Ubanski hadn't come in. He was carryin' Davis' shotgun, the AK I'd taken off the dead slope, and my '16. He stood in the door for a few seconds while my head made futile attempts to organize itself.

"Sergeant Ubanski . . ."

"I got your weapons."

"No shit. I thought you might be on your way to win the war by yourself."

"Coupla pairs of fatigues on ya bunk there. Sergeant Pyke sent 'em over." He put the arsenal next to the fatigues then dug a coupla sandwiches outa his jacket. "Case you're hungry." He put 'em on top of the dry clothes. "I cleaned the AK. After we get back I'll show y' how to break it down. Nothin' hard."

"Back from where?"

"Recon. Far's I know it's still laid on for t'morra."

"Christ A'mighty."

"The war don't stop because y' killed a coupla gooks."

"I guess not. We musta already killed a coupla *million*, and it ain't slowed us down worth a shit. You think it'll ever end?"

"Yeah . . . when the taxpayers get tired of supportin' it. When parents get tired of gettin' their kids back in bits an' pieces. Or when we blow out them bastards up North."

"Whichever comes first . . . like a war warranty?" He nodded yeah, and wha'th'fuck am I s'posed to do about it? "You want to sit a while?" I picked up the sandwiches. "Want one?"

"No, go ahead. I ate awready."

"I don't remember the last time I ate."

"Y' been busy."

I burst out laughin'. "That's the first funny thing I ever heard you say."

"That puts me one up on y'."

"You really don't like me worth a shit, do you?"

"I don't understand y', Hawkins. There's times when y' seem okay. And I misjudged y', I guess. I thought you was chickenshit through an' through. Y' coulda left Davis out there, took off. He kept sayin', 'Ol' Hawk's okay, Sarge. He stayed with me.' I don't know. I got a lot more to worry about than you." I was gnawin' at one of the sandwiches, listenin'. He wasn't speakin' like he resented me, not like he had in the past. Maybe he really didn't understand. "Tell me somethin', Hawkins . . . how come y' ain't in Canada?" I was chewin' and he didn't wait. Maybe he didn't even particularly want an answer. "There's a lotta deserters an' draft dodgers up there, right? How come y' ain't with 'em? Seems like they'd be more agreeable to ya thinkin'. Youse could all sit around together an' talk about how rotten the country is."

"Like everybody sittin' round the NCO Club talkin' about how lousy the youth of America is. Right?"

"At least we don't refuse to fight for our country."

"And the lousy youth of America never dragged us into a stinkin' war fifteen thousand miles from home just to keep a goddamn dictator in power."

"It's not for youse to decide which war is good an' which is bad. When ya country calls, y' go." I got two bottles of Dago's German beer outa the refrigerator. He took one, guzzled a long drink 'n' belched. "Y' ever think of that?"

"Ski, I *am* my country. YOU ever think of that? No, wait a minute. Listen . . . I know we don't agree, but listen for a few minutes so when you argue you'll at least know what our argument is . . . listen, okay? I *am* my country. Me 'n' Davis, Poe 'n' Garcia, Eric . . . you. So who're you talkin' about when you say 'my country'? A buncha weasel-eyed bourbon-drinkin' Southern senators who control mosta Congress . . . ? Generals who run the Pentagon? The silk-suit dudes that own the country? My country hasn't even got balls enough to declare war that they been claimin' for four years we're *about* to win . . . you ever think about that?"

He shook his head, prob'ly really sad, not so much for me as for himself. "Wha'th'fuck are y' doin' here if that's how y' feel?"

"I'll be goddamned if I know."

He finished his beer 'n' stood the bottle on a table. He sighed, rubbed his almost bald head with the knuckles of his right hand, avoidin' the ugly red scars from the rounds he'd taken. His fingers were knotty. He put his helmet on. He'd run outa things to do, so he shrugged, stood up, opened and closed his mouth twice like he wanted to say somethin' but couldn't quite make up his mind to say it. Then, finally, "I just don't understand. Y' remind me of my kid. Both of youse act like the world owes youse somethin', like responsibility an' duty don't count. Country's goin' t' hell and y' think youse got the right to say no."

No? He walked out, prob'ly as tired of me as I was of him, the war, and meaningless explanations—but Jesus H. Christ, wha'th'fuck's wrong with assumin' the right to say no to bullshit? How come I'm the only idiot on this idiotic pig farm that believes one of my most inalienable rights is the right to say no? And what's this about his kid, I wondered. But I never found out. Ah, well, fuck it. There's prob'ly gonna be lots of things I never find out. And just before I went to sleep I wondered where the Chocolate Soldier was—we'd left him at the hospital.

Dago woke me next mornin', about ten, to tell me I had guard duty at noon. "What happened to 'first light' and all that shit?" I mumbled.

"It's rainin' so fuckin' hard even the goddamn gooks won't come out, y'know? Lookit . . ."

I looked. "Christ, Dago, that's not rain. Rain falls in drops. That's gotta be a fuckin' tidal wave."

"Monsoon."

"Call room service. Have 'em send over breakfast."

"Lines are dead. Christ, I'm losin' money every goddamn day it rains. Always a line dead somewhere." He picked up the AK, played with it for a minute, opened 'n' closed the breech. "Wanna sell it?"

"You want it . . . ? Take it."

"Y' sure? I mean, y' wanna trade for somethin'?
How y' fixed for dope? Want some? Y' ever do opium?
I got—"

"Dago, for Christ's sake, I don't want anything,
okay? A cup of coffee—how's that?"

"Coffee . . . ?"

"Coffee, opiate of the masses."

"Hawk, I wouldn't go out in that goddamn rain to
get y' plasma. Dope! Here, take this." He dug out a
baggie half full of grass. "Laos. Dudes tell me y' buy it
right on the street, y'know? Ten cents a *pound*. Jesus
and Mary, I'm always in the wrong place." He jumped
up. "Hey, motherfucker, almost f'got. Y' got a letter.
Where'd I put it." He started diggin' round in a desk,
throwin' numbers slips 'n' lottery cards seven ways
from Sunday.

"Can't be for me, Dago. I don't write to people.
Nobody knows where I am. Not even my parents."

"Naw, some chick, man. Nice handwritin', too."
He banged shut a coupla drawers, yanked open another. "Yeah, here's the humper." He tossed it to me.
"Who the fuck's Susan Dancer? Never heard y' rappin'
'bout a chick."

"That's the one I married in Vegas. Remember?"

"She actually wrote y'? Man, I'd burn that goddamn
letter, y' know? Don't even open it. She wants somethin'."

"Fuck off. Let's see what Susie-Q has to say." My
hands were shakin' a little. I hadn't really forgotten her,
but I didn't like to think about her. I wasn't sure I could
handle the thoughts. I wasn't even sure I could handle
this letter. "Listen, you got some C-4?"

"Yeah, man, but y' can just burn it, y' know? C-4's
a heavy trip for a letter."

"I want a fire for some coffee, asshole." I stuck a

canteen cup into the rain. It filled in about five seconds. I made a small ball of the white plastic explosive, put it on the floor between two pieces of scrap wood, set it on fire 'n' put the cup on top. Fffffzzzzz. Instant boilin' water. I made the coffee, stirred in some sugar 'n' poured everything in another cup that wasn't so goddamn hot. Dago paced up 'n' down the bunker, grumblin'. I opened the envelope 'n' pulled out three sheets of pale blue paper folded round a Mexican bank book and a voter registration card made out to me.

"What's she want, man? What's that book?"

I opened the bank book, and started laughin'. "Hey, you fuckin' Yankee money changer, how much is thirty-five million in Mex money?"

"Thirty-five *million*? There prob'ly ain't that many fuckin' pesos in Mexico." I threw him the book 'n' started readin' the letter. I hadn't managed to get through the first paragraph before he yelled, "Ha! I knew it. Y' didn't point off. It's only three million, five hundred thousand." He tossed the book back. "Nothin'."

"No shit. Thanks." I went back to the letter. The first time through I prob'ly didn't manage to get more'n maybe five percent of what she'd written. There wasn't anything really excitin' in what she said, but just havin' the letter excited me. She said she'd had a friend make the deposit with a phony voter registration card so I could get the money anytime I wanted it, without havin' to find her. She'd spent some time at her home in California. How was my friend, the senator's son? Would I at least let her know I'd gotten the bank book? Did I want anything from the States? She used to send her brother books 'n' turtles. Anything I wanted, let her know. What I wanted she couldn't send through the mail. My mind filled up with images of her 'n' me in bed. That was the biggest reason I'd avoided thinkin' of her in the first place. I read the letter three times, and still couldn't figure out why anyone would want a fuckin' turtle in this place. "Dago . . ." He grunted. "Listen, why in hell would anyone send a turtle to someone here?"

His goddamn eyes lit up. "Turtles? She sendin' y' turtles, man?"

"She offered. For Christ's sake, we got enough problems with pigs, snakes 'n' leeches. What the hell do I want with turtles?"

"Turtles, y' ignorant redneck fucker, are candy. Jesus, Joseph an' Mary, I'd give my left nut for a pound."

"Candy?"

"Candy, man. Chocolate 'n' pecan candy."

"Wha'th'fuck they call 'em turtles for?"

"How the hell do *I* know . . . why they call eatin' cunt cunnilingus?"

"Do they?"

"Christ, Hawk . . ." He shook his head like I'd made a bad bet. "What's with you 'n' her anyway? She really a hooker?"

"She says she is." I shrugged.

"Y' must be nuts. Y' can't trust hookers. Them motherfuckers'll take everything y' got."

"She had a chance to take twenty-eight thousand dollars."

"The gold-hearted whore. Christ, man, she's crazier than you are." He snorted in disgust. "But if she's really up front, get 'er to send y' five pounds of turtles."

"She'd prob'ly just steal the money, Dago. We'd never see the candy."

"Listen, Hawk, everybody likes a little ass, but nobody likes a wiseass, y' know? Anyway, they prob'ly got lousy turtles in Vegas."

"Prob'ly."

The rain had let up. It went from a deluge to a mere fuckin' downpour. I wrapped myself in a poncho 'n' went to get somethin' to eat before I had to face two hours in a hole that sure's hell was gonna be full o' water. I could hardly wait. Two hours of guard duty is like two hours in a dentist's office. You can only expect the worst. The best that can come of it is mild discomfort. Turned out mild enough. Physically, I mean. Otherwise, it sucked. I drew a kid named Hall for a partner. I knew him to see him, but hadn't spoken ten words to him the whole time we'd been in No Man's Nam. He was a black kid from Alabama, a dumb fuckin' sharecropper's son who'd volunteered for the Army 'cause nothin' could be as bad as what he came from. Then the Army surprised him with a set of orders to Nam and he found out there's always somethin' worse. He blamed it on his oldest brother. "Tha' fuckah, he alla time writin' back how it's a helluva life, the Army. Good food 'n' money to spend on whisky 'n' women, how these slope women, they don't give a shit wha' color you is. Shee-it! He ain't met none I met."

"Where's he stationed?"

"Hospital, Fort Ord. Dumb-ass nigger." He giggled, then told me about his brother, Sergeant Abraham L. Hall, a sniper with the 101st Airborne. "He the bestest shot in Little Crik, Alabama. Fuck, man, he hunt quails wif a *single* shot .22 an' 'e al'ays come back wif a messa birds. So the Army, they make 'im a sniper. Ol' Abraham he write back he a big man. Special gun 'n' ever-'thin'. He come 'ere struttin' like Mistah Charlie with a spankin' new gun 'n' sergeant's stripes. Shee-it." He shook his head, rueful-like, smilin' at somethin' he hadn't got to.

"What happened to 'im?"

"Well, fust off, he ding 'im a buncha slopes, *wham wham wham,* you know? Ain't nuffin' to it. They done give 'im a shiny medal 'n' all. So 'e git the big head, go out father 'n' father, lookin' foh mo' gooks. One day he out theah, maybe ten, twelve miles from base camp, sneakin' round, an' 'e see 'bout two hun'ert of 'em 'an they's lookin' foh *him.* He *know* it. So he lit out. But evahwheah 'e go they was theah. Ain't nuffin' t' do but try t' hide. So he clumb up a tree an' wait foh dark. But even when it git dark he can heah 'em, walkin' round, so 'e tie 'imself in de tree an' go t' sleep. Two, three times 'e wake up. Everythin's right quiet, so 'e go off back t' sleep." Hall lit a cigarette 'n' giggled again. "So, theah 'e is, sleepin' like 'e ain't got ta worry in a world, when this ol' monkey reach ovah an' grab Abraham by 'is toe. He shake it real good 'n' Abraham shit 'is pants. 'E ain't even awake 'fore 'e fire off a round—*Bam!* Dumb fuckah blowed off two toes."

Jesus Christ! I mean it's funny, in a way, but Hall thought it was hysterical. He couldn't stop laughin'. Wha'th'fuck, we'd all laughed like hell at Whipple when he'd shredded his ass doin' that John Wayne number. But for some reason I couldn't quite connect to the story. I started feelin' lonely. Maybe it was thinkin' about the ones that were gone. Whipple was still around but Poe 'n' Garcia were dead. Davis 'n' Jinx were out of it. 'Cept for Eric 'n' Dago I didn't really relate much to anyone. Mosta Kilo coulda been people in a bus station for all I cared. It wasn't so much that I disliked them as I didn't particularly give a fat rat's ass about 'em one way or another. And vice versa. There's this bullshit fairy tale about the Army as a great melting pot, and Army buddies. That's more a myth of the movies than a fact of life. It's all crap. If the Army's a meltin' pot, what you're left with is a sticky mass of humanity as isolated inside their own prejudices as ever. A nigger's a nigger after two years in the Army as certainly as a honkie's a honkie after two years. Or ten years. Which isn't to say that you don't form friendships, but no more or less than you would anywhere else. They're no better, no longer lastin' and prob'ly, as a general rule, the people are less intelligent than you'd meet in a business, or college. I think the thing is that once you've had the shit scared outa you while you were sharin' a hole with someone you're s'posed to forever after cling to that moment. That's the myth. But the fact of it is, generally, once you've shared that moment the last thing you want is to remember it. Or be reminded of it by somebody you'd prob'ly otherwise have considered an asshole. Maybe I'm wrong. Maybe it wasn't like that before, maybe it's only *this* goddamn stupid war. Or maybe it's just me 'n' my bad attitude.

Hall had kept on talkin' while I was broodin'. Nothin' he said caught my ear till he mentioned Jinx. "Ah reckon maybe ol' Jinx is prob'ly got the right idea. Git wif winners."

"Jinx is s'posed to be MIA," I said, with a straight face.

"Shee-it!" He snickered. "Ah don' 'spect eben you believe that."

Sometimes I amaze myself. With how fuckin' dumb I am. I don't know *why* I assumed nobody else knew about Jinx but Ski, Eric 'n' me. But I did. Christ, prob'ly everybody in Kilo knew. Maybe everybody in the whole goddamn Army. Poe'd told me once that Dago'd said there was a bounty on the heads of Americans who deserted to the VC. I hadn't thought much about it, one way or the other, since I didn't really believe Americans would do that. Sounded like more of Dago's bullshit. And Eric mentioned it. The next thing Hall said was, "Ah reckon somebody'll git 'im, though. Foh ten thousand, Ah'd be right tempted *my*sel'." He showed me a mouthful of fillin's. Reminded me of a creepy undertaker, skinny cocksucker. I think maybe he felt it. He shut up and we passed the next hour in silence. When the relief came I walked off in the rain. Even the fuckin' rain was better'n havin' to cope with what passed for people around here. 'Course, the biggest problem is where to go to get away from yourself. I never figured that one. Gettin' stoned helps, but it's never enough. Nor ballin', boozin', or bangin' your head into a wall. I've tried 'em all.

It stopped rainin' durin' the night. It had to stop sometime. I mean, nothin' lasts forever. But it havin' stopped meant we had to go lookin' for the colonel's phantom army of Indians. Ski came for Dago 'n' me at five fuckin' o'clock the next mornin'. No hollerin' or any of that happy horseshit. Just a quiet shake and a few words: "Y' got thirty minutes. Get ya gear an' eat."

I was dressed before I was awake, standin' over my pack wonderin' what the hell an up 'n' comin' idiot-child takes on a long-range recon patrol. I threw in some socks, a sweatshirt, my poncho 'n' four boxes of shotgun shells. Too goddamn heavy. The fuckin' shells musta weighed ten pounds by themselves. And I knew I had that freakin' radio to tote. I threw the pack on the bunk, stuffed the socks in my pockets, tied the poncho to my ammo belt and picked up my M-16. Piece of shit, but it's lightweight. I left Dago swearin' at the Virgin Mary 'n' went to the chow hall. The smell of breakfast— ground beef in tomato sauce on toast, better known as shit on a shingle—tempted me to keep walkin'. Nothin's too good for the condemned—so fuck 'em, give 'em nothin'. I had two cups of coffee and a bowl of Frosted Flakes.

Eric came in, turned up his nose 'n' settled for milk. He sat down across from me 'n' grinned. "You look unhappy."

"No shit. Is this anything to give a man when it may be his last meal?"

"Could be worse. Napoleon got arsenic."

"I'd settle for grits, ham 'n' red-eye gravy."

"How about eggs benedict?"

"Sounds like one of Dago's buddies. Joe Bananas and Eggs Benedict."

He smiled. "You ready to leave? Got everything you need?"

"I'm travelin' light. Do we have to do this? Couldn't you convince your old man that if we go lookin' for trouble we're prob'ly gonna find it?"

"I think he's counting on that. Major Early says they got agent reports last night that claim about two thousand NVA are moving around out there."

"Two *thousand?* Two fuckin' thousand slopes?! Jesus H. Christ, nobody in their right mind'd go lookin' for two thousand anything, 'cept maybe dollars." I drained off what was left of my second cup of coffee. "Look, Lef'tenant, if the assholes *know* they're out there, why're we goin'?"

"To make sure. Let's go."

"No, wait a minute, man. Whoa." But he didn't whoa worth a shit, just walked on, laughin'. Officers and lifers are the most hardheaded people in the goddamn Army. Swear t' Christ, you'd think this was s'posed to be a goddamn Easter egg hunt in the front yard. I followed him to his bunker. We picked up Dago on the way. Ski 'n' Suchow were there, with Early. Mighty Major spent about twenty minutes talkin' about map coordinates, call signs, other patrols in the general area—whatever the fuck that meant. The general area looked like about a hundred square miles to me. Pickup points, landin' zones. Ammo, food, water. Six canteens of water, two hundred rounds of ammo, a dozen pouches of dehydrated food, two claymores each. Grenades. Like a goddamn pack mule. Whoever the hell thought up the term Light Infantry musta been a goddamn general with three fuckin' Filipino flunkies. Sure's hell it wasn't a grunt. They ought to replace the trashy-ass chaplain corps with a sorta equipment weight-watcher's organization.

We rode to battalion headquarters in jeeps, right to the helicopter pad. Big deal. Like lettin' you skateboard yourself to the gas chamber. The colonel was there for a fond farewell with Eric. I was standin' next to the Boy Ranger since I had the radio. The colonel squinted at my name tag. "Morning, Hawkins."

"Mornin', Colonel." You sonofabitch.

"All set?" he asked Eric.

"Yes, sir."

"Good hunting."

"Thank you, sir. We'll be in touch."

Then, swear t' God, they saluted. No shit. I mean Jesus Christ, his own kid goin' out to maybe have his ass blown away and the motherfucker can't do any better'n salute. Kiss my Aunt Maggie's clit, I couldn't believe it. I've heard of rigid personalities, but he had perma-press emotions. I climbed in one of the choppers. Eric got in after me. Ski, Suchow 'n' Dago were on another. Nobody had replaced Davis so we were down to five. The crew chief strapped us in. The engine started. Everything vibrated. I started to sweat and felt sick. There we were, pilot, co-pilot, crew chief, Eric 'n' me—all pretendin' we were rational, right-thinkin' people, pretendin' this wasn't the ass-end of insanity, dressed up in our play clothes, carryin' plastic guns, about to fly backwards through maybe ten millenniums in a plastic whirlybird. But even that wouldn't have been so bad if I'd believed it was necessary. I don't think I'd ever felt lonelier in my sorry-ass life. Which musta shown. The crew chief dug into a canvas bag under his seat, pulled out an orange 'n' tossed it to me with his I-know-just-how-you-feel smile. I bit a plug out of the top 'n' started suckin'.

The ride didn't last long. Maybe twenty minutes. I think we flew around more'n we had to, rather than goin' straight to the landin' zone. That's s'posed to fool the Indians. Or so I heard. I knew the ride was over when the crew chief caught our eye 'n' jerked his thumb down. I unsnapped my seat belt, grabbed some overhead straps 'n' waited for my stomach to fly out my nose. The pilot was a dropout from the Acme School of Elevator Operators. Somehow the sonofabitch managed to stop three feet above the ground. Eric was out the door before my eyes would focus, hunched over 'n' runnin'. I took off after him, like some kinda goddamn lap dog chasin' his master. When he stopped at the edge of the LZ I almost ran over him. Before I could catch my breath Ski, Suchow and Dago were there. The two choppers were gone. The pit of my stomach expanded to a five-gallon hollow in which I'd have sworn some idiotic collection of corpuscles were shootin' marbles. I wished I had another orange. Or another option.

Eric whispered, "Let's move it." That was the last intelligent sound I remember for the next two or three hours. We spent that much time climbin'. Grunts 'n' groans, half-swallowed curses, moans and muttered prayers. By the time we stopped, everybody was scratched, cut 'n' bleedin'. I wouldn't have bet ten cents on our chances of holdin' off a determined attack by a dozen Little Leaguers. When we finally reached a sorta ledge-like clearin', maybe twenty-five hundred feet up, everybody stopped, without a word. Eric took the radio 'n' unfolded his map. I took three salt tablets and went to sleep sittin' up. That lasted about ten minutes. I woke up shiverin', sweat-soaked and convinced I was dreamin' all of it. That I had done it all before, and this was a nightmare rerun. Dago was asleep. Suchow was stretched out, his eyes open but starin' into the distance at nothin' I could see. Ski was behind us, at the top of the ridge, makin' sure nobody came up and surprised us from the other side. Eric leaned over 'n' whispered, "Sack out if you want to. We'll be here a while." I wrapped myself in my poncho and conked out.

I came to with Eric's hand over my mouth. I sat up 'n' looked around. Nothin' had changed. When I was more or less awake he whispered, "Go relieve Ski." I started to get up but he held me by the jacket front. "Crawl." I crawled. Ski handed me binoculars. "Over there," he said in a hoarse whisper. " 'Bout zero-five-zero. At the base of the hill. Six-man workin' party." I did some awkward mental calculations with the zero-five-zero shit—that's about halfway between dead ahead 'n' hard right. Sure's hell, there they were. Even with the glasses you couldn't make out exactly what they were up to. "Farmers?" I whispered. He snorted and crawled away.

The view was unbelievable, in a way. A *National Geographic* shot. The valley floor was fairly good size, maybe four or five miles across from the base of the hill we were on. It was green, spotted with rice paddies, a few little hamlets, surrounded by mountains on almost every side—except toward Kilo. If the Indians planned to move a big bunch of people toward our little pig farm, or the coast, or whatever, they'd have to come through here. Or someplace like it, some other openin'.

Supposedly, there were another ten or twelve recon patrols workin' the area, mostly north 'n' west of us. Beyond the valley were more hills, just as fuckin' thick with jungle as the one we were on. You could hide half of Caesar's legions in there and never know the difference. But I wouldn't want to go wanderin' around in there lookin' for 'em.

I was there, on my belly, for an hour or so, checkin' the work party—if that's what they were—gettin' hungry, waitin' for somethin' to happen, when I got the weirdest feelin' I was bein' watched. I looked behind me, but Eric was starin' through his glasses in another direction. Ski 'n' Suchow were huddled together, whisperin'. Dago was still asleep. I checked every direction. Nothin'. But even then the feelin' wouldn't go away. I put the glasses to my eyes, checked the valley floor, the tree lines on every hill, ridges. Nothin'. Then, more by accident than design, I saw him. Jinx. Him and six, seven, eight others. All slopes. They were makin' their way toward the hill we were on, along the edge of the floor just in range of the glasses. They'd walk ten or twelve meters 'n' stop. Walk a ways 'n' stop. He was lookin' right at me. Not that he could see me. No way. But it was stone weird. They were so far away I couldn't even really see his face clearly, but it was him. Sure's God made a mistake 'n' called it man. I counted again. Nine. Eight fuckin' slopes and one of God's chosen. Fuckin' incredible. The sonofabitch was actually out there, lookin' for us. They passed outa sight for a few minutes, hidden by the vegetation. I waited. And sweated. I didn't have the first fuckin' idea what to do. I knew what I prob'ly should do—call Eric over. But I didn't know what I wanted to do. Let him go? Go get him? How the fuck could I go get him? They couldn't see us, didn't have any more idea where we were than where we weren't. A stone fuckin' coincidence. Unless they start straight up at us, I decided, I ain't gonna get him killed to satisfy the US fuckin' Army.

The point man, then Jinx, came into view and stopped. Jinx, you poor bastard, is it any better down there? Prob'ly, I answered for him. Prob'ly. 'Cause you prob'ly think you got somethin' to fight for. Or against. And I couldn't care less about the goddamn VC. I'd be perfectly happy to go home and let 'em have this whole shithole country, lock, stock 'n' Lockheed. Or Colt. Or Dow Chemical. I focused the glasses again, back 'n' forth, tryin' to get a look at his face. I wanted to see for myself if he looked any different than when he was out wadin' with us. The distance was too much. I could see him clear enough to be certain it was him, to see him turn, watch his profile BS with a slope. Like lookin' at the movie in a drive-in as you whiz past on the highway. Then my heart skipped a beat 'n' went stone cold. Some goddamn dink who wasn't even big as me came up next to Jinx, wearin' a radio. In a flash I knew why they'd come walkin' this way, why Jinx kept lookin' up . . . and why I shoulda killed the motherfucker when I had the chance.

I twisted round and pisssst at Eric. Dago was still sleepin', but the others looked up. I made a motion— a patrol leader's signal to haul ass in a hurry—and I went over the lip of the ridge on my belly as fast as I could. Hopin' to hell they'd automatically do what I'd signaled. I heard the four of 'em behind me, gruntin', cussin', equipment bangin'. We made prob'ly two hundred meters before the first shell crashed behind us, short of where we'd been. There'd be a correction. We kept movin'. Four . . . five . . . six seconds. And a

whole goddamn salvo fell where we'd been. Then another, then another. We got up and started runnin', if
you could call it that, pickin' our way through the vines
'n' shit. Quarter mile, half a mile, most of it downhill,
or we might not have made it. I stopped and they sorta
ran into each other tryin' to keep from runnin' over me.
Nobody said a word. We were gaspin' for breath, lookin' at each other's bleedin' faces. Finally Ubanski,
who'd been glarin' at me, snarled, "Wha'th'fuck was
that all about?"

"Jinx."

"Why the hell didn't you say somethin'?"

"I was too goddamn busy tryin' to save your fuckin'
ass." Fuck him.

"Hawk?" Eric was studyin' me. "How long were
you watching him before you let us know?"

"I don't know. A while."

"Y' lit'le sonofabitch," Ubanski said, tryin' to
scream without makin' any noise, which only made his
face turn purple.

"Shut up, Ski," Eric said, offhandedly.

"Y' saved the little cocksucker's ass a hundred
fuckin' times. For what? So's 'e can get us lit up? Get
us all killed to save that goddamn nigger traitor, a
fuckin' deserter? For that?" He spit on the ground between us. "I'm puttin' y' on notice, Hawkins. I get a
chance, I'm gonna kill y'."

"Get in line, you self-righteous sonofabitch. There's
a lot of people ahead of you."

"Both of you, shut the fuck up. We got enough
problems without that bullshit. Ski, take Dago and go
back up the track. Suchow, go down, see what's there.
Move it." When they were gone, he looked at me,
kinda sad. "You satisfied?"

I shrugged. "Guess so."

"I told you . . ."

"I know you told me."

"I'm sorry Hawk. It's hard." He shrugged.

"How'd he get the fuckers to do that?"

"Wouldn't be hard. If he's got the frequency, he'd listen until we made a report, get our coordinates, call sign . . . probably was out there waiting when we came in. Saw the choppers. I doubt he knew it was us. Wouldn't matter."

"I'm a sonofabitch."

"No, I don't think so. He is. Maybe I am. You're more like a disbelieving child."

"Thanks. Can I go to my room now?"

"You can get your shit together. We still got a lot to do."

"What you gonna do about Jinx? You gonna radio somebody or somethin'?"

"No. Maybe we'll get a shot at him."

I didn't say anything. I'd already made up my mind I was gonna have to kill the sorry bastard myself. First chance I got. Which, I figured, would be if and when we got the fuck outa these goddamn hills.

Ski 'n' Dago came back. Ski didn't look quite as pissed. "They're back there. Makin' enough noise to wake Westmoreland. I set some claymores." I guess the prospect of fillin' Jinx full of ball bearin's eased his sense of outrage. We took off, down the hill, up 'n' down the next, to the top of another. It was almost dark by the time we got set up. I went into a coma, straightaway, as the fuckin' Limeys say.

Rain woke me the next mornin' at first light. I was tired. We'd each done two one-hour watches on the radio, doin' a check every half-hour. Eric had gone to another frequency. Maybe Jinx would find it, maybe he wouldn't. Four times in two hours I depressed the talk button on the phone and said, "Red Ryder, Little Beaver. Over."

"Roger, Little Beaver."

"Check in."

"Red Ryder out."

No shit. Red Ryder 'n' Little Beaver. Comic book heroes. That give you any idea of where people's heads are at? The second day was mostly like the first, 'cept nobody tried to blow us away. Walk a while, sit a while. I haven't got the faintest idea how much ground we covered. Since it was mostly up 'n' down, up 'n' down, it couldn't have been much on a straight-line basis. The rain stopped 'n' started. I'd gotten so I didn't really mind. At least it was cool. By afternoon we'd set up for the night, made mush outa some dry food 'n' I went to sleep. Sometime after my second watch, which was three to four a.m., I woke with Eric's hand over my mouth. I thought I was prob'ly snorin', but he whispered in my ear, "There's about two hundred Cong on top of us. Don't even breathe hard." It was so goddamn dark I could barely see him. But I could hear *them*. Talkin', movin' slow. They couldna been more'n twenty feet away, movin' past us. We were in a tight circle. I don't know what anybody else was doin' but I was shiverin' and shakin'. If I hadn't kept my teeth jammed together they'd have sounded like chestnuts in a tin tub. I had to piss, really bad. One of the Indians stumbled and crashed into a tangle of vines, cussin'. Somebody else hit a light for a coupla seconds. I thought I'd die of heart failure. Very slowly, very quietly, I pissed, right into my pants leg. That has to be the goddamnedest feelin' I ever had. Warm water rushin' into my crotch, soakin' my leg, which was already damp from the rain. It felt good, and the relief was beyond describin'.

I'd barely finished when I felt Eric's breath in my ear. "Take this line"—he put a piece of quarter-inch rope in my hand—"When I tug start crawlin'. Slow." I got the radio on my back, my rifle in my hand and waited. The line of VC was still movin', stumblin' 'n' cussin'. The only chance we had as far as I could see was if they kept fuckin' round like that, makin' more noise than we did. I felt a tug 'n' started to crawl, one careful fuckin' inch at a time. I couldn't see Eric. I assumed he was in front of me. God, how I wished it would start rainin', a goddamn downpour, with thunder. No lightnin', Jesus Christ, anything but that. We crawled, maybe a half-foot at a time, for what seemed like forever. I don't know how many times that goddamn radio got caught in a tangle of vines, or how many times I cut myself on thorns. I twisted 'n' turned, slidin' on my belly, scared to death I'd get bitten by a freakin' snake or bang my rifle into a tree. Ten, fifteen, twenty minutes, then we stopped. Eric pulled the receiver off the radio and started talkin'. A minute, no more, and a shell crashed into the earth where we'd been, too fuckin' close for me. I could hear the shrapnel tearin' through the trees over our heads. He sent in a correction and called for a salvo. Four screamin' shells roared in over our heads, then four more, then four more. All high-explosive fireballs. He spoke again, and again, workin' the artillery up 'n' down, back 'n' forth. We were huggin' the wet earth. I was prayin'. I don't know who to, or what for, but I did some talkin'. When I thought there prob'ly wasn't another fuckin' shell left in No Man's Nam, he slammed the receiver back and hissed, "Let's get the fuck out of here." We took off at somethin' between a walk and a trot. It was a little lighter, comin' up on dawn. Gray 'n' misty.

About forty-five minutes later we came to a river, and dropped at the edge. After they caught their breath, Ski went one way along the river bank, Suchow the other. Dago started heavin'. You ever try to throw up quietly? He finally fell forward, on his face, and lay there like a beached fish. I opened a canteen 'n' poured some water over his head. He rolled over, on his back, and stared up at me. His face was as pale as the Devil's promise of righteousness, poor sick-lookin' sonofabitch. Though, to tell the truth, none of us looked too good. Suchow came back first and offered an empty hand. Nothin'. Few minutes later Ski came up with a big smile. "An ol' fucker's down there with a raft."

"One man?" Ski nodded. Eric got out his map 'n' started computin', or whatever you do when you're lost so fuckin' far from home. 'Cept he didn't seem lost. Just off course. Anyway, he musta figured out somethin' 'cause he was reachin' for the phone when we all heard a slope patrol, yakkin' 'n' laughin' off to the left. The goddamn place was crawlin' with the slanty-eyed cocksuckers. We went, belly first, into the water 'n' started easin' upstream, in the direction of the raft Ski'd found. I hadn't made it ten steps when it hit me—Dago's vomit. Christ, they'd smell it from fifty meters. I'd stopped, unconsciously, and Ski bumped into me. "Move it, Hawkins."

"Take the radio." I was shruggin' out of it while I was whisperin'. I'll give him this—he took it without a question. I went back, tryin' to hurry without makin' noise. Neat fuckin' trick, that is. Over the bank. I crawled to the smelly little pile. The voices were louder, an occasional laugh soundin' like it wasn't five feet away. I was in a near panic, tryin' to mash it into the mud. I musta looked like a cat coverin' shit. It wouldn't work, so I ripped open my jacket and scooped puke, mud 'n' God knows what else into the openin'. Jesus! At least they wouldn't smell it, if I could get back in the goddamn river. I backed away, still on my belly, tryin' to cover my tracks. My lunatic friends were hidden behind some undergrowth at the river's edge about fifteen meters from where we had first gone into the water. And there we waited, up to our necks in that stinkin' swill, kneelin' like candidates for baptism. Ten seconds, twenty seconds, a minute. I pissed again. And prayed some more. To this day, I don't know how many passed. Six, maybe seven. Maybe a dozen, but it didn't sound like it. Christ, you'd think they thought they owned the whole freakin' country. In a way it was good, hearin' them amblin' along, yakkin' 'n' fuckin' off. Made them seem a helluva lot less perfect. Like those assholes playin' frisby in the river right after we first got to Nam. God, that seemed so long ago. The idea that the North Vietnamese have the best light infantry in the world is valid, I think. They sure's hell have had the most practice lately. But what pleased me was the realization that the best wasn't based on the idea of perfection—just on who made the fewest fuckups. Could be that's generally true. We don't actually make better shoes or produce better cars than you—we just fuck up fewer in the process.

They passed and I almost busted out laughin'. My mind's-eye again. All I could see was the five of us playin' some weird game of hide 'n' seek, for the ultimate prize. If life's the ultimate. Never havin' been dead, I don't know. I mean I'm gettin' to the place where I question everything. I bit the index finger of my right hand, almost to the point of bleedin', to keep from gigglin' out loud. I was close to snappin' altogether. Pure panic was hangin' off to one side, like a goddamn thunderstorm, waitin' to move in and rain all over me. "I'm definitely not made for this cloak 'n' dagger shit," I whispered to Eric. He 'n' Ski were watchin' me like a couple of headshrinkers studying a potential basket case. Eric shook his head, as if to say no shit, what tipped you off? What he actually said was, "What in God's name were you doing up on the bank?"

"Scrapin' up Dago's vomit."

"I'll be goddamned," Ski sighed.

Eric grinned. "You amaze me sometimes, Hawk. What the hell ever made you think of that?"

"Because I don't want to die out here, you silly sonofabitch. Because I'm scared half to death. Because I don't even know why in hell we're out here, five fuckin' people against five thousand pissed-off pig fuckers, for Christ's sake."

"Damn, he sounds like a real soldier," Ski snorted, but a with a touch of disbelievin' admiration.

Terrific. That's all I need. Now I'm a fuckin' soldier. Next to bein' a goddamn martyr I couldn't immediately think of anything less impressive. I'm not even sure there's a helluva lot of difference. And mind you, all that crap was in whispers. I mean, I wanted to scream. Shit! If Hitler had been restricted to whispering there'd prob'ly never have been a Second World War. Fuck me. "Fuck you," I whispered.

"Let's go borrow a boat," Eric said. We sneaked along, still in the water, until we came to where the raft was tied up. The owner, an old man, was sittin' on the bank, workin' on a small seine. He was actually smilin' while he worked. A really fine-lookin' dude, maybe sixty or seventy, as happy as a pig in shit. I *knew* that was one dude who was absolutely unaffected by the war, at least emotionally. He coulda cared less about VC, GI, NVA, CIA, DOD, MACV, NLF or any other philosophy compressed into two 'n' three letter symbols. I loved him. Immediately. Which was good, since Dago killed him about two minutes later. Not willingly, but just as certainly. We watched papa-san mendin' his net for a few seconds. There wasn't any way to sneak up on him. If we shot him there'd be a hundred Indians to answer the call. If we didn't he prob'ly be a mite pissed about us takin' his raft, which would also tend to attract attention. So Eric pulled a thin-bladed knife outa his boot top and handed it to Dago. Dago went white, just blanched out like a nervous virgin. He managed a strangled "Wha? Listen—"

Eric snapped, "I've seen what you can do with a knife."

"Targets, man. Just targets, y' know? I never, y' know, like actually *killed* anybody with one. I mean I never even shot anybody before. Christ, I can't . . ."

"Nice and clean. If he screams we're probably all going to die here."

"Christ, Lieutenant, gimme a break."

"Come on, Dago. We haven't got all day. That patrol can come back any minute."

Dago's hands were shakin' like a spade tryin' to cash a check in a Mississippi bank. Twice he raised the knife and twice he lowered his arm. Then, seemingly without even thinkin', he let it fly. The ol' man's eyes popped open. Surprise. They rolled back in his head 'n' that was the end of him. Eric, Ski 'n' Suchow were outa the river before the ol' man rolled on his side. Dead.

Dago looked at me. "I'm gonna puke again." He didn't. He gagged a coupla times. Quietly. Then we got on the raft with the others. Ski took the pole steerin' thing in the back. If you wiggled it right the raft went in a fairly straight line. The current did mosta the work. Takin' us downriver. I stretched out on my back, watchin' Ski, wonderin' where the fuck he'd learned to operate a raft pole—I still don't know the right name for the goddamn thing. Dago was sittin' with his knees drawn up, his head restin' on his knees, still pale and prob'ly stone fuckin' weirded out. Suchow was squattin' next to Eric. They were studyin' the map. It struck me, for some dumb reason, that I didn't know diddly-shit about Suchow. Except he was a lifer and had been in No Man's Nam once before. He never fuckin' talked, least not in my presence. Maybe he talked to himself or somethin'. I studied him. He had a weddin' band, so I assumed he was married. He was prob'ly twenty-four, twenty-five. He was close to six feet, about a hundred 'n' eighty pounds, short sandy hair, brown eyes and a scar on his neck, a long, ugly crooked one that ran from the bottom of his right ear down to where his neck wrinkled when he tipped his head forward. So much for that great American myth about how close you get with your foxhole buddies. I didn't even know his first name.

Eric looked up from the map, at Dago, then at me.

"What freakin' river is this?" I asked.

"The River Styx. S-t-y-x, like sticks," he grinned. "The river of Hell, in Dante's Inferno. The Vietnamese call it Bang Mot."

"Terrific. Now I'm goin' to hell in a very large handbasket. I assume downriver means we're gettin' deeper 'n' deeper into trouble."

"Probably."

"Well, wake me when we get to the Hall of Idiots; I want to say hi to all the motherfuckers who run this war." I closed my eyes. Fuck you, Lef'tenant. Helluva thing when the goddamn officers get to be wiseasses.

In a lot less time than I had hoped for we slipped up to the riverbank, prob'ly not more'n two or three miles from where we started. Back to humpin' it. Ski unwrapped the poncho from around the radio. The sonofabitch was a lot drier than I was. I strapped it on. Me 'n' Christ with our fuckin' crosses. Off we went, up a hill, down a hill, up a hill, down a hill. Two, three, four hours. Up 'n' down, walk 'n' rest. Finally we quit, exhausted, sweat-soaked and starvin'. Eric got on the radio with battalion headquarters, then an artillery fire base. When he got off I asked him if we were covered. "Barely. Long as we don't have to run the wrong way."

"Wonderful. How many of these little slope-headed bastards we gotta find before we can go back?"

"Another thousand or two. That should do it."

"Or us."

"Or us."

"Look, why don't we hang around another hour or so, then call in about two hundred rounds on a nice hillside, tell the silly bastards we just blew away a coupla thousand and go home."

"Would you do that?"

"You think there aren't people doin' it? You think all those fuckin' body counts are for real? Shit, I'd swear we lit up ten thousand if you want. It doesn't matter, anyway. Not really. We're gonna get out of Nam soon as all the assholes can agree on how to make it look good for us. You know it, I know it, *they* know it. So why go on shittin' each other. Why die out here for nothin'?"

"It isn't for nothing, Hawk."

"Then what the hell's it for? So captains can make major, and colonels can make general? So the fuckin' manufacturers can field test their goddamn weapons? Tacticians can play with us instead of those little wooden do-dads?"

"Hawk, shut up! You don't know what you're talking about. What we're doing out here is a lot more important than the individuals involved."

"Like what?"

"Trying to save the US Army. It's falling apart. If it was just Vietnam, I'd say screw it. But this isn't the only war we're going to have to fight. Not so long as people are what they are. The Army's got to survive and this goddamn war is destroying it."

I sighed. Ain't no way to reason with a saint.

"You plannin' to save it by yourself?"

"If I have to."

"Good luck." Shit! "Listen, I think you're crazy. But as long as I'm hangin' round, you want some help?"

"Keep humping that radio"—he gave me his goofy smile—"and stay out of trouble for a while. I think I've about used up most of the reasons why you shouldn't be summarily shot."

Pure Hollywood melodrama, right? There we were, whisperin' to each other like lovers. The thing is, I liked the dumb bastard. And if he wanted to try savin' the sorry-ass Army, then fuck it, let him try. But I didn't really think he could do it. And less than two hours later I knew goddamn well he couldn't. 'Cause he was dead.

We'd been spread out on a hillside, thick with some kinda strange grass that grew about knee high in places, waist high in others. Ski, Suchow 'n' Dago were up behind us, horizontal. Eric 'n' I were watchin' a rinky-dink valley maybe a quarter-mile away, where it opened out between some knobby little hills, then bent round runnin' at a right angle to us. It was gettin' late, close to five in the afternoon. The light was already startin' to go, just a little. We saw 'em at the same time.

"Mother of God," I breathed.

Three abreast, trottin', pushin' bicycles, luggin' packs the size of hundred-pound flour sacks, mixed in with all kinds of slope grunts. They kept comin', row after row of 'em, out the bottleneck, into the openin' between the hills. Eric almost ripped the phone off the radio and started yellin' into it. Prob'ly wasn't yellin', exactly, but after three days of whisperin' a normal tone sounded like the voice of Judgment. I was only half listenin'. The numbers didn't mean shit to me. Coordinates. Coulda been stock prices for all I knew or cared. Then I heard him say, "Major, I haven't got time to count them . . . Christ!" He said to me, "How many would you guess?"

"A thousand, at least. Who the fuck wants to count?"

"Early." He went back to the phone.

What the fuck was Early doin' monitorin' our calls, I wondered. But I didn't get a chance to pursue it. Behind us Ski, Suchow 'n' Dago opened up. The shit hit the fan. I turned to see at least twenty Vietnamese movin' down the slope toward us, firin' on full automatic. I guess it woulda been our ass right there, but two of 'em tripped claymores. That thinned 'em out. Ski'd saved our asses again. One of 'em stood up to throw a grenade. I emptied a clip in his direction. He went ass over elbows and the grenade went off under his feet. Dago came snakin' down the hill on his belly. Suchow came right after him. They stopped about twenty meters from us, facin' back up the slope. Ski got up to run. A round caught him high up in the left arm, spun him around and he went backwards on his ass.

"Ski's hit," I yelled at Eric.

"Take this—" He pushed the phone into my hand and started up the hill, firin' single rounds. Dago 'n' Suchow were pourin' it on but I couldn't see wha'th-'fuck they were firin' at. Then the first round from the 175s screamed in, about three hundred meters short of the line of dinks. I panicked. I didn't know which way to correct. If I called for the wrong correction we'd get *our* asses splattered. "Right three hundred!" Eric screamed.

"Right three hundred, fire for effect," I screamed.

"Who's this?" Early yelled into the phone.

"Little Beaver, Little Beaver. Christ, they're all over the goddamn place. Fire, you sonofabitch! Fire!"

Four rounds came, right into the bottleneck, then four more. "Down fifty, Hawk . . ."

"Down fifty, down fifty, battery fire . . . tear their fuckin' ass."

"Little Beaver, keep your head, keep your head—"

I twisted around. Eric was draggin' Ski down the hill. More rounds were comin' at us from what was left of the patrol above us. Then more rounds from the 175s. I didn't know which way to turn. Eric yelled, "Work 'em up and down, Hawk. Keep making corrections . . . you can do it. Watch the valley, we'll take care of this. . ."

The valley was a mass of human sufferin'; smashed bodies, busted bags, bicycle parts . . . I was almost flat on my back, watchin' it through the glasses, my fingers wrapped so tight around the phone that my hand cramped.

"WP, Hawk! Hit 'em with WP!"

"Gimme fuckin' Willie Peter," I screamed at some poor bastard sittin' on the phones at the fire base. White phosphorus came screamin' down, burning everything it touched, searin' holes in human flesh that had never known pain like that.

"Correct, Hawk . . . work 'em up and down. Right fifty, left fifty . . ."

"Red Ryder, right fifty, right fifty . . . keep firin', you bastards . . ."

"What's your status, Little Beaver?"

"One hit . . . the cocksuckers are behind us . . ." I was starin' through the glasses the whole time, and I saw about fifty of 'em break away from the shattered columns on a dead run, headin' toward us. "They're comin' for us! We're gonna get bottled up . . . correct left, battery fire Willie Peter fire fire fire goddamn you fire . . ." I musta been screamin' at the top of my lungs but I could hardly hear myself.

Four, eight, twelve rounds smashed into the valley, close to the bastards comin' for us, but not close enough. Maybe a dozen went down. "H 'n' E, H 'n' E, correct left fifty . . . fire fire fire!" More of 'em went down . . . and still they kept comin', at the bottom of the hill. "Eric! Christ, goddamn, they're comin' up the fuckin' hill . . ."

"I'm runnin' outa ammo, Lieutenant . . ." That was Dago, I think. Suchow was steadily firin', single rounds *pop pop pop*, never sayin' a goddamn word. Somehow Eric had managed to get a bandage on Ski, who was on his belly, slow-firin'. Vaguely, off in the distance, somewhere, I heard Early yellin', "Little Beaver, can we get a chopper in there? Little Beaver . . ."

"Fuck no!" That much I knew. How the hell we'd get out I didn't know. Eric slid to a stop by me and grabbed the phone.

"Correct left one hundred, battery fire and keep firing. We're getting the hell out of here. Little Beaver, out!" He yelled at the others. "Let's go, let's go, move it." He threw a grenade up the hill. "Full automatic . . . Dago, get your goddamn ass moving . . . Suchow, move it, move it." Dago stood up 'n' took two or three rounds through the chest. He hit the ground hard 'n' didn't move. "Goddamn it!" Eric screamed, startin' toward Dago's body. The 175s were comin' steadily up the hill, gettin' closer, but keepin' the gooks' relief pinned down. Then an H 'n' E round came in less than two hundred meters downhill from us. Eric stopped in mid-stride.

"Get out, get out . . . the sonofabitch is shelling us. Di di, go go go."

Ski, his left arm draggin' at his side, and Suchow ran past me, away from Eric, both of'em hunched over, prob'ly expectin' a bullet in the back at any moment. I was kneelin', firin' automatic, load'n'fire, load'n'fire, tryin' to keep an eye on Eric. He'd gone to Dago, but Dago was dead. Eric came back, runnin', screamin', "Let's go . . . let's go." Two more rounds fell, closer, maybe a hundred meters. There was screamin' metal in the air all around our heads. We ran like crazy men. Suchow 'n' Ski, step for step, maybe fifty meters in front, then me, half a step in front of Eric. I didn't see what hit him, or when. Prob'ly shrapnel. Two more rounds came in, almost on top of us. Had to be shrapnel, to do what it did. All I know is I heard him hit the ground. His head was gone. Separated. Sliced right off, like a goddamn guillotine blade had done him in. I froze. The fuckin' shells were fallin' round us like a prophet's threats of Hell. I yelled for Ski, twice. He didn't hear. Or didn't want to hear. I don't know. I heard a freight train scream and came up ten or fifteen feet from where I'd been standin'. I still wasn't hit, but my head had stopped functionin'. I rolled on my stomach 'n' looked for Eric. He hadn't moved. Another train roared past, then another 'n' another, blindly punchin' holes in the earth, throwin' up fireballs 'n' earth clods like skid row drunks pukin' up Christmas dinner. Shock waves from the explosions mashed me into the mud. What was left of my mind screamed *move!* Move move move! Reflex dragged me up, drove me across the open ground. I grabbed Eric by the pack straps, dragged him across the ground, over the side of a shell hole. Sweet mother of God . . . why why, what in the name of God am I goin' to do . . . a headless body . . . I'm gonna be sick. IT'S NOTHIN', JESUS, GOD, it's not him, it's only a body. Sweat was rollin' off me, fear's sweat, stinkin' wet fear, oh God, save my sorry ass. Shells fell in twos 'n' fours all around us, so nobody could come for us, but we couldn't go anywhere . . . oh God, what am I gonna do with a headless body, it's nobody, nothin' . . . I've got to move, now *now*. C'mon, man, move it!

I cut off his pack, unsnapped his ammo belt, frantic, desperate, muttering, goddamn, goddamn you, you sonofabitch, you didn't have to die, you left me here in this fuckin' place alone. I was cryin'.

When I tried to get to my knees it hit me that I was still carryin' the radio. I ripped it off. Stupid piece of shit. Fuckin' junk, kick your fuckin' insides to pieces . . . I kicked 'n' kicked, but it had already been smashed. Two chunks of jagged metal were stuck in its face. I looked around for my rifle, still frantic, still full of fear. Slowly it dawned on me that I'd lost it somewhere. Eric's was gone. Christ! No fuckin' weapon, twenty miles from nowhere. It coulda been two hundred for all I knew. I didn't have the first idea of how to get out of there, or how to get back if I did. The 175s had turned back, down the hill. I grabbed Eric's body, up 'n' over my shoulder . . . I couldn't leave him. Stupid. Goddamn stupid bastard. I managed to get up, balanced, expectin' to be shot and not carin'. It didn't matter anymore. One more death just didn't matter. Not even mine. Out of the hole, up the hill. It was almost dark. I didn't look back. Fuck it. There wasn't anything to look back on.

I don't know how long we stumbled around like that. It got darker, started to rain. There wasn't sign one of Ski or Suchow. I stopped when I couldn't walk any farther, then walked farther when I could. Until it didn't make any sense to even try. We lay down for the night, without any attempt to hide. I'd gotten used to Eric. He wasn't any different from the radio. I picked him up, put him down, cussed him, dropped him, and wished to hell I'd never seen him. But I couldn't leave him out there. He wouldn't have left me and he was countin' on me not to leave him. When we finally couldn't go any further, we slept together. It was rainin' when we stopped for the night, rainin' when we got up in the morning. It didn't matter. Every kind of misery has its limits, and I'd found the ass-end of this kind.

At some point the next mornin', after we'd trudged for four 'r five hours at least, we came to the river. It was an accident. I was so freaked out I couldn't have purposely found my ass with both hands. I remember sayin', "And I don't suppose you can swim worth a shit, either . . . right?" It took an hour to find the raft. That was an accident, too. Once we were on it there wasn't any choice to be made. We went with the current. I couldn't use the pole like Ski had, so we went from bank to bank, mostly. Everytime we'd get stuck in the mud of one I'd go over the side, pull 'n' push, kick 'n' cuss, till it was free. Then we'd go off again, usually into another bank at the next turn. I was covered in slime, and leeches, but I didn't bother tryin' to get 'em off. A few leeches didn't seem like much of a problem.

We floated, drifted, ran aground, floated . . . I didn't have any idea of where we were goin'. I hadn't bothered with the map. I thought Eric would be with me, no matter what. He was, but not in quite the way I'd seen it. The River Styx . . . it ran through my head like a goddamn jingle . . . You've got a lot to live, and Pepsi's got a lot to give . . . the Pepsi Generation. Throwaway people . . . over 'n' over 'n' over, until I heard the chopper, up high 'n' movin' fast. I was wearin' the old dude's hat . . . Christ only knows how it had managed the trip . . . and maybe I really did look like a goddamn gook, and Eric like a sack of rice or a bag of ammo, or whatever tempts chopper pilots to shoot up river rafts. They came in low 'n' fast, firin' those god-awful nose-guns, chewin' up everything. I went over the side, screamin' at the sonofabitch, but he couldn't have heard me if I'd been God's goodwill ambassador, let alone a half-crazed grunt exhausted from bein' shot at more by his own people than the fuckin' dinks. The chopper came around in a tight-ass turn, raisin' hell, throwin' bullets 'n' sprayin' river water from Hell to Texas. From somewhere I got the only idea possible to save us—I stripped off my clothes, rippin', tearin', swallowin' water 'n' chokin', spittin' 'n' gaggin', until I was bare-assed. I swam to the raft 'n' climbed up. Not even that gun-happy, nearsighted sonofabitch could mistake my flashy white ass for a Cong. I mooned him, right in the middle of his fourth pass. Or maybe he wasn't makin' another pass. At least he wasn't firin' or I wouldna lasted long enough to get out of the water. At any rate, he didn't wreck his whirlybird, and managed to hover over what was left of the wrecked bundle of bamboo, while I boosted Eric up through the door, then scrambled after him. We had climbed to about three thousand feet and were flyin' away before the crew chief managed to make his mouth work. In pure desperation he finally got it together enough to ask, "Who the fuck are you?"

"Little Beaver . . . take us to Red Ryder."

He said somethin' to his microphone. The chopper changed course. Ten minutes later it settled on the landin' pad at battalion headquarters.

When I was out of the chopper with Eric in my arms, the pilot waited only until I was clear of the whirrin' blades before he lifted off and was gone. It was late afternoon. I started walkin' toward the cluster of tents 'n' buildin's, past people who stopped whatever they were doin' to stare with open mouth 'n' disbelievin' eyes. I knew they were there, but I didn't see 'em. I was lookin' for the colonel. For some reason I still don't understand, I'd decided it was important that I bring Eric directly to his father. And I had no idea of where to find him. As it turned out, he found me. The colonel, Major Early, another major, and a coupla captains. We stopped maybe ten meters apart. They were as disbelievin' as everybody else. I was so tired I couldn't go any farther. I clung to Eric 'n' waited.

To them I musta looked like the end of their world, the ultimate insult—a bare-assed buck private holdin' a headless body without even a free arm to salute. So this is it, this is what our army has come to, from Valley Forge to Vietnam, two hundred years of tradition to produce a madman. I don't know. Maybe they were just pissed that I hadn't had the decency to get myself killed.

"Get this man clothes. And a medic!" the colonel yelled. A dozen people ran frantically in six different directions. The colonel came forward, by himself, closed the distance between us until we were no more'n five or six feet apart. He stopped, finally, starin' at me. "Who are you?"

"Little Beaver, Colonel. I'm lookin' for Red Ryder."

He shuddered. "Hawkins . . . ?"

"I've brought Eric, Colonel. He's dead."

I put Eric's body on the ground and stood up. Still the bastard's face hadn't cracked, or even frayed around the edges.

"What happened?"

"What happened? No shit, wha'th'fuck do you think happened? Jesus H. Christ! We found the fuckin' Indians, that's what happened. Then Major Early tried to kill us is what happened."

"Major Early was under the impression that you were being overrun. He tried to save you."

"I think we mighta done better if he'd tried to save the fuckin' slopes."

A buncha people ran up 'n' stopped outside the confrontation area, unsure what to do.

"Cover the body," the colonel said. "Come with me, Hawkins."

Somebody tossed me a poncho and I followed the colonel to his tent. It was dark inside. He snapped on a light.

"Sit down."

"I'd rather stand."

He shrugged, opened a desk drawer 'n' pulled out an envelope. It was open, but you could see it had been sealed at one time. "My son apparently thought very highly of you, Hawkins."

"An obvious failure of the system."

"Hawkins, let's not forget, regardless of the circumstances, that you are a private and I am a colonel."

"Colonel, you also ought not forget that you are the biggest jerkoff I've ever seen."

"Hawkins, I'll have you court-martialed."

"For what? Insubordination? Shit! Listen, you just wait a coupla days 'n' you can get me for murder. Lot easier to prove. I'll even bring you the body if you want."

"Exactly who, Private, do you intend to murder?"

"A sonofabitch. A couple of 'em. One's named Jinx—"

He sighed. "Ah, yes. Jinx." He actually looked like he might be interested.

"And the other's that sorry motherfuckin' major out there, named Early."

"You're tired, Hawkins. I'll have someone drive you to the battalion aid station." He looked down at the envelope, then pushed it at me. "This is for you. I opened it in error. I thought you were dead, too." He shrugged. "I'm sorry."

I took the envelope and looked at my name on the front like I'd never seen it before. I remember vaguely wonderin' if when the colonel had said he was sorry he meant sorry he'd opened the letter or sorry I wasn't dead. I spent an hour in the aid station, with people askin' me stupid questions and shootin' me full of whatever. Then a corpsman drove me back to Kilo. I went straight to the bunker without seein' anyone. It was completely dark now, so it wasn't hard. I walked in to find two fuckin' kids I barely knew sittin' on my bunk, drinkin' Dago's German beer, listenin' to a tape of Leon Russell.

"Wha'th'fuck are you doin' here?"

"Hawkins . . . ? Man, you're supposed to be dead. Sergeant Suchow said Dago, you 'n' the lieutenant got lit up."

"I'm sure's hell sorry to disappoint you, but I'm not quite dead, so haul your fuckin' ass outa here."

"Hey, man, wait a minute, okay? Will you wait a

fuckin' minute . . . ?"

The Greener was standin' next to the wall inside the door. I picked it up. "You two jerkoffs got ten seconds . . . one . . . two . . . three . . ." They started grabbin' their shit. The one, Madison, a skinny kid from Oklahoma I'd heard BS'in' in the chow hall, about his daddy's hog farm 'n' how he could run this place better'n anybody around, got really PO'ed.

"You got no right . . ."

I laid back the hammers on the shotgun. "You got the right to move in? That right? The fuckin' bodies ain't fuckin' cold and you come waltzin' in . . ." They were gone. My hands were shakin'. I ripped off the poncho 'n' laid down. I remember thinkin', so Ski made it. Then I slept.

The next day I spent mostly in the bunker. Suchow came by for a few minutes, to say Ski was gonna be okay. He was in the hospital with a fucked-up arm, and would be evaced out soon. Suchow hadn't got a scratch. He started to tell me how they got out, but I told him I didn't give a shit, I just wanted to be left alone. Jefferson 'n' Whipple came by, stood around for a few minutes 'n' left. Nobody else came. Prob'ly the word was I was crazy as hell, stay away. I drank coffee, smoked 'n' tried to decide when to go get Jinx. I figured I had one shot at it and I didn't want to waste it. Early would be easy. Just frag him one night. Coupla grenades in his tent. Goodbye.

It was late afternoon before I got to Eric's letter. I pulled the paper out.

Hawk—this is just in case I don't make it. Take care of yourself. Keep struggling. Don't let the bastards wear you down. And whatever happened to bring this about—forget it as soon as you can. Go on with your life.

He signed it "The Boy Ranger." I hadn't even known he knew I called him that. I read it again, but it wasn't real, or it was too real. I opened the envelope to put the letter back 'n' saw the medal on the gold chain he always wore, the star. It was months later before I found out what a Star of David is.

Late in the afternoon I went to the battalion machine shop 'n' laid the Greener on a counter in front of a bored-lookin' corporal. "Can you shorten the barrels?"

"Yeah? How short you want 'em?"

"Eighteen inches. And cut about four inches off the stock."

"It's a nice-lookin' piece. Sure you wanna fuck it up like that?"

"I'm sure." He shrugged 'n' disappeared into a back room. A few minutes later he brought it back. "Listen, do me a favor, drill a hole through the stock, at the butt, on top. Okay?"

"Sure."

When he'd finished I went back to the bunker 'n' made a sling outa heavy cord, tyin' one end to the butt, through the hole he'd drilled, the other end around the shortened barrels. Short barrels would make it less accurate, but I figured to transact my business at very short fuckin' range. The only question was when.

Somebody else made the decision for me. Maybe Jinx. Maybe some slope bright-boy tactician. I suspect the business with the hogs was Jinx. It was the kinda thing he'd think was fittin' and funny. I could see him sittin' back there in that hut with his goddamn electric blender 'n' GE toaster, perkin' a pot of coffee, laughin' like hell. Whoever was responsible for it at least had a sense of human life value if not a sense of humor. What they did, come first light the followin' morning, was drive a herd of hogs through the mine fields. Swear t' Christ, you never heard such oinkin' and hell-raisin' in your life. I'd been awake since about four a.m., smokin'—chain smokin', actually—tryin' to decide when to go for Jinx. Or more likely, tryin' t' decide if I had the balls to walk back into that hamlet and hunt him down. I mighta sat there all day, given a choice. But some crazy fuckin' slope changed the whole thing around. First I knew of him, or them, was this weird sound—fuckin' Vietnamese yellin' "Sooooeee . . . soooeee pig pig, soooeeeee pig."

Now, it's a fact, sure's Christ made crab apples, that there ain't hardly a damn Yankee that can call pigs like that 'n' make it sound good. But a fuckin' slope with that nasal sing-song way of talkin' they got just ain't got the right kinda voice. I mean, I can't yodel, and Uncle Ho's children can't soooeeeee pigs. Plain as day. But they tried, and what with some switchin' and random gunshots they drove about three dozen hogs right through the wire 'n' mines, makin' a helluva mess in the process. At first I didn't hear any of us firin' back, and couldn't figure what the hell was goin' on. Then I heard the M-60s open up, then some AKs, some explosions that had to be sappers with bangalors 'n' sachel charges. I loaded the Greener 'n' sat down on my bunk, waitin'. If they wanted to bring the war to me, okay. But I wasn't goin' lookin', not even to walk outside. I listened to the yellin', the whinin' ricochets, '16s pop pop poppin', the thumpin' from the heavy shit, stutterin' automatics, few grenades, and figured fuck 'em.

It didn't last long anyway. From my perspective, I mean. Sittin' it out makes a big difference. Thirty seconds, tryin' to hide behind a buncha sandbags somebody's tearin' to shreds with an AK can seem like a lifetime . . . but sittin' in that bunker wasn't much worse 'n' sittin' in a theater with your eyes closed listenin' to a soundtrack. No wonder generals don't mind fightin' wars.

When mosta the hootin' 'n' hurrahin' died down I walked outside with the shotgun hangin' from my right shoulder, under the poncho. I had extra shells in both pants pockets, and my rifle hangin' from the left shoulder, outside, visible, without a clip. I made a straight line, through the torn-up earth 'n' shredded pig meat, past the wire, through the hamlets, never lookin' right or left, never lookin' back. Nobody paid any attention to me. They were countin' the dead, patchin' the wounded 'n' feelin' fairly good. In the hamlets there wasn't a soul to be seen, and prob'ly wouldn't be until they were sure both sides had finished tryin' to fuck each other over. Two hundred, three hundred meters, a normal pace for a man walkin' through Indian country not really expectin' to meet any Indians. I know somewhere in my short, troubled life there musta been fantasies about hot-doggin' for history, grandstandin', bein' a football hero—which I never was—grabbin' glory in one idiotic stunt from which, naturally, I would escape relatively unharmed. A *little* blood was good for the cameras. But there wasn't any of that now. I didn't intend for anyone to ever really know what happened. I wasn't even sure I could do it.

Two of Jinx's new-found friends picked me up comin' into the hamlet where he made his home, the same one where I'd found him before. They came up behind me, took the '16 and we went on walkin'. Like a three-man arrowhead. I recognized the hooch and went in without knockin'. My pair of escorts stopped behind me, fillin' up the door, half-smilin'. They both were carryin' their AKs like those East Germans with burp-guns you used to see in photographs, slung around the neck, weapon at the ready, finger on the trigger. Inscrutable Orientals. Or smug fuckin' slope-heads. Depends on how you see it.

Jinx looked up . . . impassive, I guess is as good a word as any. We were about ten feet apart. I nodded at the inscrutables. "Friends of yours?"

"They want you, man." He shrugged.

"So much for guarantees, huh?"

"One of 'em's the father of that kid you lit up." He said somethin' in Vietnamese to the closest one. I guess it was Vietnamese. Wasn't pig latin. The dude's face lost the silly little half-smile. My hand tightened on the shotgun. "You also wasted his brother."

"I thought all this was impersonal. I mean, *he* wired his kid, right? For that matter I could be really pissed with him." I was tremblin'. "Luke got hit with frags." The non-involved partner snickered 'n' said something to Jinx.

"He says you shakin' like a heartless dog . . . I think he said 'heartless.' I still have lots of trouble with idioms."

"I know what you mean. I still have trouble with idiots too." I was really shakin'. "And liars 'n' friends that betray you."

"Hawk, man, I'm really sorry. But you know, man, they're like *testin'* me . . . dig it? Everyday I get put to the test, and I can't afford to fail. You know? These dudes ain't shit, man, they ain't goin' to do anything. Take you to see the head man. Coupla weeks, a month . . . no more'n a month, you'll be free. Nothin' heavy, right?" He shrugged.

Without a flinch, emotional or otherwise, I raised the barrels of the Greener in one smooth movement, and blew both slopes into oblivion. Double-barrel 00-buckshot, no more'n ten, twelve feet. They went through the doorway into the muddy yard. Their chests looked like fleshy confetti. I'd palmed two new shells before I fired. In a single flick of the thump-snap of the wrist I popped open the shotgun, dumped out the used shells and thumbed in two new ones. I closed the breech usin' two hands. I just ain't meant for that Wyatt Earp shit. It took maybe five seconds, prob'ly closer to two.

Jinx hadn't moved. I'm not sure he believed it. I swung the barrels round, so he could look into 'em. His eyes got about as big as saucers. "Yo, wait . . . listen, man . . . hold it." His hands were up, arms extended, protestin', tryin' to push away the barrels from a distance of at least three arms' length. "Oh, man, why'd you hafta go 'n' do that? Jesus Christ, Hawk, wait . . . listen, man, why don't you take a walk, man . . ." I laid back the hammers and he paled out . . . "Hey, c'mon, you my main man, Hawk . . . listen, we smoked dope 'n' fucked together, we been *buddies, Hawk*—!" I lit off both barrels 'n' blew him through the goddamn wall, right into the mud 'n' rain that had started again. When I stepped through the new, wider doorway, his chest, what there was of it, was smokin'. I stepped over him, turned toward the interior of the hamlet. Two more slopes came tear-assin' out the door of a hooch about ten meters away. If they'd been five yards apart I'd prob'ly have died right there. But they were in each other's pockets and went to hell together. I reloaded.

Later, I walked back to Kilo, collected some personal stuff 'n' started for Atlanta. I was still carryin' the Greener. I told everybody the war was over, that I was goin' home. Nobody started arguin' with me till I got to Danang. The farther away I got from the fightin', the harder it was to make people believe the war was finished.

A lot later, maybe three months, back in the States, I saw the official report on "Subject Hawkins," which I took to be me cleverly disguised as a nonentity. Subject Hawkins killed fourteen people in the aforementioned hamlet, includin' several armed members of the National Liberation Front, also known as Viet Cong. I couldn't remember that. Jinx, four Indian grunts . . . and a blank. Subject Hawkins also burned down some "dwellings." Subject Hawkins then returned to his company and killed a large number of hogs, threatened several officers and noncoms, went absent without official leave and refused to return to his post, in violation of a direct order. That seemed like something I might have done. Subject Hawkins, in the meantime, also had been recommended for a second Silver Star and promotion to corporal. Subject Hawkins was obviously under great stress, and suffering from severe emotional strain (see psychiatrist's report, pp. 25–31). Subject Hawkins was being considered for a general court-martial, or immediate discharge "for the good of the service."

Discretion won out over valor, plus the very excellent prospects for some very bad publicity, and Subject Hawkins was discharged as a Private E-1, with two Silver Stars, one Purple Heart, some junk medals given to any soldier who can stand on his feet long enough to pass inspection by a visitin' general, and instructions to report to the nearest VA hospital for psychiatric rehabilitation. Subject Hawkins, with discharge in hand, told them to go fuck themselves, because about the only thing Subject Hawkins had left was his unshakable bad attitude.

PUERTO VALLARTA 1972